A BODY AT THE DANCE HALL

BOOKS BY MARTY WINGATE

A BODY AT THE DANCE HALL

MARTY WINGATE

bookouture

Published by Bookouture in 2024

An imprint of Storyfire Ltd.
Carmelite House
50 Victoria Embankment
London EC4Y 0DZ

www.bookouture.com

ISBN: 978-1-83525-198-0
eBook ISBN: 978-1-83525-197-3

To Leighton

PROLOGUE

All the gaiety of the Palais de Danse had vanished, and the trumpets and trombones sat gleaming and silent at the musicians' feet. The black-lacquered latticework glittered in the light from the silk lanterns that swayed in currents of warm air.

Men in evening jackets and women in wisps of dresses and headbands adorned with a jewel or a single feather sat stiffly, as if at school and awaiting instruction. A low tide of murmurings rose and fell, but amateur sleuth and foxtrot enthusiast Mabel Canning heard just one whispered word as she crossed the vast dance floor: murder.

At the beginning of a corridor leading away from the dance floor was a wall of police officers. Never one to let a man get in her way, Mabel pushed through the crowd of burly men for a better look. Blinking in the flash of a photographer's light, she shuddered as she saw the body: sprawled in a pool of blood on the tile floor, its arms and legs askew, as if caught in the middle of a rather lively dance.

When Mabel had been assigned to accompany a glamorous young American to a light-hearted evening of dance and entertainment, she never expected it to turn on a sixpence to tragedy.

A person with whom she had been speaking not all that long ago now lay dead at her feet. She was supposed to be a watchful eye, to protect her feisty young ward from danger. She had failed. Was she in some way responsible for this act of violence?

As shaken as she was, Mabel mustered all her courage. For her skills went far beyond the dance floor – she was the intrepid leader of a private investigations group. She was determined to solve this gruesome murder, but she would need the help of her friends in the London Ladies' Murder Club.

ONE

LONDON

January 1922

Mabel reached a hand out to grab the pole and leap onto the tram only for it to pull away from the stop without her. It rang its bell in a mocking tone as it trundled off.

'Damn!' she exclaimed and stamped her foot right in the middle of a puddle, splashing muddy water onto her stockings. What had been a light mist only a moment ago when she'd walked out of New River House had become a heavy shower catching the curls in her brown bob haircut that peeked out from under her cloche. She should've worn the hat with a wider brim.

A passing man popped open an umbrella, nearly poking Mabel's eye out, and a crowd of people jostled her as they surged towards an approaching bus. The wrong bus for Mabel, but at this point, she would be late whether she took a tram, bus or the Underground.

She stepped out of the fray and hailed a passing taxi.

'Piccadilly,' she said to the driver through the window, and got in.

. . .

Since she began working at the Useful Women agency five months ago, Mabel had made it her policy to arrive at the office by nine o'clock as a show of her dedication to the job. She followed this practice whether her assignments were of the ordinary variety, such as mending lace, restringing pearls or reading to invalids, as well as when they fell within the remit of the Private Investigations division.

Mabel proudly led this section of the agency whether the job meant finding a lost dog, a lost relative or a misplaced note to the butcher. Very occasionally a serious case came along. When that occurred, Mabel called on one or two other Useful Women for assistance or, more likely, her crew of associates whom she considered honorary Useful Women. Especially the man.

Today it was nearly half past as she raced up the stairs of 48 Dover Street. At the first-floor landing, she paused when she saw a cluster of five or six women waiting outside the office door. Mabel recognised one of them as Miss Gregory, who had regaled them the previous pay packet Friday with the story of her first assignment, which had been to teach a dog to walk on its hind legs. Miss Gregory seemed game for any job, and Mabel had recognised a kindred spirit.

Seeing Mabel approach, Miss Gregory nodded at the closed door and said, 'No sign of her yet.' Inside the office, the telephone rang. 'It's been going like that since nine o'clock.'

Miss Lillian Kerr owned the Useful Women agency and ran a tight ship. Mabel didn't believe the woman had ever missed a day of work or had even been late. Certainly not this late.

'I do hope she isn't ill,' Mabel said, which prompted concerned murmurs from the others. The telephone stopped ringing, its last jangle echoing in the silence.

'Wouldn't she ring the exchange and tell them she was indisposed, I wonder?' one of the women said.

'I wonder should one of us try to ring the exchange,' said another.

'I wonder where there might be a telephone nearby,' said a third.

'The office at the end of the corridor has a telephone,' Mabel said, becoming a bit annoyed at all this wondering. 'I'll go and ask them.'

But before she could move, there came a clattering on the stairs and they turned to see Miss Kerr herself racing up to the landing where she stopped, breathing heavily and gripping the newel. A damp lock of her hair had come loose from its bun and dripped over one shoulder, the grey hairs among the dark standing out like silver ribbons. Her brimmed hat sat askew, and the cluster of silk snowdrops tucked into the band drooped.

The women at the office door drew closer together. Could this bedraggled and flustered personage be the same Miss Kerr who dealt out assignments as if she were playing bridge and who could sweet-talk a client on the telephone while raising a warning eyebrow at one of her Useful Women?

Miss Kerr sniffed in an officious manner, threw back her shoulders, straightened her hat and marched forward, giving them a brusque 'Good morning.' The telephone inside the office started up again. She drew the key from her coat pocket, unlocked the door, and had it answered by the third ring. World order, as far as it concerned the Useful Women agency, had returned.

Mabel spent most of the morning assisting with the table seating for a dinner party. This was no mean feat as the guest list comprised a variety of quarrelsome family members.

'Look here for example,' said Mrs Mortmain to Mabel. 'My

great aunt Janet would turn her soup into my father-in-law's lap if she were seated next to him.'

At last, they settled on an arrangement where no one would be happy. 'That way,' Mabel said, 'you can't be accused of playing favourites.' She left, but not before advising Mrs Mortmain to serve a clear soup at the dinner.

Mabel returned to Useful Women by a bus that went the long way round Hyde Park. She walked up the short way from Piccadilly to 48 Dover Street and glanced up at the building that seemed wedged in along the terrace of shops and offices. Built a century ago and remodelled before the war, the building aspired to be of the Palladian style with heavy use of Portland stone on its edifice and in the arch over the door. The interior remained modest to serve those with the need for office, not ornament. At least the coal fires had been replaced with piped-in gas, although it could be said Miss Kerr did not overindulge when it came to creature comforts.

The first floor lay empty and quiet as workers behind office doors up and down the corridor got on with the business of the day. But when Mabel neared Useful Women, she could hear a voice emanating from within – the sound slipped under the door and flowed out over the transom. A man's voice.

What was this about? Mabel didn't remember ever seeing a man in the office – an unwritten, albeit understood, rule of the Useful Women agency. Would a man make arrangements for his son's birthday party or even be aware that embroidery on table linen needed restitching? Mabel's steps slowed so that she could listen in on this extraordinary event.

'I'm sorry to have to ask again, Lillian,' he said, 'but as I explained earlier, it's an emergency. You can understand that, surely. Please, could you, for the sake of what was, see fit to—'

'It's too late to play that card, Rupert,' Miss Kerr replied crisply.

His voice dropped in reply and Miss Kerr murmured something in return. Disregarding the idea she was eavesdropping, Mabel crept closer, but the telephone jangled, making her jump and knock against the wall. She heard footsteps and, fearing that this Rupert would look out to find her in a compromising position, Mabel made a run for it to the far end of the corridor nearly colliding with Mrs Fritt, who came rattling round the corner pushing her tea-and-bun trolley.

'Oh, Mrs Fritt,' Mabel said, panting as she stepped out of the line of vision from the Useful Women office, 'you've saved the day. That is, I'm gasping for a cup of tea.'

'You didn't have to come all the way down here, Miss Canning,' Mrs Fritt said, her voice rattling nearly as much as her trolley. She adjusted her starched white headpiece that looked like a miniature mob cap perched on the top of her head. She tucked a stray frizzled wisp of hair back in place. 'I was on my way to Miss Kerr's.'

'Well then,' Mabel said, 'I'll just follow you there, shall I?'

Mabel stooped behind Mrs Fritt on their way down the corridor. When she peeked round the woman's shoulder, she saw a man emerge from the Useful Women office. He was a well-dressed, fine-looking fellow in his late forties or early fifties with a stern look and stiff brown hair that either pomade or strength of will kept in place. He looked back into the office. He didn't speak but smiled – a charming smile that curled up the corners of his mouth – and then turned to go.

'Tea and a bun, sir?' Mrs Fritt called after him.

'No, thank you,' came the reply as he hurried down the stairs.

The office door had remained open, and so Mrs Fritt rattled her way in and Mabel followed.

'Here we are now, Miss Kerr. And look who it is I've found way down the other end of the corridor – Miss Canning.'

Miss Kerr gave Mabel a sharp look and then glanced towards the door, out of which that fine-looking man had exited only a moment ago.

'I was afraid I'd missed Mrs Fritt,' Mabel said, 'and ran to catch her at the far end of the corridor' – Mabel waved her arm as if the distance was too great to quantify – 'because I'm in that much need of tea. And a bun.'

'Ooh, look at the flowers, Miss Kerr,' Mrs Fritt said, nodding to the short vase of pure white freesias sitting at the corner of the desk. 'Don't they have the loveliest fragrance.'

Wherever did they come from? Mabel thought, but didn't ask, noting the high colour that came to Miss Kerr's cheeks.

Mrs Fritt kept up a one-woman conversation about the weather as she served and collected her five pence each. Mabel took her usual seat across the desk from her employer and, at last, Mrs Fritt rattled off.

Mabel imagined that Miss Kerr longed to tell her about the fine-looking man. Certainly, Mabel longed to ask, but some lines could not be crossed. In the suffocating silence, Miss Kerr shifted the candlestick telephone to the side, adjusted the vase an inch and picked up her fountain pen.

'Such a busy morning,' Mabel said, hoping for a side-entry into the topic on her mind.

Miss Kerr tapped the pen on the edge of her saucer and didn't reply. Then, she pushed her teacup aside, laid the bun over the top and pulled the Useful Women Jobs log over, opening it to a blank page.

'Miss Canning, you've no investigations going on at this present time, do you? The search for Mr...'

'Tinkles,' Mabel said. 'The search for Mr Tinkles ended successfully. He was discovered living like a king in the next flat up from the client's where no one asked him to chase down a mouse for his own dinner.' Mabel reminded herself not for the first time that not every private investigation carried with it excitement, danger or secret plots.

'Good, good. As it happens' – Miss Kerr's voice became nonchalant in the extreme, sending up a red flag in front of Mabel – 'there is a job available that may last several days. It is of a somewhat delicate nature and will require discretion and patience, both qualities you have displayed in the past.'

Mabel, usually game for any job, realised that if Miss Kerr felt she needed buttering up, it might be best to ask for details.

'Just what is the job, Miss Kerr?'

'A companion is needed for a young American woman visiting London. She came over on the *Olympic*.'

'Is she travelling alone?' Mabel asked.

'No. Yes. Apparently, there has been some confusion about that,' Miss Kerr said with a vagueness Mabel had never witnessed.

Miss Kerr said no more and the lack of particulars both intrigued and worried Mabel, but in the end, she trusted her employer and didn't mind taking a chance. It had been a rather dull January thus far.

'I'd be happy to take the job.'

Miss Kerr sighed as if a great weight had been lifted from her shoulders and she took up her tea and bun with relish. 'I'm sure there will be little to do apart from being a pleasant companion and showing her the city. Taking foreigners on a tour is, after all, one of the services we offer.'

'Who is the client?'

A bit of Miss Kerr's good cheer seeped away. 'Useful Women have been engaged by Mr and Mrs Arkwright.'

'Was that Mr Arkwright here earlier?' Mabel asked boldly, but in an innocent tone, as if she hadn't heard their 'Lillian' and 'Rupert' exchange.

'Yes,' Miss Kerr said as she unscrewed the top of her fountain pen and stared at the blank page of the logbook.

'And Mr and Mrs Arkwright are relations of—'

'Yes, yes, Miss Canning, relations. I'm sure all will become clear when you arrive this afternoon at four o'clock at the Arkwright residence in Mayfair.' Miss Kerr wrote down the address without consulting her notes and handed it over. 'This is strictly a business arrangement, but you may need to be available during the day and evenings as well. Please do keep me abreast of things. Now, perhaps you'd like to take the afternoon to prepare.'

Mabel took Miss Kerr's comment to mean she'd best smarten herself up for the job. She looked down at her legs, splattered with dirty water, and the mud crusting on her boots. She would change her stockings and brush her boots off and hope that would be enough.

The telephone jangled, Miss Kerr gave her a nod of dismissal and Mabel departed with half a bun in hand, nearly running into Miss Gregory on the landing.

'Oh, I say,' the woman gasped, 'sorry. I didn't see you.'

'It's all right,' Mabel said. 'Are you late for something?'

'No,' Miss Gregory said, pulling off her gloves and stashing them in a pocket. 'It's only that the more jobs I do in a week, the—'

'—fatter the pay packet on Friday,' Mabel finished. 'I completely agree.'

Miss Gregory grinned, and a smattering of freckles danced across her nose. 'So, it isn't pin money for you, either,' she said. 'Some of us need to work for a living, don't we? Although I'm not entirely sure I'm making the best impression on Miss Kerr. Already this morning I delivered a dress to the wrong house.'

'I'm sure it wasn't as bad as my debacle at a game of bridge when I first started,' Mabel said. 'Miss Kerr can be very forgiving.'

'Good thing, too,' Miss Gregory said. 'You off on another job?'

'Yes, for the Arkwright family in Mayfair. I'm to be a companion to a young American woman visiting London.'

Miss Gregory's eyes widened. 'I say!' She glanced at the Useful Women office door. 'Missed out on that one, didn't I?'

The assignment did sound pleasant, Mabel thought as she continued on her way. A young American relative comes to meet her older English cousins and they are at a loss as to how to entertain her. Her? Mabel looked down at the paper Miss Kerr had handed over. No name, only the street and house number in Mayfair. Well, never mind. She would learn the young woman's name soon enough.

Mabel dropped the shillings into the cabbie's hand and, as he pulled away, turned to study the Mayfair house in the afternoon's fading light. Detached red brick trimmed in Portland stone with a portico. Frosted glass panels flanked the door and above, running the length of the first floor, was a balustrade that allowed just enough room for planters of trimmed yew. There were streets in London, Mabel thought, where everything looked just so.

When she pulled the bell, it went off loud enough to wake the dead. She jerked her hand back as if scorched by a hot iron. The bell stopped, but an ear-piercing shriek continued coming from in the house. Did someone need help? Should she run to find the nearest constable?

The door opened at the exact moment silence fell. There stood a butler, a middle-aged man with black hair marked by grey at his temples and a face that betrayed nothing.

'Hello, good afternoon,' she said. 'I'm Mabel Canning from the Useful Women agency. I believe Mr and Mrs Arkwright are expecting me.'

'*You can't make me!*' came a scream from within.

The butler winced slightly, but said with perfect calm, 'Yes, Miss Canning, please do come in. If you would be so kind as to wait for a moment.'

Mabel went as far as a round Queen Anne tripod table that held a tiered arrangement with pots of narcissus. The butler disappeared into the lion's den.

After a mere moment of quiet, Mabel heard a man's raised voice followed by a shrill retort—'*I won't! I won't! I won't!*' Out of the room burst a flash of kingfisher blue. Mabel barely glimpsed the figure pounding up the staircase before it disappeared down a corridor followed by a door slamming so violently that she felt it under her feet.

The butler emerged from the same room and without batting an eye said, 'May I take your coat and gloves, Miss Canning?'

She handed them over, adjusted her hat and followed him into a sitting room where the curtains had been drawn, a merry fire blazed in the grate and lamps everywhere had been switched on. Mr Arkwright stood at the mantel and a woman sat in an armchair, her hands neatly folded in her lap and her head bowed.

'Miss Canning,' the butler announced.

Arkwright's stern look Mabel had seen earlier at the Useful Women office had vanished to be replaced by a flushed face and nervous hands that went in and out of his jacket pockets.

'Thank you, Trigg,' he said. 'Will you tell Dorcas to bring in the tea?'

The butler nodded and backed out.

'Miss Canning, I'm Rupert Arkwright.'

Mabel saw no flicker of recognition, so perhaps he hadn't noticed her fleeing down the corridor that morning. She crossed the room and held her hand out, which he shook.

'Hello, Mr Arkwright, pleased to meet you.'

Arkwright turned to the woman sitting in the chair. 'My dear, may I present Miss Canning. Miss Canning my wife, Mrs Arkwright.'

Mrs Arkwright did not raise her gaze and her husband looked round the room as if searching for a rescue. Swallowing her nerves, Mabel extended her hand to the woman.

'Mrs Arkwright, how do you do? May I say how lovely the arrangement of narcissus is in your entrance hall. It's quite like a breath of spring in the middle of winter.'

Good manners pushed their way to the surface. Mrs Arkwright glanced up with heavy-lidded hazel-coloured eyes, giving the impression she looked down on Mabel who stood above her, and shook Mabel's hand with a weak grip. 'Thank you, Miss Canning.'

No one spoke, and so Mabel plunged into the deep. 'Thank you both for choosing Useful Women to help with your' – she faltered for a moment – 'domestic needs.' She cringed at her own words, which made it sound as if she were there to polish the silver.

'Yes,' Arkwright said, recovering as he offered Mabel a beguiling smile. 'I hope you will pardon the outburst you witnessed. As you can see, we are at sixes and sevens, but it's only that Roxanne is still settling in from her journey.'

Roxanne. Well, at least I have her name now.

'I'm sure it's quite exhausting, all those days on a boat,' Mabel said. 'Is Roxanne a cousin of yours?'

Mrs Arkwright sat bolt upright. 'She didn't tell you? Rupert—'

'Yes, Adelaide, yes. Miss Canning, Roxanne is my daughter. She is Roxanne Arkwright. She lives in America with her mother and has come for a visit.'

Pennies were dropping quickly in Mabel's mind. Mr Arkwright was divorced, and his wife had fled to America and then he had remarried. In these modern times, this sort of thing happened, of course it did, even if Mabel rarely encountered it. Now here came the couple's grown daughter, who appeared none too happy to be in London. And who was the 'she' of Mrs Arkwright's accusation? It could be none other than Miss Kerr, who had deftly neglected to give Mabel any relevant detail of her assignment.

'She's from America?' Mabel asked pleasantly. 'What part?'

'Chicago,' Arkwright said.

'Lovely,' Mabel said. That topic exhausted, the three stood in silence until Dorcas arrived with the tea.

'We shouldn't pour until she's down,' Mrs Arkwright said after the maid had left.

'No, we can't let her think she can run this household by throwing tantrums,' Arkwright replied, frowning.

'How old is Roxanne?' Mabel asked.

'Eighteen,' her father said.

Too old for a tantrum.

'Shall I go up and see about her?' Mabel said. 'A fresh face can sometimes help.'

'No, Miss Canning,' Arkwright said, 'you shouldn't have to—'

'Yes,' Mrs Arkwright said quickly. 'Thank you, Miss Canning. It's the second floor, turn right to the end.'

Mabel tapped lightly on the door.

'Go away!' came a shout from within.

'Miss Arkwright?'

'*I said*' – a pause – 'Who is it?'

'I'm Mabel Canning. May I come in?'

'Yes.'

Roxanne sat in an upholstered armchair with her knees drawn up to her chin and her stockinged feet tucked under a pillow and a scattering of magazines on the floor round her. She turned away, but still Mabel had caught sight of her face, blotchy from crying. She had a long, elegant neck and wore a collarless dress, setting off her straight auburn hair cut in a short bob. An uneven cut that went up and down and down and up, as if done in a hurry by an amateur hand. Perhaps this was the style in Chicago, America. Regardless, she looked fairly miserable, and Mabel's heart went out to her.

'Miss Arkwright, I've been engaged to be your companion and show you around town while you're visiting. Did your father tell you?'

Roxanne turned a venomous look on Mabel. 'I don't need a nursemaid,' she said, biting off each word, 'and I told him so. I'm twenty years old and can do as I like. I don't want to see London. So, you can leave the way you came.'

Mabel's sympathy evaporated. She wanted the job, but then again, she didn't want it if her days would be filled with childish tantrums.

'Very well,' Mabel said, exuding a calm she did not feel. 'I'm sure that will suit your father. Think of the aggravation you will save him if you lock yourself up in this room for your entire visit.'

She turned to go.

'Wait,' Roxanne said and then paused for a moment. 'Where would we go?'

'Museums, galleries,' Mabel said. 'Anywhere you like.'

Roxanne smiled and the corners of her mouth curled up just like her father's. 'That sounds swell, Miss Canning.'

Mabel smiled at Roxanne's American accent. It reminded her of an American officer who ended up convalescing at Fellbridge Hall where Mabel volunteered as a nurse during the war. In Mabel's limited experience, Americans always sounded so cheerful. It was Roxanne's first day in England – perhaps she was just out of sorts from the travel.

'Good,' Mabel said. 'Now, I'm going downstairs for a cup of

tea. Will you join me?'

'I suppose I will.'

'By the way,' Mabel said, 'your father told me you were eighteen.'

Roxanne's smile evaporated and she leaned over to pull on her shoes. 'What does he know?'

Mrs Arkwright served the tea and passed round plates of cinnamon cake.

'Isn't the maid supposed to do this?' Roxanne asked as she took the cup and saucer from Mrs Arkwright and set it down, shaking her head at the cake. 'I had to fill my own plate at breakfast, too. What's happened to your servants, Father? You haven't lost all of Mama's money, have you?'

Rupert Arkwright didn't answer, in part, Mabel thought, because he was grinding his teeth. No explanation came from Mrs Arkwright either, and so Mabel, who grew up with no servants, explained to Roxanne that the lady of the house served the tea.

'Perhaps that's different from how it's done in Chicago,' Mabel said.

Roxanne drank her tea and said nothing.

Rupert turned to Mabel. 'How long have you been with the Useful Women agency, Miss Canning?'

'Since September,' Mabel replied.

'It must be interesting and varied work,' he said, sitting back with a smile.

'Miss Canning and I will have a lovely time, I'm sure, Father,' Roxanne said. 'We're going to a museum and a picture gallery and' – she gave Mabel a sly look – 'the Palais de Danse.'

Rupert slammed his cup down on the table, and tea sloshed onto the rug below. He pointed a finger at his daughter and said, 'You are not going to a dance hall.'

TWO

'We're going to a dance hall.'

Mabel sat on the sofa in Cora and Skeff's flat on the third floor of New River House. Cora, next to her, looked up from her handwork – sewing a needle-felt robin onto the brim of a bucket hat. She worked at Milady's, a milliner's on the King's Road, and often brought work home with her. In fact, the flat had hats hanging from pegs and lined up along the back of the sofa and anywhere there was space – all Cora's designs and quite creative.

'The Hammersmith Palais de Danse,' Mabel added.

'Oh, the Palais,' Cora said, her apple-cheeks glowing.

Skeff leaned back in her armchair and exhaled, blowing a stream of cigarette smoke towards the ceiling.

'Cora and I enjoy tripping the light fantastic,' she said. 'We'll put a record on the gramophone here or occasionally go out to a dance hall.'

'Men are in such short supply,' Cora said in a matter-of-fact tone, 'that no one minds two women dancing together. Much.'

Skeff leapt up and extended her hand to Cora. 'Shall we?'

Cora took Skeff's hand and was swept up in a tango, the

couple striding the short distance across the sitting room and into the kitchen cheek to cheek before pausing, whipping their heads round and gliding back again, all the while Skeff humming a steady beat. When they reached the end of their makeshift dance floor, Skeff threw Cora back and gave her a sound kiss.

'Well done!' Mabel said, clapping.

Skeff's dancing with Cora in addition to her quite short hair and her penchant for wearing trousers might give some people pause, but Mabel didn't mind it. When she'd first arrived in London and met these neighbours, she had decided to take their arrangement in her stride, because it wasn't her place to ask questions. Now, they'd become the sort of true friends you could rely on no matter what.

'Won't Winstone go with you?' Skeff asked.

'He's in Southampton until sometime tomorrow,' Mabel said, doing a poor job of hiding her disappointment because, if she were to dance with anyone, she'd prefer it be Park Winstone. Park was her neighbour from the first floor. He had been involved in what started out to be just another one of her Useful Women assignments not long after she'd arrived in London. He was one of the first friends and allies and now... now what were they? Mabel wasn't entirely sure.

'He said it was something about a man who swears he sent the army forty crates of unfilled artillery cases, but actually had sent forty crates of Huntley & Palmers wartime biscuits.' Park described his post with the diplomatic service as 'reading other people's letters', but Mabel suspected there was more to it than that.

'And regardless,' Mabel said, 'I'll need to keep an eye on Miss Roxanne Arkwright – this will not be the time to enjoy myself.'

'Arkwright?' Skeff asked.

'Rupert Arkwright is her father,' Mabel said. 'Have you heard of him?'

Skeff, a journalist on her uncle Pitt's newspaper, the *London Intelligencer*, kept abreast of both people and events in town.

'Arkwright, Arkwright,' she muttered. 'Steel. American steel, I believe. Do you want me to see what I can find?'

'Yes, please,' Mabel said.

'What will you wear to the Palais?' Cora asked.

There's the rub. Her wardrobe, satisfactory in general, specifically lacked an evening dress suitable for her to wear when she accompanied a rich American – because weren't they all rich? – to the Hammersmith Palais de Danse. But she couldn't afford a new frock, and so what else was there?

'My best dress could use some help,' Mabel said. 'A ribbon at the waist? You know, to spruce it up a bit. It's all I can do before tomorrow evening.'

'Hmm,' Cora said, tapping her forefinger on her chin. 'I might have an idea.'

Skeff grinned. 'There you are, Mabel – sorted. When Cora has an idea, it's best to pay attention, doesn't matter if it's hats, dresses or disguises.'

'Well, I don't need a disguise this time,' Mabel said, although she knew Cora would be up for it. 'But perhaps one of your hats?'

'I'd say I can do better than that. You see,' Cora said with a touch of mystery, 'Mrs Norrell has decided to enter holy orders.'

Come Friday morning, Mabel arrived at the Useful Women office to collect her pay packet. She took her place at the end of the queue in the corridor and chatted with the other women as they inched their way up while inside, Effie Grint sat at the plain deal table pulled over next to Miss Kerr's desk. Just before

Mabel crossed the threshold, she looked back down the queue, saw Miss Gregory and waved.

After signing for her packet, Mabel moved to the other side of Miss Kerr's desk and explained about going to the Palais. Miss Kerr replied that seemed well within her remit as companion and there would not be a problem with Mr Arkwright's fee.

'Now, Miss Canning, if you are free this afternoon, I do have a job going.'

Miss Gregory had collected her own pay packet by that time and moved closer.

'Good morning, Miss Kerr.'

'Miss Gregory,' Miss Kerr said in a closed manner.

'I'm very sorry about Mrs Vickers' coat,' Miss Gregory said, and then added in an obsequious tone, 'I'm eager to take anything today that you have available.'

Mabel, feeling a bit like an older sister to Miss Gregory who looked about ten years her junior, asked, 'What happened to Mrs Vickers' coat?'

Miss Gregory wrinkled her nose and her freckles jumped. 'She wanted the buttons replaced and I accidentally sewed them on the inside of the coat.'

Mabel snorted a laugh, but then noticed Miss Kerr didn't look all that amused. 'For one of my first jobs, I was meant to repair the lace on a camisole and ended up sewing it to my own skirt. Sometimes it takes us a while to find our specialities, don't you think, Miss Kerr?'

Miss Kerr pressed her lips together.

'What was the job you had for me?' Mabel asked.

'Mrs Neame,' Miss Kerr replied.

'Ah,' Mabel said. 'I hope I'm not speaking out of turn, but I'd be happy to give this assignment over to Miss Gregory. You would be hanging her Millais. Sort of. She tells wonderful stories about the Pre-Raphaelites.'

'That's kind of you, Miss Canning,' Miss Kerr said, conceding with a nod. 'All right, Miss Gregory, if you're willing, I'll send you to Mrs Neame.'

Miss Gregory broke out in a huge smile and took Mabel's hand for a moment. 'Thank you!'

Mabel spent her day on mundane assignments – hanging pelmets and arranging flowers. She was home in her flat by afternoon and had taken out her best dress wondering if she might truly have to wear it to the glamorous Palais when she heard a knock.

There stood Cora holding a brown-paper parcel as if it were a presentation cushion. 'Here we are now.'

'Come in,' Mabel said.

'It's Mrs Norrell, you see,' Cora said, picking up the conversation from the day before as she unwrapped the parcel on the sofa. 'She's one of our customers at Milady's, and she comes down with a bout of religious fervour about as easily as you or I take a head cold. When she does, she wants me to give all her clothes away—or sell them for charity. Then, when she's left with almost nothing to wear, she changes her mind and must buy an entirely new wardrobe.'

'She's done this more than once?' Mabel asked.

Cora closed the door and unwrapped the paper parcel. 'This is the third time I know of.'

'Her husband doesn't object?'

'Her husband doesn't have a say in the matter,' Cora said with a giggle. 'It's her money. Now, take your things off. You don't wear a corset, do you? Good. Take off your camisole, too.'

Mabel's hand went to her chest. 'But Cora—'

'It's all right,' Cora said, holding up what looked like a strip of velvet. 'You'll have this on. It's sort of a strapless brassiere.' Once Mabel had been secured, Cora held up the dress.

The fabric, a royal blue chiffon velvet, felt like silver slipping through Mabel's fingers. She slid it over her head and it fell gracefully down just below her knees. Once on, Mabel turned to the mirror.

'Oh my,' Mabel said, a bit breathless. 'There isn't much to it, is there?'

Cora stood behind her, fussing with the hook closure. 'Bare arms are acceptable on an evening dress,' she said.

'These straps are no wider than my finger.'

'It's from Paris,' Cora said as if that was an answer. 'Mrs Norrell brought it home with her only last week. And look here – it comes with its own bertha.' She held up a delicate, open-work crocheted shawl and draped it over Mabel's shoulders. It barely covered them.

'And see it has an extra inner layer of artificial silk. Oh Mabel,' Cora said, clasping her hands, 'you look stunning.'

Did she? Mabel shivered.

'Once you're dancing, you'll warm up,' Cora said. 'Now, I've a headband that'll look perfect against your hair.'

Mabel, her coat buttoned up to her chin, slowed her steps as she reached the first-floor landing at New River House. She listened for the sound of a piano or a friendly *woof* from behind the door to Winstone's flat – an indication that he and Gladys, his terrier, had returned home – but there was nothing forthcoming.

She continued downstairs and out the door but hesitated on the pavement. The cold January air seeped through her coat and the flimsy Parisian dress. Surely she was wearing clothes more suitable to a taxi than a tram? Mabel marched to the kerb and hailed the first one she saw.

At the house in Mayfair, Roxanne, lips painted red and cheeks rouged, had buttoned her coat, too – a lovely double-breasted emerald plaid that set off her dark red hair still with its ragged ends showing beneath a stylish beaded cloche. Instead of a hat, Mabel wore Cora's headband – a circlet of small, golden leaves.

Both Mr and Mrs Arkwright stood in the entrance hall with them, the father with a stern expression but the stepmother with a small smile that faded in and out.

Arkwright took a five-pound note from his pocket and said, 'Miss Canning, perhaps you would keep account of—'

'Is that money?' Roxanne asked, eyeing the large white paper with black stamping.

'Yes, it is,' her father said, 'and—'

Roxanne snatched it out of his hands and from her coat pocket, took a square flat envelope purse – brown leather with a tooled design. She folded the note up and inserted it into her purse.

Arkwright frowned and then turned to Mabel. 'Miss Canning, I will expect the both of you back here by eleven o'clock.'

'Rupert,' Mrs Arkwright began.

'Eleven?' Roxanne sounded as if she were choking. 'The Palais doesn't close until midnight. I'm not a child, you know.'

'You'll have plenty of time to dance,' Arkwright said in an appeasing tone.

Roxanne breezed by them to the waiting taxi.

Arkwright sighed. 'Have a lovely evening.'

The streets were wet from an earlier rain and the air smelled of cold and that mix of petrol, exhaust and horse carts that Mabel thought peculiar to London. Roxanne peered out the window at the bright lights of the city.

'Curfew,' Roxanne scoffed. 'The truth is, I could die and he wouldn't care.'

'That can't be true,' Mabel said. 'He's your father.'

'It is true,' Roxanne insisted, suddenly looking sad and much younger than her years. 'He's never wanted anything to do with me. All my life I've wanted to come see him. Mama begged him again and again, but he would always say no.'

'When did you and your mother move back to America?' Mabel asked.

'I was three,' Roxanne said and stuck out her bottom lip as if that child still lurked just under the surface.

'Well,' Mabel said to Roxanne, 'you're here now – that must count for something. Is this the first time you've met your stepmother?'

'And the last, if she has anything to say about it.'

'Why would you say that?'

'She's not all that happy I'm here, surely you can see that?'

Mabel believed Mrs Arkwright's hesitancy was more due to treading carefully around the stepdaughter she'd never met.

'How was your crossing to Southampton?' Mabel asked.

Roxanne gave her a cautious look under heavy lids. 'Boring,' she said.

'Did you meet anyone interesting?'

'No.'

'Didn't your mother want to take the journey with you?' Mabel asked.

'How old are you, Miss Canning?' Roxanne asked abruptly, putting an end to the topic.

'Thirty-two,' Mabel said. 'How old are you?'

Roxanne's cheeks flushed. 'I'm twenty – I told you that.' She looked out the window again. 'You've never married?'

'No.'

Roxanne turned wide eyes on Mabel. 'Never been asked?'

'Yes, I have been asked,' Mabel said. 'Twice. I turned them down.'

'You what?' Roxanne asked, aghast. 'Why?'

'I had other plans,' Mabel said. 'I wanted to move to London, be independent and run my own life.' She shrugged. 'Perhaps I'll marry someday.'

'Leaving it a bit late, don't you think?' Roxanne asked as they pulled up to the Palais.

The stone building sat at the corner as if it owned the street. A former skate rink Skeff had said, and Mabel didn't doubt it. Now, it oozed elegance and charm and from its high arched windows emanated a warm, inviting glow. Come in and dance.

By the time they'd reached the cloakroom and Mabel had taken off her coat, Roxanne dropped the bored act.

'Hot dog, Miss Canning,' she said and gave a low whistle. 'You did all right.'

Mabel wasn't certain if this accolade made her more or less comfortable in Mrs Norrell's Parisian frock, but she felt well-covered compared to Roxanne, whose daffodil-yellow dress exposed shoulders, arms and most of her back with no bertha as even a pretence of covering.

'Thank you,' Mabel said. 'You look lovely. That's a striking hat.'

They turned to gaze out across the expanse of the Palais. The bright lights reflected in Roxanne's wide eyes, her lips were slightly parted and her breath quickened.

It impressed Mabel, too. The former ice rink had been transformed with a vast dance floor framed at four corners by black-lacquered columns with matching fretwork and a pagoda roof. Silk Chinese lanterns hung from the ceiling and there were two low bandstands, one at each end, and enormous parlour palms stood in the corners. Tables and chairs filled the edges of the room and a bar ran down the side of one entire wall. Already, at just past eight o'clock, there were groups of men and women gathering as the bands warmed up in a minor cacophony of horns.

'Do you have dance halls in Chicago?' Mabel asked.

Roxanne clicked her tongue. 'We're not rubes, Miss Canning.'

A man in a dark evening suit led them to a table at the edge of one of the lattices and asked if they'd care for drinks.

'A bottle of champagne, my good man,' Roxanne said.

'What?' Mabel said. But the waiter disappeared before she could protest.

'My father is a big cheese, Miss Canning,' Roxanne said, 'I assure you he can afford it.'

Perhaps he could, and he hadn't put any restrictions on their evening apart from asking Mabel to keep account of costs – five shillings each entrance fee and a bottle of champagne an eye-popping one pound.

When the waiter returned, popped the cork and poured, Roxanne extracted a one-pound note from her purse and handed it over.

Mabel sipped her glass of fizz, but Roxanne swigged half of hers down in one go – followed by a coughing fit. Nevertheless, she continued drinking as they both surveyed the room. Roxanne's head went round and round as if she were a lighthouse. Mabel caught the frenetic excitement that filled the air with lively chatter and the band playing loud enough to be heard above it all. The men looked dashing in their well-cut suits and many of the women were wearing slinky dresses similar to Roxanne's – Mabel didn't think there was a corset in the place. Most women wore headbands or cloches – this was no place for an overwrought picture hat.

Roxanne paused in her survey of the room and frowned.

'What's he doing here?'

Mabel looked over her shoulder towards the door. 'Who?'

'The blond,' she said, 'built like a brick. He was on the boat.'

Mabel spotted him. A man in his twenties who had stepped aside to take in the room. When he glanced their way, he blinked, but then passed over them and made for the bar.

'Do you know him?' Mabel asked.

Roxanne shook her head. 'He was always lurking. He never spoke to me, but he gave me the creeps.'

Mabel spotted the young man at the bar, watching them. He had a mild, innocent face and he nodded to Mabel then looked away.

'Have you seen him since you arrived in London?'

Roxanne shook her head. 'No, but he was on the train up from Southampton.'

'You didn't come up on the train on your own, did you?' Mabel asked.

'Are you saying I couldn't be trusted?' Roxanne shot back.

Heaven forbid Mabel should imply what looked very much like the truth. 'I'm saying wouldn't it be difficult to find your way.'

'Oh. Well, I didn't, as it turned out. Father and his wife were waiting for me when I disembarked, and we came up on the train together.'

And what a delightful journey that must've been.

Still, was it a coincidence that this young man who had been on the *Olympic* and on the same train with Roxanne just happened to come to the Palais the very same evening they did?

'Oh, I'd love to,' Roxanne said to a beetle-browed man who had come up and asked her to dance. 'See ya, Miss Canning,' she said, making sure to take her purse with her.

Mabel looked back to the bar, but the lurker had gone, and when a man came up and asked her to dance, she accepted, thinking she could keep a better eye on Roxanne on the floor.

For the next hour or so, they were never back at the table at the same time. Mabel seldom went to dances in the country, apart from the Christmas dance at nearby Fellbridge Hall, but she did enjoy it and so she may have become distracted until she passed Roxanne and noticed the young woman's flushed face and bright eyes. Mabel returned to the table to discover the level of champagne in the bottle had dropped to less than half and she'd had only a few sips from her own glass. She gave up dancing altogether, had the waiter take the bottle away and sat.

The music ended and Roxanne made her way back accompanied by the beetle-browed man. She stared at her empty glass.

'Hey, what's the big deal?' Roxanne said, hands on her hips.

'Shall we order food?' Mabel asked.

'I don't want to eat. Waiter,' she called, raising her hand and swaying slightly. 'Another bottle of champagne.'

Mabel shook her head at the waiter and said to Roxanne, 'We'll have lemonade.'

'Don't you tell me what to do!' Roxanne shouted over the music. 'You're as bad as that old bat, and I took care of her, didn't I?' She pointed a finger at Mabel across the table. 'You'd better watch yourself, Miss Canning!'

Roxanne pivoted on the spot and strode out to the dance floor with the beetle-browed man in her wake.

Mabel drank lemonade and declined further invitations as she kept an eye on her charge until she saw Roxanne disappear down a corridor behind the far bandstand. Mabel knew that wasn't the way to the lavatories, and so she went in pursuit, but by the time she started down the same corridor, it was empty.

'Roxanne!' Her voice echoed. She came to an intersection with another corridor, and there was still no sight of Roxanne. Hearing a noise to the right, she turned in that direction and came to a wide opening into a vast kitchen where everyone shouted, and food seemed to be flying through the air.

Someone grabbed Mabel's arm from behind and whirled her round. She found herself face to face with the lurker – the young man Roxanne had recognised from the crossing.

'Miss Canning,' he said in a low voice. 'We need to talk.'

Mabel pulled her arm away. 'Who are you?' she demanded. 'How do you know who I am?'

He tapped a finger on the side of his nose and said, 'It's all right. We're both working for the same person, aren't we – although we don't want that spread around.' He fished in the breast pocket of his jacket and pulled out a calling card that read:

OSWALD DEUCHAR, PRIVATE DETECTIVE
PINKERTON TRAINED

Below that came a telephone number.

Deuchar – a Scottish name, although he sounded upper-class London to Mabel's ears. 'What do you want with me, Mr Deuchar?' Mabel asked.

There was a shout from the kitchen – something about the beef being like shoe leather. Deuchar glanced round quickly and then nodded further down the corridor. 'In there.'

Mabel followed him to an opening with a thick wooden door that slid back and forth along tracks and now stood open just wide enough for Deuchar to enter. Inside, a single bulb hung on a flex cord, giving light to whole dry hams hanging from the ceiling and crates of fruit and vegetables on shelves and stacked on the floor. The restaurant's larder.

'Come in, Miss Canning, where we can talk without being seen,' Deuchar said with some urgency. 'Please – you're in no danger from me. Let me explain.'

He backed away and Mabel took one step inside. 'Pinkerton trained,' she said. 'What does that mean?'

'The Pinkerton Agency – it's only world famous. And they have lady detectives. Have you never heard of it?'

'No.'

'Mr Pinkerton was a Scot,' Deuchar said with great earnest, 'and he went to America and started a detective agency.'

'And he trained you?'

Deuchar's mouth worked as if he couldn't quite get the words out. 'Not... as such.'

'Then, what does that mean?'

'My great-uncle met the man!' Deuchar exclaimed as if that was all that needed to be said, but when Mabel didn't respond, he added, 'I'm a great admirer and I've modelled my own detective agency after his.'

'But he didn't train you, and so your calling card is a lie.'

'You know how it is, Miss Canning, because you're a detective, too.'

That brought her up short. How did he know that? 'I don't lie about my credentials,' she said. 'Were you on the *Olympic* – the same crossing as Miss Arkwright?'

'Yes, I was on the boat.'

'Were you following her?'

'Not following, as such,' he said. 'I was hired only to keep an eye on her. Easy job, I thought, but then the telegraph came about the old woman being left behind and there Miss Arkwright was, on her own. Well, that could've been trouble.'

'Why? Why would that be trouble?' Mabel knew nothing of Roxanne's voyage. Was Deuchar's *old woman* the same as Roxanne's *old bat*?

'A young lady should not be travelling alone,' Deuchar said. 'Any father will tell you that.'

'Did something happen on the crossing?' Mabel pressed him.

'No,' he admitted, sounding just a bit disappointed. 'She showed a fondness for her food, but mostly she kept to her rooms. She did look a bit lonely.'

'Why are you here this evening?'

'Again, Miss Canning, an extra pair of trained eyes never hurts, does it?' He glanced out the door towards the hall.

'There's something peculiar afoot – I fear trouble from a particular quarter.'

Cold fear washed over Mabel. 'Is she in danger? Then we must telephone the police.'

'Danger? No, nothing you and I can't take care of. But first, there's someone I need to have a word with. Give me ten minutes – twenty at the most. We don't want to play our hand too early, do we? You stay here and I'll be back to get you.'

'I'm not staying in here,' Mabel said.

But without her noticing, Deuchar had moved in a way to draw her further into the room. Now, he swung one of the hanging hams at her. It knocked her on her bottom as if she were a ninepin and gave him just enough time to shove the sliding door closed on its tracks. Mabel scrambled up, but heard the clang of iron as it fell into the hasp, locking her in.

'You open this door immediately,' Mabel shouted, slapping the thick wood and then shaking the sting out of her hand.

'Twenty minutes, Miss Canning,' he called back. 'I promise you.'

Mabel continued to beat on the wood, but no one came. She tried to slide the door open but succeeded only in rattling the iron hasp and chain on the outside. She paced up and down, back and forth in the room, dodging hams as she went. Her mind spun in a confusion of fear, anger and bewilderment and she sat down on a crate of oranges in order to still her thoughts, but eventually the cold seeped in. She rubbed her bare arms and returned to pacing, beating on the door every time she passed.

A look at her wristwatch told Mabel the twenty minutes had come and gone. Would Roxanne notice that she had disappeared, or had too many glasses of champagne clouded her mind? Time slowed to a crawl, but even after an hour, Mabel remained hot with anger and cold with the temperature. Past eleven now, and the Palais closed at midnight – would anyone look for her?

At last, Mabel heard voices in the corridor. She ran to the door.

'Help me! Let me out of here! Let me out now!' She beat on the wood and was finally rewarded with the sound of clanking iron. She began shouting at Deuchar. 'How dare you lock me in here and walk away! You'll be lucky if I don't ring for the police!'

The door slid open and there stood Detective Inspector Edmund Tollerton of Scotland Yard, wearing his usual bowler hat and buttoned-up coat. He had a face that never gave anything away, but now it was awash in relief.

'Well, Miss Canning,' he said, 'I'm very happy to see you.'

Mabel, stunned, could only reply, 'What are you doing here?'

He took off his hat. 'I'm afraid there's been a murder.'

THREE

'A murder?' Mabel whispered. 'No, not Roxanne!'

She ran past Tollerton and two police constables.

'Miss Canning, wait, please—' Tollerton called.

Mabel outran his words. She burst out of the corridor into the vast hall and held up at the edge of the empty dance floor, teetering as if on the rim of a precipice.

No music played. Band members at each end had put down their horns and the dancers now sat in every available chair while others crowded at the end of the room near the bar and the door. The sound of shuffling and low voices rose and fell like waves, and there was an air of sorrow in the place that struck at Mabel's heart.

Silence fell and movement ceased upon Mabel's appearance. In a moment she took in the room – uniformed police were scattered about the place and the dancers' finery appeared gaudy and mocking. Mabel's gaze searched the crowd for Roxanne and her looks were returned with a mix of alarm and suspicion.

Then, across the floor Roxanne stepped forward. Her beaded cloche was gone, and she wore a man's coat that she held closed with clenched fists. Her father stood next to her and, behind him, Detective Sergeant Lett talked with two police constables.

When Roxanne caught sight of her, she let out a wail.

'Maaaaabel!'

Arkwright reached out and touched her shoulder, but she shook him off and flew across the dance floor. Mabel met her in the middle and Roxanne threw herself into Mabel's arms.

'Oh, Mabel, there you are. I couldn't find you,' Roxanne said through sobs. 'And then – it was horrible. The blood. I couldn't... Mabel, you disappeared. Where were you?'

Overwhelmed with relief and stunned by Roxanne's emotional outburst, Mabel could barely speak. 'I was here, but—'

'I was worried,' Roxanne choked out. 'I said those awful things to you and then you disappeared. The police have been looking for you.' She swept away the tears streaming down her face and wiped her nose on the back of her hand. A handkerchief appeared, held out by her father.

'It's all right now, Roxy love,' he said quietly. 'Miss Canning is here. Go sit down.'

Arkwright nudged Roxanne the rest of the way across the dance floor to a table, and Mabel followed. When he'd sat his daughter down, he whirled round and shoved a finger in Mabel's face.

'You were meant to keep your eye on her,' he said in a furious whisper.

'Then why did you need Mr Deuchar here, too?' Mabel whispered back and Arkwright recoiled as if she had slapped him. He turned back to his daughter, and Mabel stood, bewildered.

While locked in the larder, Mabel's fear had grown and so when Tollerton said there had been a murder, she had jumped to the conclusion that Roxanne was the victim. But Roxanne was alive, and so who had been murdered? And why was Arkwright even here – surely they weren't that far past their curfew? Had he not trusted Mabel to look after Roxanne?

Mabel noticed a group of men standing nearby at the entrance to a service corridor. She turned to Tollerton, who had come up behind them.

'Inspector, who was—'

But Roxanne had come back for her. 'I thought something terrible had happened to you,' she said. She gripped Mabel's arm and pulled her away from Tollerton, holding her coat closed with the other hand. When Roxanne swayed slightly, Mabel was reminded of how much champagne she had drunk.

'But I'm fine,' Mabel assured her. 'Here, you sit down.' She gently pushed the young woman into a chair. Roxanne's shoulders sagged, and with her rouged cheeks and red lips against a face drained of colour, she looked like a dejected porcelain doll.

'Here you are now, Miss Arkwright.' A young woman police constable with small brown eyes that could pierce steel set a cup and saucer down on the table. 'Tea.'

'Constable Wardle,' Mabel said. 'How very good to see you.'

'Miss Canning,' Wardle said, nodding. 'I'm happy you're all right.'

'I don't want any tea,' Roxanne said.

'You'll drink it nonetheless,' Wardle instructed in a sharp tone.

'Here now,' Arkwright said to the WPC in protest, but Roxanne followed orders.

Mabel turned again to Tollerton. 'Inspector, tell me—' she started, but was interrupted by a commotion and raised voices near the front. Several constables scuffled with an intruder who broke through their barricade, then stopped and scanned the crowd. It was Park Winstone.

'Tolly!' he shouted.

Tollerton raised his arm and gestured. 'Here!' Winstone

barrelled towards them, followed at his heels by a brown shadow with a dark saddle marking. In a low voice, Tollerton quickly said to Mabel, 'Miss Arkwright became frantic when she couldn't find you, and when her father arrived, he confirmed you should be here. We instituted a search of the building, and I rang Park, because if I hadn't let him know there would've been hell to pay.'

No further explanation was necessary. When Winstone reached her, she held out her hands to him.

'I'm fine,' she said hurriedly. 'Look, I'm fine. Really I am.'

Winstone, on the other hand, looked dreadful – his face ashen, more than just that one errant curl broken free of pomade, and his glasses, sitting slightly askew, were speckled with rain. He held tight to her hands and was out of breath, as if he had run all the way from Islington.

'Tolly said a man was dead and you were missing,' Park said.

At Mabel's feet, Gladys sniffed and wriggled and *woofed*. It came to her that Gladys was the sort of terrier used during the war to carry messages – and to search for bodies on the battlefield.

'Oh no, Park,' Mabel said, touching his cheek. 'I wasn't really missing, it's only that no one knew where I was. No one except that man, the one who...' An unpleasant sensation like a spider crawling up her arm caused Mabel to shudder. She turned round to the others. 'Where is he? Roxanne, where is the man you saw on the ship?'

Roxanne's hands flew to her face causing her coat to fall open, and Mabel saw a large, dark red stain on the front of her daffodil-yellow dress.

A fresh flood of tears began. 'He's dead.'

Now that Mabel was accounted for, Tollerton got busy.

'Miss Arkwright,' Inspector Tollerton said, 'if you would come with me.'

'Inspector,' Arkwright said, putting a hand on his daughter's shoulder, 'may I have a word with you first?'

The two men stepped away, and Roxanne's eyes, wide and hollow, followed. 'Father?'

Arkwright turned back. 'I'm just here, Roxy. Stay with Miss Canning for a moment.' Arkwright raised his eyebrows at Mabel.

'Roxanne,' Mabel said, 'here let me button that coat up, all right?' Hiding the bloodstained dress wouldn't make it go away, but at least Roxanne wouldn't have it in front of her. 'Would you like to meet Gladys?' She led the dog over. 'Gladys, this is Roxanne.'

Gladys sat and held out a paw.

A small smile curled up the corners of Roxanne's mouth. She leaned over and shook the proffered paw. 'Gladys,' she said. 'Aren't you a smart girl? Our Digger knows this trick, too.'

'You have a dog?' Mabel asked.

'He isn't really mine, he's more...' Roxanne looked up, her gaze darting about until they rested on her father, who was still talking with Tollerton. She let out a small huff and turned to Winstone. 'Now Mabel, who is this kind gentleman?'

Mabel carried out the introductions.

'Pleased to meet you, Miss Arkwright,' Winstone said.

'Oh, Mabel,' Roxanne said, with a touch of her old self, 'you are full of surprises, aren't you?'

Mabel's attention was drawn away to the corridor beyond where a cluster of scene-of-crime officers gathered. There was a burst of light as the photographer's flash tray went off.

'Roxanne, would you look after Gladys for a moment?' Mabel asked.

Roxanne readily complied, scratching the dog behind the ears and talking in baby tones. While Tollerton and Arkwright were still in conference, Mabel nodded to Winstone and the two of them moved closer to the activity around the body. When one of the officers moved, Mabel had a clear view.

There Oswald Deuchar lay, awkwardly sprawled on his stomach with his arms spread as if he'd tried to break his fall. The back of his head had been bashed in, his blond hair matted and dark with blood that had pooled beneath him. Even in death, his face, half turned up to the garishly bright light above, held that mild look of innocence.

A well of emotion rose in Mabel and she shook her head to regain control of herself. 'He couldn't've been more than twenty-five,' she said. 'He told me he was a detective working for Rupert Arkwright.'

Winstone stood behind her, put his hands on her shoulders, bare but for the lacy bertha, and his warmth was a comfort.

Roxanne's voice came from behind them.

'I want Mabel there, too.'

She turned back to Roxanne, standing in defiance with her arms crossed and her purse in one hand. Next to her was her father and Tollerton – the latter looking none too happy.

'Miss Arkwright, I can understand you wanted to be sure that Miss Canning was safe before you went through the events of this evening,' Tollerton said, 'but—'

'If my daughter would like Miss Canning to be present,' Arkwright said, 'I see no reason why she shouldn't be.'

Tollerton heaved a resigned sigh. 'Fine. Lett, see that no one leaves until I say so. I don't care who they are – dancers, band members, Palais staff. Winstone, go with him.' He nodded towards the sergeant.

Winstone – previously of Scotland Yard and still unable to shake its last vestiges – said to Mabel, 'Keep Gladys with you,' and went off to assist.

'Drake,' the inspector said, and the police constable followed them as they paraded after the manager of the Palais,

Mr Bryars – a fretful man in a dinner jacket and slicked-back sandy brown hair. He gestured them into a large office with a sofa in the corner near a small coal fire, burning bright. In the middle of the room, a large mahogany desk with papers scattered about its surface.

'Oh dear,' Bryars said when he saw the disarray. He dashed over to the desk and began gathering up sheets and straightening them into a neat stack. 'A gust of wind from the door and this is the result.' Bryars looked on the floor and in the corners.

'All right, Mr Bryars?' Tollerton said, waiting to take a seat at the table.

'Yes, of course.' Bryars then opened the door of a cabinet behind the desk, reached in and brought out a glass paperweight. He took a look at it, muttered something and set it on the stack of papers. 'There now, that's better,' he said and circled round to stand near the mantel.

Tollerton sat behind the desk and Mabel, Arkwright and Roxanne in the chairs across from him. Gladys sat at – or rather, on – Mabel's feet.

The inspector took a notebook out of his inner coat pocket, flipped through several pages and dug in another pocket for a pencil. Mabel noticed Arkwright kept a concerned watch on his daughter, whose eyes followed Tollerton's every move, her brow furrowed. The start of a police interview, Mabel had learned, engendered such a response, because what did Roxanne know of the inspector?

But Mabel knew that, although gruff at times, Tollerton had proved to be a good and fair copper. On previous occasions he had – albeit rather grudgingly – acknowledged she'd been a help to the police. He and Park were friends, and she suspected that Park had played a role in getting Tolly to realise just how useful one of Miss Kerr's Useful Women could be.

'All right,' Tollerton said, then looked up and noticed the

manager. 'That'll be all for now, Mr Bryars. I'll call if I need you.'

'Yes, of course,' Bryars said. He didn't move. 'Drinks?'

Mabel remembered the nearly half bottle of champagne Roxanne had consumed earlier in the evening.

'A cup of tea would be lovely,' she said.

'Yes,' Arkwright said, looking not a little disappointed. 'Why don't we all have tea.'

When the manager still didn't move, Tollerton said, 'Please send a tray of tea over, Mr Bryars.'

'Tea,' Bryars said, and sidled out the door.

Once he'd gone, Tollerton said, 'Well, Miss Arkwright, we know Miss Canning is safe and here she is sitting next to you. Now, we can begin. Tell me, how old are you?'

Roxanne dropped her gaze to her lap. 'Eighteen, sir,' she said in a small voice.

Tollerton made a note. 'I want you to go through your evening, leaving out no detail.'

Roxanne swallowed. 'Mabel and I arrived and handed over our coats.' She looked off into the distance as if that moment had been long, long, ago. Mabel certainly felt that way. Then, Roxanne sniffed and with a resolute jut of her chin, continued. 'We were sitting at our table when I saw him come in. The man...' She looked up in a panic. 'I don't even know his name!'

'His name was Oswald Deuchar,' Mabel interjected and felt both Arkwright and Tollerton's eyes on her.

'Oswald Deuchar,' Roxanne repeated. 'I didn't see him again, because I was dancing. I was on the dance floor the entire time, wasn't I, Mabel?'

When she hadn't been shouting at Mabel. Roxanne might've remembered that, too, because she blushed.

'Then,' Mabel prompted, 'I saw you go into a corridor at the end of the bar.'

'Yes,' Roxanne said. 'I went looking for the powder room. I

walked down a long hallway, went past the kitchen and I turned again and ended up coming out the other end of the bar. I looked for you, Mabel, but you weren't at our table so I asked the lady who took our coats, and she pointed across the dance floor to another hallway. It was busy in the powder room, and I got to talking with a woman who had come in after me. We laughed about how she puts a forward partner in his place by stepping on his foot a time or two.' Roxanne shot her father a wary look. 'Not that that has ever happened to me. Then I talked to another woman from a town called Up Mudford, can you imagine? And then, I left. When I came to the end of the hallway, he stumbled out of a side passage' – she gestured with her hand as if seeing it again. 'It all happened so fast. I could see blood on him, and he fell into me and then onto the floor and I... I screamed.'

For a sullen young woman who had until that moment said very little about anything, it was quite an explanation and must've taken all her energy because at the end, Roxanne slumped back in her chair.

'Roxy, love,' her father whispered and put a hand on her arm.

She sat up again and took a sharp breath. 'I'm all right, Father. Mabel, what did he do to you?'

'He didn't do anything,' Mabel said, unsure if knowing the details would set Roxanne off. 'He only wanted to talk.'

At that moment, the tea arrived, Mr Bryars himself carrying the tray and setting it on a low table by the fire. He proceeded to pour and distribute cups, ask about milk and sugar and offer round a plate of Marie biscuits. Tollerton tapped his pencil on the edge of the desk, looking as if he'd like to be tapping it on Bryars' head to get the manager out of the office. When Bryars finished, he took up his previous post by the mantel, but Tollerton's brusque 'Thank you – I'll have a word with you later' sent him on his way.

'Now, Miss Arkwright, do you remember your dance partners? Do you know the men's names?'

Mabel peered at Tollerton, hoping to read something into the question. Did he believe Roxanne had danced with a murderer?

'We didn't introduce ourselves,' Roxanne said. She leaned forward and set her tea on the desk.

'I remember one man you danced with several times,' Mabel said. 'It looked as if he were showing you a dance step.' The beetle-browed man.

'Yes,' Roxanne said. 'The schottische – I didn't know that dance. He said he was an instructor.'

'You would recognise him again?' Tollerton asked.

'I suppose.'

'I would,' Mabel said.

'Miss Arkwright,' Tollerton said, 'Mr Deuchar never attempted to speak with you?'

Roxanne shook her head.

He spoke to me, Mabel thought, as she drank her tea. She sensed it would be best to give Tollerton the details after Roxanne and her father had gone. Had Arkwright sent Deuchar to the Palais that evening, as the private detective had told her?

Finished in Bryars' office, Tollerton led them out to the hall full of a waiting crowd of dancers, musicians and servers where Mabel and Roxanne studied the faces of the men in the hall. Some returned their gazes with steady looks, others with furrowed brows. A few pasty-white fellows looked as if they could do with a sit-down. None of them was the beetle-browed man and when they asked the manager, who waited at the end of the bar, Bryars said he didn't sound familiar. *Descriptions can go only so far,* Mabel thought. *What we need is a drawing.*

Passing one of the tables, Roxanne nodded at a dark-haired woman.

'She's one of the ones I talked with in the powder room,' Roxanne said to Mabel. 'Up Mudford, not the funny one.'

Tollerton heard the exchange and sent Lett over to talk with the woman but dismissed the rest whose details had been taken. He then called to PC Drake and instructed him to drive the Arkwrights home. While WPC Wardle took Roxanne to the cloakroom to claim her coat, Mabel took advantage of the moment and approached Arkwright.

'As you can imagine,' she said, 'I must inform Miss Kerr about the events of this evening as soon as possible, but as tomorrow is Saturday and the Useful Women office is closed, I am unsure how to contact her.'

Mabel watched Arkwright consider her statement. His face revealed nothing, but neither did he act innocently confused about the subject of Miss Lillian Kerr. 'Yes, of course, Miss Canning. Why don't you let me take care of that. And Miss Canning,' he added, 'I'm terribly sorry about earlier.'

Roxanne returned wearing her double-breasted emerald-green plaid coat. She slid her purse into its pocket and held out her father's coat to him. Dark rings had appeared under her eyes and she blinked heavily. She leaned down to the dog and said, 'Lovely to meet you, Gladys. Perhaps you'll come for a visit?'

Her father smiled at this exchange. 'Roxy, do you remember your little dog, Boodles?'

Roxanne looked up at her father and frowned. 'My dog? I've never had a dog.' She turned to Mabel. 'I'll see you tomorrow, Mabel. We'll go to a museum.'

Her father's smile faded. 'You should stay in tomorrow.'

'I want to go to a museum. What's the beef – it's her job, isn't it?' Roxanne snapped and then her eyes filled with tears. 'Please, Father. Please, Mabel.'

'I'll see you tomorrow afternoon,' Mabel said, 'and we'll decide then, shall we?'

When Roxanne and her father left, Mabel, Winstone and Tollerton returned to Bryars' office. Gladys stretched out before the dying fire as Mabel told her story.

'He locked me in the larder beyond the kitchen,' she said. 'He implied that Roxanne was in danger or that something puzzled him, and he needed to sort it out. He made it sound as if we were working together and then he locked me in.'

Winstone leaned forward with his elbows resting on his thighs, his hands clenched as she gave her account. But Mabel's emotions had reached steady ground and, apart from a bitterness at being duped by Deuchar, she gave her statement in a firm voice.

'He wasn't violent and seemed rather apologetic,' she continued. 'He'd seen someone he wanted to talk with – it might've been someone from the crossing on the *Olympic*, but then again...' Mabel thought hard about Deuchar's words. 'No, he said it was something from "a particular quarter" as if it was something different.'

'And he told you he was working for Rupert Arkwright,' Tollerton said.

'What does Arkwright say to that?' Winstone asked.

'He admitted knowing Deuchar would be here this evening, but said his only concern is his daughter's welfare,' Tollerton replied. 'It isn't much of an answer, but I told him I'd see him first thing tomorrow.'

'He didn't come with us this evening,' Mabel said. 'When did he arrive?'

'The fellow at the door said about half past ten,' Winstone said. 'He said Arkwright was concerned when he couldn't find you or his daughter.'

'Our curfew was eleven,' Mabel said, 'so he was jumping the gun.'

Tollerton made a note.

'How concerned was he?' Tollerton asked. 'Angry? Annoyed?'

'The doorman told me it was as you'd expect a father would be.'

'Lett has found a couple sitting at the table nearest the corridor,' Tollerton said. 'The man was standing and could see Miss Arkwright coming down just as Deuchar stumbled out of a side passage, so it looks as if she's in the clear.'

'In the clear?' Mabel repeated, incredulous. 'Did you actually suspect her?'

'Everyone's a suspect,' Winstone reminded her.

'Yes, yes,' she said. It was the policeman in him, she knew. Winstone hadn't been with Scotland Yard since just before the war when he left as a detective sergeant – but Mabel knew he still felt the call and that Detective Inspector Tollerton welcomed Park sticking his nose in a case. Most of the time. Former colleagues, but still friends.

Tollerton opened his pocket notebook on the desk and flipped several pages, stopping at one half full. *What had he learned about the victim? What else did he know about Arkwright's movements?* Mabel straightened her posture and let her eyes casually fall onto the page, but Tollerton noticed and slapped the notebook closed, apparently remembering that reading upside down was one of her special skills.

'Is the blow to the head what killed Deuchar?' Mabel asked.

'I'd say so,' Tollerton said. 'Fairly bashed his skull in. Something flat, probably whatever was to hand. I've got men looking outside and in for the weapon. The murderer attacked from behind and so might have blood on him. Still, we haven't found anyone with that telltale sign. I've got an officer checking the coats, too.'

Attacked with something flat. A brick? A frying pan? The image of Deuchar's smashed-in skull rose up in her mind and Mabel forced herself to breathe evenly and slowly. She had asked the question, after all.

Well after midnight, PC Drake drove them back to Islington. Park and Mabel settled in the back. He took her hand and tucked it into the crook of his arm. They didn't speak, apart from the occasional thoughts that floated to the surface of Mabel's mind.

'Mr Arkwright and Miss Kerr are acquainted.'

'Socially?' Winstone asked.

'They are Lillian and Rupert to each other.'

Mabel's attention drifted off and she might have dozed for a second or two, before coming back to the moment. 'Cora found me this dress. Mrs Norrell has decided to go into holy orders.' She realised she should join up these two random-sounding thoughts but hadn't the energy. 'I suppose it's too late to wake them.' She meant Skeff and Cora, leaving it to Winstone to understand.

'Probably.'

She rested her head against his shoulder, dislodging her golden-leaved headband. She took it off and put it on Park, where it sat atop his curls.

'Now I'll be mistaken for Julius Caesar,' he said.

'Was it planned? Did someone want Oswald Deuchar dead, or was it a fight that went too far?' She yawned, feeling overcome with tiredness. Gladys yawned, too. Before Winstone could join them, the car had pulled up to the door of New River House.

'Thank you, Constable,' Mabel said, and Winstone shook Drake's hand.

· · ·

In the foyer, they tiptoed past the porter's office so as not to wake him in his private quarters beyond. Mabel knew Mr Chigley to be a conduit of information about her well-being to her papa in Peasmarsh – the two men had worked together in India with the Army Service Corps – but she also knew he could be discreet. Mabel, thirty-two years old, understood that as an unmarried daughter and only child, she remained her father's chief concern. There was no sense in causing undue worry.

'Will Roxanne want to be on the next sailing to America?' Mabel asked herself aloud when they reached the door of her flat on the second floor.

'She will need to stay until the end of the enquiry,' Winstone said.

'Well then, perhaps my Useful Women assignment isn't finished.'

Winstone handed Mabel back her golden-leaved headband and kissed her. They stood quietly until Gladys offered a throaty comment.

'I'm sorry I didn't know you were at the Palais,' Winstone said, 'or I would've been there sooner.'

'To save me from Oswald Deuchar?'

'To ask you for a dance.'

FOUR

Mabel stood inside her flat leaning against the closed door, unsure whether she wanted a late supper, a glass of the blackberry wine she'd brought back from Peasmarsh at Christmas or Park's arms round her. Perhaps all three. Instead, she took herself off to bed, although not to sleep. Not immediately. As weary as she felt, the evening's events kept repeating in her mind. It was as if she sat in some dreary cinema forced to watch a nightmarish film again and again until oblivion finally overcame her.

An early riser only when necessary, Mabel arose late the next morning and lingered over her second cup of tea, still in her dressing gown at eleven o'clock.

She'd accomplished little that morning, apart from writing home. Worried that a reporter from one of the 'rags' as Skeff called them might somehow find the thread that led from Deuchar to the Arkwrights to Useful Women to her, Mabel thought it best to tell her papa first. She had fretted over the phrase 'unfortunate incident'. Hadn't she used that before? She said nothing about being locked in the larder and ended the letter with an amusing story about Gladys and a squirrel.

Mabel wrote a separate letter to Mrs Chandekar, their housekeeper, full of their usual chat. She told her about Mrs Norrell's dress and about how Miss Kerr and Mr Arkwright seemed to know each other. Not that Mrs Chandekar wouldn't be as worried as Papa about Mabel's well-being, but the housekeeper understood Mabel's need to strike out on one's own. Hadn't Mrs Chandekar done the same herself many years before, when she began working as baby Mabel's ayah and journeyed with them to England from India?

Perhaps that's what Roxanne was trying to do – be independent. She didn't seem entirely prepared for it, but that could be her age. Eighteen, not twenty. Mabel seemed to recall being sixteen and trying to pass for eighteen one year at the Christmas dance at Fellbridge Hall, so she couldn't blame Roxanne for that.

Mabel read the letters over before sealing them then retrieved her notebook from the leather satchel she had bought second-hand to accompany her role as private investigator within the Useful Women agency. In the notebook, she started on a detailed account of the evening at the dance hall and ended with a list of questions she wanted answered. But as she had been engaged as a companion, not a detective, she didn't believe she'd have the opportunity to ask them. *Not your case,* she told herself with some regret.

A knock at her door nudged Mabel back to the moment. She should've dressed by now. But when she opened the door to Skeff and Cora, she relaxed.

Skeff had a large brown envelope tucked under one arm and nodded approvingly at Mabel's dressing gown. 'Late evening, was it? Enjoy yourself?'

'Was the dress all right?' Cora asked.

'The dress was perfect, the evening was late and as for enjoying myself do you have a minute to come in? Tea?'

'Another cup for me this morning and my back teeth will be floating,' Skeff said. 'Cora, my love?'

'No, thank you,' Cora replied.

They settled on the sofa. Mabel put a few pennies in the gas heater and stood at the mantel. 'Well, here it is,' she said, and told her story, watching Skeff and Cora's expressions shift from friendly interest through concern to shock.

When she finished, Skeff let out a low whistle. 'You don't half have an evening out, don't you?' she asked, probably referring to a séance Mabel had attended in the autumn where the spirit to be contacted had turned up freshly dead. Skeff reached in the pocket of her coat and brought out a small notebook. 'It'll be in the police log by now, but I'll ring Uncle Pitt just to be certain. What was his name?'

'Oswald Deuchar,' Mabel said. Skeff wouldn't print details that the police would prefer to keep quiet about – she was a competent and fair reporter and Uncle Pitt's *Intelligencer* didn't go in for sensationalism. Still, Mabel wasn't sure just what Tollerton would want kept quiet at this point in the enquiry. Perhaps she should ask him.

'Cora, let me get Mrs Norrell's dress for you. It's so lovely. Good thing I wasn't the one Deuchar stumbled into.' She thought of Roxanne's daffodil-yellow frock splattered with blood.

'Why don't you keep it here for now,' Cora said. 'It might be called into service again.'

Mabel thought about this. 'Yes, thank you.'

Skeff handed her the brown envelope. 'You had asked if we had anything on Arkwright when you were hired to accompany Roxanne, and here's what I found in the morgue,' she said.

Mabel looked up in alarm. 'He isn't the one dead.'

'No, no, of course not,' Skeff said. 'Not that sort of morgue. In America morgue is what they call the newspaper's library.

Uncle Pitt heard it from a fellow visiting from *The Sun* in New York City. It does make it easier to write up an obituary – having this to hand.'

In light of last evening's events, it sounded a bit gruesome to Mabel.

'This might help, too,' Skeff had handed over an issue of *Tatler* from a month earlier. 'Cora dug it up.'

'You are both priceless,' Mabel said, clutching the envelope and magazine to her chest and feeling a bit weepy.

'We're happy to oblige,' Cora said.

'Might this affair be one for the London Ladies' Murder Club?' Skeff asked, eyebrows raised.

Skeff and Cora were vital members of Mabel's unofficial team of private investigators for important Useful Women enquiries. Skeff for her newspaper connections and Cora not for her fashion sense—although that was unique—but for her ability to create a disguise from whatever was to hand. They, along with Park and of course Gladys, had helped immeasurably on several occasions in the past.

Mabel gave a nod. 'I certainly hope so. I want to do whatever we can to aid the Yard's work without—'

'Stepping on Inspector Tollerton's toes?' Cora offered.

'Exactly,' Mabel said. 'I may know more later. Come by this evening and I'll open a bottle of blackberry wine.'

'We'll be here,' Skeff said. 'Your father's country wines are exceptional.'

Mabel laughed. 'You only taste the successes – be glad you missed the parsnip cordial.'

They started out the door of the flat just as Winstone and Gladys arrived.

'Ladies,' he said to them. 'May I take you all to lunch?'

'Midday lecture at the Methodist Hall on the life of women astronomers,' Skeff said. 'Perhaps another time.'

'You can take me to lunch,' Mabel said. 'And then I'm going to call on Roxanne.'

'I've a day dress from Mrs Norrell for you to try,' Cora said. 'I'll just nip up and fetch it, shall I?' And off she went as Mr Chigley came up the corridor.

'Morning,' he said. 'Miss Canning, telephone. It's your Miss Kerr.'

Miss Kerr ringing her on a Saturday – an unheard-of occurrence, before Rupert Arkwright.

Mabel looked at her dressing gown. 'Mr Chigley, I shouldn't keep her waiting. Is there anyone about? Do you think I could dash down?'

Mr Chigley nodded, giving half a wink on the scarred side of his face – injuries received decades ago in India. 'All's quiet at the moment,' he said. 'You come down and I'll keep a look out.'

Cora returned to her flat, and Winstone and Skeff lingered on the first-floor landing with Gladys while Mabel descended to the ground floor, picked up the earpiece and leaned into the mouthpiece on the wall phone. 'Hello, Mabel Canning here.'

'Miss Canning, good morning, it's Lillian Kerr. I hope I'm not disturbing you.' Miss Kerr's voice sounded as liquid as it did when she spoke to clients on the Useful Women office telephone, but did Mabel detect a note of... what? Uncertainty? She wondered if Miss Kerr was sitting at home wearing her dressing gown.

'Not at all, Miss Kerr,' Mabel replied, deciding to be direct. 'You have heard about last evening?'

Mr Chigley stood at the counter inside the porter's office with the newspaper spread out before him. He stopped turning the pages.

'Yes,' Miss Kerr said, 'I have been apprised of the situation and I'm dreadfully sorry for all involved. I can imagine young Miss Arkwright was quite affected by events. Not that you weren't, Miss Canning, but with your experience, you bring a more circumspect attitude, I'm sure.'

'It was a shock for Roxanne, that's true,' Mabel said. 'I plan to stop by this afternoon and see how she's doing.'

'About that,' Miss Kerr said. 'I have spoken with Mr Arkwright, and he wants you to know that you are in no way obliged to continue as companion for his daughter while she's in London.'

Miss Kerr paused long enough for Mabel to worry.

'Am I being dismissed? Is that what Roxanne wants?' Mabel asked.

'No,' Miss Kerr replied. 'I spoke further with Mr Arkwright who eventually conceded that it may be in his daughter's best interest for you to continue as her companion.'

If only Mabel could've listened in on that telephone conversation. Or perhaps Rupert Arkwright visited Lillian Kerr at her home? Mabel whisked those images away to concentrate on the subject to hand.

'Mr Arkwright is aware of your speciality within Useful Women,' Miss Kerr said, 'but would prefer you address yourself to diverting his daughter's attention away from the events of last evening. He wants you to stay away from the enquiry.'

'He what?' Mabel sputtered. The door to the street opened and in strutted Mr Jenks, bobbin salesman, who gave Mabel in her dressing gown the once-over. She glared at him, and he skittered by her and up the stairs.

'Well, I don't know how I would do that and yet stay by Roxanne's side. Am I to put cotton wool in my ears? Wear a blindfold?' Mabel's burst of anger dissipated when she remembered to whom she spoke. 'I'm terribly sorry, Miss Kerr.'

'No apology needed. Mr Arkwright is unable to see the wood for the trees, which I pointed out to him. I explained that if you continue as Miss Arkwright's companion, you should do as you see fit. I wouldn't say he agreed with me, but he didn't forbid it. You carry on and I will take all responsibility.'

Carte blanche given by her employer against the wishes of a client who might just possibly be a former beau. Yes, Mabel had got that far in her imaginings.

'Thank you, Miss Kerr,' Mabel said. A smile threatened to take over her entire face. 'I'm happy to remain on the job. Roxanne can be a bit cantankerous, but she seems a lovely girl at heart.' Mabel, stirring with magnanimity, would be generous.

'Do you think so?' Miss Kerr said with unusual enthusiasm. 'Oh, I am glad.'

That settled, they rang off. Mabel dashed up to the first-floor landing where Skeff and Winstone waited as Cora came down to meet them, carrying another brown-paper-wrapped parcel.

'Here you are,' Cora said, holding out the parcel. She handed Mabel a cluster of silk violets. 'And this is for your brimmed hat. I know the dress is a good colour for you. You will exude a sort of calm and I'm certain anyone you meet would know you to be a responsible, competent person capable of solving a murder.'

Mabel basked in another vote of confidence.

'Give me a minute to dress and then come up,' Mabel said to Park. 'Thanks, you two – enjoy the lecture.'

In her flat, Mabel set to unwrapping the latest frock from Mrs Norrell. The day dress, made of soft velvet, came in a shade of mauve that reminded Mabel of the blackberry wine in her kitchen. Straight lines, square neckline and a sash for a belt. She appreciated Mrs Norrell's taste. Mabel pinned the silk violets onto the band of her hat, put it on and looked at herself in the small wall mirror by the door. Her brown eyes peered back. She smiled – Mrs Chandekar had always said Mabel had a 'winning' smile, whatever that meant. Pleasant, at least. That would just do for an afternoon in Mayfair.

. . .

'Look what Skeff brought me,' Mabel said to Park when he'd come back up to her flat. She held out the brown envelope. 'Articles about Rupert Arkwright. I'd asked her on Thursday to see what she could find, because I was curious about him and my assignment, but now I wonder if there could be clues about the murder here.'

They sat side by side at the small table by the kitchen and read through the dozen or so articles that described Rupert Arkwright as an astute businessman with holdings in railways, land, automobile design and American steel manufacturing.

There was the announcement of his 1902 marriage to Mary Louise Fortuna Harvey from Chicago, the only child of a man who had made his fortune in steel.

'There's nothing on Arkwright before his marriage,' Winstone pointed out, 'so it's looks as if it was Mary Louise's money that got him into steel. He certainly did well from it.'

In the wedding photo, a young, serious Rupert looked out at the camera with his hands behind his back. In the stillness of the photo, she noticed his nose appeared a bit out of kilter. Mabel pointed it out and Winstone said, 'Broke his nose, most likely.'

Arkwright stood next to a seated, pleasant-looking woman wearing a long dress with a high neck and a straight-brimmed hat with so much tulle piled on the top it looked like she had put the wedding cake on her head.

No article mentioned the divorce, Mary Louise's return to America or the couple's daughter, Roxanne. Had Rupert taken his wife's money and then divorced her? Had he started an affair with the current Mrs Arkwright while still married?

'What's this?' Winstone asked as a small clipping slipped out and onto the floor. Mabel picked it up.

The clipping announced the marriage of Arkwright to Mrs

Adelaide Patrice Jeffers, widow of Major Thomas Jeffers, Ret.
They had married not quite three years ago, and Mary Louise
and Roxanne had moved back to America fifteen years before
that.

Mabel opened the *Tatler* – the first issue after Christmas
three weeks ago – to the marked page to find a full-page photograph of Roxanne Louise Fortuna Arkwright.

The photo had been taken before the disastrous haircut.
Roxanne's long hair had been swept back into a low bun,
leaving a short halo of curls round her face. She had that
charming smile that turned up at the corners of her mouth. Her
father's smile.

'She's a sweet girl,' Mabel said. 'Until she isn't.'

The caption reported that in the New Year, Miss Arkwright
would be sailing on the *Olympic* from New York City and
would visit her father, Rupert Arkwright, in London.

'Alone?' Winstone asked.

'She wasn't meant to be travelling alone,' Mabel said.
'Somehow Roxanne made it on the ship and her companion
didn't. But Deuchar was there.'

'It's possible Deuchar's murder had nothing to do with
Arkwright,' Winstone said. 'A private detective can collect
enemies along the way.'

'He couldn't have been at this profession for long – he was
too young.' Mabel began flipping through the pages of the magazine in a nonchalant manner. 'I suppose Tolly knows all about
Oswald Deuchar by now.'

'Possibly. Will you ask him?'

'I will. Rupert Arkwright wanted me to stay away from the
case, but Miss Kerr has somehow persuaded him that I should
continue on the job as I see fit.'

Winstone screwed up his mouth, but still she could tell he
was smiling. 'And so, you will carry on with the enquiry?'

'Of course. I won't shirk my duty as companion to Roxanne,

but I am certainly going to look into a few things. What do you think?'

'What do I think of your employer going against the wishes of a client in order for you to solve a murder?' Winstone stood and offered his hand. 'I think it's time for lunch.'

FIVE

Mabel and Winstone went to the café on the other side of Angel station, which was just as well, because icy rain beat on their faces during even that short journey. Mabel had an omelette and Park the mixed grill and, thus fortified, they went their separate ways – Winstone to see Tollerton and Mabel to Mayfair. Gladys accompanied Mabel, because Roxanne had been taken with the dog, who knew how to make herself welcome in any situation.

Trigg answered the door and gave that butlerish impression of a bow to Mabel and then also to Gladys.

'Good afternoon, Miss Canning,' Trigg said. 'Please come in. Your arrival has been much anticipated. Mrs Arkwright is in the drawing room and hopes to speak with you.'

At that moment there was the sound of galloping from above, and Roxanne appeared at the banister on the first floor.

'Oh, gosh, Mabel, there you are,' she said, breathless. 'And Gladys! Could you come up for a moment? There's something I need to ask.'

'Let me say hello to your stepmother, first,' Mabel called up as she took off her coat and gave it a shake before handing it to Trigg.

'No!' Roxanne squeaked, and then whispered, 'Please, will you come up first?'

The cloche that she had worn to the Palais lay on her dresser like an exhibit in a museum with Roxanne standing next to it, arms wrapped round herself as if afraid of the headpiece. From the doorway, Mabel's first thought was that perhaps the beading had come loose, but as she neared, she realised the problem. The rim of the light-coloured satin had been stained a dark brownish-red, and she could see several distinct fingerprints the same colour. Blood.

'I think I might've...' Roxanne said, her voice wobbling. 'He fell towards me and I put my hands out and' – she held out her now-clean palms – 'and I must've...' She pantomimed putting her hands to her head. She took a ragged breath. 'What do I do now?'

Mabel clasped Roxanne's hands and shifted her to the side, away from the cloche. 'I'm so sorry that happened. How are you feeling this afternoon?'

Roxanne's shrug moved through her body like a shudder. She bent over and patted Gladys. 'Father is out, and I was afraid to go downstairs.'

'Why?'

'Because the hat is hers,' Roxanne said.

'Your stepmother's? It isn't as if you'd ruined it on purpose,' Mabel said. 'She'll understand. Let's go now and you can explain.'

Roxanne shook her head. 'I shouldn't be talking with her. Don't fraternise.'

She said it as if she were repeating instructions. 'Who told you that?' Mabel asked.

'She could trick me by being nice,' Roxanne said. 'She wants me to call her Mother Adelaide.'

'How is that a trick?' Mabel asked.

Roxanne frowned but didn't reply.

'At your age, Roxanne, whatever age that might be' – Roxanne had the good grace to blush at that statement – 'I'd say you could decide for yourself if your stepmother is tricksy or not. Now, I'm going down. You come when you're ready and bring the hat.'

'Will you leave Gladys with me?'

'No, she'll be waiting, too.' Mabel walked out. Gladys gave a snort and trotted after.

Mrs Arkwright sat at a writing desk near the window and looked up expectantly when Mabel entered.

'Good afternoon,' Mabel said, keeping just inside the door. 'I've brought a friend's dog with me – I hope that's all right. Her name is Gladys.'

Capping her fountain pen, Mrs Arkwright said, 'Yes, certainly. Please do come in. I'm terribly sorry, Miss Canning, for all the trouble caused—'

'I'm all right,' Mabel said. 'But how distressing not only for Roxanne, but also for you and her father.'

'Thank you,' Mrs Arkwright whispered. She cleared her throat and continued. 'He's been looking forward to her visit for months and now—'

'Is Mr Arkwright at home?' Mabel asked.

'No, he has gone to see the detective inspector.'

Would Mabel hear about his interview through the grapevine – Tolly to Park to her? She hoped to fill the gaping holes in her knowledge of Oswald Deuchar and his arrangement with Rupert Arkwright.

Mrs Arkwright gestured Mabel to the sofa in front of the

fire and sat in a chair next to it. 'Roxanne is quite taken with you, Miss Canning, and I appreciate that you're willing to remain in your post. You come highly recommended.'

'Do you know Miss Kerr?' Mabel asked.

Mrs Arkwright smiled – half a smile accompanied by what might have been half a laugh.

'Yes, Lillian and I have known each other for years. We belong to the same club.'

Mabel believed there were few straight lines in one's life, but rather meandering paths that crossed and recrossed as one met people here and there until it could almost be said that one stood a mere three or four people away from knowing the king. Here must be a prime example. Who had met whom first and through what circumstances? And where did Roxanne's mother fit in?

Gladys, who had settled at Mabel's feet, lifted her head and looked at the door. Mabel looked, too, and in a few seconds, it opened just wide enough for Roxanne to slip in.

She held her hands behind her back, her eyes shifting between the two women until at last she spoke.

'Mmmm...'

Roxanne sounded as if she were humming a song with no tune. She stopped and started again.

'Mmmother Adelaide, I'm terribly sorry, but I've ruined your cloche.' She held it out and it dangled between thumb and fingertip.

Mrs Arkwright rose, went to Roxanne and took the hat. She examined it for what seemed like ages before she looked up and said, 'Roxanne.'

Roxanne shrank back.

'Dear girl,' Mrs Arkwright continued, and her voice caught, 'how dreadful for you. I don't care a whit about the hat as long as you weren't hurt.' She dropped the cloche on a side table and took Roxanne's hands in hers. 'You're quite cold. Come and sit down by the fire.'

Roxanne allowed herself to be guided to the sofa and placed at the end, nearest Mrs Arkwright's chair, and the three of them sat quietly for a few moments.

'Will we go to a museum this afternoon, Mabel?' Roxanne asked.

'There's a cold, icy rain today,' Mabel replied. 'Not really an afternoon for an outing.'

'Shall we have tea, instead?' Mrs Arkwright asked.

Roxanne gave a little nod. 'Yes, all right, but could I have a cup of coffee?'

'Of course you may.'

Mabel felt a decided warmth in the air as if the fire had started to melt a large block of ice in the room.

'I'll ring for Dorcas.' Mrs Arkwright rose.

'Dorcas has gone into my room to clean,' Roxanne said. 'She said she'd been waiting half the day to get in.'

'It's no concern of hers how long you stay in your room,' Mrs Arkwright said. 'You may stay all day if you like, although it's much more pleasant having you down here with us.'

Roxanne smiled.

Mabel popped up from her seat. 'Shall I go back to the kitchen and ask Cook? It's only that I'd like to get Gladys a drink of water. You'd like a drink, wouldn't you, girl?'

Gladys obligingly opened her mouth and panted slightly.

As she left, Mabel heard Roxanne ask, 'Mother Adelaide, I don't remember much from when I lived in London – I was such a little girl. Did you know me then?' and her stepmother replied, 'No, dear, I only met you for the first time when you arrived.'

. . .

Mabel wandered off to the back of the house and found the kitchen on the ground floor. A Welsh dresser took up most of one wall with a good-sized cooker on the opposite, a generous worktable in the middle and the usual array of pots and pans hanging overhead. At the sink stood a thin woman no taller than Mabel with wisps of grey hair escaping her linen cap.

'Hello,' Mabel called tentatively, but in a voice loud enough to be heard over the sound of the tap running into a metal pot.

Cook whipped round, took in Mabel and Gladys with beady black eyes and set her hands on her hips. 'You're not another one of those Dorcas has brought in? No, wait now – you're the one here to be a companion to the young lady, that's who you are.'

'Yes, I'm Mabel Canning from the Useful Women agency. This is Gladys.'

Gladys' nose twitched wildly at the intoxicating mix of food aromas. She trotted over to Cook, sat and offered a paw.

'Think you can try that on me, do you?' Cook asked. 'I see what you're on about.' Gladys gave a throaty reply and kept her paw in the air. Cook produced a thin grin and gave it a shake. 'I suppose I should find you a scrap of something.' She whipped a tea cloth off a cutting board on the table to reveal the remains of a roasted beef joint. She picked off more than a few scraps, put them in a dish and set it on the floor. 'Now,' she said to Mabel, 'what'll you have?'

'Miss Roxanne has come downstairs,' Mabel said, but before she could go on, Cook picked up in what seemed like the middle of a different conversation.

'We've got too many hands or we don't have enough, that's the trouble, and it doesn't do anyone any good Dorcas acting hard done by. Who could we find for it, that's what I want to know. The thing being we don't need a scullery maid but for evenings and first thing in the morning, and we don't need a between-maid all day long. More char than not, I suppose. Still, we've had a run of so-called scullery maids who couldn't tell the back end of a mop from a coal scuttle and wouldn't know how to peel a potato if it hit them on the head. Except for her angel that Dorcas brought in, although she's no girl, and now where has she got to? I tell you, if a day ran smoothly, I'd fall down dead with the shock of it.'

Cook paused to take a breath and Mabel leapt in.

'Dorcas is cleaning Miss Roxanne's room.'

'Is she now,' Cook said and began counting the eggs in a rack in a muttering voice.

'And Mrs Arkwright has asked for tea and also coffee.'

Cook stopped counting and looked up at her. 'Why didn't you say so in the first place?'

Trigg brought in the large tray and left again. Gladys stretched out in front of the fire but kept one eye open on the plate of seed cake while Mrs Arkwright poured. Roxanne said, 'Mother Adelaide, I am truly sorry about your lovely hat.'

'No matter, dear. Perhaps we'll save the beads.'

'May I take the hat with me?' Mabel said. 'I have a friend who designs hats and she's terribly creative. If the cloche can't be saved, perhaps she could use the beads on another design you might like.'

The business of the hat settled, they turned to other topics, and although conversation didn't quite flow, at least it didn't run into any dams along the way.

'What do you and your friends like to do in Chicago?' Mabel asked.

'My friend Juliet moved away and now all it seems I ever do is get dragged to luncheons with Mama and her friends,' Roxanne said with little enthusiasm. 'Mabel, tell me about where you live.'

'I live in Islington.'

'Is that London?' Roxanne asked.

'Yes,' Mabel said. 'Here, I'll show you.' She took her Bacon's walking map from her satchel, unfolded it and under lamplight, pointed out a few key features. 'See, here's about where your father's house is in Mayfair. Here's Islington. There's St Paul's Cathedral. You see the Thames winding through the city.'

'And the bridges?' Roxanne asked.

'Yes, the bridges,' Mabel said. There were a great many and she hadn't learned them all yet. 'That one is Blackfriars and that one Westminster. And Tower Bridge is there. It's near St Katharine Docks and the Waterman pub.'

'A pub?' Roxanne asked. 'You've been there? Can we go?'

'Why don't we visit the Tower, instead?' Mabel asked.

'But I want to go to a pub,' Roxanne insisted.

Mabel heard her emotions rising but didn't believe pubs were the issue. Roxanne hadn't recovered from a man dying at her feet.

'I know so little about your home in Chicago,' Mrs Arkwright said, trying to steer the conversation into calmer waters. 'Does your mother have any relations nearby?'

'No, there's no one,' Roxanne said. 'No one at all. Only the two of us. No one. This is lovely cake.' She stuffed a large piece in her mouth.

Mabel and Mrs Arkwright exchanged glances and the latter offered a small shrug. 'You aren't a Londoner by birth, Miss Canning?'

'No, I come from Peasmarsh, in Sussex.'

'Did you have snow at Christmas?'

And so, the talk turned, inevitably, to the weather. They heard the bell at the front door and paused. There was the sound of Trigg answering but when he didn't come to the drawing room to announce anyone, they continued with their idle chat until the bell went off again, and Mabel realised it was time for her to be going.

'Stay, Mabel,' Roxanne said. 'Please – stay to dinner.'

'Yes,' Mrs Arkwright said. 'That would be lovely.'

Mabel had no time to reply, because Rupert Arkwright walked in. The butler followed him in and went straight to the drinks cabinet, poured a whisky and took it to his master on a small tray.

Arkwright's face was drawn and grey and he clutched a paper in his hand. But then he caught sight of the women, and a warmth came over him.

'Well, now, good afternoon, ladies.'

Roxanne leapt up as if on a spring.

'Father, I remember Boodles now,' she declared. 'He was the palest cream colour and so soft.' She touched her cheek. 'And he would stick his wet nose right in my ear.'

A smile spread slowly across her father's face. 'You screamed when he did that – and then you screamed when he stopped.'

Roxanne's brows drew up at the memory as if it pained her. 'How could I forget Boodles?'

'You were quite young,' Mabel said.

'I should've remembered,' Roxanne said, her face clouding. 'Mama said—'

'Your mother,' Rupert cut in.

His good humour dried up and he looked down at the paper in his hands as if he'd never seen it before. He held it out. It was a telegram.

'Your mother is on her way.'

SIX

A stunned silence fell.

'Is Mama coming alone?' Roxanne asked, sounding slightly out of breath.

Her father frowned at the telegram. 'She doesn't say. Perhaps she'll be travelling with Miss Hawksley who had, after all, been promised a trip across the ocean.'

Roxanne cowered at this statement and her father softened. 'Now love, don't worry.'

'Does she know what happened?' Roxanne asked. Her face had taken on a green cast.

'I don't see how she could,' Arkwright said, looking again at the telegram as if it held secrets it was unwilling to relinquish. 'She sent this from the boat, so she'd already left before yesterday.'

'She was meant to be in Florida for the winter,' Roxanne said glumly.

'She's arriving into Glasgow on Wednesday and says she'll make her own way. That most likely means she'll be here on Thursday, Adelaide—'

'I'll let Dorcas know we'll need a room ready,' Mrs Arkwright said, pulling the cord by the fireplace. 'What about the rose room next to yours, Roxanne?'

Roxanne screwed up her face but didn't answer.

'Or perhaps the honeysuckle room on the first floor at the end of the corridor?'

Roxanne nodded.

The news of the first Mrs Arkwright's impending visit seemed to settle on top of them like a wet blanket. It couldn't be a comfortable situation for the current Mrs Arkwright to welcome a former wife as a houseguest, but at that moment, Adelaide Arkwright appeared to be the least bothered by the prospect. Had Miss Kerr known the first Mrs Arkwright, too?

'I'd better send a reply as soon as I can,' Arkwright said.

His wife pulled the cord by the fireplace and Trigg came into the room. 'Sir?'

When Arkwright gave him the news, the butler's only reply was, 'Yes, sir.'

'Trigg,' Mrs Arkwright said, 'would you ask Dorcas to come in?'

'Dorcas isn't here, ma'am. Gone out to return soon.'

Out of the corner of her eye, Mabel saw Gladys tiptoe out of the room. The dog had impeccable timing.

'Oh now, where has Gladys got to?' Mabel asked, looking round in bewilderment. 'I'd best go back and make sure she isn't bothering Cook. I'm so sorry.'

She found Gladys in the kitchen with her eyes fixed on Cook, who stood at the worktable slicing an apple. She cut off a piece, tossed it in the air and laughed as the dog leapt straight up and caught it.

'I've come to fetch Gladys,' Mabel said.

'No bother,' Cook said. 'We haven't had a dog about the place for donkey's years – since Boodles, little Miss Roxy's dog she had to leave behind. Do you remember the fellow, Mr Trigg?' she asked the butler, who had come in behind Mabel.

'How could one forget?' Trigg replied.

'Were you both here when the first Mrs Arkwright and Roxanne lived here, then?' Mabel asked.

'We were indeed,' Cook replied. 'All those years ago, Trigg here was a footman, and I was a scullery maid, if you can believe it. I've been here all along, but Trigg was away during the war driving an ambulance.'

'Won't it be nice for you to see Mrs Arkwright again?' Mabel asked.

Cook and butler exchanged looks, but said nothing, and that was enough for Mabel.

'I'd best be off. Come along, you,' Mabel said to Gladys, giving the dog a scratch behind the ears.

The drawing room door opened as she approached and out came Roxanne.

'Oh, there you are, Mabel,' she said, putting a hand to her chest.

'Here I am and here I go,' Mabel said. The afternoon had nearly passed, and with Roxanne's father home bringing surprising news, it seemed hardly the time to set off to a museum.

'Will you be round tomorrow?' Roxanne asked.

Her father came out behind her. 'Roxy, we mustn't take up every minute of Miss Canning's life.'

'But tomorrow's Sunday,' Roxanne said. 'What do you do on Sundays, Mabel?'

'I may go to church and then I'll probably be washing out my stockings,' Mabel said. 'Would you like to help?'

Trigg came out with her coat just as there were voices from the kitchen, then Dorcas burst out, straightening her apron. Mabel had seen her only briefly on Thursday, but now took a closer look. She had wide-set eyes, a narrow, pointed nose and black hair scraped back and mostly hidden under her white starched cap.

'I'm terribly sorry, sir,' she said, sounding not terribly sorry. 'It was only that I'd not had my lunch and instead took a walk for the air.'

'It's all right, Dorcas,' Arkwright said. 'Mrs Arkwright wants to talk with you. Roxanne, will you help? You will know how your mother likes things.'

'Yes, sir, I do know – she likes them "just so",' Roxanne said and went back into the drawing room with Dorcas.

Once the door closed, Mabel asked Arkwright, 'Miss Hawksley was Roxanne's companion who was meant to accompany her on the boat? How did she get left behind?'

'Wouldn't we all like to know the details of that caper?' Arkwright asked with chagrin. 'I don't suppose you could wheedle the details out of Roxy?'

'If the opportunity arises, I certainly will. Now, won't Mrs Arkwright...' *There's a problem.* Two Mrs Arkwrights in one house. 'Does she know Roxanne travelled without Miss Hawksley?'

'I had to send that telegram, didn't I?' Arkwright asked, as if still arguing with himself whether he should've or shouldn't've. 'That's what will have spurred her to come and rescue her daughter.'

'Now she will need to be told about what happened at the Palais.'

Arkwright's shoulders drooped. 'I've waited fifteen years to see my daughter and after this, the minute MaryLou arrives she'll probably take her away again.'

Mabel nearly objected to his statement – hadn't Roxanne said she had begged to visit her father again and again and that he'd put them off? That was a question for another time. Mabel thought she'd best get to the point.

'Mr Deuchar told me that you had engaged him. Were you worried about her safety?'

'Adelaide says that all those years I missed out on normal fatherly concern were pent up inside me.' He shrugged. 'I couldn't even wait until the curfew I'd given you myself but had to go and collect the two of you from that dance hall. Or try. You see, I thought that after she arrived here, it might be a good thing to have someone keep an extra pair of eyes on her. MaryLou had warned me that she might try to go out on her own.'

'Because to you, she was still a three-year-old?'

'I suppose it was like that, yes. I can see now that perhaps I overreacted by engaging the fellow, but when I saw his advertisement in the *Gazette* and I rang and explained the situation, he was so enthusiastic. He had very good references – I made certain to check.'

'But you also engaged Useful Women,' Mabel reminded him.

'Adelaide's suggestion, and it made great sense. She pointed out that Roxy would need a companion while she visited – someone a bit closer to her in age – and that we should ask Lillian. I put her off on that matter – I admit my pride got in my way. Years ago, you see, Lillian and I were...' He narrowed his eyes at Mabel as if she'd lured him down a path he'd rather not go.

'It seems rather extreme to send the man all the way to America so that he could come back on the same boat.'

Arkwright held up a forefinger. 'That was entirely his idea. When I explained the situation, he told me that he had business in New York just after Christmas and would arrange to return on the same sailing. I thought it couldn't hurt. And then, of course, I sent a telegram to alert him when we realised Roxy was alone on the ship.'

'Did you argue with him last night at the Palais?'

'Argue?' Arkwright took a step towards her. 'Are you accusing me of murder, Miss Canning?'

Mabel declined a taxi home. The rain had let up, and she and Gladys walked out to Piccadilly to catch a tram, her gloved hands stuck in her pockets for extra warmth. The streetlamps blazed and she found that walking in a crowd and sitting on the tram as it trundled along conducive to thinking. She had a great deal to sort out.

She admitted to herself she'd felt threatened at his reaction to her question. But there had been no time to clear the air because Roxanne had popped out of the drawing room to give her the bloodstained cloche. Mrs Arkwright had followed, and a search had ensued for paper to wrap the cloche in, and by the time Mabel walked out the door, Arkwright was no longer in the entrance hall.

Mabel arrived at New River House just before five o'clock and thought this would be as good a time as any to telephone Oswald Deuchar's detective agency.

But first to get past Mr Chigley, who had a late edition of one of the papers open on the counter. As the porter greeted them and Gladys slipped under the counter and straight to Mr Chigley's heater, Mabel glanced down briefly and read the one-column headline upside down.

DEATH AT A DANCE HALL

Hammersmith Palais de Danse
scene of murder

No arrests made

She'd best get this out of the way. 'Mr Chigley,' Mabel said, nodding to the article. 'I was there last evening – a Useful Women job to accompany a young woman visiting from America. I may have mentioned it to Papa, and so I thought you should know, in case he rings to check on me.'

'I see,' Mr Chigley said. 'Might this involve your ladies'... club?'

Her *ladies' murder club* as she called it, but only as a little joke. She knew Mr Chigley walked a thin line between not lying to her papa yet not worrying him needlessly. He was the soul of discretion, but there was no need to tax him.

'It's possible that it may,' she said, 'but not as yet.' Not until she could figure out how she could make it so.

The door to the street opened and in came a stream of residents all stopping to collect their post from the porter. Mabel moved over to the telephone and under cover of general chatter, picked up the earpiece and asked the exchange to ring the number on Oswald Deuchar's calling card.

She didn't really expect anyone to still be in the office of his detective agency at five o'clock on a Saturday afternoon, but there was no harm in trying.

A woman answered with, 'Regent 3782.' An older woman. So, not an office, but perhaps his home. Was this Oswald Deuchar's mother? Did she know what had happened to her son?

'Hello, my name is Mabel Canning. This is the number I was given for Oswald Deuchar's private detective agency.'

There was a small gasp. 'I will not tolerate being badgered in this time of grief.'

'I'm terribly sorry,' Mabel said, 'it's only that I'm with the Useful Women agency and last evening I was at the Palais and met Mr Deuchar and I'm telephoning to say—'

'Scotland Yard advised me not to speak to the newspapers,' the woman said in a crisp fashion. 'Not yet.'

'No, I'm not from the papers,' Mabel said. 'I spoke with Mr Deuchar, and I only wanted to express my—'

'You what? Wait – what did you say your name was? Miss Canning?'

'I'm with the—'

'Oh, Miss Canning,' the woman said in a rush, 'what a relief to hear from you. Please, can you come to me tomorrow? Morning would be best. Shall we say ten o'clock? We shouldn't be bothered that early.'

'Yes, of course, I can be there,' Mabel said, 'but please, can you tell me, are you Mr Deuchar's—'

'Housekeeper. I'm Mrs Fredericks.'

'Mrs Fredericks—'

'Freddy, please – it's what the dear boy called me. Hanover Terrace, Regent's Park.' She gave the house number and rang off.

'Come along, Gladys.'

Stunned at the ease with which she had gained access to Deuchar's house, Mabel climbed the stairs slowly with Gladys at her heels, her mind already at work as to how to handle the interview with the grieving housekeeper. 'The dear boy' she had called him. Perhaps Mrs Fredericks had begun as Deuchar's nanny, just as Mrs Chandekar had started as Mabel's ayah. Mrs Fredericks could have been privy to the inner workings of the detective agency if Deuchar used his own home for the business.

Mabel knocked on the door of Winstone's flat, but there was no answer. With a sigh, she continued up to the third floor to Cora and Skeff's, invited them down, and returned to her flat on the second floor where Gladys stretched out in front of the cold heater.

She had just opened the blackberry wine when the two

women arrived and so she poured three glasses as she told them about her afternoon.

'I'm to stay on the job as Roxanne's companion,' she concluded, 'but with Mr Arkwright's knowledge, if not blessing, that I am involved in the murder enquiry.'

'I'm sure Mr Deuchar would've wanted you to investigate his murder,' Cora said. 'Too bad you can't ask him.'

'Arkwright isn't complaining about paying the fees, though?' Skeff asked.

'Miss Kerr worked a bit of magic there,' Mabel said.

'Good,' Skeff said. 'Even staying as companion to Miss Arkwright puts you close enough to nose around a bit, doesn't it?'

'As long as I don't step on Detective Inspector Tollerton's toes.'

'You'll want to look compassionate, empathetic, won't you?' Cora asked. 'Put Mr Deuchar's housekeeper at ease. I might have a hat for you.'

'Yes, thanks. Oh, and Cora, what about this? Can anything be done?'

Mabel took the parcel with the bloodstained cloche from her satchel and laid it on the table.

'Oh dear,' Cora said.

'Yes,' Mabel agreed. 'It belongs to Mrs Arkwright, and she gave it to Roxanne to wear and... well, you see what happened. I thought you might do something else with the beads. You have free rein.'

'Hmmm.' Cora picked up the cloche and took a closer look at the handwork and Mabel could see her mind already at work.

'Now, Skeff,' Mabel said, 'there was a man at the Palais who asked Roxanne to dance several times. He wasn't there after the murder and no one recognised his description – not even the manager. If we had a drawing of his likeness that we could show round at the Palais, we might get a lead. We need an artist who is quick with his pencil.'

'Ah,' Skeff said, tapping her finger on the side of her nose. 'We know just the fellow for that, don't we? I'll find him for you.' She swigged down the rest of her wine. 'Shall we, Cora?'

The two left and Mabel went to her larder – a single shelf in the kitchen. Gladys joined her and they contemplated what she might make of her store. The entire contents included five more bottles of blackberry wine, a jar of stewed chicken, a tin of tomato soup and an open packet of cream crackers.

As she studied this still life, a light knock at the door lifted her heart and promised more than just a distraction from a dismal meal. Mabel opened the door to Winstone.

'Busy?' he asked.

He looked pleased with himself. Mabel detected behind his glasses a gleam in his eye, and he smiled as if he didn't mean to but couldn't help it. The errant curl that defied pomade spilled out onto his forehead.

'Not busy,' she said. 'Would you like to come in? I've just opened a bottle of blackberry wine.'

'Why don't you come down to ours?' he asked. 'Bring the wine.'

She retrieved the bottle and followed. Perhaps he had news of the murder enquiry to share. But when Winstone opened the door of his flat with a flourish, and Mabel took one step inside, she saw the cause of his buoyant air – an oak box on the coffee table.

'Park, you have a gramophone!' she exclaimed.

He lifted the lid. 'I saw it in a shop window this afternoon for a very good sale price.'

A record already lay on the turntable. Mabel leaned over and read the label aloud. 'Santos Cassevetti and his Band.'

'Care to dance?' Park asked.

'I'd love to.'

Mabel set the bottle of wine down as he cranked the machine and opened the two small doors in the front of the cabinet. He set the needle on the spinning disc and took her in his arms.

A foxtrot. Slow, slow, quick-quick they danced round the close quarters of his flat. When too close to the furniture, Winstone changed direction, but still they knocked into the bookcase, the piano stool and finally Gladys, who snorted and sprang up onto the sofa, out of the fray.

'Sorry, girl,' Winstone said over his shoulder.

Mabel closed her eyes as they danced, guided by his hand on her back. She imagined they were in Paris, but when she opened her eyes again and saw Park watching her, she was happy to be just where she was.

The song ended and they stopped dancing but stayed in each other's arms.

She tilted her head up and kissed him, a long, soft kiss. Then she said, 'If you tell me about your afternoon, I'll tell you about mine.'

With glasses of wine in hand, Mabel gave Winstone a précis of the Mayfair household and its tenor the day after Oswald Deuchar's murder.

'Rupert Arkwright's announcement that the first Mrs Arkwright is, at this very moment, on her way to England put a stunning end to the afternoon. The news has certainly put the wind up Roxanne and her father, I can tell you that.'

They drank their wine in silence for a moment, then Mabel refilled their glasses and said, 'Now, what do you have?'

'Very little,' Winstone said. 'I offered Tolly my services and then spent hours checking the names of those present at the dance hall against police records. I came up with next to nothing. As far as I know, there's no motive, no weapon, although certainly opportunity for nearly everyone present.'

'Not Roxanne,' Mabel said.

'Not Roxanne,' Winstone agreed. 'But what about Arkwright?'

'He told me he has little practice being a father and couldn't wait until our curfew.'

'Tolly is looking for the taxi driver who took Arkwright to the Palais. It would've been easy enough for him to arrive twenty minutes before he said he did, come in the back and track Deuchar down. Perhaps they argued, Arkwright struck him and left.'

'Struck him with what? I don't suppose the chef at the Palais restaurant counts his pans, does he?'

'Police are searching the area for a likely weapon, but it's only a ten or fifteen-minute walk to the river and the murderer could've pitched it into the Thames. That's assuming there was a plan. If it was an opportunistic attack, the murderer, confused and frightened, may have taken the weapon home with him and put it under his bed. I've seen it happen.'

'Arkwright didn't like it when I asked if he and Deuchar argued,' Mabel said.

'What did he do?'

'He did nothing,' she said. 'I asked a question, and he took exception to it. Is he really a suspect?'

'Early days.'

Mabel tapped her wine glass. 'Oswald Deuchar lived in Hanover Terrace near Regent's Park.'

Winstone raised his eyebrows. 'How did you come by this piece of information?'

'Deuchar gave me his calling card and so I telephoned this afternoon. The housekeeper answered – Mrs Fredericks. She sounded fairly broken up about it.'

'Tolly was off to talk with her this afternoon, but I didn't see him again.'

'Mrs Fredericks invited me to call tomorrow.'

'Why would she do that?'

'She knew who I was,' Mabel said. 'Oswald Deuchar must have told Freddy – that's what he called her – about me. I suppose Miss Kerr could've touted my qualifications to Arkwright and he told Deuchar.'

'The housekeeper knows a great deal,' Winstone said.

'Yes, there's no telling what I'll learn – possibly details that are difficult to elicit in a formal police interview.'

'You aren't going alone? You know nothing about the woman or the household.'

'I can hardly come to harm on a Sunday morning at Regent's Park, can I?' Mabel asked.

'Certainly not – especially if Gladys and I are patrolling along Regent's Park just over the road.'

'Good,' Mabel said, 'that's settled. Dinner? I have a jar of stewed chicken.'

Gladys raised her head and sniffed.

'Can you find shelter if it starts to rain?' Mabel asked Winstone on Sunday morning as they stood beside Regent's Park. At their feet, Gladys strained against her lead, ready for a romp. Across the road and on the other side of a strip of bare trees and shrubs, stood Hanover Terrace, a row of white stucco houses imposing in their Palladian grandeur.

'We'll be fine,' Winstone said.

Mabel made her way to number 9 and paused at the door. She adjusted her hat – she wore one of Cora's with the brim turned slightly under along the edge. 'It will give you a suggestion of sympathy.' With a deep breath, Mabel rang the bell.

The woman who answered wore a formal uniform –

starched white cap covering grey hair and an apron over a black
dress that went to her ankles, showing only a bit of black stock-
ing. She had a soft face poorly disguised by a stern look.

'Hello, good morning, I'm Mabel Canning.'

'Miss Canning,' she said, full of emotion and her watery
blue eyes watered even more. She extended her hands as if
wanting to take hold of Mabel's, but then withdrew them. 'How
kind of you to come. I am Mrs Fredericks, but you will call me
Freddy, won't you? There's no one else left who will do so.'

It warmed Mabel's heart to know that Oswald Deuchar had
someone to mourn him, but she felt sad that it had to be so.

'Mrs – that is, Freddy. I have a friend who will be waiting
for me. He's over there on his way into the park' – Mabel turned
and waved, and Winstone doffed his hat in reply – 'but he may
call after a bit. Is that all right?'

'Dear girl, you should've invited him in. Did he know
Ozzie?'

'No, I'm afraid they didn't have the opportunity to meet.'

'Regardless, he's welcome. Is he part of your detective
agency?'

A member of the London Ladies' Murder Club? Mabel
snorted a giggle. 'He is, actually. Rather an honorary member.'

Freddy insisted that Mabel take a seat by the fire in the small
morning room congested with heavy, lumbering furniture, flock
wallpaper in deep red and paintings so muddy with age and
coal smoke that they seemed to be dark holes engulfed in gold
frames. She had glimpsed an expansive dining room and
surmised the drawing room, bedrooms, in fact, the rest of the
house, lay on floors above with the kitchen below. The house
spoke of old money.

When the housekeeper returned with a tray and a plate of

plain biscuits, Mabel said, 'Are you on your own here now that Mr Deuchar is gone?'

The housekeeper cast a glance over her shoulder and said, 'Yes, all alone. I'm not accustomed to that yet. I keep expecting the dear boy to come down the stairs and say, "What ho, Freddy!"' Freddy smiled sadly, 'Milk and sugar?'

'Milk, please.' As Freddy poured, Mabel said, 'I suppose after his estate is settled, you'll need to leave. That's too bad. It's a lovely house.' Although a bit too Victorian for Mabel's taste.

'Oh no,' Freddy said, 'I won't need to go anywhere – he's left everything to me.'

SEVEN

'Mr Deuchar left everything – including the house – to you?' Mabel asked, thinking she couldn't have heard the housekeeper clearly.

'Yes,' Freddy said. 'Such a dear boy.' She became engrossed in stirring sugar into her own coffee, and then passed Mabel the plate of biscuits. 'I'm not saying it isn't unusual. But poor Ozzie had no one else. He was only a babe when his grandfather took him in after his parents were killed in a skiing accident in Switzerland.'

'Were you here at the time?' Mabel asked.

'Oh yes,' Freddy said. 'Brought the boy up as if he were my own. His grandfather may have footed the bills, but you know how men are – they leave the tending of children to women.'

Not always. Mabel's papa had had a strong presence in her growing up and she had the memories to prove it.

Freddy went to the mantel, retrieved a small photograph and gave it to Mabel. She held it under the dim light of a lamp to see an old man with a mane of white hair and enormous moustache, seated, and next to him a young boy in a suit wearing a collar too tight for him. There was no mistaking that mild expression.

'How old is he here?'

'Thirteen – it was taken ten years ago.'

Except for growing a few inches taller, little Ozzie hadn't changed one whit.

'The elder Mr Deuchar died when the boy was barely eighteen and as there was no other family, it all came to him. Ozzie hadn't been taught to work and the money is all in investments, so there was nothing for him to do. He had to seek distraction where he could and so he became a gentleman detective.'

'He opened his own business?' Mabel asked.

'Oh yes. He advertised in the papers and occasionally he'd be called in to look for a missing grocery order or a misplaced letter or lost pair of—'

'Spectacles,' Mabel said. This was sounding much of a muchness to many of Mabel's private investigations for Useful Women.

'But mostly he read a great many stories,' Freddy said. 'He saw himself as Dupin, as Inspector Bucket, as Holmes. Perhaps not the priest, but certainly that new fellow – the Belgian. He even loved those tawdry novels you see on the racks outside of bookshops. He was lonely and so those detectives became his friends. Poor boy.'

'He put "Pinkerton trained" on his calling card.'

'Yes,' Freddy said with a smile. 'He admitted to me that he was stretching the truth a bit, although I have no idea who this Pinkerton is.'

'You said he spoke of me,' Mabel said. 'Was that on Friday?'

'No, the day before that,' Freddy said, frowning up at the ceiling as she thought. 'The ship docked on Tuesday, and he came up on the train Wednesday.'

'Did he say how he knew of me?'

'It was because of this case he had – oh my, he was ever so

excited. He was keeping watch on a young woman coming to visit her father. He said that the father told him you would be his daughter's companion and that you were a lady detective in London, and that you had your own agency.'

'No,' Mabel said, quick to correct that misperception, 'I don't have my own agency. I work for Miss Kerr's Useful Women. She has a register of women who can take on all manner of temporary jobs. It's just that private investigation is my speciality.'

'Nevertheless,' Freddy said, 'Ozzie was quite impressed. His enthusiasm may have got the better of him – as it often did – and he may have assumed you would be working together on a case.'

Mabel had seen first-hand Oswald's enthusiasm for his job. And now, she saw his generosity. 'It was kind of him to make sure you would be looked after.'

'I didn't want this place.' The housekeeper looked round as if the walls were closing in. 'I told him so. I said I'll be gone long before you and even if I'm not, all I need is a bit of money to go live in the country. But Ozzie said it was a dangerous job being a detective, and he must be prepared. He said if I had the house, too, I could do as I pleased and not be bothered by anyone.' She clicked her tongue. 'That was pie-in-the-sky thinking.'

'And what about the others on staff?' Mabel asked.

'There's no one but me,' Freddy said. 'After the elder Mr Deuchar died, they all left one by one – the upstairs maid, the cook and the rest. There didn't seem any reason to replace them, but now, I don't know. The char woman comes in, of course, and occasionally someone will knock on the door at the back and ask for work.' The housekeeper sighed.

Mabel opened her satchel to give Freddy a copy of the Useful Women booklet – she liked to have a few handy to pass to potential clients – but found she'd run out.

A sound came from the rear of the house – a door opening

and closing. There was a shuffling noise and then a falsetto voice calling, 'Come out, come out wherever you are!'

The kind, soft Mrs Fredericks disappeared, and she hardened as if bracing herself against an anticipated blow. 'I'm very sorry, Miss Canning—'

She got no further when a man appeared in the doorway. He saw them and a leer of a smile grew wide on his face as if his lips were made of rubber. He ran a hand over his lank, thin dark hair. He wore an unbuttoned coat over a collarless shirt that had a stain down the front. At the waist his trousers strained against the button.

'Here she is being lady of the manor,' he said, his voice warbly and oleaginous. 'And a visitor! Will you introduce me, and shall I join you for coffee?' He rocked back and forth on his heels, appeared to lose his balance and grabbed hold of a nude bronze statue nearly his same height to steady himself.

Freddy didn't look at him, but said to Mabel, 'Miss Canning, this is my husband, Mr Fredericks.'

'The pleasure is all mine, Miss Canning,' Fredericks said, sidling up to Mabel. He leaned over to take her hand and she was nearly overwhelmed by the odour of stale beer and a body long overdue for a wash.

'Hello, Mr Fredericks,' Mabel choked out.

'Call me Fred, will you? She's Mrs Fredericks but called Freddy and I'm Fred Fredericks and called Fred. That's a kind of joke, isn't it?' He chuckled and glanced round the morning room, his eyes settling on the drinks tray in the corner. 'Might we have a nip of something to celebrate your glorious inheritance, dear wife?'

'No, we may not,' Freddy said through clenched teeth.

'All right, all right,' he said, seemingly unbothered. 'As long as I have a shilling or two to send me on my way.'

Freddy reached into the pocket of her apron and drew out a

small purse. She took two coins and handed them over. 'Here. Now, off you go.'

'No need to get shirty,' Fredericks said. 'Not after the favour I've done you.'

'Go on,' Freddy said as if shooing away a stray dog. 'Get out.'

He spun round and walked off, knocking his shoulder into the door post and setting the wall sconce to shake.

The housekeeper turned her back on him. Her cheeks were glowing red, but she drew herself up and in a dignified tone said, 'I'm so very sorry, Miss Canning.'

'There's no need to apologise,' Mabel said. 'Was your husband employed as part of the household, too?'

'Certainly not. At least I could put my foot down about that. Fred lives elsewhere and works as a street cleaner. When he works at all.'

Mabel heard a door open and close, and Freddy leapt up. 'Dear God, he went out the front. What will people think? Thumbing his nose at me, as usual.'

'Does he worry you?' Mabel asked. 'Is he... violent? Because you could tell the police.'

'Little good that would do,' Freddy said. 'When have you ever known police to tell a husband he needs to stay away from his own wife?' She shook her head as if to be rid of the thought of him.

They were quiet as Mabel thought about her next move. 'Did Mr Deuchar say anything before he left for the Palais that made you think there would be trouble?'

'Trouble?' Freddy asked. 'No, I can't think – wait. Earlier in the day, he'd been to see Mr Arkwright and came back quite excited. "Something's afoot, Freddy" he told me. "It's peculiar," he said. "I saw someone that got my mind to whirring. I can sense these things." He always admired the detectives who could pull a clue out of thin air.'

Peculiar was just the word Deuchar had spoken before he'd locked Mabel in the larder. What had he seen or heard? Had that peculiar clue resulted in his murder?

'Wait now' – Freddy put a finger up – 'later, Mr Arkwright arrived here and he and little Ozzie went off to the study. They didn't want coffee and they closed the door, but I could hear raised voices.'

Mabel waited for more, but nothing further came. 'They argued?' she asked. 'What about?'

The housekeeper lifted her hands, palms up. 'I heard no words and didn't see Mr Arkwright leave. Afterward, Ozzie made light of it. "Emotions can run high," he told me, "where loved ones are concerned."'

Had Arkwright admitted this to Tollerton?

'Now Miss Canning,' Freddy said, 'I want you to know that I give you permission to go through Ozzie's detective bits and bobs and do whatever you like with them.'

'Did he keep a notebook?'

'He wrote voraciously.'

'Thank you, Freddy, I would very much like to read his most recent notebooks, because they might have clues that would lead to the person who did this terrible thing. Mr Deuchar's death may have nothing to do with the Arkwrights – it could be another of his cases.' *Murder over missing spectacles?*

'And I would hand them over this minute if I could,' Freddy said, 'except that Detective Inspector Tollerton from Scotland Yard took them away.'

'Ah well,' Mabel said, disappointed, but not surprised. 'They are in safe hands. I know Inspector Tollerton and he's a fine policeman. It's his job to find out who murdered Oswald.'

'I don't see why it can't be your job, too,' Freddy said. 'I could pay you.'

Wouldn't that be a boon to her post office savings account?

For the briefest of moments, Mabel contemplated working for two masters – or would that be one master and one mistress?

'Rest assured, Freddy, that I will work for the same answers as the police, but you won't have to pay me to do so. I'm already involved in the case, and Scotland Yard has grown accustomed to me hanging about.'

The bell went off and the housekeeper flinched but recovered quickly. 'He would never ring the bell,' she muttered as she went off to answer.

It was a man at the door, but not Freddy's husband. Mabel heard his voice and so went out to see Winstone and Gladys on the doorstep. The outdoors – even with grey skies – looked bright and inviting against the dark entrance hall. Behind them, a taxi waited.

'Did you learn much?' Winstone asked as the taxi sped down Marylebone Road. Inside with the windows closed and the cabbie up front, Mabel felt free to talk.

'Oh, yes. Did you see a man leave a few minutes ago?'

'I did, and that's when I decided to hail a taxi and come for you. Who was it?'

'That was Mrs Fredericks' husband. Two more unlikely people to be married I've never seen. She works and he... sponges. Wait now, I should start at the beginning.'

She went through what she'd learned about little Ozzie from the housekeeper, keeping the best for last.

'It's possible his murder has nothing to do with Arkwright,' she said. 'Oswald Deuchar left everything to Freddy.'

'Everything? And I take it, that's a vast amount?'

'The house and money – piles of it, probably. And just now, Freddy's lout of a husband wandered through looking for a drink to celebrate her inheritance and to remind her of a great favour he'd done her.'

Mabel watched Winstone's face as the comment sank in. 'There's a turn-up for the books,' he said. 'I wonder does Tolly know.'

'I wonder what sort of alibi Mr Fred Fredericks has for Friday evening.'

By the time they reached New River House, Mabel itched to sit down with her own notebook. Gladys hopped out of the taxi ahead of them and they went to the door while Winstone paid the driver. The minute they set foot in the foyer, Mr Chigley appeared at the counter.

'You have a visitor, Miss Canning,' he said, giving a small nod behind him.

Mabel looked past him into the porter's office and there, wearing her double-breasted emerald-green plaid coat and perched on the desk chair with cup and saucer in hand, was Roxanne.

EIGHT

'Hi, Mabel,' Roxanne said brightly, popping up and setting her drink down. 'Thanks so much, Mr Chigley, you're a doll for letting me wait in your office.'

Mr Chigley turned scarlet and sputtered something that might have been 'No trouble at all.'

'Roxanne,' Mabel said, 'this is a surprise.'

Roxanne ducked under the end of the counter before Mr Chigley could raise the drawbridge.

'Hello, Mr Winstone. Hello, Gladys.' She gave the dog a pat and Park a big smile.

'Good morning, Miss Arkwright,' Park replied. Gladys *woofed*.

'Have you three been to church?' Roxanne asked.

Mabel ignored the question. 'I didn't realise you were coming to call. On your own. Unless you've brought your father or stepmother along with you?' Mabel made an exaggerated survey of the empty foyer.

A bit of Roxanne's bravado leaked away. 'Oh, please don't sound like Mama, Mabel. I hardly needed to be escorted between Father's house and yours. I took a taxi.' She pulled her flat leather purse from her coat pocket and opened it to show two pound notes and a few coins. 'I let him pick out the fare, but I suppose I'd better learn what these things are.' She held up a half crown. 'Is this the same as a fifty-cent piece?'

'I have no idea,' Mabel said. 'Did you tell your father you were coming?'

Roxanne's lower lip popped out. 'I hope I'm not intruding.'

'I'm delighted to see you,' Mabel said, 'but that's beside the point.'

'I left a note,' she said in a defensive tone.

The telephone on the wall jangled and Roxanne flinched.

'Excuse me, won't you?' Mr Chigley said as he lifted the end of the counter, walked out of his office and to the telephone.

'Hello, good morning,' he answered. 'New River House.'

Neither Mabel, Winstone nor Roxanne – whose face had lost all colour – spoke as they listened to Mr Chigley. Mabel, who had a knack for filling in details of the unheard half of a telephone conversation, believed anyone could've done it on this occasion.

'Yes, good morning, sir... Chigley is the name, sir. I am the porter here.' He glanced over at the trio plus dog. 'Yes, sir, I believe she is and appears quite well... Let me just...'

Roxanne shrank behind Mabel as if needing a buffer between herself and the telephone. Mabel patted her hand and walked over. 'I'll take it,' she said to Mr Chigley, who handed her the earpiece and scooted out of the way.

'Mr Arkwright?' Mabel asked.

'Miss Canning,' Arkwright spat out, reminding Mabel very much of her old and highly disagreeable schoolmaster. 'Please explain to me why my daughter is there when you were both given explicit instructions that she should stay indoors today?'

In the background, Mabel could hear a woman talking in a calm voice. 'Rupert, there's no need to. ' It was Adelaide. If only she were on the telephone.

'I don't remember any such explicit instruction, Mr Arkwright,' Mabel said. 'I remember you suggesting I might not want to be bothered on a Sunday.'

Like a steam engine that's pulled into the yard, its *chuff-chuffing* petering out to nothing, Arkwright began with a bluster. 'The point was to...' and then there was Adelaide's voice again and he sighed and said, 'Yes, yes. Is my daughter all right?'

'She's fine,' Mabel said.

'I'll be over directly,' Arkwright said.

'I'd like it if Roxanne stayed for the afternoon – I'm sure we'll find something to do. I might need help washing out my stockings.'

She probably shouldn't have said that to Rupert Arkwright, but it made Roxanne giggle.

'Adelaide,' Arkwright said away from the mouthpiece, and the next voice Mabel heard was hers.

'Miss Canning, all is well?'

'It is, Mrs Arkwright. I'm happy to have Roxanne visit and I'll be sure to escort her home personally.'

'Thank you. There really seemed no point in confining the poor girl to the house. I'm not surprised she made a break for it. We'll see you later.'

Mabel had barely replaced the earpiece on its hook before the door to the street flew open and Skeff and Cora came tumbling in, laughing. The two stopped when they saw them.

Skeff spread her arms and said, 'This is a grand gathering.' She looked at Roxanne with raised eyebrows.

'Skeff, Cora, this is Roxanne Arkwright,' Mabel said.

Hands were shaken all round, including Gladys' paw, even though she'd already met everyone.

'We've just come to find you, Mabel,' Skeff said. 'Remember you wanted a drawing done.' She said nothing more, but rocked on her heels and gave Mabel a significant look.

'Yes, I do,' Mabel said. 'Where is he?'

'Down at the churchyard. I thought we'd nip back here to make a few sandwiches.'

'Are we going on a picnic?' Roxanne asked.

They went off to their respective flats to glean what they could from their larders. Roxanne followed Mabel, and when the door was opened she took two steps in and cast her eyes over her surroundings as if she'd entered an enchanted forest.

'This is just yours,' she said. 'You live here.'

'It is and I do,' Mabel said.

'You have your own kitchen and sitting room and you can be alone if you want to be,' Roxanne said with awe. 'No one can tell you you're too old to keep a rag doll on the bed or not old enough to come to London on your own. No one can tell you to come downstairs this instant and eat your dinner even if you hate liver. No one can tell you anything.'

Mabel hated to burst the bubble of Roxanne's idealised version of her life. Plenty of people could still tell her what to do. Or at least try.

'It's just a flat,' Mabel said.

'Yes, but it's *your* flat. Here's your bedroom,' Roxanne said. She went to the window. 'Look! I can see down to the street.' She turned to Mabel with a sly look. 'Does Mr Winstone visit you in your flat, Mabel?'

'Yes, he does.' Mabel attempted without success to keep from blushing at Roxanne's innuendo. 'And I visit him in his.'

'What do you do to while away the hours?'

'We play the piano,' Mabel said abruptly. Roxanne narrowed her eyes, as if trying to sort out whether that meant something else, which it didn't. Yet.

'Oh, Mabel,' Roxanne continued to wax, 'this is so... modern. Juliet has moved to New York and has a flat, but Mama would have a fit if I wanted to live on my own.'

'Remember I'm a bit older than you.'

'But still, didn't your mother object?'

'My mother died when I was a baby.'

Roxanne looked stricken. 'How terrible. You must miss her.'

Mabel shrugged. 'I miss what I imagine she would've been like. It was certainly terrible for her and for my father. We were living in India, and Papa engaged an ayah – like a nanny – to take care of me on the return journey. Once here, she stayed and became our housekeeper.' The story carried with it more layers than that, but Mabel was accustomed to giving only the highlights. 'Mrs Chandekar was like a mother to me.'

'India! Mabel, you never cease to amaze me.'

'We've known each other for only four days, Roxanne. I daresay there are quite a few stories about your life in Chicago that would amaze me.'

'Like what?' Roxanne asked, her good humour gone. 'I haven't told you anything.'

'No,' Mabel said, 'you haven't. Are you not allowed to?'

Roxanne, chastened, looked down at the bowl of winter pears Mabel had carried in from the kitchen. 'Are those for the picnic?'

Winstone stayed behind but sent Gladys along with the rest of them to St Mary's churchyard up the road. They were all bundled in coats, scarves and hats and their breath shot out in clouds of fog when they spoke.

'Not too cold for you?' Skeff asked Roxanne.

'Too cold?' Roxanne said. 'You don't know cold until you've lived through a Chicago winter.'

'We've a bit of sun,' Cora said, squinting up at the pale yellow orb. 'At least we have the illusion of warmth.'

The churchyard hadn't been used for burials for ages and much of the space had been given over to a garden with trees, grass and a few benches. It appeared empty until out from behind a wide beech trunk leapt a boy of about fourteen. He had a solemn face and a cross-hatched scar on his right cheek, and he wore a floppy newsboy hat, a thin coat and trousers that came just to his ankles. He carried a battered cricket bat.

'Hello, Flea,' Mabel said, 'How are you?' Flea nodded a few times and then raised his eyebrows at Mabel. 'I'm well, thanks,' she said.

Skeff had introduced Mabel to Flea in the autumn, when he helped with her first case of private investigation for Useful Women. Flea seemed to live off his wits, although Skeff had told her he had a bed at a pub down at the docks. The young man didn't speak, but he communicated quite well nonetheless through head nods, finger snaps, whistles and gestures. He had a fine talent for drawing and with an economy of pencil lines could produce an easily recognised picture of a person or place.

'Roxanne, this is Flea, a friend of ours,' Skeff said. 'He doesn't talk, but he makes himself understood.'

Mabel held her breath, poised to intervene if Roxanne was rude to the boy.

'Hi, Flea,' Roxanne said and held out her hand.

Flea looked at her hand, wiped his own on his trousers and shook.

Roxanne's gaze fell to the battered cricket bat in his hand.

'That's a funny-looking baseball bat you've got there,' she said.

Flea put a hand to his chest in mock surprise. He held the cricket bat up shoulder-high and swung it, but then shook his head, lowered the bat and swung again.

'Cricket, is that it?' she asked. 'Where's the ball?'

Flea produced a worn red ball from his pocket and made to toss it to her once and then did it, in fact.

Roxanne caught it with one hand. 'I don't know cricket, but

I was pitcher on my school's softball team. Let's see if you can hit this. Back up a ways, now.'

Mabel, Skeff and Cora could only watch as Roxanne wound up her right arm – round and round it went like a pinwheel and then she let the ball go underhanded. Flea swung at it and missed as it sailed waist-high straight past him. It ricocheted off a gravestone, hit the ground and skittered past Gladys, who had found something fascinating at the base of a birch and ignored it.

'Strike one!' Roxanne shouted as Flea chased the ball and threw it back to her. 'Ready?' She wound up again and this time the satisfying *thunk* of leather on wood echoed in the cold air.

The two players then engaged in a heated discussion and a great deal of laughter about running the bases and scoring. The exchange was heavy with Roxanne's voice although Flea held up his side of the conversation after his own fashion.

Mabel turned to Skeff and Cora. 'I can't say I expected that.'

'Aren't they sweet together?' Cora asked. 'Well, who's for a sandwich?'

They laid the blanket in a patch of winter sun and pretended to be warm as they ate ham sandwiches and the pears Mabel had brought. Skeff produced a flask of tea and they shared one cup, and soon it came time for Flea to get to work.

'I'm hoping Flea will draw us a picture of that beetle-browed man who kept asking you for a dance,' Mabel explained to Roxanne.

'Why?' Roxanne asked as she watched Flea produce a small drawing pad and a pencil from his pocket.

'Because it's important to talk with everyone who was at the Palais Friday evening,' Mabel said. 'That fellow might hold a vital clue without even knowing it, but he had already left by the time the police arrived. Perhaps with a good likeness, we can track him down.'

Instead of a witness, he could be the killer, but Mabel didn't think there was a need to bring that up.

'Once we have a drawing, I'll hand it over to the police,' she said, 'so they can ask their own questions. But it would be nice to have my own copy, so, would you draw it twice, Flea?'

Mabel gave the beginning of a description and Flea went to work.

Roxanne added a detail or two. 'I think he might've been wearing a' – she dropped her voice to a whisper – '*toupee*.' She snickered. 'I could see the line at the top of his forehead.'

Flea finished up and held the pad in front of his chest to show them.

'That's him, isn't it, Mabel?' Roxanne asked. 'You're a real artist, Flea.'

'There's someone else I'd like you to draw,' Mabel said, and described Fred Fredericks.

Flea frowned at the finished portrait, Roxanne made a face at it and Cora said, 'Oh dear.'

'Yes,' Mabel said, 'that's him. Could you do another of the same?'

'And after that, could you do a drawing of Gladys?' Roxanne asked.

Gladys, after devouring half a sandwich from Roxanne, had found her own patch of sun on a nearby path and sat posing. The artist and his assistant moved off closer to their subject. Skeff stretched out on the extra blanket space and put her head in Cora's lap.

Roxanne was far enough out of earshot for Mabel to say, 'Her mother will be here in a few days, and I may be dismissed. What would Roxanne need with a companion then? But I'll stick with it in the meantime.'

Cora ran her fingers through Skeff's short hair and said, 'She needs you, Mabel. You're like an older sister to her.'

Mabel blushed at the compliment.

Skeff lit a cigarette. 'Oswald Deuchar's name will be in all the papers by tomorrow,' she said. 'Or perhaps he'll be described as "the grandson of George Deuchar", because it's the old man who made the money. Tollerton is letting out few details, as usual.'

'I don't believe he has many details yet,' Mabel said. 'I'll see if I can talk with him tomorrow.'

Roxanne darted over to them. 'Mabel, do you have your map with you? May I borrow it for a moment?'

Mabel retrieved the Bacon's from her satchel and Roxanne returned to Flea where she unfolded the map, took the boy's pencil and began pointing to various places. When the tour of London had apparently ended, Flea took his pencil back and got to work making one quick drawing after the other at Roxanne's request. She talked and laughed and punched the boy in the arm in a playful manner. When they finished, Flea began tossing his cricket ball for Gladys, and Roxanne came over to Mabel, her hand full of drawings. 'Look at this one, Mabel – it's me.'

'It's lovely,' Mabel said, standing and holding out the drawing. Flea had managed to catch that elusive spirit of Roxanne's that bounced between joy and frustration. 'You should show it to your father and stepmother.'

Roxanne watched Flea with a smile. 'I like him,' she said. 'You hardly notice he doesn't speak, because he talks in so many other ways. He reminds me of Tommy.'

'Who is Tommy?' Mabel asked.

Roxanne flinched as if an invisible hand had slapped itself across her mouth.

'Roxanne?' Mabel put a hand on her elbow, because it looked as if she might collapse on the spot.

Her eyes wide and dark, Roxanne shook her head violently. 'No, I can't—'

At that moment, Flea threw the ball in a high arc and

Gladys, eyes on the prize, ran flat out in a straight line that took her flying across the picnic blanket and between Mabel and Roxanne, knocking them both out of her way. Cora leapt up and caught Roxanne as she let go of her handful of drawings. Skeff wasn't quick enough to save Mabel, who fell on her bottom. After a moment of shock, everyone laughed. Flea put his hands up, palms out, as apology, and Gladys returned with the ball, dropped it at the boy's feet and sat, tongue lolling out the side of her mouth in triumph.

The sun, such as it was, dipped below the tree line, and Cora shivered.

'Time to pack up, don't you think?' Skeff asked.

Mabel bent over and retrieved one of Flea's drawings. 'Look, here's Gladys.'

With only a curly mark here and there, the boy had captured the dog's stiff coat and brown saddle marking, and her noble pose, with her head turned to the side and chin raised.

Roxanne scrambled to collect the other drawings off the grass and put them in her coat pocket. 'Flea says I can keep these. I want to buy him a new drawing pad. We'll see him again, won't we, Mabel?'

On the pavement outside New River House, Flea tugged on his cap, gave Roxanne a light punch on the arm and headed down the road.

'Won't he come in?' Roxanne asked, adjusting her brimmed hat and tucking in a ragged end of her hair.

'Not really his milieu,' Skeff said as she pulled open the door and they filed into the foyer.

'Have a good afternoon, did you?' Mr Chigley asked.

'A fine afternoon,' Mabel said. 'Is Mr Winstone in?'

'Out,' the porter reported. 'He said he's gone to see a man

about a horse.' Gladys made a throaty comment. Mr Chigley looked down and added, 'Don't worry, it's just a saying.'

Gladys ducked under the counter, went directly to the gas heater on the wall, stretched out on the small hearth rug and sighed.

'All right to leave her with you?' Mabel asked.

'Always,' Mr Chigley said.

'I promised your father and stepmother I'd see you home,' Mabel said to Roxanne, 'but before we go, I wanted to tell you that Cora is the one who cut my long hair into a bob when I first arrived in London in September. Didn't she do a wonderful job?' Mabel patted the curls that came just to her chin.

'Your hair is lovely, Roxanne,' Cora said with a tentative tone to her voice.

Roxanne's hand went up to the ragged ends. 'It's dreadful,' she said. 'I cut it myself on the boat. Mama has insisted that I keep my hair long, but I wanted it short. She won't be happy about it when she arrives.'

'Well, I'd say your cut is quite original,' Cora said, 'but if you like, I could even it out for you.'

'Cora's a dab hand with a pair of shears,' Skeff said.

That settled it. They went up to Cora and Skeff's flat and soon Roxanne looked like any other modern young woman with her dark auburn hair in a sleek bob.

'Oh my,' Roxanne said as she gazed at herself in the mirror on the wall by the door. 'Thank you, Cora.' She turned to face them. 'Thank you all. I've had such a lovely afternoon...' The last word petered out to a whisper as tears filled her eyes. 'You've been so kind and...' Her chin quivered and Mabel put an arm round the girl's shoulders. 'I shouldn't cry. When she arrives, Mama will tell me I brought this all on myself. I'll have to own up to tricking Miss Hawksley, and Juliet will get in trouble for helping me, and Mama has had to interrupt her winter in Florida... and that poor man died.'

'That had nothing to do with you,' Mabel said, speaking, of course, only about Oswald Deuchar's murder. 'And surely your mother is coming because she's worried about you, not because she's angry.'

Roxanne caught hold of herself, sniffed and coughed, which was halfway to a laugh. 'Sometimes it's difficult to tell the difference.'

Mr Chigley hailed a taxi for them, and Mabel and Roxanne spent a quiet journey to Mayfair. But when they arrived at the house and Mabel reached to open the door, Roxanne put a hand on her arm.

'Mabel, do you think my father truly wanted me to visit?'

'He told me he's wanted it for years.'

Roxanne frowned. 'Mama has always said he threw us out. That we were forced to move back to America. That he took all of her money.'

Mabel had taken note of the wide variation in the stories about MaryLou and Roxanne departing for Chicago. 'I don't know what went wrong in your parents' marriage, but perhaps it was an emotional time for both of them. As the years go by, it can be convenient to change the past to suit our own purposes. When your mother arrives, perhaps they can put that to rest.'

'Will Mother Adelaide be all right, do you think, about Mama being here?'

Mabel marvelled at this growth in Roxanne in the few days since they'd met – here was the young woman concerned about someone else's well-being.

'I believe your stepmother wants the best for you,' Mabel said, 'and if that means having your mother here, then so be it.'

Roxanne nodded in an absentminded fashion. 'And really, Mama doesn't mean to scare people,' she said. 'At least, not all the time.'

The curtains to the side of the door twitched, followed by Trigg emerging. He opened the taxi door and Roxanne stepped out.

'There you are,' Mabel said, 'safe home.'

'Won't you come in?' Roxanne asked through the taxi's window.

'Not this time. I'll see you soon.'

Trigg paid the cabbie for the full fare, including taking Mabel back to Islington, but then told the driver to wait. Adelaide Arkwright came out and approached the taxi.

'Mother Adelaide, I knew where I was going the entire time,' Roxanne said. 'I can show you on the map in the library where Islington is. It wasn't as if I was going off half-cocked as Mama says.'

'Good, I want to see it,' her stepmother said. 'You go on in and I'll be right there. I only want to thank Miss Canning. And Roxanne, your hair looks lovely.'

Roxanne's hand went up to touch her new bob. She smiled, waved at Mabel and disappeared.

'We had a lovely afternoon,' Mabel said through the open window. 'I think Roxanne quite enjoyed herself.'

'I can see it on her face and I'm so grateful. So is her father.' Mrs Arkwright smiled and tapped a finger on the edge of the taxi door. 'Miss Canning, I would like to have a longer talk with you. I wonder if you would be willing to meet me tomorrow afternoon at my club?'

'Yes, I'd be happy to.'

Mrs Arkwright gave the taxi a firm pat as if sealing a deal. 'Good. It's the Minerva Club in Brunswick Square. Shall we say half past five?'

Upon her return to New River House, Mr Chigley announced that 'Mr Winstone hopes you will join him at the Old Ivy' in such a formal manner, it didn't sound at all as if she were being asked to meet a man at a pub on a Sunday.

'I'll just fetch my satchel and be on my way,' she said.

Mabel had seldom had such a busy Sunday. She still hadn't got to washing out her stockings, but had decided they could wait, because she felt fairly certain that Detective Inspector Tollerton would be at the Old Ivy, too.

They'd met there before, and so Mabel had no qualms walking into the pub – already doing good business having just opened for the evening. The man behind the bar nodded to her and then down the corridor towards the back room.

Tolly sat at a table with his coat still on – Mabel wasn't sure she'd ever seen him with it off – and Park across from him, flipping through his pocket notebook. They both had pints of beer in front of them with one waiting for her. Gladys, instead of being stretched out in front of the fire, sat attentively at Park's elbow, her nose close to the table's edge and not far from the platter holding several small pork pies, bread and cheese, and a few apples.

The men stood briefly and sat when Mabel did. They exchanged 'Good evenings' and, pleasantries done, set to eating as they went over what they had discovered so far. Mabel asked, 'Is Rupert Arkwright a suspect?'

'Should he be?' Tollerton asked in that police fashion of never answering a question. Mabel now knew how to work round it.

'Does Deuchar's murder have anything to do with the Arkwrights – with Roxanne?' If she couldn't get answers, she could at least ask the questions on her mind.

'If we had anything solid on the murder, I might be able to answer that,' Tollerton said. 'As it is, Miss Arkwright needs to be careful.'

'She was with me all afternoon,' Mabel said, 'and I rode in the taxi back to the house in Mayfair.'

'Her father needs to be watched, too,' Park said, and at Mabel's furrowed brow added, 'It's the nature of an enquiry, isn't it?'

She knew it was. 'You've been to see Oswald Deuchar's housekeeper,' she said to Tollerton, 'and she told you the two men argued.'

'Too bad she didn't listen at the door so we could know what it was they were arguing about,' Tollerton replied.

'Did Arkwright have the opportunity Friday evening?' she asked.

Winstone flipped a page of his notebook. 'There's a twenty- to twenty-five-minute discrepancy in Arkwright's account of what time he arrived at the Palais and what time the cabbie said he was dropped off.'

'Witnesses saw him walk into the Palais almost the moment Miss Arkwright screamed when Deuchar fell towards her,' Tollerton said. 'It would be close, but he could've done it.'

'And any sign of the weapon?' Mabel asked as she peeled an apple.

'I have the pathologist's report,' Tollerton said. 'He was struck repeatedly, all blows to the back of the head.'

Mabel set the apple down and took a long drink of her beer, then asked, 'Any idea how large an object the weapon was?'

'Nothing too unwieldy,' Tollerton said. 'Perhaps something the murderer could put in his pocket and walk away with.'

'So, possibly a brick – or half a brick,' Mabel said. 'But not a frying pan.' At Tollerton's raised brows, she added, 'The kitchen is on the other side of the dance floor.'

'Kitchens are full of potential weapons,' Winstone said. 'Knives, mallets, heavy tins of food.'

'Rolling pins,' Mabel added. 'No, too large.'

'A tin of soup might've done it,' Tollerton said, 'but weren't all the tins in the larder with you? Still, I'll have someone go through all the kitchen equipment piece by piece with the chef – make sure everything's accounted for.'

'Could it have been a robbery gone wrong?' Mabel asked. 'Oswald surprised the thief?'

'The safe is in the office and Bryars told me he keeps his office locked at all times,' Tollerton said.

'He also said the safe was the first place he looked when Roxanne found Deuchar and the commotion began,' Winstone said. 'No money missing. None taken from the bar either.'

'That's not to say Deuchar didn't surprise someone doing something he shouldn't,' Tollerton added.

'What about Mr Bryars himself?' Mabel asked.

'Yes,' Tollerton said, 'what about him? He's got one of the most air-tight alibis of anyone that evening. It's his style to circulate, so that his employees from cloakroom to kitchen to doorman will know to be on their toes. We mapped his movements. He looks clean as a new pin, and I don't like it.'

Mabel opened her satchel and pulled out Flea's drawings.

'Here is the beetle-browed man who asked Roxanne to dance several times and was gone by the time you arrived.'

Tollerton held it out for inspection. 'Who did this drawing?'

'Why?' Mabel asked.

'It's quite good. He wouldn't want a job with the Metropolitan Police?'

'I'll certainly mention it to him,' Mabel said and smiled as she imagined Flea's reaction.

'I don't know him,' Tollerton said and passed the drawing to Winstone, who looked at it and frowned.

'Do you know him?' Mabel asked.

Winstone squinted at the image of the beetle-browed man. 'I may.'

'Where do you know him from?' Tollerton asked. 'Someone we arrested before the war?'

'I'll have to think about it.'

'I'll turn this drawing over to a couple of the PCs to go through the books,' Tollerton said. 'They'll need to see it at the dance hall, too.'

'I have an extra copy,' Mabel said.

'Good,' Winstone said. 'You and I could show it round the Palais tomorrow evening.'

'Yes, we could,' she agreed. She reminded herself that this would be part of an enquiry, not an evening of dancing.

Winstone tossed the last bite of pork pie to Gladys, gathered their empty glasses and asked, 'Same again?'

Tollerton agreed, but Mabel said, 'Could I have a cup of tea?'

As Winstone went out to the bar, Mabel showed the drawing of Fred Fredericks to Tollerton.

'Do you know this man?' she asked. 'He's the husband of Oswald Deuchar's housekeeper.'

Tollerton took a sharp look at the drawing. 'She told me no one else lived there.'

'Strictly speaking, he doesn't live there, and she made it quite clear she wished she could have nothing to do with the man, but he appears to wander through at will. Dodgy doesn't half describe him.'

'You've met him?' Tollerton asked.

'Mrs Fredericks asked me over this morning.'

'As much as I appreciate your assistance, Miss Canning, you should not—'

'Park was across the road the entire time, you can ask him. You took Oswald's notebooks.'

'I did.' He rested his forearms on the table. 'Five of them chock-full of his close, careful writing. Would you like to take a look and see if you can pick up a tune from it?'

Tollerton made reference to one of Mabel's special skills – when she looked at a person's handwriting, she often heard music and that music seemed to reflect the person.

'I don't see it would help Oswald now,' she said. 'But, can you tell me, what did he write?'

'Stories.' Tollerton rolled his eyes. 'Detective stories, of course. All starring himself and all quite fantastic. Nothing connected to an actual case.'

'I don't believe he had much in the way of an actual case apart from finding missing grocery orders and lost spectacles,' Mabel said. 'What did he ever do to anyone to deserve this?'

They drank in silence for a moment, then Tollerton said, 'How did you know about the housekeeper?'

'Deuchar gave me his calling card, so I rang the number on it, and discovered it was the telephone at his house, not at a detective agency. Mrs Fredericks said little Ozzie, as she calls him, had talked about me and so she hoped to... I'm not sure. Either learn what I knew or enlist me in finding his murderer. Her husband interrupted us.' Mabel felt a stirring of purpose. 'She wasn't happy to see him, but at the same time, perhaps she wanted me to meet him so that he would become a suspect without her coming out and saying it.'

'A suspect?'

'In Oswald's murder. Mr Fredericks seemed to take great joy in reminding his wife that he'd done her "a favour".'

'Why would killing Deuchar be a favour if the woman doted on her employer?' Tollerton asked as Winstone returned with two pints. A girl followed with a tea tray and Mabel waited until she had gone.

'Because Oswald Deuchar left Freddy everything – did she not tell you?'

Mabel took no pleasure in knowing more than Scotland Yard. Oh all right, perhaps a bit of pleasure.

As Mabel, Winstone and Gladys walked home, she said, 'It might help if Scotland Yard sent a woman to talk with a woman sometimes. It helped with Freddy, didn't it? He should send WPC Wardle to do interviews.'

'Wardle is a good officer,' Winstone said. When they reached the doorstep of New River House, he paused. 'You don't think this Freddy and her husband are in it together and she's playing the innocent?'

'It's a possibility, I suppose. We'll need to show Fred's drawing around the Palais, too, won't we?' Mabel hoped Freddy wasn't involved but couldn't discount it entirely. She could, however, change the subject for the rest of the evening.

'How about a glass of blackberry wine and an evening with the piano?'

NINE

On Monday morning, Mabel looked forward to sitting in her usual chair across from Miss Kerr and having a good chinwag. This would be the perfect time, Mabel thought, to ask a few pointed questions about the Arkwrights.

But she caught Miss Kerr on the telephone and in the middle of taking the details about a job. When that conversation finished, the telephone jangled again. So, Mabel went to the cabinet and took a few more copies of booklet number eight for her satchel. At last, Miss Kerr replaced the earpiece on the hook, and said, 'Good morning, Miss Canning. I must say, you do look as if you're holding up well.'

Mabel could only nod in reply, because the telephone went off again. She gave her employer a wave and left. Out on Dover Street, she plunged her hands in her pockets and took stock of her day. She would look in on Roxanne, take Freddy a Useful Women booklet, then return to Islington for some much-needed shopping – she'd had tea with no milk that morning.

. . .

When Mabel rounded the corner on Piccadilly, she was met with a wave of pedestrians flowing towards her and she felt rather like a lone Scottish salmon swimming upstream. Then she saw, standing in the nearest doorway, Miss Gregory and so pushed her way over to the shelter.

'Bit of a crush today, isn't it?' Mabel commented.

Miss Gregory started at the sight of her. 'I didn't see you coming.'

Mabel touched her bucket hat—a rusty velvet with a cluster of russet silk oak leaves at one side. 'It's my hat. My friend Cora designs them. She says that a different hat can change your entire appearance.'

'I'd say she's right there,' Miss Gregory replied. 'Yes, the pavement is full of people intent on getting to where they are going. I stepped in here so that I wouldn't be run over. I needed to catch my breath before I go up to Miss Kerr.'

'Has another assignment gone wrong?' Mabel asked, then blushed. 'I mean—'

'No, no, it's all right,' Miss Gregory said. 'It was lovely of you to put a good word in and Miss Kerr has given me more jobs. Today, I will unstick the drawers on a Welsh dresser.'

'Ah,' Mabel said. 'I advise candlewax on the runners.'

'Duly noted.' She glanced sideways at Mabel. 'What about you?'

'Oh, well, I...' Should she really be talking about the murder?

'The thing is,' Miss Gregory said slowly, as if being cautious, 'the woman who runs the boarding house where I live gets all the papers in, and you must admit the word "murder" in a headline is a real eye-catcher. And Arkwright – isn't that the client you mentioned?'

'Yes, course,' Mabel said. 'But it's a police matter now.'

Miss Gregory looked surprised. 'But you run private investigations for Miss Kerr.'

'Yes,' Mabel said, 'and we do all we can to work with Scotland Yard on these matters.' Mabel hoped she didn't sound officious, but a murder enquiry wasn't fodder for casual chat.

'They're lucky to have you,' Miss Gregory said. 'Look, you wouldn't fancy coffee and cake at the Corner House – with absolutely no talk of murder?'

Mabel's schedule was her own until four o'clock that afternoon. 'I'd love to.'

'Good,' Miss Gregory said. 'Only, you do look a bit peaky.'

'Do I?' Mabel asked. Perhaps Miss Kerr had been too kind when she commented about Mabel *holding up well*. Coffee and cake should put her to rights.

One of the waitresses raised her chin in greeting when she saw Mabel, and the waitress who came to take their order greeted her in a friendly way.

'Everyone seems to know you,' Miss Gregory said. 'Do you come here often?'

'Probably too often for my budget,' Mabel said. 'Lunch, tea, coffee. Although surely a sixpence lunch of devilled sardines isn't too extravagant.'

Over slices of Battenberg and the general chatter and clatter in the café, they exchanged stories about being one of Miss Kerr's Useful Women.

'You have more to tell than I do,' Miss Gregory said. 'I started a fortnight ago and already have a reputation.'

'You'll bring Miss Kerr round, I'm sure.'

'Are you in digs?' Miss Gregory asked.

'I have a proper flat,' Mabel said, 'and am incredibly lucky. It's at New River House in Islington. It's turned out to be the best place I could possibly have landed in many respects. Where do you live?'

'Stuffy lodgings with Mrs Oates in Fulham just off the

King's Road,' Miss Gregory replied. 'I have a fine view of the yard out back of the Elm Tree pub.'

'King's Road? I have a friend who lives upstairs from me and works at Milady's on the Chelsea end. This is her hat I'm trying.'

'The both of you should thank your lucky stars. I've a room and two meals of sorts. But I'm lucky to have a room of my own – several of the other girls share.'

'Keeping to a budget is what makes us among Miss Kerr's best workers.'

'I do have a bit of money that's supposed to be mine,' Miss Gregory confided in a low voice, 'but I won't touch it.'

Mabel had a bit of money she didn't want to touch either. It had come from her mother and if money could embody love, that's what the pot represented to Mabel – a way for her mother to watch over her.

'We can't be profligate with our money, can we?'

'Too true. Mine could be taken away any time,' Miss Gregory said. 'I've been thinking about that since my mum died.'

'I'm sorry,' Mabel said. 'When was that?'

'October.'

'Had she been ill?'

'It went on for years after my father died. She could never work. It's because of her that I can do so many different things – I had to, didn't I, because there was no one else. Cook, clean, repairs – I nursed her through that whole last year as the pain got worse and worse. I learned how to manage it for her – how many drops for this, how many drops for that. She was so brave.' She looked into her bag, brought out a folded photograph frame and handed it to Mabel. 'Here, see?'

On one side was a photograph of a woman who looked much like an older Miss Gregory – Mabel even imagined she could see freckles scattered across her nose. The other frame held a death notice. 'Winnie Frances Gregory, widow of John George Gregory, died peacefully in her sleep, 20 October 1921.'

'Peacefully in her sleep, my eye,' Miss Gregory said as she gazed out the window, with a vacant look as if she were not sitting in the Corner House with Mabel, but at her mother's deathbed.

'What about your father?'

Miss Gregory examined the pink and yellow cake crumbs on her plate. 'Yes, what about my father? He died when I was ten. An accident in the rail yard.' She took the double frame from Mabel and carefully pulled out a one-paragraph news-paper cutting.

COAL CAR DEATHS

Two men were found dead at the bottom of a coal car on the rail line at Victoria Docks. Police say the men had climbed into the car when it was empty with a bottle of whisky and had fallen asleep unseen before a load of coal was delivered.

Miss Gregory looked out across the room. 'That's coming up to twelve years ago – an anniversary of sorts. What am I supposed to do,' she said, in a sharp tone, 'mark the occasion by wearing a black mourning band?'

It didn't sound like the happiest of families. The story tugged at Mabel's heart, and she determined to ring home to Peasmarsh. She would wait until evening, after her papa had closed his greengrocer's shop and he and Mrs Chandekar had finished their evening meal. She called up the image of their evenings at home with no trouble.

They would be sitting near the fire, reading and drinking

their cocoa. After, Papa would climb the stairs to bed – had he been moving more slowly when she'd visited at Christmas? – and the housekeeper would wash out their cups before retreating to her own room just off the kitchen. They would be surprised to hear from Mabel, but she felt compelled to tell them how grateful she was for their love and care.

'Not like the father of your American,' Miss Gregory said, bringing Mabel back to the moment. 'He was there at the right moment to defend his daughter.'

'Is that what the papers say?' Mabel asked.

'Why, don't you fancy him for it?' Miss Gregory asked. 'Seems like a story old as time. Father suspects forward young man – and one he'd hired, to boot – had crossed the line with his daughter. He tells him to stay away and when he doesn't, well...' Her hand flew to her mouth and her nose wrinkled. 'What am I on about?' Miss Gregory waved her hand as if clearing the air. 'That's the story in one of those romances I've been reading, so you pay me no mind. Tell me, Miss Canning, do you have another name? I'm Evangeline.'

Mabel walked to the Arkwright house counting her blessings and with admiration for Evangeline Gregory who'd had a much tougher path to independence than she had had. She may be having a rough patch getting started, but with her good humour and willingness to work, Evangeline should make a go of it.

'Good morning, Miss Canning,' Trigg said, blinking at her hat. 'I'm afraid Miss Roxanne isn't at home. She's gone out shopping with Mrs Arkwright.'

'Has she?' Mabel asked, alarmed. 'The two of them alone?'

'Yes,' Trigg said, and frowned. 'Was that unwise?'

Mabel couldn't say. Surely shopping on Oxford Street with your stepmother would pose no danger for Roxanne. Was she in danger?

'No,' Mabel said. 'No, I'm sure it's fine.'

But Trigg apparently didn't believe Mabel's statement and neither did she. 'Shall I ring the shop? It's Mrs Montagu's Fashions. They know madam there.'

'Yes, why not,' Mabel said, trying and failing to sound nonchalant.

She waited in the entrance hall next to the table of narcissus while Trigg went off and returned in only a few minutes.

'They are there. All is well and they will lunch out before returning.'

Mabel breathed a sigh of relief. *Don't get overwrought,* she told herself. What was there to worry about?

'They will return this afternoon before teatime as Mrs Arkwright has a previous engagement,' Trigg said. Yes, Mabel knew about that engagement.

Without Roxanne to keep company, Mabel looked on this as an opportunity to hear more about the Arkwrights. She could learn about Rupert Arkwright as an employer and any tendencies he had towards rage. She might hear from the staff about Oswald Deuchar's visits to the house. There were clues to be mined here, Mabel thought. But who would speak freely to her?

'Might I have a word with Cook?' Mabel said.

Trigg returned to stoic butler. 'I'm afraid Cook has much to do and is at this moment poring over her recipes and sending orders to the butcher, the baker and the greengrocer.'

'Trigg, about the first Mrs Arkwright's impending arrival' – Mabel paused to give him time to comment, but he didn't – 'I hope it won't be too much of an imposition on the household staff.'

'We eagerly await the occasion, ma'am.'

'But it does mean more work for all of you, and Dorcas may particularly be feeling the weight of it. Perhaps Useful Women could help.' Mabel pulled a copy of booklet number eight from her satchel.

'Yes, ma'am, Useful Women,' Trigg said, taking neither the bait nor the leaflet. 'Mrs Arkwright is quite familiar with the agency.'

'Of course she is,' Mabel said and gave up.

TEN

Freddy opened the door at Hanover Terrace barely wide enough for Mabel to see her face.

'Miss Canning,' she said, 'what a delight. Will you come in?'

'I'd love to, thanks,' Mabel said.

The answer seemed to take a moment to register with the housekeeper, who finally opened the door wide enough for Mabel to enter.

A small fire did its best to take the chill out of the air in the morning room, and Mabel stood beside it.

'I've brought you a copy of the Useful Women booklet number eight,' she said, reaching into her satchel and handing it over. 'You might want to engage someone for all those jobs you no longer want to do yourself.'

'How kind of you.' Freddy placed the booklet on a side table and gave it a pat. 'It seems I cannot even apply myself to the simplest of tasks at the moment – sorting out the larder, fixing the latch on the scullery door, ordering coal. I do believe I've found someone but will keep your Useful Women in mind. Would you like coffee?'

As the housekeeper served Welsh cakes along with the coffee, Mabel took out the drawing of the beetle-browed man.

'Do you know this man?'

The housekeeper examined the drawing. She got up, went to the window and held it up to the light. She frowned. 'Isn't that odd?'

'Is it?' Mabel asked.

'Oh yes,' Freddy said. 'This man worked for little Ozzie.'

'Worked for him in his detective agency?' Mabel asked, shocked that she'd hit a mark.

'In a manner of speaking,' Freddy said and smiled indulgently. 'Ozzie never had very much for him to do but would pay him a shilling here and there to carry out the "footwork" as Ozzie said.'

'Do you know the man's name?'

'No, I'm afraid I don't. Ozzie did enjoy his little intrigues.'

'Does your husband know this man?'

Freddy recoiled. 'Oswald would never associate with anyone who would associate with Fred. At least, not knowingly.'

There came a sound from downstairs of a door closing, and Freddy started.

'It's been lovely to see you, Miss Canning,' she said as she gathered the dishes. 'Please do stop any time.'

'Yes,' Mabel said. 'Thank you.' She'd barely buttoned her coat and put her hat back on before she found herself outside with the door closing behind her.

Mabel stood on the pavement along Russell Square smoothing down the jacket of Mrs Norrell's latest contribution – a chestnut brown wool suit. She gazed, open-mouthed, over the road at the grand hotel. It towered over its surroundings, boldly standing out in a façade made of shades of pale terracotta.

Mabel had found Bloomsbury, new territory for her, by studying her Bacon's walking map of London. From reading Baedeker's, she'd learned the area to be rife with intellect and art. Why, one could rub shoulders with the likes of Dickens in Bloomsbury – if he had still been alive. Who might Mabel encounter at Mrs Arkwright's club?

Brunswick Square lay not far beyond the grand hotel. Mabel found number 28a and stopped at the door long enough to read the small brass plaque: Minerva Club, Members Only. Then a tall woman with broad shoulders and wearing a rolled turban came up behind her and cleared her throat. Mabel pushed the door open and stepped in.

She took in her surroundings as two women came down the stairs in front of her and went through into the café – a spicy aroma and the clinking of china dead giveaways. There were a few chairs in the foyer and landscapes hanging on the papered walls. The top counter of a two-tiered desk held a lamp, telephone and vase of willow stems with grey fuzzy catkins.

The woman behind the desk said, 'May I help you?'

'Hello, good afternoon,' she said, hurrying over. 'I'm Mabel Canning and I believe Mrs Arkwright is expecting me.'

'Yes, of course, Miss Canning,' the woman said, flipping pages of a large register in front of her. Mabel cut her eyes to the stack of newspapers at the corner of the desk.

THE VOTE
The Organ Of The Women's Freedom League

'Here you are,' the woman said to Mabel, turning the register and offering a fountain pen. She tapped on the top line, which she had partially filled in with 'Guest of A. Arkwright'.

Mabel signed and the woman smiled. 'Welcome to the Minerva Club. May I ask, are you a working woman? It makes no difference to us, of course, except to help us keep a finger on the pulse of womankind today.'

'Yes,' Mabel said. 'I work for the Useful Women agency.'

'Do you indeed?' the woman said, lifting her eyebrows. 'Well, then. Your coat and gloves?'

Mabel relinquished them but kept her satchel with her. The woman gestured to a doorway out of which drifted the sound of many conversations and a fair amount of cigarette smoke.

'Do go in.'

Mabel paused at the door. She saw women of all ages and in various styles of dress from suits to day dresses to trousers and wearing all manner of hats – toques and picture hats and tasselled turbans. She wished Cora could be there to see them. A few of the designs reminded Mabel of Cora's, especially the brimmed hat with a cluster of needle-felt snowdrops.

Two women wearing aprons moved through the room taking orders and serving drinks and tea. Chairs and settees crowded the room, and a fire blazed in the grate. Small tables were dotted about, and straight down the middle of the room ran a long, narrow refectory table with what looked like a copy of every newspaper printed in London.

There was not a man in sight. Odd how that relaxed her. Then she saw, on the far side of the room in the recess of a bay window, Mrs Arkwright raise a hand. Mabel made her winding way through the room and when she reached the bay window, she found Adelaide Arkwright sitting with Miss Kerr.

'Good afternoon, Miss Canning,' Mrs Arkwright said. 'Please do sit down. This isn't an ambush. Lillian and I thought it would do us all good if we had a quiet chat.'

'If you are at all uncomfortable,' Miss Kerr said, 'I will understand and leave with no repercussions.'

'No,' Mabel said. 'I'm delighted to see you both.'

Miss Kerr looked as she always did, neatly dressed in skirt, blouse and cardigan – a dark navy today, which set off the few threads of grey in her hair rather well – and her reading glasses still dangled from the chain round her neck. Yet Mabel had never seen her outside of work and so although the same Miss Kerr, she seemed different. A bit looser perhaps.

One of the waitresses circled round to them. 'Anything?'

'I'll have another gin and Dubonnet,' Mrs Arkwright said.

'Yes, and for me, too,' Miss Kerr said.

'Miss Canning,' Mrs Arkwright said, 'will you join us?'

'Oh yes, thank you.' Should she ask for tea? Or a sherry? 'I'll have the same.' When the waitress had gone, Mabel asked, 'Are you both members here?'

'We are and have been from the beginning,' Mrs Arkwright said. She explained about the Women's Freedom League, its work for women's suffrage and its support of non-violent protest. Mabel pictured Miss Kerr organising demonstrations and carrying placards. Had she chained herself to a railing outside the Houses of Parliament?

'I'm acquainted with Lady Fellbridge,' Mabel said, 'and her work for equal citizenship for women. Fellbridge Hall is near Peasmarsh.'

'Lady Fellbridge is a vital member of the effort,' Miss Kerr said.

Mabel's mind flashed back to her beginnings with Useful Women, and she recalled Miss Kerr being impressed with her letter of recommendation from Ronald Herringay, vicar of the church in her village. Now she understood it was not because he was a vicar, but instead because he was the second son of Lady Fellbridge.

The waitress appeared with their drinks, which were bright red. Mabel took a cautious sip. She recognised the gin, along with a herbal quality and an intriguing bitter note. The drinks signalled a change of topic.

'About the enquiry,' Mrs Arkwright said.

'I think you can understand why Roxanne's father wanted

to help ensure she had an uneventful and pleasant visit,' Miss Kerr said.

'Not that he expected anything untoward to happen,' Mrs Arkwright said. 'Certainly not a murder.'

'It's because he saw this as his one chance to get to know his grown daughter without interference,' Miss Kerr said.

Mabel took another sip.

'MaryLou Arkwright will blame Rupert for what has happened,' Miss Kerr said, 'no matter who the murderer is. It's likely she'll demand Roxanne leave immediately.'

Mabel noticed the two women watching her and realised she'd not said a word. But what could she say? She had no control over MaryLou Arkwright.

'I'm sure the police would rather Roxanne remain until after the enquiry.'

The two women sighed and nodded, as if Mabel had arrived at the crux of the matter.

'Detective Inspector Tollerton has come to the house Saturday, Sunday and this morning,' Mrs Arkwright said. 'He has also asked Rupert to go to Scotland Yard twice. Each time he's asked the same questions.'

Badger the suspect, Mabel thought. *Wear him down.* She knew it to be a useful technique.

'There are certain events in Mr Arkwright's past,' Miss Kerr said, 'that could be misinterpreted.'

'Events?' Mabel asked.

Adelaide Arkwright sat back in her chair, as if Lillian Kerr were the expert on the matter.

'He boxed as a young man,' Miss Kerr said. 'While working his way up in the company from mail room to his own office, he spent his nights in the ring.' She shook her head. 'He would come to work the next day, swollen nose, blackened eye and delighted with himself. He said it was the antithesis of his job and he enjoyed the extremes.'

'Why would Scotland Yard be interested in that?'

'Because a man died.'

In the stunned silence that followed, the waitress stopped by. 'Anything else?'

Mrs Arkwright answered for them. 'No, thank you.'

'Mr Arkwright...' Mabel began. 'In the ring?'

'No,' Miss Kerr said. 'He'd had a bout one evening against a fellow no one liked and who picked fights outside the ring with anyone who looked at him crosswise. Rupert won the bout, but afterward this fellow attacked him outside on the pavement. Rupert defended himself. Later that night, the man died.'

Rupert Arkwright had killed a man.

'At the inquest,' Mrs Arkwright hurried on, 'an open verdict was declared. The coroner couldn't decide if death was caused by Rupert's blows, by the earlier fight in the ring or previous injuries. But even after thirty years, he still lives with the uncertainty. It's filed away in his mind, the idea that he could...'

'He couldn't and he didn't,' Miss Kerr said.

Try as they might to excuse him, Rupert Arkwright was coming across as a hothead.

'Wouldn't it be better to admit this to Inspector Tollerton rather than let him find out?' Mabel asked.

'Yes, it would,' Mrs Arkwright said. 'Cards on the table, as it were. But Rupert isn't convinced.'

'If the police were told by someone they trusted,' Miss Kerr said, 'it might go over better.'

Now Mabel understood the reason she'd been invited. She needed a moment to think and so instead of answering, picked up her glass, disappointed to find her drink nearly gone. 'After this happened, Mr Arkwright kept his job with – what company?'

'He worked in the London offices of West Midland Steel. He was well-liked and the directors supported him throughout the ordeal,' Miss Kerr said.

A slight gap appeared in the conversation until Mrs Arkwright laughed and said, 'You're too modest, Lillian. Go on and tell her. Miss Canning is a detective – she will find out regardless.'

'I know this,' Miss Kerr said, 'because I was a telegraphist for the company and later worked in the telephone exchange. In fact I was there the day he met MaryLou, who was visiting with her father from Chicago. He was in American steel.'

'Mr Arkwright had stopped boxing by then, I suppose?' Mabel asked.

'Yes.'

'What was the name of the man who died?'

Both Mrs Arkwright and Miss Kerr frowned and shook their heads. 'We've been trying to come up with it. Keating, perhaps?' Miss Kerr offered.

'When did it happen?'

'February 1899,' Miss Kerr said. 'I don't recall the precise date, but I do remember the night he showed up on my doorstep, bloodied and in tears.'

As Mabel finished her drink, she took out her notebook and wrote the month and year of Rupert Arkwright's deadly fight. It had occurred in Willesden, which was west from London, not really the city, but near enough. She knew the coroner's report would be held locally.

In the foyer as they waited for their coats, Mrs Arkwright stood talking with the woman at the desk, and Miss Kerr and Mabel moved to the side.

'Miss Kerr,' Mabel said, 'I hope you don't think I've been prying into your personal affairs. I certainly don't mean to.'

'My personal affairs with Rupert Arkwright are long over.'

Mabel leapt to her employer's defence. 'Well, I can't imagine him throwing you over for anyone, and so I assume it was your decision that set him free to pursue Mrs Arkwright, that is... Harvey. Miss Harvey as she was.'

'I would've had a fine life with him, I know that,' Miss Kerr said, 'but in the long run, I decided that I was not the right woman for Rupert. Neither was MaryLou – but please don't let on to her that I ever said that. No, in the end, Miss Canning, it's Adelaide who is the perfect match.'

'Here we are now,' Mrs Arkwright said, coming towards them with coats in her arms. 'Miss Canning, this is yours? Yes, good. Thank you, Lillian. I wish you would reconsider coming over while MaryLou is here.'

Mabel almost added her tuppence to that plea, but only if she could be present when all three of Rupert Arkwright's loves would be in one room.

'You won't need me, Addy,' Miss Kerr said. 'You'll do just fine.' And with that, she was gone.

'Before you go, Miss Canning – Mabel,' Mrs Arkwright said, 'I know you and Lillian are on business terms, but would you consider calling me Adelaide?'

Mabel had returned from the Minerva Club and was on her way up to her flat when Park opened his door on the first-floor landing. She stopped and, ahead of their visit to the Palais, told him what she'd learned from Freddy – the beetle-browed man had worked for Oswald Deuchar.

'Did Oswald know the beetle-browed man would be at the Palais? Had Oswald hired him as a sub-agent to keep an eye on Roxanne?'

'Maybe Bryars will have an answer for us,' Winstone said.

'I'll go dress.' Mabel had Mrs Norrell's Parisian gown with the bertha and Cora's golden-leaved headband to wear. She was happy to give it another outing

She glanced downstairs to the empty foyer at New River

House, and then stepped quite close to him. His arms, as if they had a mind of their own, automatically circled her waist.

'I had an interesting time this afternoon,' she said, 'but that will keep until later.' They kissed. And kissed again.

'Mmm,' he said and licked his lips. 'Is that gin?'

'Gin and Dubonnet. And I'll have another when we're at the Palais. But before we go' – she came to her senses – 'I'll have tea and toast.'

'Then you'd better hop to it.'

Where had the time gone? Mabel dashed up to her flat.

'Gin and Dubonnet and I'll have a whisky,' Winstone said to the waiter. They sat on the opposite side of the dance floor from where Mabel and Roxanne had been, and for a moment, Mabel relaxed. Lights glittered off the black lacquer latticework and at other tables people laughed over glasses of champagne. A foxtrot ended and dancers paused, painting a still life of men in well-cut suits and women in gay colours and with skirt hems that Mabel could've sworn had risen two inches since her previous visit. When the band struck up a waltz and the men took their partners in their arms, Park rose and offered his hand to Mabel.

They had questions for Mr Bryars, but he hadn't come in yet, although the man behind the bar said he was expected. No matter. While Mabel had eaten her toast, she'd thought about what she wanted to do and see at the Palais besides talk to Mr Bryars. She wanted to retrace her steps down the corridors when Deuchar had followed her and locked her in the larder. She wanted to walk the corridors that Roxanne had when she went to the powder room and then encountered Deuchar. But for the moment, she would dance.

Circling and gliding across the floor, she lost herself in the music and when Winstone slipped his hand up under Mabel's bertha just enough to rest his fingertips on her bare back, she smiled.

They had two dances then sat down to dinner – Winstone steak and fried potatoes and Mabel Dover sole. Then, they showed the drawing of the beetle-browed man about. He was not one of the instructors, as he had told Roxanne. A couple of the regular fellows remembered him but didn't know his name. The band members only shrugged.

But at last, one of the bartenders said, 'Yeah, I see him sometimes. Friday, he was talking to another fellow, arguing it looked like, but in a quiet way.'

'Who was the other man?' Winstone asked. 'A regular?'

The bartender shrugged. 'I didn't see his face.'

'Did you take a look at the man who was killed?' Mabel asked.

'Why would I want to do that?' the bartender asked with a grumble. 'I had enough of dead bodies during the war.'

Late in the evening, Bryars appeared, and Winstone and Mabel followed him back to his office.

'Mr Bryars, I'm Winstone and this is Miss Canning. We were here Friday evening with Detective Inspector Tollerton.'

Bryars threw a fretful look at one and then the other.

'I'm the one Mr Deuchar locked in the larder,' she said, just as a reminder.

'Yes, of course. Dreadful. What can I do for you?'

'We'd like to talk with you, if you wouldn't mind,' Mabel said. 'We'll take only a few minutes of your time.'

Bryars looked as if he would indeed mind, but he opened the door and said, 'Come in.'

The lights were on, but the fire had long gone out, leaving a smell of cold ashes. The desk was bare except for tidy stacks of papers at two corners, topped with glass paperweights. As he walked by to sit down Bryars patted each paperweight.

'Monday is meant to be my day off,' Bryars said, 'and yet I'm here every Monday regardless. I had a meeting with the owners and had to smooth things over as best I could, and now I've returned because I must finish last week's accounts. Police have been in and out since Friday night – I can't say it's been good for business.'

Mabel didn't believe it had been bad – Monday evening and the Palais teemed with dancers and diners. But Bryars didn't seem like the type who would accept commiseration. Instead, Mabel leaned forward.

'Look at that,' she said, peering at the closest paperweight. 'It's a castle, isn't it?'

Bryars smiled indulgently and picked up the glass to give her a closer look at the colour print encased within. 'That's Carnarvon Castle and this one' – he took it back and picked up the other – 'is Arundel Castle. It's my favourite.'

'Are you a collector?' she asked. Mabel had known a woman in Peasmarsh who collected silver spoons with images of the royals on the handles.

'Mementoes from my travels,' Bryars said with affection. He pulled a drawer open, rummaged round and pulled out another. 'Dover Castle. My favourite.' He did the same with another drawer, this time sticking his entire arm in and scratching round until he located the Scottish home of J.M. Barrie. He rose from his chair and opened the cabinet behind him. Paperweights populated the shelves, posing on stacks of ledgers and folders and books. He began to recite the origin of each.

'My, you do get around, don't you?' Mabel asked. 'How many do you have?'

'Thirty. Nearly thirty. Thirty or so.' Bryars clutched a paperweight to his chest. He opened another cabinet and looked in. 'Let me show you the Royal Pavilion at Brighton. It's my favourite.' He instituted a search of drawers and cabinets, growing frustrated as he talked under his breath. 'Not here, where? Not here.'

'Sit down, please, Mr Bryars,' Winstone said, and the manager sat, looking nervous.

Winstone pulled the drawing of the beetle-browed man out of his inside jacket pocket, unfolded it and laid it out on the desk. 'Did you see this man here on Friday?'

Bryars picked the drawing up, flinched, and let go as if afraid of being bitten. The paper fluttered to the desk. 'Was *he* here?'

Winstone leaned forward. 'Do you know him?'

'I don't know where he came by that hair,' Bryars said, 'and so it may not be him, but he looks very much like a person I wish I didn't know, by the name of Ned Kettle.'

'Ned Kettle?' Winstone exclaimed. He grabbed the drawing, glared at it, and then slapped his hand on the desk. 'By God, it's Ned Kettle.'

ELEVEN

'Ned Kettle. I should've known,' Winstone said with frustration. Bryars had been called away by one of his staff, allowing Mabel and Park a moment to themselves. 'But I haven't seen him in years. Tolly was on the right track when he asked if I'd arrested him before the war. I never did. Ned was a low-level thief, but useful for information. He was always quite a pleasant fellow.'

'He didn't seem odious on Friday evening,' Mabel said. 'Roxanne danced with him, and she didn't seem bothered.'

'I don't see him as a murderer,' Winstone said. 'He was never violent – he'd rather talk a bracelet off a woman's wrist than take it by force. Not that he had much luck either way, but he was always full of plans. I'd heard he joined up at the beginning of the war.'

Bryars came hurrying back in. 'Kitchen staff – they are as difficult to pacify as they are to quantify. The owners are on at me about that – why such high costs in the kitchen? Now, as I said, I don't know where Ned Kettle is and I don't want to know. He nearly got me collared for a crime I had nothing to do with – lifting a tiara right off a woman's head! That was two years ago. He's a rough sort and I want no part of that. A tiara, I ask you! If the owners get even a hint of trouble about me, I'll be out on my ear.'

'You say he was violent?' Winstone asked.

'I'm sure you know the sort,' Bryars said. 'No argument that fists couldn't sort out.'

Winstone and the manager discussed Ned Kettle further, but Mabel's mind wandered as she looked behind Bryars to the cabinets he'd left open when he showed off his glass paper-weight collection. She counted, but lost track. Then, she reached out and took the Arundel Castle paperweight off the desk. Winstone watched as she weighed it in her hand, feeling its size and heft. Their eyes met.

'Mr Bryars,' Mabel asked, 'where is the Royal Pavilion at Brighton?'

Nearly an hour later, the three of them stood looking down at the desk covered in glass paperweights – twenty-seven of them all told. They had been on shelves, in drawers, put away in boxes and corners and one was found inside a humidor. Bryars fretted during the search and when it was finished, he swore what lay before them was his entire collection. All bar one – the Royal Pavilion at Brighton had gone missing.

'Where has it got to?' Bryars asked in distress. 'It's my favourite.'

'Mr Bryars,' Mabel said, 'are you certain that is the only paperweight missing?'

'Yes, of course I'm certain,' he said. 'I wouldn't forget what I have. I wouldn't.'

His insistent tone made her think he was trying to convince himself as well as them.

'Mr Bryars,' she said, 'how did you know Oswald Deuchar?'

Like a candle too close to the fire, Bryars melted into his

desk chair and covered his face. 'I didn't do it,' he wailed. 'I didn't do it.'

'No one is accusing you of anything,' Winstone said.

There's an old saw, Mabel thought. *The policeman's proverbial way of calming a suspect.* And it worked – Bryars' agitation eased.

'So, you did know him?' Winstone asked.

Bryars nodded mutely, and then sighed and said, 'It was a misunderstanding. He was investigating the disappearance of a gold watch from a... a former friend of mine. I had been wrongly accused, but when Mr Deuchar came here to question me, I didn't want it getting round. I thought Mr Deuchar understood that if a hint of this sort of thing got out, my position would be jeopardised.' He lifted his eyes long enough to look at each of them. 'A delicate issue, if you take my meaning.'

'When was this?' Winstone asked.

'A year ago,' Bryars said. 'Not quite.'

'And so it was quite a surprise to see Mr Deuchar again,' Mabel said.

'I did not kill him,' Bryars said firmly. 'And I don't know what's happened to the Royal Pavilion at Brighton.'

Someone used it to bash Oswald Deuchar's head in and then dropped it in his coat pocket and strolled out of the Palais. Did Bryars truly not know? That would be a special skill she'd like to have – detecting a liar.

'I'll ring Tolly,' Winstone said. 'May I?'

Bryars waved his permission to use the telephone.

While Winstone went through the exchange, Mabel decided to take Bryars at his word. At least, for the moment. 'Did you see the Royal Pavilion paperweight on Friday night?'

'Yes,' Bryars said with fervour, as if she'd got to the crux of the matter. 'Yes, I'm certain it was here. It's my favourite.'

'When we came into the office with the inspector, the door was not locked.'

'What? It's always locked,' Bryars said, but Mabel knew from his defensive tone that it wasn't. 'No money was taken!' he pointed out. 'If I had, by mistake, left the door unlocked – and I'm not saying I did, mind you – why would someone come in and steal a paperweight?'

A murderer who needed a weapon, perhaps to stop Oswald from... telling someone something? The corridor where Roxanne found Deuchar was on the same side of the dance hall as the office. The kitchen, a source for all manner of possible weapons, was further away, so the murderer looked closer and found a door unlocked and inside, his choice of heavy, handy weapons.

When Detective Inspector Tollerton arrived, Winstone gave the floor to Mabel, who shared her thoughts about the weapons. Tollerton gazed at the collection on the desk.

'Little point in fingerprinting now,' he said, 'but we'll try it. Well done, Miss Canning. Now Mr Bryars, what about your door being unlocked?'

Bryars was obsequious with his apologies, after which the three men discussed Ned Kettle, his penchant – or lack thereof – for violence and the reasons he might be lurking round the Palais.

Mabel wondered had he targeted Roxanne for dances? He hadn't spoken to her beyond a word or two. Had he been sent by Deuchar?

Once they'd worn out these possibilities, the barman found a small crate and the glass paperweights were boxed up for the police, cushioned upon Bryars' insistence in a copious amount of wood shaving.

They left the manager slumped in the chair behind his desk, looking bereft. The doorman hailed a taxi for Winstone and Mabel. Tollerton, who had a police car waiting, stopped.

'Anything else interesting?' the inspector asked Mabel.

'From me?' she asked. 'No.'

Mabel did have something interesting – her discovery of Rupert Arkwright's past as a boxer and the man who died, but she decided she'd rather tell Park about it first.

'I believe I'll spend tomorrow with Roxanne,' she said. 'We've quite a few more museums to tick off our list. Or perhaps we'll go out to lunch.'

'She shouldn't be out and about,' Tollerton said. 'We don't know if this murder had anything to do with her or not, but best be safe.'

'She's safe with me,' Mabel said, but, at his sceptical look, added, 'I don't suppose you could lend us a constable for the day as a chaperone? WPC Wardle?'

'Yes,' Tollerton said, but drew out the word as if unsure. 'Why Wardle?'

Two reasons, Mabel thought. First, Wardle could have heard things round the station that Tollerton didn't want to become general knowledge even to Mabel – speculation, gossip. She might be willing to share. Second, what about Wardle's potential to add more to an investigation? One of only a few WPCs with Scotland Yard, Wardle's usual assignment was making tea. If she had been one of the Useful Women, Mabel would've recruited her to the Private Investigations division.

'Three women would look less conspicuous than two and a uniformed man. But only if you allow her to wear plain clothes.'

Tollerton shrugged. 'I'll send her to Arkwright's tomorrow.'

'Good. Eleven o'clock?'

In the taxi, Mabel at last told Winstone about meeting Adelaide Arkwright and Miss Kerr at the Minerva Club.

'So,' Winstone said, 'they were defending Rupert Arkwright, yet letting you know what he was capable of?'

'It seems so,' Mabel said. 'They want the police to know about it sooner rather than later. Strike first, and all that.'

'But they've no name for the dead boxer?'

'No – possibly Keating, but they weren't sure. I have the month and year – Miss Kerr was quite certain about that.' Mabel's imagination had already taken off with the vision of Miss Kerr sponging the blood from a young Rupert's face, easing the pain in his heart. 'Before we left this evening, I stopped by and asked Skeff to look up death notices for that month and from that she can find newspaper reports.'

'Well done,' Winstone said. 'Then, you can hand that to Tolly. When does the first Mrs Arkwright arrive?'

'Thursday, they say. She'll be coming into port at Glasgow and so will need to come down on the train. She's made the arrangements herself.'

'Arkwright didn't do that for her?'

'He seemed to want to leave it to her – as if he were a bit afraid,' Mabel said, and laughed. 'Really, how much of a monster can she be? I do hope I'm invited over as soon as she arrives.'

Mabel brushed Mrs Norrell's chestnut wool suit down before she went to bed. In the morning, she would ask Cora if she might keep it a bit longer. Was Mrs Norrell still in the 'letting go' phase as she readied herself to enter holy orders, or had she abandoned the idea once again? Mabel wished she were able to buy Mrs Norrell's frocks. She sighed. *If wishes were horses.*

She slept well that night. Pleased at the progress in the enquiry, she cooked herself an egg for breakfast and looked ahead. Winstone would run this Ned Kettle to ground and find out his involvement in the murder of Oswald Deuchar. Mabel had discovered what the murder weapon might have been. Now, Scotland Yard could search for a glass paperweight that had encased within it a print of the Royal Pavilion at Brighton. Search where? Every corner of the Palais. The pockets of Ned

Kettle, when they found him, and of Fred Fredericks. Rupert Arkwright, too?

Flea's second drawing of Ned Kettle had been safely tucked away in Mabel's satchel. She looked one more time to be sure, then buttoned up her coat, pulled on her hat and started downstairs.

No need to knock on Winstone's door. He had planned to be up and out before dawn to catch those sources that might do more business during the night than in the light of day. So Mabel continued down, but before she reached the ground floor the door opened and in walked a short fellow wearing a hat that may have started life as a bowler but now teetered on the edge of shapeless anonymity.

'Where's Winstone?' he asked Mr Chigley in a loud voice. The sound echoed off the foyer walls and the man winced. 'Sorry,' he said in a near whisper. 'Where's Winstone?'

Mr Chigley, who brooked no quarter with dodgy types, set a hard line to his mouth. 'Mr Winstone isn't in.'

Mabel took the last few steps slowly. 'I'm acquainted with Mr Winstone,' she said. 'Would you like me to tell him you called?'

'Who are you?' the man said, looking Mabel up and down.

'I'm Miss Mabel Canning,' she replied, taking on the Sunday-school voice that worked so well with eight-year-old boys. 'Who are you?'

'All right, all right,' he said in a conciliatory tone. 'Tell him Bootsie might have something for him.'

'Bootsie?' Mabel asked.

The man nodded to his feet and Mabel looked down to see he wore one brown and one black boot.

'Right,' she said, 'Bootsie. We'll let him know, won't we, Mr Chigley?'

· · ·

Mabel went off to Dover Street a bit worried that there would be an awkwardness between her and Miss Kerr, now that they had met in a social setting. But when she arrived at the Useful Women office, she realised her concern had been unfounded. Behind the desk, Miss Kerr appeared her normal, businesslike self, although that could've been in part due to the presence of Miss Gregory and another one of the Useful Women.

'Good morning, Miss Canning,' Miss Kerr said as she turned the pages of the Jobs ledger.

'Good morning, Miss Kerr,' Mabel said. 'Morning.' She nodded to Miss Gregory – Evangeline – and the other, who sat along the wall with cups of tea and buns. 'Mrs Fritt come and gone?'

'I went on a search for her first thing,' Miss Gregory said. 'The cooker at the boarding house went out and the porridge was cold.' She shuddered. 'Shall I find her for you?'

'No need,' Mabel said.

'What are your plans for today, Miss Canning?' Miss Kerr asked in a neutral tone. The other two women stopped talking – Miss Kerr wasn't known to consult with her Useful Women, but rather assign.

'A quiet day, I think. Shopping, lunch.' Escorted by WPC Wardle, but Mabel didn't think she needed to spread that news around.

'Good,' Miss Kerr said.

Mabel gave the two women a nod and left, but Miss Gregory followed her out.

'I'm off to collect two dresses from the drapers and deliver them all the way out on Hampstead Heath. Not much, but it's work, as we say. Miss Kerr is giving me more chances. and I must thank you for your help.'

'Not a bit of it,' Mabel said. 'You only needed to find your feet.'

Evangeline stopped when they'd got to the street and

studied Mabel's face. 'You all right? This murder business not bothering you?'

'No,' Mabel said. 'Really nothing to do with me.'

Miss Gregory lifted an unbelieving brow. 'But isn't the father around when you go to the house to collect your young charge? Isn't he still a suspect?'

Had the newspapers really slapped that label on Rupert Arkwright?

'Yes, all right,' Mabel said, 'a bit to do with me. But we don't talk about it, because I don't want Roxanne to be affected by the business.'

'Right,' Miss Gregory said with a smile, 'that's your job every day until Scotland Yard solve this murder – to show the girl a good time. And you're just the one to do it, I may say. You have an abundance of patience.'

'Do you know, she isn't that bad,' Mabel admitted. 'She's young and changeable as the weather, but so full of life. I admit I do enjoy her company.'

Mabel arrived at the house in Mayfair earlier than eleven – she wanted to have time to explain to Roxanne why WPC Wardle would be accompanying them about town. How had Wardle taken it when given the assignment, Mabel wondered? Had she bristled at what looked at first glance to her little more than making tea? Being chaperone instead of having a more serious role in the enquiry?

Trigg opened the door and Mabel barely had time to shed her coat and gloves before a cheerful Roxanne put her head out of the drawing room and said, 'Mabel, Hildy is already here – where've you been? Come in – Dorcas has just served coffee.'

In the drawing room, Adelaide sat in a chair near the fire. Next to her on the sofa, Mabel saw the back of a young woman with straight brown hair cut in a short bob.

'Good morning,' Mabel said, and the young woman stood and turned. For just a moment, Mabel didn't recognise WPC Wardle out of uniform. She wore a deep red jersey wool day dress and seemed to have lost a few of her sharp edges. Her small dark eyes were curious, not cautious.

'Good morning,' Wardle said.

Roxanne shut the door and went back to pouring coffee and distributing cups. 'You didn't tell me about this, Mabel – having a police*woman* along for the day. Sounds odd, doesn't it? Still, I think it's a fine idea. Hildy is a like a spy or something, isn't she. Working undercover, as they say in those detective magazines.'

It was as if Roxanne had forgotten just why it might be necessary to have the police keep an eye on her, but Mabel wouldn't be the one to burst her bubble of good cheer.

'I've heard that Miss Canning has done a bit of undercover work,' Hildy said.

Mabel, both surprised and pleased that a member of the Metropolitan Police would know she had done anything of the kind, said, 'Thank you, Constable.'

'None of that today,' Roxanne said, holding up a finger before taking a slice of Dundee cake. 'Wouldn't we look foolish going to lunch at the Savoy saying Constable this and Miss Arkwright that? No, we're all to use first names. All righty?'

'Yes,' Mabel said. 'All right-ee.' Especially helpful, because if people overheard the surname Arkwright, they may remember seeing it in the newspaper – and not because Rupert was an astute businessman.

Roxanne looked at her stepmother. 'I've tried my best to persuade Mother Adelaide to come along. I really want you to.'

Adelaide blushed and looked so pleased at being asked that Mabel didn't believe anything could top that.

'Thank you, Roxanne, but I'll let you three enjoy your lunch.'

. . .

They left soon after and shopped along Piccadilly. In a bookshop, Roxanne bought a copy of Bacon's walking map of London.

'Here, Mabel, I want you to have this new one,' Roxanne said. 'I'm afraid I drew on yours when we were at the picnic – I was asking Flea to show me where he lived. So you should have an unmarked map.'

'I hadn't even noticed,' Mabel said. 'It doesn't matter, you keep your new one.'

'Well, all right, I do like to know where I'm going.' They stood at the till and Roxanne unfolded her map and ran a finger across it. Within a minute's study, she said, 'We're right here, Hildy. Look, Mabel, there's Islington where you live.'

'So it is,' Mabel said, looking where she pointed. 'You seem to enjoy map reading.'

'I did well in geography in school, but Mama said what good would it do me.' Roxanne took a pencil from the counter and circled a few places on the map, then brought out her flat purse, but found she needed one extra fold before her Bacon's would fit inside it. Once secured, she looked down Piccadilly. 'Is there a stationer's nearby?'

There was, and Roxanne bought a new drawing pad and a set of pencils for Flea.

'His name is Flea?' Hildy asked as they emerged out onto the pavement again.

'He's an artist,' Roxanne said. 'He drew my picture and Gladys' – do you know Gladys, Hildy?' Wardle nodded that she did. 'And he drew my friend Juliet and some others. All I needed to do was describe someone to Flea and even if he'd never seen the person, he would come up with their likeness.'

They walked to the Savoy and when they'd been seated, Mabel gazed at the posh surroundings.

'I feel like a fish out of water here,' she confessed. 'I'm more accustomed to sardines on toast at the Lyons' Corner House in Piccadilly.'

'Lyons' Corner House?' Roxanne repeated. 'Let's go there next time, why don't we? I'm sure it's lovely.'

They ordered only one course – Mabel the Welsh rarebit, Roxanne cold pork roast and Hildy egg croquettes. When the dishes came, Roxanne laughed.

'I thought you asked for *rabbit*, Mabel,' she said, 'not cheese toast.' She peered at the browned top. 'Looks pretty good.'

Roxanne finished her meal in a flash while she told Hildy about playing softball. She became so involved in describing how she 'wound up' for a pitch that she hit a passing waiter, who merely bowed and went on his way.

'Oops,' Roxanne said, and snickered. 'Got him right in his breadbasket. I brought along a photograph of my team from school. I'll show you when we get back. Look, you two stay here while I go back to that men's shop we passed and buy Father a tie. I won't be long.'

Roxanne rose and Mabel and Wardle, in chorus, said, 'No!'

'Why not?'

'We'll go back with you,' Mabel said.

'You aren't finished with your meal,' Roxanne pointed out. 'It's only down the street, it isn't as if I'll get lost.'

'You shouldn't be alone,' Hildy said. 'That's the truth of it.'

The murder of Oswald Deuchar didn't need to be spoken of, but it was in the air. Even if nothing pointed to Roxanne being in danger, Mabel would rather be too cautious than not.

Roxanne's high spirits evaporated, and she sank back into her chair.

'It's only that you should be with someone you know,' Mabel explained as she covered Roxanne's hand and gave it a squeeze. 'London can be quite overwhelming.'

'Yes, all right,' Roxanne answered weakly

A great annoyance rose in Mabel at Roxanne's acquiescence at the situation. Wasn't the girl allowed some fun?

They returned late afternoon to find the house in Mayfair bustling with activity – additional staff had been taken on to make ready for the arrival of Mrs Arkwright the first. After Trigg had relieved them of their coats, Roxanne paused in the entrance hall, observing the comings and goings – dusting and polishing, scrubbing the skirting board, straightening pictures, shaking out table linens and carrying stacks of bedsheets from the laundry.

'Why don't we go up to my room?' Roxanne asked. Her good spirits had returned, and she ran ahead of Mabel and Hildy. 'C'mon,' she called over her shoulder.

They followed and settled at the end of the bedroom near the fireplace and a low table stacked with issues of *Tatler*, *Picture Show* and *Woman's Weekly*. At the other end of the room, Mabel could see Flea's drawings pinned round Roxanne's mirrored dressing table. She recognised Gladys amid a sea of faces.

Roxanne went to a drawer in the wardrobe and searched until she drew out a flat, square black box – the sort that a necklace might be kept in. But when she opened it, Mabel saw a stack of photographs.

'Here I am with my softball team at school last year,' Roxanne said, holding up the first one. 'And there's my friend Juliet – she was my catcher. That's her mom and dad beside her.'

The girls had gathered for a team photo and adults and children gathered round and behind them. 'Which one is your mother?' Mabel asked.

'Mama didn't like me playing softball, so she never came to the games,' Roxanne said. 'She says it made me look like a tomboy. "Don't be a tomboy, Roxanne Louise, or no man will ever be interested in you."' Roxanne clicked her tongue. She flipped through the photos, saying, 'Don't do this, Roxanne Louise, don't do that. Don't take off all on your own, Roxanne Louise. A lady doesn't walk through town by herself. I don't see why not — I always know where I'm going.'

'Who is this lad here?' Hildy stopped Roxanne's photo shuffling by sticking her finger into the mix and pointing to a boy of about fourteen. 'He's been in almost every photo. Look, there he is beside you.'

Roxanne put the photos in the box, closed it and held it to her chest. 'Mama didn't want me to bring any photos with me.' She glanced across the room to the pinned-up drawings. 'But I brought the photos because I wanted something to remind me of home, in case I was miserable when I got here.' She laughed. 'I was miserable, wasn't I, Mabel? And I made you all miserable, too. But here it is not even a week later... and now I'm not.'

A muffled clamour came from downstairs and they all three lifted their heads as if to listen better. WPC Wardle stood, moved quickly to the door and opened it a few inches and the noise became clearer. Voices mingled with clattering, but one female voice rose above it all like the delightful sound of bells pealing.

Roxanne made a choking noise and ran to the door, threw it open and went to the banister, leaning over and looking. In a second, she reared back, plastered herself against the wall and edged her way back into the bedroom where she shut the door carefully. She turned, and Mabel could see perspiration break out on her forehead.

'It's Mama,' Roxanne whispered. 'She's here.'

TWELVE

'Isn't she a day early?' Mabel asked after a stunned moment of silence.

'Yes, and on purpose, probably,' Roxanne said. 'The advantage of surprise.'

'I should be on my way,' Hildy said, looking at her wristwatch.

'I should, too,' Mabel said.

'*No!* Please no,' Roxanne said. 'It's all right, Hildy, I understand, but Mabel, it's different with you, don't you think? Because you know Father and Mother Adelaide and you were there at the Palais and she's going to have to be told and so you're actually part of it all, aren't you? Please don't leave. I'm begging you.'

'Is your father at home?' Mabel asked.

'I don't think so,' Roxanne said and cast a fearful look towards her bedroom door and what lay beyond. 'Oh no, Mother Adelaide is alone. We should go down.'

The commotion had quieted, and no one was about when the three made their way carefully to the entrance hall. Trigg came out from the back.

'It's Mama, isn't it?' Roxanne asked, keeping her voice low.

Trigg nodded and replied at a similar volume. 'Yes, Mrs Arkwright has arrived and is in the drawing room with Mrs Arkwright.' He frowned slightly.

'I'll take my coat and hat, Mr Trigg,' Hildy said quietly, her manner returning to that of a WPC. He nodded and fetched her coat. As he helped her on with it, Mabel tried to see some reaction on the butler's face to this unexpected event. He remained stoic, but she noticed his eyes dart here and there, as if he feared that MaryLou Arkwright might be looking over his shoulder.

They said goodbye to Hildy, and when the door had shut, Roxanne turned to Mabel. 'Thank you for staying, Mabel. Ready?'

Ready for what? She wasn't going to the firing squad, was she?

'Yes,' Mabel said, hooking her arm in Roxanne's. 'I'm ready to meet your mother.'

In contrast to the noise in the entrance hall only a few minutes earlier, the drawing room was quiet as the tomb. Yet not as cold. The fire burned brightly in the hearth, the curtains were drawn and the lamps round the room were switched on, banishing the darkness from every nook and cranny. The two Mrs Arkwrights sat on either side of the fire – the first in the leather wingback chair Mabel thought to be Rupert's and the second in a wing-back upholstered with a subtle print in duck-egg blue.

'Oh, my darling!'

MaryLou Arkwright leapt up, rushed to Roxanne and threw her arms round her.

'Mama!' Roxanne said, holding her mother close. The meeting gave Mabel a moment to study the first Mrs Arkwright.

She had dressed for travel in a sensible dark green wool suit.

Mabel thought she had put on a bit of weight since her wedding photo, but she wore it well. She'd kept her auburn hair long and pulled back into a low, twisted bun that accentuated the silver streaks at the temples. Her eyes were closed and she embraced her daughter with a look of rapture on her face. When she opened them, her gaze alit briefly on Mabel, who had remained near the door.

'Roxanne Louise,' MaryLou said, pulling away. She smiled at her daughter. 'What have you done to your hair?'

Roxanne's hand shot up to her bobbed cut and smoothed it down. Then she threw her shoulders back and said, 'I cut it off, Mama. I told you I wanted to cut it and so I did.'

'Did that Juliet talk you into it?'

'No, Mama, she didn't. It's all my doing.'

MaryLou touched her daughter's cheek. 'Where were you when I arrived? There was no one to introduce Adelaide to me.'

'I'm sorry, Mama, we were upstairs. We didn't expect you until tomorrow.' Roxanne's head swivelled round as she checked all four corners of the room. 'Did you come alone?'

MaryLou gave her daughter a hard look that disappeared almost as quickly as it had appeared. 'I tried to persuade Miss Hawksley to join me, but she's gone right off ocean voyages. I can't imagine why.' Roxanne dropped her gaze. 'She deserves an apology, you know.'

'Yes, ma'am. I'll write to her tomorrow.'

'Where is your father?'

'I don't know. Mother Adelaide—'

Her mother made a movement and Roxanne flinched.

'He's at his office,' Adelaide said. 'I've asked Trigg to telephone.'

It was the first time the second Mrs Arkwright had spoken since they'd walked in the room.

MaryLou turned to Mabel. 'Hello.'

'Oh!' Roxanne said. 'Mama, this is Mabel Canning. Mabel, this is my mother, MaryLou—'

'Miss Canning,' MaryLou said and extended her hand. 'How do you do?'

Mabel approached and shook her hand. 'Please to meet you, Mrs Arkwright. I hope you had a pleasant journey.'

'As pleasant as could be, I suppose,' MaryLou replied. 'How do we know you, Miss Canning?'

Mabel thought that for an American, MaryLou had a good grasp of the royal 'we'.

'We asked Miss Canning to be Roxanne's companion,' Adelaide said.

'Companion?' MaryLou echoed.

'I work for Useful Women,' Mabel said. 'It's a—'

'Domestic agency?'

'She isn't a maid, Mama,' Roxanne said crossly. 'Useful Women do all sorts of things. Mabel is a private detective.'

Mabel, watching MaryLou's eyes widen and mouth open, wished they could've worked their way up to that designation.

'A *lady* detective?' MaryLou asked, biting out the words. 'Have we fallen into one of those magazine stories that your—'

Her mouth snapped shut so fast, it was a wonder she didn't bite her tongue.

'I'm a companion for your daughter,' Mabel said. 'Useful Women are capable of doing all manner of jobs, Mrs Arkwright – cataloguing libraries, repairing lace, showing visitors around London.'

'Didn't he already have one detective watching you on the ship?' MaryLou asked her daughter while watching Mabel.

The mention of Oswald Deuchar, even in an oblique way, shut them all up, but MaryLou didn't seem to notice, because at that moment, the door to the morning room flew open and there was Rupert Arkwright, one arm out of his coat and Trigg behind tugging on the other sleeve.

'MaryLou? We didn't expect you until tomorrow.'

'You must've misunderstood my telegram,' she said. 'And hello to you, too, Rupert.'

'Yes, of course,' he said. He straightened his collar, passing Mabel as he went further into the room, took MaryLou's hand for a moment and then kissed her cheek. 'I'm sorry. Did you have a good voyage?'

A high colour came to MaryLou's cheeks. 'Tolerable. Now, why does my daughter have a lady detective as a companion?'

Arkwright sighed. 'Can we all sit down? Where is Trigg?'

Trigg came in on cue with a drinks tray that held a whisky for the man and glasses of sherry for the women. He left and Arkwright gestured them to sit – he in the leather wingback and Adelaide in the duck-egg blue wingback. Mother and daughter took the sofa and Mabel sat in a carved oak armchair.

'MaryLou, there has been an incident and the first thing I want you to remember is that Roxanne is safe and is in no danger.'

'Dear God,' MaryLou said and grabbed her daughter's hand, squeezing hard enough for Roxanne to wince at the pain and shake free.

Arkwright continued in a measured voice as he told – with the barest minimum of detail – what had taken place at the Palais on Friday evening. Mabel and Roxanne went to the Palais, he said. A man was killed. This man happened to be the detective Rupert hired to watch Roxanne. Scotland Yard are investigating. Mabel admired his clean, emotion-free account.

MaryLou maintained silence throughout and even after the explanation. It looked as if Roxanne might say something, but stopped when Trigg came in to ask if dinner should be served or held. Adelaide told him they would go in soon and asked Mabel to stay. She tried to wriggle out of it, but Roxanne pleaded. In the end Mabel acquiesced, even though she longed to be in Park's flat playing his portable piano while he wrote one of his reports for the diplomatic service with Gladys stretched out at his feet.

After Trigg left, no one spoke. Mabel sipped her sherry, Roxanne looked at her hands, MaryLou glanced round the room. Adelaide watched her husband, who got up and stabbed a few pieces of burning coal with the poker.

Mabel jumped when the doorbell rang, its shrill tone piercing the silence in the drawing room. Trigg answered, and Mabel heard a man speak in return. Her hearing wasn't as good as Gladys', but it was good enough to recognise who had come to the door. She rose just as the butler entered and said, 'Sir, Detective Inspector Tollerton to see you.'

Tollerton stopped short when he saw Mabel and then looked at the other women before saying, 'Mr Arkwright, may I speak with you privately?'

Beyond Tollerton and Trigg, Mabel could see PC Drake and another constable in the entrance hall.

'Yes, of course you may,' Arkwright said smoothly. 'Why don't we go to my office?'

They disappeared, leaving confusion and fear in their wake.

'Who was that?' MaryLou asked.

Roxanne stared at the closed door. 'He is Detective Inspector Tollerton, Mama, didn't you hear?'

'Yes, I heard that,' MaryLou said sharply. 'Why is he in this house?'

'Perhaps he has news of the investigation,' Mabel said.

'Then it's too bad the inspector didn't invite the lady detective along, isn't it?' MaryLou said, raising her eyebrows at Mabel.

The door opened and they gasped, but it was only Trigg. 'About dinner, ma'am?'

'Trigg,' MaryLou said and then stopped.

'We'll wait,' Adelaide said. 'Please tell Cook I'm sorry.'

More waiting. When Mabel heard the men back in the

entrance hall, she abandoned her sherry and without excusing herself went out. Making sure to close the door behind her, she remained where she stood and watched as PC Drake handed Tollerton something wrapped in a handkerchief. Tollerton looked inside and felt the heft of the object in his hand. Mabel could not see, but from the way he handled it, she could guess what he held – a glass paperweight with a print of the Royal Pavilion at Brighton encased in it.

Tollerton put handkerchief and object in his pocket. 'Mr Arkwright, I'd like you to come with us.'

'What was that?' Arkwright demanded. 'Where did it come from?' He tried to push his way past Drake to Tollerton, but the constables grabbed him. He fought, but they pulled his arms back with a jerk and he gave up. The scuffle was short-lived. 'All right, fine.' They let him go. 'I'm happy to go and clear up whatever misconceptions you have. May I speak to my wife first?'

Tollerton nodded and Mabel moved out of the way as Arkwright went to the drawing room and opened the door.

'Adelaide,' he announced, 'I'm going with Detective Inspector Tollerton to discuss a few matters. I'm sorry I'll miss dinner – please do go ahead without me.' He turned and walked out, escorted by the two constables. Through the open front door, Mabel watched Arkwright get into the waiting police car.

She hurried forward and whispered, 'What is this?' to Tollerton.

He glanced over her shoulder and said in a low voice, 'I'll ring Park and explain. You should go home.'

The door closed. She turned to find both Mrs Arkwrights and Roxanne in the entrance hall watching her.

'What have you to do with this?' MaryLou asked.

'It isn't Mabel's fault they took Father away,' Roxanne said.

'They didn't take him away,' Mabel said. 'He went with them.'

Trigg hovered at the edge of the entrance hall. 'Dinner, ma'am?'

'I couldn't eat a thing with Rupert gone off to Scotland Yard,' MaryLou said. 'I'll have a sandwich in my room.'

'Yes,' Adelaide said, 'that's the best thing to do. I'll ask Cook to make up trays for our rooms. I'm so sorry, Mabel.'

'Don't worry,' Mabel said. 'Why don't I go and ask Cook about the trays and you can... sort things out here?'

'Thank you,' Adelaide said. 'Trigg, where is Dorcas?'

Dorcas appeared from the dark corridor behind the butler.

'I'm here, ma'am.' She crept into the entrance hall, but not far.

'Dorcas,' Adelaide said, 'show Mrs Arkwright to the honeysuckle room and then you can take her bags up.'

'The honeysuckle room?' MaryLou said. 'How sweet.'

Adelaide went back to the drawing room and Dorcas led the first Mrs Arkwright up the stairs. Mabel stayed in the entrance hall, watching their journey to the first floor and down the corridor where she heard a door open and MaryLou say, 'Oh, is this what happened to the box room?'

An uproar from the kitchen – shouting and the banging of metal – came from only one person, Cook.

'Serve dinner, hold dinner, serve, hold – what do they think the state of the chicken will be at the end of this parliamentary debate?' Cook said, slamming down an empty pot on the worktable.

'Mrs Arkwright has asked for trays to be sent to their rooms,' Mabel said, making sure to stand in the doorway in case she needed to dodge a flying pan.

'The proper Mrs Arkwright, I hope you mean,' Cook said, and when Mabel didn't answer, she looked up and in a quieter tone added, 'not the one's just arrived.'

'Yes, the proper one. But not a tray for Mr Arkwright because he's gone out for the evening.' Mabel hoped it was only for the evening and he wouldn't be locked up.

'And what about you?' Cook asked.

'I'm happy to help with the trays, and then I'm going home.'

'Not that anyone can blame you,' Cook said. 'After all the work we put in today, we still weren't ready for her and here she is, and don't you think we won't hear about it. We called in everyone we could think to help.'

While she talked, she worked. Mabel assisted where she could and soon three trays of chicken and a few other bits sat ready to go.

'Where's that Dorcas?' Cook asked.

Mabel looked out of the kitchen and saw, at the end of the corridor, a white cap duck back into a room. 'Dorcas?' she called.

Dorcas looked out, saw Mabel and dusted herself off. 'Here, ma'am.' She marched into the kitchen.

Cook handed her a tray. 'To Mrs Arkwright.'

'Which one?' Dorcas asked in a shaky voice.

'The proper one,' Mabel said quickly, because she thought she saw steam coming from Cook's ears. 'I'll take the first Mrs Arkwright her tray and return for Roxanne's.'

At the bottom of the stairs, Dorcas said in a small voice, 'Is she a terror as they say?'

MaryLou didn't look like a terror, but Mabel could already see how she might be labelled as one. 'It's just everyone's a bit upset.'

Dorcas went off to Adelaide's room. As Mabel approached the honeysuckle room, she heard Roxanne inside and hesitated.

'Mama, I had a dog when I was a little girl here. A dog named Boodles.'

'Roxanne Louise, where do you get these outrageous ideas – did your father tell you this?'

'Father reminded me,' Roxanne said, 'but then I remembered myself. Did you know Trigg worked here when we lived in London? Except he wasn't the butler. I've remembered that he made dollies from clothes pegs and gave them to me. Did I leave them behind?'

'You've always had such an imagination,' her mother replied.

'These are true things, Mama. Don't you want me to remember?'

'I want you to remember you live in Chicago – that is your home.'

'I'm not saying it isn't,' Roxanne replied in a hurt tone.

Mabel knocked lightly on the door. 'I've brought your tray.'

Roxanne answered, her face screwed up in indignation. 'Mabel, you shouldn't be doing this,' she said, taking the tray and setting it on the dressing table. Behind her, MaryLou sat up in bed on top of the counterpane with a pile of pillows behind her.

'I don't mind,' Mabel said lightly. 'That's the thing about being one of Miss Kerr's Useful Women – we manage whatever needs to be done.'

'Miss Kerr?' MaryLou asked.

'Yes,' Mabel said. 'Miss Lillian Kerr. Useful Women is her business.'

'Miss... Lillian Kerr?' MaryLou asked again.

'I'll come down and help, too,' Roxanne said.

'Roxanne Louise, you will do nothing of the sort,' MaryLou said. 'I need you here.'

'I'll bring your tray up,' Mabel said.

Mabel returned and handed the cold supper to Roxanne over the threshold. 'I'll be on my way now.'

'Oh, don't you live in?' MaryLou asked.

Mabel didn't answer.

Before she reached the bottom of the stairs Roxanne slipped

out of her mother's room, came halfway down and sat on a step, leaning her head against a railing.

'I'm sorry about earlier, Mabel,' she said. 'For not introducing you right off the bat. Mama pushes things right out of my head, you see, and I... That's no excuse. I'm sorry.'

Mabel put her hand on the newel and leaned down closer to Roxanne. 'It's all right. It was a bit of a shock, seeing her?'

'Yes, a shock. Will my father be all right? He isn't in trouble, is he?'

'I'm sure the inspector just had a few questions for him.' She was sure of nothing of the kind. 'Police believe it's best to take care of things as they come up – it helps the enquiry move along.'

Roxanne threw a quick glance over her shoulder back towards her mother's room. 'Mama... Mama is the kind of person who doesn't have any confidence in herself and so she thinks she needs to act like she does, so she puffs up and sort of bullies people.'

'That's quite a grown-up thing to know about your mother,' Mabel said. 'Did you figure it out or did someone explain it to you?'

'Look,' Roxanne said, 'there's something I have to tell you.' Her hands trembled and she clasped them together and threw another furtive look up the stairs. 'Remember the boy in the photos? The one Hildy asked about?'

'Yes, I remember. He's about the same age as Flea.'

'That's Tommy,' Roxanne whispered. 'He's my brother.'

THIRTEEN

Mabel stood bolt upright. 'You have a brother?'

Roxanne nodded and smiled. 'I miss him. And Tommy would like Flea, I know he would. I wish they could meet.'

'But Roxanne—' Mabel began, only to be interrupted.

'Roxanne Louise!' MaryLou called from her bedroom.

'Yes, Mama, coming,' Roxanne called, then whispered to Mabel, 'Mama said Father would take all her money away if he knew about Tommy and... and... Look, Mabel, I'll explain tomorrow. I'll see you, won't I? We could meet at the Corner House.'

'I think it would be best to give you and your mother a day to recover.'

'Roxanne!' MaryLou called again.

'Yes,' Roxanne said with regret. 'She'll probably say the same thing, and so I'll have to be brave without you for a whole day. The next day then. We'll go to the Corner House. And a museum!' She dashed back up the stairs.

Mabel stood in the entrance hall considering this new addition to the Arkwright family tree when there was a knock at the door. It startled her, but at least it wasn't the shrill bell. Trigg came out to answer, and on the doorstep stood Park with Gladys.

'Taxi for Miss Canning,' Park said, nodding to the one waiting at the kerb.

'Yes, sir,' Trigg said and added, 'Please do come in while I retrieve Miss Canning's things.' He closed the door behind man and dog and went off to the boot room.

While he was gone Mabel greeted Gladys and whispered to Park, 'I hope you can tell me what's happened. And I have news for you, too.'

Winstone glanced round the entrance hall. 'Where is everyone?'

'In their rooms.'

'Roxanne?'

'Worried.'

Trigg returned with Mabel's coat, hat and gloves. 'I'm sorry to take so long,' he said. 'They've left the boot room in disarray.'

Mabel buttoned her coat and, as they left, said to Trigg, 'I wish you a quiet night.'

From upstairs, MaryLou called out in a loud and firm voice, 'Trigg, tell Dorcas to run a bath for me.'

Trigg turned to Mabel. 'Chance would be a fine thing, Miss Canning.'

'You run an excellent taxi service,' Mabel said as she snuggled up to Park on the bench seat and Gladys jumped up next to her.

'My pleasure.'

'Tolly found the glass paperweight in the boot room, didn't he?'

'Yes,' Winstone said. 'In Arkwright's coat pocket. Police received an anonymous tip. Tolly didn't tell me anything more except that you were here.'

'How reliable are anonymous tips?'

'They come in throughout enquiries that have been in the papers,' Winstone said, 'and vary widely – outrageous, vindictive, downright ridiculous. The postman did it. The victim was my grandfather in another life. A mentalist committed the murder without ever being present. But a tip about a glass paperweight that hadn't even been mentioned by police? That's suspicious.'

After a moment, Mabel said, 'Roxanne's mother surprised everyone by showing up a day early and seemed to enjoy the chaos that ensued – but that's the least of my news. Roxanne just told me that she has a brother, and he must be three or four years younger. His name is Tommy. His existence is – was a secret. At least from everyone on this side of the Atlantic.'

'Three years younger,' Winstone said. 'That would be fifteen years ago, when Roxanne and her mother left England.'

'Timing is everything,' Mabel said with a flick of a brow. 'I'll find out more, but not tomorrow – I will leave the Arkwrights to themselves for a day.'

Mabel went straight to the Useful Women office the next morning and offered herself for any job going as well as to deliver the news – or at least find out if Miss Kerr had already heard.

'Thank you, Miss Canning,' Miss Kerr said. 'Adelaide rang last night to tell me. MaryLou always did enjoy a grand entrance.'

'I thought it best to let them be today,' Mabel said. 'Did she tell you about Mr Arkwright as well?'

Miss Kerr nodded. 'But she had no details.'

'Miss Kerr, I want to explain about Mr Arkwright's boxing story,' Mabel said. 'I haven't mentioned it to the police yet, because I've asked Skeff to look into the details – there must've been something in the papers about it, but as we aren't certain of the man's name, the one who died, then it may take her longer. Perhaps in the meantime, Mr Arkwright has told the police himself,' she added.

'It's a part of his past he wanted to forget, so I doubt if he would bring it up voluntarily.'

'It seems unlikely that it has anything to do with what's gone on,' Mabel said, 'but I will let you know when I have all the facts.'

'Thank you, Miss Canning. Now if you're free and willing to work, I've a Mrs Gantry needing help with wallpaper selection.'

'I'm happy to take it, but perhaps Miss Gregory could try that.'

'You are a worthy advocate for Miss Gregory,' Miss Kerr said, 'but she was not to be found when I rang her boarding house and spoke to a Mrs...'

'Oates,' Mabel said. 'It's good of you to give her a second chance. She's no family, apparently, and trying to make her own way. She has a spirit and determination about her. Well, all right then, wallpaper it is.'

And so, Mabel filled her day on an assortment of mundane but time-consuming Useful Women assignments. It was past seven before she finished, having been delayed struggling to take down a dinner party shopping list from a French cook who spoke little English. They had come to an impasse over shellfish. What was French for winkles?

At last, Mabel trudged up the steps to New River House. She longed to talk through the muddle in her mind until it became clear, but at the same time, wanted to be alone to write in her notebook.

'Good evening, Mr Chigley,' she said and heaved a great sigh.

'Miss Canning, you look done in,' the porter said.

Gladys appeared behind him and instead of going under, leapt into the air and onto the counter and licked Mabel's face.

'Oh, Gladys,' she said and giggled, 'sausage for your tea, was it?'

Gladys sprang onto the floor and *woofed*.

'I'd say she'd like a turn round the green if you've got the time,' Mr Chigley said. 'That Bootsie returned, and Mr Winstone went out with him a while ago. He said it was all right and would you look after Gladys because he wasn't entirely sure when he'd return.'

Mabel scratched the dog's head. 'Did you hear them mention any names?'

Mr Chigley screwed up his face in thought. 'Ned.'

Good. 'Thank you, Mr Chigley. Let's go, Gladys.'

They took a quick circuit of the green across the road, and dashed upstairs where Mabel put pennies in the gas heater and Gladys stretched out in front of it, snorted and promptly fell asleep. Mabel poured herself a sizeable glass of blackberry wine and got to work with her notebook.

Had Arkwright bashed in Oswald Deuchar's head with a glass paperweight and then kept it in his coat pocket or had the real murderer set him up? It seemed unlikely a disgruntled client would be involved – Deuchar's cases were prosaic in the extreme. Who stood to gain by Deuchar's death, and would he be devious enough to point a convincing finger at Arkwright? An image of Fred Fredericks with his leery smile rose in her mind. Fredericks – by way of his wife – would certainly benefit. The thought of it infuriated Mabel. Would she let this Fredericks get away not only with murder but with tearing apart the Arkwright family? No, she would not.

By ten, Mabel's fury had given way to pain – a cramp in her hand and a twinge between her shoulder blades. One more turn round the green and with no sign of Winstone, she and Gladys went to bed.

· · ·

The next morning, Park came to the door of his flat half-dressed and squinting as he put on his glasses. He looked at Mabel through bloodshot eyes as Gladys, her first run of the day behind her, slithered past him to her empty food dish and sat next to it.

'Had a good evening, did you?' Mabel asked, feeling all the better for a walk first thing in the morning, but not wanting to lord it over him too much.

Winstone grunted.

'Did you find out where Ned Kettle is?'

'I've put the word round I want to talk with him.'

'And how much whisky did that take?'

'Too much,' he said, but she got a grin out of him at least.

Mabel checked her watch. 'Now that I've given them time for breakfast, I'm off to Mayfair. You can tell me your details later – when you can think straight.'

He reached over, took her gently by the wrist and pulled her close. She leaned across the doorstep and they kissed.

'Ah,' she said, 'and it was cheap whisky, at that.'

An icy gust hit Mabel square in the face when she walked out of New River House. Well, at least it wasn't raining. She pulled Cora's black velvet toque down firmly on her head and set off for her day. She'd given the Arkwrights – Roxanne, her father, mother and stepmother – a day to get accustomed to each other and Mabel could contain her curiosity no longer.

Trigg answered the bell a bit out of breath.

'Forgive me, Miss Canning, I've just returned from the cobblers.'

'The cobblers?' Mabel asked.

'Mrs Arkwright – the previous one – asked me to take her boots in first thing this morning,' Trigg said.

'Where is Dorcas?'

'Yes, where is Dorcas?' the butler replied. 'Please do come in. Shall I ask Miss Roxanne to come down or will you go up?'

'I'll go up,' Mabel replied. 'Is Mrs Arkwright at home?'

'Mrs Arkwright had a meeting this morning. The visiting Mrs Arkwright' – Mabel tried to keep a straight face at this designation – 'has yet to rise, I believe. Mr Arkwright is working in his office here for the morning and asked not to be disturbed.'

Probably unwilling to face MaryLou, Mabel thought, and she could hardly blame him.

Trigg retreated to the back of the house and Mabel went up to the second floor to Roxanne's room where she knocked but received no answer.

'Roxanne?' She knocked again then opened the door and went in.

The curtains had been opened and a cup of tea placed beside the bed. Mabel felt the teacup – cool. Roxanne's bed had been slept in, but she wasn't in it now, which meant that most likely she had gone down to her mother's room. Mabel left and closed the door, but then opened it again and looked around for what, she didn't know and when she didn't see it, closed the door again and went down to MaryLou's room.

She tapped lightly and when no answer came, knocked. Still no answer. She opened the door a few inches and heard a delicate snoring. The curtains were closed and Mabel waited a moment to let her eyes adjust to the dim light. She could see MaryLou in bed wearing a mask over her eyes, but no Roxanne.

MaryLou stirred. 'Coffee,' she said and then returned to snoring.

Mabel went downstairs and found Trigg sitting at one end of the worktable in the kitchen with Cook standing at the other, beating on a great lump of dough.

'I haven't found Roxanne yet,' she said to them.

'Miss Roxanne's gone out,' Cook said. 'Dorcas said a friend

called for her earlier.'

'What friend?' Mabel asked.

Cook shrugged. 'You should ask Dorcas, she'll know.'

'Where is Dorcas?' Mabel asked.

Cook stopped punching the dough and there was a moment when time seemed suspended as the three of them looked from one to another. Roxanne had nowhere to go and no one to see. Where was she?

Trigg sprang from his chair and Mabel's heart thumped in her chest.

'Dorcas?' Trigg shouted and rushed out the door.

Mabel followed him. 'Perhaps we should ask Mr Arkwright,' she said, and Trigg pivoted on the spot and pointed to the right.

She followed the butler down a service corridor that ran nearly the length of the rear of the house and came out on the other side of the main staircase.

Trigg knocked. 'Sir?'

Mabel knocked, too – this was no time to stand on ceremony. 'Mr Arkwright?' and when there was no reply, knocked again at the same time she opened it, saying, 'Mr Arkwright—'

Rupert Arkwright lay on a blue floral Axminster in front of a broad oak desk. The hair on the back of his head was matted with blood and underneath, a dark stain had soaked into the rug.

FOURTEEN

'Trigg!' Mabel shouted then dropped to her knees at Arkwright's side and felt for a pulse.

The butler rushed in and shouted, 'My God!'

'He's alive!' Mabel said. 'Ring for an ambulance, then the police.'

'No, ma'am,' Trigg said. 'You ring and I'll take care of Mr Arkwright – I've more than enough practice for it.'

They exchanged places. Mabel stumbled in her haste to reach the telephone on the desk. Her shaking hand depressed the hook too many times, and the exchange answered with, 'All right, all right, I'm here.'

'Ambulance! Please, we need an ambulance immediately.' She gave the address. 'You've got that?'

'Yes, love,' said the exchange, a woman who sounded younger than Mabel. 'On their way. What else do you need?'

'Scotland Yard.'

Inspector Tollerton was not at his desk and Mabel waited for what felt like an excruciating amount of time while he was found. All the while, she watched Trigg's careful attention to his employer.

He checked the wound first and reported, 'Bleeding has stopped,' before slowly turning Arkwright over.

'Good,' Mabel said. 'That's good, isn't it?'

'Miss Canning, can you reach that cushion?' Trigg nodded towards an upholstered chair by a floor lamp.

'Yes.' Mabel moved the telephone as far down the desk as it would go, but her reach fell short by several inches. She set the earpiece down just as she heard Tollerton answer. 'Wait, Inspector,' she called. 'It's Mabel – wait.' She pushed the pillow under Arkwright's head when Trigg lifted it.

'All right?' Mabel asked and Trigg nodded, so she leapt up and grabbed the phone. 'Inspector, someone has attacked Rupert Arkwright – hit on the back of the head by the looks of it. And... and Roxanne may be missing.' In as even a voice as she could muster, she told him the little she knew, and he rang off.

Now what? Mabel thought. 'Trigg?'

'He's still breathing, Miss Canning. I'll stay with him – will you look in on Cook?'

Mabel found Cook standing stock-still in the middle of the kitchen, her hands clasped in front of her. When she explained, the woman gasped. 'But Miss Roxanne?'

'Did you ask Dorcas?' Mabel asked.

'Dorcas isn't back yet.' Cook turned to the sink and took hold of the rim as if she might collapse.

'Are you all right?' Mabel asked.

'Where is the girl?' Cook asked.

Mabel swallowed hard and steeled herself. 'I don't know, but the police will find her,' she said. 'They'll need to talk with each of us.'

Cook took a stiff breath. 'They'll need tea.'

Mabel couldn't be still and wait for the ambulance to arrive, and so she instituted a search of the house, ignoring the voice in her head that said Arkwright's attacker could still be on the premises. 'I hope he is,' she muttered.

She took a fire poker and went into every room, but caution caught up with her and she did so quietly, listening at the door first. She didn't dig into wardrobes, but she did pause long enough to confirm nothing had been disturbed. It turned out to be a useless activity, but expended her pent-up nerves and kept her mind busy. She even went back into MaryLou's room. The light snoring continued and so Mabel closed the door quietly. Let someone else deal with her.

She stood waiting in the cold on the doorstep when the ambulance arrived, and she remained there until they carried Arkwright out on a stretcher. Three police cars pulled up at the same time. Tollerton hopped out of the first and the other police cars emptied four constables, including WPC Wardle, and the plainclothes scene-of-crime officers.

'This way,' Mabel said and led them in.

'Anything on Miss Arkwright?' Tollerton asked as they walked back to Arkwright's office. Wardle moved closer to listen.

'Cook said that Dorcas said she went out with a friend.'

'Is that possible?' Tollerton asked.

'With whom?' Mabel demanded and then caught herself. The same question kept going round and round in her mind. 'She knows so few people in London.'

'Wardle, you and Miss Canning gather whoever is here in the...?'

'Kitchen?' Mabel offered. 'It's only Trigg and Cook. Mrs Arkwright is out, and Mrs Arkwright is upstairs asleep.' At Tollerton's raised eyebrows, she added, 'The first Mrs Arkwright – Roxanne's mother – arrived the night before last. She's the one still asleep.'

Tollerton didn't pursue the matter. He followed his officers into the drawing room. Mabel and Wardle joined Trigg and

Cook in the kitchen where they sat in silence until the inspector came in. Then they went through their mornings for him, and in each telling, the absence of Dorcas loomed larger in Mabel's mind, like a silent and invisible deadly fog seeping in.

Mabel followed Tollerton out of the kitchen leaving Cook, Trigg and Wardle making tea.

'Do you know anything about Mr Arkwright's injury yet?' Mabel asked.

'It looks as if he were hit only once,' Tollerton said.

'A paperweight?'

'Might've been.'

'And that was a glass paperweight you took out of his coat pocket Tuesday evening?'

Tollerton nodded. 'Royal Pavilion at Brighton.'

Mabel had feared an empty day ahead of her full of fear and worry, but now she seized on a purpose. 'Perhaps there's another one missing from Mr Bryars' collection. I'll go and ask him to count them again. Wait, have you returned them?'

'Yes, the crate was returned yesterday,' Tollerton said. 'They were all clean of prints except Bryars'. Right, go ahead, as long as Winstone goes along, too.'

Both Mabel and Tollerton knew she would not have waited for police permission, but still, she realised it was good of him to grant it.

'Park is looking for Ned Kettle,' she said. 'He's the beetle-browed man.'

'Kettle.' Tollerton nodded. 'Now that I hear the name, I remember Park knew him, but this was before the war. I never met the man.'

'I'd say you'll get your chance,' Mabel said. 'He must know something – he had gone to Oswald Deuchar's house. Freddy – the housekeeper – saw him.'

'Yes, that much I know.'

'Is it all right if Constable Wardle and I go up to Roxanne's room?' Mabel asked.

At that moment, one of the scene-of-crime officers called to Tollerton and so the inspector nodded to Mabel and left.

She put her head in the kitchen. 'Hildy? Come up with me.'

They climbed the stairs and stood just inside the room. Mabel seemed to hear an echo of Roxanne as she remembered how the three of them had enjoyed themselves on Tuesday afternoon.

'Would she leave on her own?' Hildy asked.

'I suppose it's possible. But Dorcas said she left with a friend. Who would that be?'

A shriek pierced the air and for one glorious moment, Mabel thought it was Roxanne refusing to do something or go somewhere or... Then the shriek dwindled into shouts and she realised it was MaryLou. She must've awakened to find a PC at her bedside.

Mabel and Wardle went out to the landing to see Adelaide Arkwright arrive home and be confronted with a constable at the door.

'Could you help with Roxanne's mother?' Mabel asked Wardle. 'And I'll talk with Adelaide.'

They sat in the drawing room near the fire with a tea tray between them. Mabel had told Adelaide briefly what had occurred and ended with, 'They've taken him to hospital.' It was paltry comfort.

'I need to go and see him,' Adelaide said. She tried for the second time to pick up her cup and saucer, but her hands shook so violently, she set it down again.

'Of course, but speak to the inspector first,' Mabel replied.

'I shouldn't have gone anywhere this morning,' Adelaide said with a severity that did little to hide the fear in her voice.

'Whoever did this to your husband slipped in and out,' Mabel said. 'If Trigg didn't see him, how would you have?'

'Trigg went to the cobblers?'

'Mrs Arkwright – MaryLou, that is – had asked him to take a pair of boots in first thing,' Mabel said.

'What could've happened to Roxanne?' Adelaide said. 'Did someone attack Rupert and then take her away?' With hope in her voice, she asked, 'Or could she have gone to visit you?'

The same hope had occurred to Mabel, and she had telephoned Mr Chigley as soon as her mind had been clear enough.

'No, she hasn't been there.'

Adelaide suppressed a sob and searched for a handkerchief. 'What can I do – must I sit and wait? How?'

Tollerton had questioned Trigg and Cook and sent constables up and down the street to knock on doors. No one had noticed anything of significance. Police dusted what seemed like every surface in the house for fingerprints. When Dorcas came back, she'd have a job of it cleaning up.

Mabel and Adelaide were sitting quietly when Tollerton came into the drawing room.

'Your maid is missing,' he said. 'Do you have any idea of her whereabouts?'

'Dorcas' grandmother is dying,' Adelaide said, 'and she has no one else in her family except for a cousin in Chester. I told her to take as much time as she needed, and so she has been going off to spend every moment possible at her bedside. I hadn't told anyone the reason – not even Cook or Trigg – because Dorcas is a private person and preferred it that way.' Adelaide watched as Tollerton wrote in his notebook. 'It seemed like a kindness at the time,' she added.

Tollerton asked Adelaide a few more questions – where

she'd been, when she'd left, how Roxanne had seemed that morning.

'I only saw her as I was leaving,' Adelaide said. 'As happy as she was to see her mother, I believe it's put a bit of a strain on her. And just when she was settling in, thanks to you, Mabel.'

Dorcas returned while the three of them were still in the drawing room and either Trigg or Cook had given her the news, because she burst into the room without a knock, tears streaming down her face.

'I should never have gone,' the maid said to Adelaide between sobs. 'But Gran's time was near and so I stayed until the end. It's only after she passed that I came back to this terrible news. What am I to do now? I need to ring the undertaker for her.'

'Sit down, Dorcas,' Adelaide said, gesturing to the sofa. Dorcas looked aghast at the suggestion, but when it was repeated with more force, the maid perched on the edge of the cushion. 'I'm so sorry about your grandmother. It was right of you to be with her.'

But Dorcas was inconsolable. 'Miss Roxanne gone? No, it's all my fault. But how could I be in two places at once?' she cried.

'What time did this friend call for Miss Roxanne?' Tollerton said, needing to raise his voice over Dorcas' wails. 'And what time did you go out?'

'It was nine o'clock, sir. It's an early household, this. Mrs Arkwright off to her meeting, Mr Arkwright closing the door to work in his office. I came out of the kitchen with the other Mrs Arkwright's breakfast tray, and Miss Roxanne was in the entrance hall. "I'm going out with a friend," she says to me. Through the frosted glass I could see someone out on the pavement waiting for her.'

'How did Roxanne seem?' Mabel asked.

'She seemed like herself,' Dorcas said. 'I shouldn't've let her go.' She sobbed into her apron. Cook appeared and put a cup of tea in front of Dorcas and, after Tollerton had walked out, pulled a flask from her pocket and added a tot of whisky to it.

MaryLou's hysterics upon being informed of the situation continued – rising and falling like the moaning of the wind – until a doctor had been called to give her something. She had returned to bed, and Trigg had taken her tea and toast.

Adelaide had left for the hospital where she would wait for her husband to regain consciousness and her stepdaughter to be located. Scotland Yard had finished with the crime scene, the photographer setting off a final flash in Rupert's office. WPC Wardle, bless her, had stayed behind with Cook, Trigg and MaryLou to help as needed.

That left Mabel to her own devices. Tollerton had offered a police car to take her home, but, at sea with her thoughts, she had declined. Now, she stood in the quiet entrance hall of the Mayfair house and considered her options.

She needed to talk with Park, to sort through what had happened and help her think where she might look for Roxanne – but Winstone had not been home when Mabel had telephoned Mr Chigley earlier. She checked her wristwatch – the morning had gone and it was mid-afternoon. She rang Mr Chigley again.

When she got hold of him, Mabel spoke only a few words to Park – all that had been needed for him to get the gist of the situation. Shortly thereafter, she walked into the back room at the Old Ivy. He and Gladys were waiting for her with a plate of bread, cheese, ham, butter, pickle, a few apples and a full pint of her own – Park's was near finished. Mabel's tummy growled, but at the same time, her eyes filled with tears. She'd been calm enough up to that moment, but now how could she eat anything with Roxanne missing?

Park stood and took her in his arms, pulled off her brimmed hat and kissed her hair. She didn't mind crying in front of him, but still, she forced herself to get through it and onto the business at hand.

'Where is she, Park? Who would take her, and why didn't it look as if she'd been taken under force? I can't imagine Roxanne would've gone quietly with a stranger.'

'The maid didn't see anyone?'

'A figure outside on the pavement, that's all. Who does Roxanne know? She knows us, she knows Cora and Skeff, she knows Hildy Wardle. That's it.'

'She knows Flea,' Park said.

'Yes, she knows Flea.' Mabel thought for a moment and a warm rush came over her. 'And Flea reminds her of her brother, Tommy. Roxanne and Flea got on so well on Sunday. She wanted to see him again and has even bought him a new drawing pad and pencils. That's it – Roxanne and Flea have gone off for the day to play cricket or softball or something.'

'Would he know where to find her?' Winstone asked.

But Mabel had no use for common sense. 'She must've told him. Yes! Her disappearance has nothing to do with what happened to her father.'

'She didn't leave a note?'

'She...' Mabel faltered for a moment. 'It didn't do any good leaving a note when she went to New River House, did it? They worried regardless. I'll telephone the Arkwright house and Hildy can go look in Roxanne's room for the drawing pad and pencils she bought for Flea. If they're gone, then we'll know they're together.'

The pub's telephone was on the wall down at the end of the dark narrow corridor, no doubt to discourage people from using it. Trigg answered and then extracted Hildy from MaryLou's room.

But the constable came onto the line with the worst news – the drawing pad and pencils were still in Roxanne's drawer.

Next, with a pounding heart, Mabel rang Cora at Milady's and explained.

'I mentioned your shop when I said you could do something about the beaded cloche.'

'She's not come here,' Cora said, 'but I will keep an eye out, and I'll do whatever I can to help. Are you going to search for her any place dodgy where you might need to look not yourself?'

'I might do,' Mabel said, but couldn't imagine where that might be. 'I'll let you know.'

Next, Mabel rang Skeff at the *Intelligencer*.

'I'll wait until Tollerton decides what he thinks best for Roxanne's safety,' Skeff said. 'If it's an abduction, there may be a ransom demand. He may or may not want it reported.'

'Yes, good,' Mabel said. 'There is the slimmest chance that she and Flea are off together. I know it doesn't seem likely, but could you find out?'

'Right,' Skeff said. 'I tell you what, let me nip down to the Waterman and I'll ask round for you. Shall I ring Mr Chigley with any news?'

'Yes, please, and thanks ever so much, Skeff.'

Mabel and Winstone returned to the back room where the cold platter awaited, and the pint stood untouched. Mabel sank onto the bench.

'Here now,' Park said, 'eat or you'll be no good for Roxanne. We've got a lot to do.'

She willed her chin to stop quivering, took a swig of beer and got out her notebook and pencil. She ate and drank and wrote as she gave Park her account – leaving out not the least detail, because such busywork structured her mind and kept her fears at bay. Winstone broke in occasionally to ask a question.

'So, that's it,' Mabel said at last. 'The hospital rang before I left to say that Rupert is still unconscious. Can we discount Rupert Arkwright in Oswald's death now?'

'We can discount him using the Royal Pavilion paperweight that was found wrapped in a handkerchief in his coat pocket,' Winstone said.

'Yes, what about that?' Mabel said.

'There was dried blood on it, but not on the handkerchief, except for a few flakes that had sloughed off. Arkwright identi- fied the handkerchief as having his monogram, but it was old and frayed and one that he said would've been on the rag heap. There were fingerprints on the glass, but not his.'

'Planted,' Mabel said. 'Mr Arkwright had a similar wound to Oswald's, Tolly said, but thankfully he'd only been hit once. Could a different paperweight have been used this morning? I told Tolly we would make Mr Bryars count his collection again. Where should we go first? Have you found Ned Kettle?'

'I have and that'll be our first stop,' Winstone said as he carved up an apple and began throwing wedges in the air for Gladys to catch.

'I should've left something for Gladys,' Mabel said, surprised to see scant remains on the platter. She drank down the last of her pint.

'I'd say Gladys will be well-fed. I've asked Mr Chigley to keep an eye on her for us and I'm sure he's got something for her tea. It could be...' He stared at Gladys, and she stared back. 'Sausages.'

Woof!

On the walk to New River House, Winstone did his best to keep the conversation light, but Mabel's mind would have none of it. It was one thing to make plans, talk about plans and write about plans, but as soon as ever it could, terror crept in and all sense vanished. She began to imagine the worst. Roxanne abducted. Roxanne tied up and left for dead. Roxanne thrown in the river, really dead. *No!* A voice inside her head would shout.

Winstone stopped on the doorstep to their building and looked at Mabel, who realised she had been asked a question but didn't know what it was.

'Never mind,' he said, and ran his hand down her arm. 'We'll find her. They'll make contact – demand money. Tolly's on this.'

In the foyer, Mabel asked Mr Chigley if Skeff had telephoned – she knew there hadn't been enough time for her to get down to the Waterman pub near the Tower Bridge and look for Flea and Roxanne, but Mabel couldn't help herself.

'I've not heard from her, Miss Canning. Is something amiss?'

'Yes,' Mabel said, 'but perhaps I could explain it later. If Roxanne walks in' – her voice caught in her throat – 'don't let her out of your sight.'

'And here's Gladys for you, Mr Chigley,' Park said. 'Thanks for this.'

'You're very welcome.'

Mabel looked at her wristwatch – gone six o'clock. Roxanne had vanished between nine and ten that morning. She'd been missing for eight hours.

FIFTEEN

Ned Kettle wasn't wearing his toupee when Mabel and Winstone met him at the Cornerstone boarding house. He looked older, sadder and smaller than he had at the dance hall. The Cornerstone had a sign by the door that read: 'A boarding house for gentlemen of reduced circumstances'. Women weren't allowed upstairs, but because several of said gentlemen now occupied the sitting room – reading and smoking – Mabel and Winstone met Ned in the dining room. It had already been laid for breakfast, although Mabel detected the lingering smell of boiled cabbage from the evening meal. But even though the dark woodwork had a nick or two, it shone with polish, and the table linens, frayed at the edges, gleamed bright white with bluing.

'You're very welcome to the Cornerstone,' the landlady, Mrs Timpkins, said to Mabel and Winstone. She clasped her hands in front of her and smiled at them, her grey hair in a long braid wound round the top of her head like a halo. 'Mr Timpkins and I are always happy to show visitors how kindness, a hot meal and a place to lay your head can help a man remember the good in the world. Now Ned here has been with us for... how long is it?'

'Nine months, Mrs Timpkins,' Ned offered.

'Nine months and, after a rough start, he has been an exemplary boarder and has even taken it upon himself to assist Mr Timpkins in keeping the boiler from breaking down completely, a task I can tell you that would try the soul of a saint. I'll leave you alone now, but just a reminder, Ned, that the coalman will be here tomorrow afternoon.' She cocked her head towards Mabel. 'Ned stands out on the pavement to make certain the coal goes down the right chute.'

Ned smiled. 'I don't mind helping where I can.'

'And all we ask,' Mrs Timpkins said, 'is that our gentlemen abide by the rules of the house, which are few and easy to follow. Breakfast at eight, no smoking in the bedrooms and the door is locked at ten o'clock every night. I'll say good evening to you.'

Mrs Timpkins left and then Winstone said, 'Ned, this is Miss Canning.'

'Pleased to meet you, Miss Canning.' Ned nodded.

'And you,' Mabel said. 'Do you remember seeing me at the Palais last Friday?'

'I do indeed. You were with that lovely young lady from America.' He looked at Winstone. 'I don't mean anything by it, Mr Winstone – dancing. I don't do anyone any harm. All the ladies leave with the same number of rings on their fingers, if you know what I mean.'

'Roxanne thought you were one of the instructors,' Mabel said.

'I help out where I can, but I'm not official-like. I couldn't be – not with that fusspot Bryars in charge.' He cut his eyes at Mabel and when she smiled, he did, too. 'We had a bit of a set-to a couple of years ago, before I got myself straightened out.'

'What happened to you, Ned?' Winstone asked. 'You were always happy as Larry.'

'The war, Mr Winstone, as you might expect.' Ned sighed. 'I went to war one man and came out another. Didn't everyone – at least, those of us who came out at all. It wasn't as bad for me as it was for others, but still I had a rough time of it for a while. Then one afternoon, I wandered into some little dance hall and the music just sort of... picked me up. It's the dance hall what kept me from going over the edge of beyond, not the church – although I'd prefer if you didn't say that to Mrs Timpkins, if you don't mind, because they're very good people and all.'

He'd looked at Mabel for this, and so she said, 'Not a word.'

'The one time I feel like myself again is dancing,' Ned continued, 'and so that's where I go every afternoon and evening I can. I'll go to any dance hall, although, that Palais is something, isn't it? When I'm there, I try to stay out of Bryars' way. I've cottoned on to his routine, you see, and I know when I can be out on the dance floor and when I shouldn't. Also, two years ago I didn't have my' – he patted his head, now bare of his toupee. 'But we have a curfew here, and so I always leave before the place closes down, so I didn't hear about poor Mr Deuchar until later.'

'About Oswald Deuchar,' Winstone said. 'How did you know him?'

'I worked for him.'

'Freddy told me she'd seen you at the house,' Mabel said.

'The housekeeper? Yeah, I've been there a few times.'

'Do you know her husband, Fred?' Mabel asked.

Ned recoiled at the question. 'He's a bad 'un, Miss Canning. Just the sort I steer clear of these days.'

'What sort of work did you do for Deuchar?' Winstone asked.

'Did you know he was a private detective?' Ned asked and they nodded. 'Well, months ago, not long after I'd moved in here, he put an advertisement in the newspaper – Gumshoe seeks assistant.' Ned laughed. 'I didn't know what a gumshoe was, but I was eager for work and so I answered. Turns out gumshoe is what they call a detective in America. He loved American detectives, did Mr Deuchar.'

'What did you do for him?' Winstone asked.

'Very little. He was a kind man, and I'd see him every week. He never had much going, but even so, he'd always pay me a shilling even if all I did was to go through a rubbish bin looking for something someone had lost.'

'You saw him at the Palais Friday evening,' Winstone said.

'Yes, sir, I did and that was a surprise. He caught me partway through the evening in that service corridor. Not the one on the kitchen side, the other one. Mr Deuchar said he was glad to see me and that there was someone he wanted me to watch.'

'Roxanne?' Mabel asked.

'The young American lady? No, not her exactly, but someone he suspected might be trouble for her. I stopped him right there. I couldn't do it, you see.' Ned's face reddened. 'I explained to Mr Deuchar that I had my curfew, but also I couldn't watch whoever he wanted me to watch and still keep an eye out for Bryars. If he saw me, there would be hell to pay.' He sucked in a breath. 'I'm very sorry, Miss Canning.'

'It's all right,' Mabel said. She remembered Bryars hadn't been too happy to learn that Ned had been at the Palais. 'Why doesn't he like you, Ned?'

'A mix-up,' Ned muttered. 'It had to do with a lady's tiara.' He looked up earnestly. 'Like I said, that was two years ago at least. But still, I'd rather avoid Bryars if at all possible, and I've got good at it. He's all over the hall, but he's predictable in his movements.'

'And so,' Winstone said, 'after you talked with Deuchar, you left? What time?'

'It must've been about ten o'clock,' Ned told them, looking miserable. 'And it turns out it wasn't Miss Roxanne who needed protecting, it was Mr Deuchar himself.'

'When you were standing in the corridor talking with Deuchar' – Park's gaze darted to Mabel, and she knew the significance. It was the corridor where Deuchar was killed – 'did you see anyone when you were talking with him?' Winstone asked.

Ned Kettle thought hard, his beetle-brow furrowing. 'It seems to me someone from the kitchen went by. Wearing one of those white aprons and a white hat sort of, but tied on, you know? Buttoning up his white coat as he hurried by.'

By ten o'clock, Mabel had been locked in the larder near the kitchen, which was on the entire other side of the dance floor. Why would someone from the kitchen be dashing down the corridor where Oswald had been killed?

'You didn't see a face?' Winstone asked.

'I didn't, no, I'm sorry, Mr Winstone, only the back of him.'

'Tall? Short?'

'Well, I've not got much height myself, so most people seem tall.'

'And this morning, Ned,' Winstone said. 'Where were you?'

Ned didn't seem to take offence at such a police sort of question.

'I was here all morning, Mr Winstone. The boiler needed attention.'

Mrs Timpkins came to the door. 'We'll be having cocoa soon, Ned. Would your friends like to stay?'

'Thank you, Mrs Timpkins,' Mabel said, 'but we'll need to be on our way.'

'Very well then, good night.'

Winstone pulled his notebook from his breast pocket, wrote something on a page and tore it out. He handed Ned the paper and a shilling. 'Here you go. You ring me next week, will you? I might have some work for you.'

'Thank you, Mr Winstone, that's very kind. Good evening, Miss Canning.'

'Good evening, Ned. Take care.'

When they walked out of the Cornerstone, the taxi they'd arrived in still idled at the kerb – Winstone had asked the driver to wait. Good thing, because Mabel wasn't entirely sure where they were – south of the Thames along a questionable road where the streetlamp outside the boarding house was the only light for a long stretch. She wouldn't've wanted either of them to go out searching for a taxi.

'Hammersmith Palais,' Winstone told the cabbie.

'Ned admitted to being at the Palais at ten o'clock,' Mabel said, 'but curfew at the Cornerstone is at ten.'

Winstone lifted his eyebrows in reply. 'Ned knows how to open a locked door and he knows how to jimmy a window. Perhaps Timpkins gives him a bit of leeway, because he doesn't want to lose his best boiler man.'

'So he might not be totally redeemed,' Mabel said. 'But it doesn't seem that he would march into Bryars' office and steal a glass paperweight, does it? Not when he's avoiding the man.'

'I believe him when he said he saw someone,' Winstone said. 'He might've seen the murderer only minutes before he attacked. But what would someone from the kitchen be doing on that side of the building?'

'We'll ask Bryars if he saw a kitchen worker out of place that evening,' Mabel said.

But then, out of the blue, panic nearly took Mabel's breath away. If the kitchen worker meant to harm Roxanne and Deuchar met his demise because he intervened, then perhaps the attempted murder of Mr Arkwright was also intended to stop him from protecting his daughter? And if the murderer was behind Roxanne's disappearance, would Mabel be able to find her before it was too late?

At the Palais, Winstone paid the five shillings each while Mabel looked past the doorman to the dance floor, teeming with couples doing a fast foxtrot – spinning around, deftly avoiding collisions while laughing and chatting. The band played and no one had a care. Another world, Mabel thought.

They went directly to Bryars' office, but he didn't answer. Winstone looked at Mabel and she looked at his hand on the door handle. He tried it and the door opened.

'What's he playing at, telling us it's always locked?' she asked, although inside, it did appear as if he had just stepped out. The lights were on, papers and ledgers covered the desk and the fire looked about midway through its evening.

'We'll come back,' Winstone said. 'Let's go to the kitchen.'

As they passed the bar, he asked, 'Have you seen Bryars?'

'Oh yeah,' the barman said, 'he's about. Likes to put his nose in every corner, making sure we're doing our jobs.'

They walked down the back corridor that led to the kitchen, and as they passed the larder where Mabel had been trapped, she showed it to Park.

'How did he manage to close the door on you?'

Mabel nodded to the hanging Italian ham. 'Bowled me over with that.'

At the wide opening to the kitchen, they stepped aside and waited as a string of waiters came out with plates in hands. When a break came, Mabel peeked in. As on Friday evening, the place was a hive of activity – chopping, mixing, stirring, assembling plates, washing dishes, cleaning up spills on the floor, all accompanied by a great deal of shouting orders.

'There must be twenty people in here,' Winstone said.

'May I help you?' said a man in a toque and with a tone that told them he really did not want to help them at all.

'I'm Winstone and this is Miss Canning. We were with the police on Friday.'

'Friday?' he asked. 'Oh, that business. They've been back since then counting my mixing bowls.'

'Have you seen Mr Bryars?' Winstone asked. 'He should be expecting us.'

The chef looked past them and down the corridor. 'He'll be around any minute and so I'd like to keep this lot working.'

'Are all these permanent staff?' Winstone asked.

'There's no one under fourteen works here – I won't abide that.'

'It isn't a question of child labour. Are they all permanent or do you take in workers as needed?' Winstone asked again.

The chef shrugged. 'I do, yes. Some nights are busier than others, and a few cooks know to look in on me in case I need the extra hands.'

A metallic crash followed by a 'Bloody hell!' came from a fellow at the head of a long work counter. He wiped his hand across his apron leaving a wide purple streak behind. 'That's the end of the blackcurrant sauce,' he called over.

'It certainly is a messy job, working in a kitchen,' Mabel said.

'Yes,' the chef said, and swept a hand down the front of his own apron that carried splotches and streaks of brown, orange and red. 'As the French say, you cannot make an omelette without breaking a few eggs.'

'You must have a laundry service,' Mabel said.

'Of course we have laundry service,' the chef replied. 'Did you think we took our own aprons home every night to wash out?'

Mabel glanced over at Winstone, who said, 'Who is it?'

The chef frowned. 'It's Bradford's in Norwood. Look, why the interest in—'

'How often do they come round to collect?' Mabel asked.

The chef gave up. 'Midweek – Wednesdays.'

'How do they get all that out?' Mabel asked, nodding to the chef's apron.

He shrugged. 'I have no idea what sort of miracles they work.'

'Mr Bryars, there you are,' Winstone said in a loud voice.

The manager had appeared at the door and the volume in the kitchen rose as everyone picked up their pace.

'Mr Bryars,' the chef said, his nose in the air, 'I don't see how I can serve food while—'

'Why are you questioning my kitchen staff?' Bryars asked.

'We aren't here to question *them*, Mr Bryars,' Winstone said, 'we're here to question *you*.'

Bryars took a step back. 'Why? What now?'

'It's about that fine collection of paperweights,' Winstone said. He put an arm round the manager's shoulder, turned him and they headed off, giving Mabel a quick look as he did so.

She stayed back and once the manager was down the corridor, the chef sighed.

'How many casual workers do you take in at a time?' Mabel asked.

'Never more than three or four.'

'Are they regulars? Do you get their names?'

'Why would I do that?' the chef asked. 'If I give them a job and they do it, that's all either of us cares about. Some are regulars and occasionally someone new turns up.'

'How many did you have Friday last?'

'Friday last, Friday...' The chef narrowed his eyes. 'Why?'

'Because I'm a private detective and have the ear of Detective Inspector Tollerton, that's why.'

'All right, all right,' he said, 'I'm only asking. Four to start with. They'd all vanished before the police arrived.'

The chef turned out and shouted, 'Vickers, don't burn that chop to a crisp!' Mabel decided she'd learned all she could and left. As she walked down the corridor, the chef started on someone else. 'Pay attention, Annie, there's a reason it's called bread sauce and not bread loaf.'

Mabel walked out to the bar, stopping to make a note about the laundry. Ned told them he had seen someone in kitchen garb while he stood talking with Deuchar. Had the murderer worn the uniform as disguise and protection, then stripped off the bloody thing and left it with the rest of the soiled kitchen laundry? It wasn't that easy to get blood out of linen or cotton – perhaps this Bradford's laundry service would've tossed it aside.

She crossed the edge of the dance floor to the other side of the building and walked into the office as Mr Bryars finished laying out his treasures on the desk.

'There should be twenty-seven, I swear to it,' the manager said as he counted. 'Or twenty-nine?'

Park, standing over the desk, looked up at Mabel as she gazed at the collection. *Rupert Arkwright is lying unconscious*, she thought with irritation, *and Bryars can't remember how many paperweights he owns.*

Bryars finished counting. 'No, wait. Something is missing.' He lifted one glass paperweight after another, confirming the identity of each. 'Buckfast Abbey in Devon,' he said, 'such a haunting place.'

And where is Roxanne? Time is passing and every minute is counted.

'And here's the home of J.M. Barrie – he was Scottish, you know.'

Perhaps Arkwright had awakened and could say who attacked him, where Roxanne had gone. What are we doing listening to Bryars witter on. Mabel trembled with rage. If the man didn't shut up, she would scream.

'I brought it back three years ago, but I returned to Scotland last year and found a lovely one of... hang on.' He ran his finger down each row of paperweights, reciting their names in a low mutter. When he got to the end, he began again.

'What is it?' Mabel shouted.

The question shot out of her and Bryars jumped back.

'Well, there's a puzzle,' he said. 'What's become of Holy-roodhouse?'

SIXTEEN

They rang the police and the three of them sat in Bryars' office over cups of tea until Tollerton and PC Drake arrived.

Now, in the taxi on the way back to New River House, Mabel asked, 'Were the two paperweights taken on the same night? Do you think Holyroodhouse was used on Rupert Arkwright?'

'If it was Holyroodhouse,' Winstone said, 'whose pocket will it be found in?'

They had told Tollerton what they knew, and before they left had peppered him with questions. They learned Rupert Arkwright had yet to regain consciousness, although doctors were optimistic. When questioned on Tuesday evening, Arkwright had told police that he had not recently worn the coat where they'd found the paperweight, and the butler had confirmed that. Police were now working on the idea that the murder weapon had been deliberately planted there by one of the many temporary staff taken on to get the house ready for MaryLou Arkwright's arrival, but it had been a motley crew and no one, not even Dorcas, could remember every name.

Adelaide had taken the blame for this, saying she had given

Dorcas a free hand in finding extra help, not realising the maid was in such a state because of her grandmother that she could barely remember her own name. It had been the perfect set-up for the murderer, making it easy for him to sneak in, leave a false trail of evidence and then ring the police with a tip. But perhaps Arkwright had discovered the murderer's identity and so became the next intended victim.

Mabel wiped the fog from the inside of the window as the taxi wove its way in and out of traffic down Marylebone Road. 'There are four kitchen workers unaccounted for the night Oswald was killed,' she said.

'But was Deuchar the target?'

Or was it Roxanne? The question hung in the air. And now, a week later, had the murderer bagged his prey?

Gladys performed a little dance for them in the foyer of New River House. Mr Chigley came out of his private quarters carrying a cup of Bovril and the dog gave his hand a grateful lick. While Winstone took her out for a turn round the green, Mabel asked if Skeff had rung.

'She did.' Mr Chigley's cautious reply told her not to expect much. He tapped the open page of his day diary. 'I wrote it down – Miss Skeffington said you would know what she meant. "Flea says no but will watch out."' When he saw her face, he asked, 'Bad news, was it?'

'Not the news I had hoped. Oh, Mr Chigley.'

Mabel told him the state of affairs.

'You mean, she's been abducted?' he asked. 'Dear God. You're keeping yourself safe, aren't you, Miss Canning, because I would never want to have to tell your father—'

'There will be no need to tell Papa anything,' Mabel said firmly. 'I know you understand that. If you see or hear something that might help, just tell me or Mr Winstone, or Cora and Skeff. Or telephone the police – whatever it takes.'

'I will be vigilant,' Mr Chigley said.

Park and Gladys returned, the latter giving herself a good shake and spraying Mabel with cold rain. They said their good nights to the porter and Mabel led the way, trudging up the stairs, her steps getting slower and slower. What was she to do now? How was she to get through the night?

On the first-floor landing, when Winstone paused, Mabel took his hand and they continued to her flat. While he poured a handful of pennies into the gas heater and Gladys stretched out in front of it to dry off, Mabel opened a tin of tomato soup and put out bread and butter, but when they sat down at the table, she found it a great effort to eat. Park watched her and after the meal, such as it was, suggested he leave Gladys with her and go back to his own flat.

'Please,' Mabel said, 'I know it's late, but can't you both keep me company for a while?'

'Do you have a deck of cards?' Park asked.

Mabel gave a brief laugh and covered his hand. 'I'm sure you and Gladys know a few tricks to entertain me.' She nodded to the sofa. 'Go on, have a seat over there.'

Park stretched out on the sofa while Mabel tidied the kitchen then put the kettle on. When she came out, he was asleep.

She smiled down at him, brushed that errant curl off his forehead and took his glasses off. When she leaned closer and touched her lips to his, he stirred, but she wouldn't wake him. She brought out the extra blanket from the wardrobe, covered him and went to bed.

The next morning, Mabel woke and thought it amazing that she had slept at all. A warm body lay next to her and she tried to remember what had happened – until a wet nose touched her arm.

'Good morning, Gladys,' she said and then she heard a rattling in the kitchen. 'Good morning,' she called.

'Tea?' Winstone asked. He came to the door, but politely looked in the other direction.

Mabel wished Gladys and Winstone could switch places so that the dog would be brewing the tea and Park would be...

'Yes, please.' She rose, threw on her dressing gown and went out. 'Thank you for staying,' she said. 'I hope you weren't too uncomfortable.'

'No, it was fine, fine.' He stretched his shoulders back. 'Fine.'

There was a knock at the door.

'Mabel?' Cora asked. 'It's only us.'

She opened the door to them. 'Good morning, come in.'

'Morning, Winstone,' Skeff called over to Park in the kitchen alcove. She stepped past Mabel and gave Gladys a scratch.

'Morning, ladies,' Park called.

Cora followed and presented Mabel with a hat she'd been holding behind her back. 'Just something I had to hand. Last evening, I was inspired to make an adjustment or two.'

'Thanks, Cora,' Mabel said. The picture hat had a wide blue ribbon wrapped round the band with such a generous posy of sky-blue silk gentian that the brim hung down slightly on one side. She put it on and went into the bathroom to look in the mirror. The hat framed her face and the soft curls of her bob, but unfortunately did little to hide her wan complexion and hollow eyes. She pinched a bit of colour into her cheeks.

'It's lovely,' she said when she came out. Cora grabbed her hand and gave it a squeeze.

'I don't want to call it a lucky hat,' Cora said, 'because you are better than luck. But I believe it will imbue you with confidence and a sincerity that will persuade even the most recalcitrant people to tell you what you need to know.'

'You'll find her,' Skeff said. 'You'll find her safe.'

Mabel nodded but couldn't speak.

'Tea?' Park asked.

'Not for us, thanks,' Skeff said. 'Mabel, I'm sorry I didn't have better news from Flea, but it was a good idea you had. I rather think Flea wouldn't mind if Roxanne visited him.'

Fear shot through Mabel as she thought of Roxanne wandering lost somewhere along the Thames with its rabbit warren of docks and danger. Mabel knew from experience how easy it was to knock a person over the head and push him – or her – into the river. Anyone could end the same way even by accident. She shut her eyes tightly to banish the thought.

'Now, I've a few bits for you from the paper,' Skeff said, handing over a brown envelope. 'About Arkwright's boxing incident.'

'Yes, of course,' Mabel said, realising the revelation about Rupert Arkwright's past had gone clean out of her mind. 'And here, I'll return the other packet you gave me.'

'I don't know if it matters,' Skeff said, 'but you'll see there's a later article about West Midland Steel and Arkwright's reach expanding into railways. There had been trouble at the rail yard he bought. The article makes mention of it but gives no details. I'll keep looking into that if you like.'

'Yes, please do,' Mabel said. 'Better to have too much information than not enough.'

'We'll be off now,' Skeff said. They walked out into the corridor, but Skeff stopped and added, 'Oh by the way, it wasn't Keating. The name of the boxer who died. It was Kettle.'

Mabel closed the door and leaned against it, stunned.

'Kettle!' She looked up at Winstone. 'He's Kettle.' She couldn't get any other words out.

They sat on the sofa and Mabel opened the envelope,

turning it over and giving it a shake. The clippings drifted out onto the coffee table and they got to work sorting them. Park found the item about the boxer, Harry Kettle. It looked as if he'd been in plenty of fights outside the ring before his last one and he had started them all. The open verdict at the inquest had let the young Rupert Arkwright off. Mabel scanned the clipping and finally found her voice. 'Could he be related to Ned? Could Ned want revenge? But why, after all these years?'

'Deuchar told Ned about the Arkwright case,' Winstone said. 'Perhaps Ned let slip about this relative, Deuchar realised he was plotting revenge and they argued about it. Ned could have been planning to punish Arkwright by harming his daughter.'

'Ned told us he'd had a hard time after the war, but he'd recovered.'

'I'm not certain anyone can fully recover from that,' Winstone said. 'Did I get taken in? Could he hide his true nature that well?'

'He seemed so sincere. And contrite.'

'Good cover, that,' Winstone said. 'But sometimes the most dangerous people are the ones who hide their true nature best. The question is, has he taken Roxanne somewhere? Is she still alive?'

He had been speaking as if half to himself but stopped and cut his eyes at Mabel. But her mind had gone in the same direction, even leaping ahead to the same dreadful conclusion. She steeled herself and asked, 'Where would he have taken her?'

'Miss Canning?' came Mr Chigley's calm and quiet early-morning voice. He followed it with a light knock. 'Miss Canning? Detective Inspector Tollerton would like to speak with you. He's on the telephone.'

Tolly would've asked for Winstone first, Mabel knew, but when Mr Chigley had knocked at Park's door and received no answer, the inspector must have asked for her.

Gladys went to the door, snuffled and greeted the porter with a low *woof*.

'Thank you, Mr Chigley,' Mabel said through the door. 'On my way.'

A letter had arrived at the house in Mayfair, Tolly said. A threatening letter. Mabel's heart sank.

She passed the earpiece to Winstone and let him finish the conversation with Tollerton while she went back to her flat to dress. Her hands trembled as she buttoned her coat, but when she put on Cora's picture hat with the sky-blue silk gentians, it steeled her will. In a short time, they met back in the foyer.

'There you are, girl,' Winstone said to Gladys, who trotted under the counter and jumped up into the porter's desk chair. 'And thank you, Mr Chigley.'

'It's always a pleasure to have Gladys keep me company.'

Out on the pavement, Winstone said, 'I'll run Ned to ground. I have to say, a threatening letter has never been his modus operandi. In fact, none of it sounds like him, and yet he's the one with the best motive.'

'I'm off to Mayfair,' Mabel said. 'I want to see Adelaide to let her know we're doing everything we can and... and that we'll find Roxanne. After that, I'll go to Hanover Terrace to show the drawing of Ned to Fred Fredericks. Ned visited Oswald, and it sounds as if Fred is always loitering nearby, despite what his wife says. What if he and Ned were in this together because Fred wanted money and Ned wanted revenge? And what if Freddy knew what they were up to and that she would benefit? What if they have Roxanne *there*?' She heard her own words and paused. 'Is that too far-fetched?'

'It never hurts to be thorough.' Winstone frowned at her, but it was a thinking look, not an objection. 'You'll ring Tolly if you find anything?'

'I will.'

'It came by hand and was put through the letter box under cover of darkness,' Trigg said to Mabel the moment she arrived. 'The coward.' Quiet fury – it was the first emotion Mabel had seen from the butler.

'What did it say?' Mabel asked.

'It read thus,' Trigg said, and stood looking off into the distance as if performing a school recitation. 'You killed long ago and went on with your life, but no more. You will pay.' He shuddered as if the words had left a bad taste in his mouth.

'Do you still have the letter?' Mabel asked. 'I'd like to see the handwriting.'

'The police took it, ma'am. And it was typewritten.'

No chance there, then, for Mabel to employ her eye for associating a person's hand with music and recognising it easily.

'Is the inspector still here?'

'No, ma'am, he's gone.'

'Where is Mrs Arkwright?' Mabel asked. She felt sure Trigg would understand her question referred to the proper one.

'Upstairs in the morning room,' the butler said, 'and I believe she would very much like it if you looked in. I'll take up coffee.'

'And the other Mrs Arkwright?' Mabel asked.

'Keeping to her quarters. She was ringing for Dorcas every two minutes until the maid was nearly run ragged. She's escaped by going off to the undertakers.'

Trigg went back towards the kitchen.

'Well,' Mabel said to herself as she climbed the stairs, 'at least I won't have to worry about MaryLou if she stays in her room.'

She paused in the door of the morning room. 'Hello, good morning.'

Adelaide, who had been staring at a piece of needlework in her lap, sprang up, her face full of fear and hope.

'Oh, Mabel, is there news?'

'No, I'm sorry,' she said. 'But there will be. In the meantime, I wanted to look in on you.'

'Come and sit,' Adelaide said, and dropped back into her own chair and stared at the fire. 'The one thing he wanted in all the world – to have his daughter here – and for it to end like this.'

'It hasn't ended,' Mabel said with more force than she intended.

'The letter that arrived,' Adelaide said, 'there was no demand for money.'

Yes, Mabel had noticed. *You will pay* – but if not in money, then... No, she wouldn't believe that. She couldn't.

'When Mr Arkwright wakes and when Roxanne is home,' Mabel said, 'you will all need to ask MaryLou a few questions.'

'You aren't saying she has anything to do with Rupert's injury and Roxanne's disappearance?' Adelaide asked. 'She may not be the easiest person to get along with, but I can't imagine that.'

'No, of course not. But she does have a secret that is unfair to keep,' Mabel said. 'On Tuesday evening, Roxanne told me that she has a brother. I believe he's about three years younger than she is.'

Mabel watched as Adelaide's thoughts were laid bare on her face. Confusion, disbelief, anger.

'Rupert has a son he never knew about?' she asked.

'That's not certain,' Mabel said, 'not until we know the timing or until MaryLou explains. What is certain is that MaryLou had another child. And she told her daughter not to breathe a word about him.'

At that moment, the door opened, and there she stood – mother of two – MaryLou Arkwright.

'Oh, I see there's a party going on while my daughter is God knows where,' she said, her voice uneven and her hair coming loose from its pins. 'Don't let me disturb you.'

'Good morning, Mrs Arkwright,' Mabel said, standing. 'I've only stopped briefly. Would you like coffee? Trigg is bringing up a tray.'

'I couldn't possibly,' MaryLou said. 'I'll go back to my room.'

'Please do stay, MaryLou,' Adelaide said and sounded as if she meant it.

'Is there news?'

'I don't believe so,' Mabel said.

'My poor baby,' MaryLou said and covered her mouth.

'Roxanne is strong and brave,' Mabel said, 'and that's because of you. She will be all right.'

Trigg appeared from behind MaryLou with the tray of coffee, cake and three cups, as if he'd known all along she'd be there. He set the tray on the table in front of the fire and backed out.

Having been coaxed into the room, MaryLou sat on the sofa between Mabel and Adelaide's chairs and poured the coffee.

They managed to sit for at least ten minutes without anyone saying a word other than 'Milk and sugar?' 'Yes, thank you' 'Cake?' and 'Please.' China clinked as coffee was stirred. A lump of coal in the fireplace cracked and fell, sending out a burst of sparks.

'MaryLou... does Roxanne have a younger brother?'

Adelaide had had the good sense to ask the question after MaryLou had swallowed her coffee, but the answer came out sputtering, nonetheless.

'What? How dare you—' Her head snapped to Mabel. 'This is your doing, isn't it?'

'Yes, it is,' Mabel admitted.

'Private detective indeed,' she said, her voice rife with

contempt. 'Inventing lies, trying to extort even more money out of Rupert only to—'

'Roxanne told me,' Mabel said.

MaryLou shot out of her chair, but then held still, an ominous quiet gathering round her person. 'I will not be treated in this manner,' she said, then plonked her cup and saucer on the table and stalked out.

'What was she afraid Rupert would do?' Adelaide asked. 'And what else has she filled her daughter's head with?'

It may have been a rhetorical question, but Mabel had an answer. 'For one thing, Roxanne believes that if her father finds out about Tommy, he will take all their money away.'

'Is that it?' Adelaide asked. 'Money? Now you say it, Roxanne made several references about money to her father since she arrived. "Have you spent all of Mama's money?" – that sort of thing.'

'Was it MaryLou's money?' Mabel asked.

'Yes,' Adelaide said. 'MaryLou brought money into the marriage – a large amount – and Rupert used it wisely. By the time they divorced, he'd already doubled it and so he gave MaryLou back what she had brought to the marriage, and he added to that the rate of interest for those years. They moved back to her family house, and Rupert sent money for Roxanne every month. It doesn't sound as if she's mentioned that to her daughter, does it?'

'No, it doesn't, and it doesn't seem as if she's willing to admit it,' Mabel said.

'She can say what she likes, but there's an abundance of proof. Lillian signed the documents as a witness.'

Mabel laughed. 'This was when Miss Kerr worked on the exchange at his office?'

'She was Rupert's secretary by then,' Adelaide said. 'But that's all she was during the time he and MaryLou were married.'

'But before and after?'

Adelaide smiled. 'That isn't my story to tell.'

Enough of an answer for Mabel – for the moment. 'I don't know if I could ever gin up the nerve to ask her,' Mabel said, finishing her coffee.

'Did the boxing story come to anything?' Adelaide asked as she walked Mabel to the morning room door.

'It may,' Mabel said. 'Park has gone to look into something related.'

'Your Mr Winstone,' Adelaide said. 'I've yet to meet him.'

'You will. I must go now. You'll be all right?'

'I will. I'm going to sit with Rupert after lunch,' Adelaide said. Her chin quivered.

Mabel reached over and covered Adelaide's hand with hers. 'He'll know you're there and he'll be glad of it.'

She left but went to the kitchen instead of out the front door. No Trigg, no Dorcas, but Cook sat at the table, lost in thought.

'How are you all here?' Mabel asked.

'It's as if we're moving through treacle and getting further behind.' Cook shook her head. 'Why didn't Dorcas tell us about her granny? Here I was complaining and there she was miserable – what she must think of us. People shouldn't be like a closed book about family.' She searched Mabel's face. 'Is there any word about Miss Roxanne?'

No word, no word. It was depressing to repeat. *Buck up, Mabel.*

'There'll be something by later today,' she said with false bravado. She felt the panic rise within her, took a sharp breath and said goodbye.

SEVENTEEN

'Oh, Miss Canning, it's you,' Freddy said, looking more than a bit disappointed. 'I thought you might be the coalman changed his mind. You see him down there, delivering.'

Mabel looked down the road to where a lorry piled high with bags of coal, sat at the kerb. The iron lid on the coal hole in the pavement had been lifted and two men were taking turns pouring bags of coal down the opening.

'Couldn't he spare a bag or two for you?' Mabel asked.

'Exactly my question to him and you'd have thought I'd asked for the moon. He told me he his orders are to deliver here on Saturday at eleven o'clock and he couldn't disappoint other customers just because I wanted to push ahead in the queue. A bit of a cheek, if you ask me. I wonder should I try again. Do come in.'

Mabel walked in before she asked, 'Freddy, is your husband about?'

The housekeeper drew herself up, pulled her cardigan together and crossed her arms. 'Although Fred may try to make a habit of it, I do my best to deter him.'

'So, he is here? Because I'd like to speak with him.'

'Is it about little Ozzie?' she asked. 'I've heard nothing else from the police.'

'Yes, it is,' Mabel said. 'Remember you asked me to carry on investigating.'

'I did,' Freddy said, her gaze darting about the entrance hall rather than looking at Mabel. 'Although I didn't think you'd agreed to it.'

'I told you I would stay involved but that you needn't pay me.'

'Ah yes, that was it,' the housekeeper said. She cast a sideways glance towards the back of the house where Mabel thought the servants' stairs might be that led down to the cellar.

'Is your husband downstairs?' Mabel waited and then added, 'The gathering of evidence is an ongoing process in an enquiry, and I will leave no stone unturned. I need to speak with him.'

'Yes, yes, all right,' Freddy said. 'He may be here. You're welcome to go and see. When you've finished with your questions, you may tell him to be on his way.' The telephone on the entrance hall table rang. 'Do forgive me – this may be the undertaker.'

That was the second mention of an undertaker in one day and Mabel didn't like it.

At the back of the house, stairs led down to a dim, shadowy corridor, the only light coming from high windows that faced out the back of the house. The light grew brighter at the end of the corridor, and when Mabel had passed the kitchen and what might've been the pantry, she went through an opening into a room. On her left, there was a scullery sink, a few shelves with broken pots and the door to the back garden. Off ahead of her, in a dark place in the far corner, a camp bed, neatly made with a rough blanket and a small pillow.

Freddy, thou doth protest too much. She not only lets her dodgy husband into the house, she allows him to sleep there. Mabel looked round the rest of the space. On the right, towards the front of the house, a solid wooden door was held fast with an iron rod that slid across it. At the bottom of the door, she saw a sifting of coal dust had spilled out. All right, he sleeps next to the coal cellar, but still, he has a bed.

A sound from behind made her turn, and there was Fred.

'My, my, Miss Canning,' he said in that unctuous tone as his rubbery smile widened. 'To what do I owe this pleasure?'

'Good afternoon, Mr Fredericks.' Mabel handed him the drawing of Ned Kettle. 'Do you know this man?'

Fred took the drawing from her. He held it out at arm's length and then brought it close to his eyes. He walked over to the window and cocked his head as he studied it. Then he handed it back to her.

'No, I'm terribly sorry, I don't believe I do.'

'You've never seen him?'

'Now Miss Canning,' he said, wagging a finger at her, 'you didn't ask me that, did you?'

Mabel clenched her teeth. 'Have you ever seen this man before?'

'I may have done,' he said. 'Once or twice. I believe he might've been visiting Mr Deuchar – little Ozzie as my wife likes to call him.'

'Did you ever speak to him?' Mabel asked.

'No,' Fred said, shaking his head. 'I know where the line is drawn, Miss Canning, and I know when it's safe to cross it and when it isn't. I didn't put my nose into Oswald's affairs. To my Freddy, Oswald Deuchar was the son we never had and, although you may not believe it, I would never have touched a hair on his head.'

He was right there – she didn't believe a word that came out of his mouth. Why hadn't she shown the drawing of Fred around the Palais?

She left Fred to his camp bed in the cellar and went up to the entrance hall where Freddy stood idly brushing the newel post with a feather duster.

'I hope you found what you were seeking,' she said.

'I had a word with your husband, yes.' Mabel said. She glanced round the narrow space. 'It's a lovely house.'

'Yes,' Freddy said. 'The elder Mr Deuchar's wife did the decorating. Years ago, that was. I've been told I should re-decorate, but I am so fond of the place.'

'Could you show me the other rooms? It's only my curiosity about furniture and wallpaper – I love that sort of thing. I often take Useful Women assignments to help women decide what fabric to choose.' That was the truth, although Mabel wouldn't say it was one of her specialities.

Freddy's eyes lit up. 'I'll give you the grand tour, shall I?' she asked, and off they went.

Mabel's intention was to be certain Roxanne wasn't being held captive in the house. Freddy's enthusiastic reply was reassuring, but still, she wondered if a tour of the house might reveal some clues. They went into every room on three floors. Freddy threw open cumbersome curtains and the doors of wardrobes and linen closets. She spoke lovingly of the heavy Victorian mahogany and walnut chairs and bedsteads and used her feather duster to point out features. No sign of Roxanne.

'Fascinating,' Mabel said with disappointment as they at last made it back to the ground floor. 'Now, best of luck with your coal delivery.'

'Coffee, Miss Canning?' Freddy asked, hurrying after her.

'No, thank you. I really must go.' But something in the

housekeeper's tone gave her pause. 'How are you doing in yourself?'

'At sea, as you may have noticed,' Freddy said. 'I confess I am a bit uncomfortable in my new situation. How people live with so much wealth is quite beyond me. It was one thing when it belonged to Ozzie and I worked for my wages, but now, look at me – I'm even taking on what I call an under housekeeper. I've let her order the coal for me and I've allowed that scoundrel to sneak back into my life.'

Was Freddy's uncertainty in her new situation just that? Or was she using it to divert Mabel's attention, when in fact something far more sinister had her nerves on edge?

'On my first visit,' Mabel said, 'your husband said he'd done you a favour. What did he mean by that?'

'Nothing,' Freddy said. 'A jest. I tell him, "Do me a favour and stay out of my way," and he brings it up as if he's bestowed some great kindness on me. Silly man.'

'Why don't I look in on you tomorrow?' Mabel asked.

'Would you?' Freddy asked. 'Now I have two things to look forward to tomorrow – the coal delivery and coffee with you.'

Mabel hurried off, holding up at the end of the terrace to think. Uppermost in her mind was what Park might be uncovering about Ned Kettle's connection to a long-ago death involving Rupert Arkwright, and what Tollerton had learned about the threatening note that asked for no money. But for the moment she would do the one small thing that may not help find Roxanne's captor but would help Roxanne's family – she would ask Evangeline, under the guise of Useful Women, to be a comfort to the Arkwright household while Mabel occupied herself with the case. At the least, perhaps Evangeline could sit with MaryLou. Mabel would pay out of her own pocket for that if need be.

. . .

Evangeline Gregory's landlady, Mrs Oates, wore all black with her black hair pulled tightly into a bun, accentuating her beaky nose and closely set beady eyes. Standing against the dim entrance, she nearly disappeared, leaving behind only her face glowing like the Cheshire cat.

'I'm full up,' she said to Mabel, who stood on the doorstep. 'Unless you'd like to share?'

'I'm not in need of accommodation,' Mabel explained. 'I'm looking for Miss Evangeline Gregory.' The woman stared at her. 'She's one of your lodgers.'

'Yes, so she is,' the woman said. She smiled briefly, as if that was required of the situation. 'I'm afraid I haven't seen her since breakfast. Perhaps she's gone out.'

'Are you certain? Could anyone else have seen her? I just need a quick word.'

'Friday is not a cleaning day,' she replied as if that explained all. Behind her, a young woman skittered across the corridor and the movement caught the landlady's eye. 'Sibylla!'

The young woman froze. 'Yes, Mrs Oates?'

'You don't clean Miss Gregory's room on Friday, do you?'

'No, Mrs Oates.'

'Off you go then,' Mrs Oates said, and Sibylla skittered away. 'There you are now. I can't keep after every one of my lodgers every minute of the day, can I?'

'Well, thank you,' Mabel said. 'Will you tell Miss Gregory I was asking for her?'

'I'm told this, I'm told that,' Mrs Oates said as she shut the door. 'I'm sick and tired of being told what to do no matter what the price a bottle of gin.'

Mabel stopped on the pavement outside the Elm Tree pub on the corner. She remembered Evangeline saying she had a view of the pub's yard from her room, so Mabel walked alongside the building past precariously stacked beer casks and looked up. Not quite three o'clock, but the sun came straight into her eyes. She held up a hand to shield them against the glare and studied the windows at the back of the boarding house, trying to guess which one might be Evangeline's. There, on the third floor, Mabel saw movement. She squinted. Was someone waving at her?

She went out of the yard and back round the corner towards the boarding house, and there came Evangeline, pulling on her coat.

'Mabel, what are you doing here?'

'I came to...' It was at that moment Mabel realised she hadn't only come to offer Evangeline a job – she had come to be cheered up. To find herself in company instead of sitting on her own, imagining the worst. 'Mrs Oates said you were out.'

Evangeline hooked her arm through Mabel's and gave the boarding house a backward glance. 'Well, that's because she's not the sharpest knife in the drawer, if you take my meaning. You should've come on up. You're welcome anytime, no matter what she says.' She looked towards the King's Road. 'I could just do with a cup of tea. What do you say? There's no Corner House nearby, but we've a café to hand.'

The café sat just across the King's Road from the Elm Tree pub. It was a modest establishment with a clean counter, two wizened slices of cake on a platter, and the only table occupied was by an old man along the wall reading a newspaper.

Evangeline greeted the waitress with familiarity. 'Not too busy, I see. Lunch crowd just leave?'

'Yeah,' the waitress replied without any sign of humour. 'A mob of them, it was.'

'Two cups of tea, please,' Evangeline ordered.

The waitress glanced at Mabel and back at Evangeline. 'All right,' she said. 'I'll bring them over.'

'No, I'll come up and collect them.' Evangeline made for a table at the back, but the waitress called out, 'Sorry, I'm cleaning back there. You could take one of the window tables.'

'Thanks,' Mabel said. 'I always like a window seat – you can see so much going on.'

They settled at the table, Evangeline with a grumble. 'I feel like I'm on display,' she said. 'A puppy in the window, you know. Which reminds me, do you know Miss Kerr had me grooming rabbits yesterday?' Evangeline's hand went to her throat, and she coughed. 'I'm still swallowing fur!' They both laughed and she added, 'At least I didn't misplace any. You can't imagine what they're worth – I had a lecture from the owner as we combed the little beasts.'

'You're proving yourself game,' Mabel said. 'Miss Kerr likes that.'

Evangeline looked past Mabel to the counter. 'Hang on,' she said. 'Here's our tea.'

She went up to the counter and Mabel heard her ask the waitress, 'Any fresh cake in the back?'

Mabel turned round to them. 'Bread and butter would be lovely. I've not had time for lunch, myself.'

The waitress looked over at Mabel and then across the counter at Evangeline. 'Yeah.'

She disappeared through a swing door into the kitchen and Mabel turned back to the table. She opened her satchel, thinking she'd take her notebook out in the event anything important occurred to her, but she ended up only staring at a blank page until Evangeline came back carrying the teacups and sat down. The waitress came out of the kitchen not far behind with the bread and butter.

'Thanks,' Evangeline said. The waitress paused for a moment, then returned to the counter. 'And what about you,' Evangeline said to Mabel. 'Have you done anything nearly as exciting as grooming any rabbits lately?'

The light-hearted moment sank along with Mabel's heart like a lead weight. How could she even think of being cheered up when Roxanne was God knows where?

Evangeline frowned and leaned over the table. 'Mabel?'

'Sorry,' Mabel managed to say. 'It's just that... some things have happened, and I can't really say...'

'Then don't say.' Evangeline reached out and patted Mabel's hand. 'Don't let's talk about whatever it is. Drink your tea.'

Mabel pulled her tea closer – it was a thick mahogany colour and had an odd smell. Stewed, she thought.

'Roxanne is missing, and her father was attacked and he's still unconscious.'

The words tumbled out and lay there on the table between them.

'Your American?' Evangeline asked, her brows knitted and the freckles bunched up. 'Why? How?'

'Yesterday morning at their house,' Mabel said. 'No one saw anything.'

'Nonsense,' Evangeline said with force. 'Someone must've seen something. Aren't the police on it?'

'Yes,' Mabel said, 'and they will find her, I know they will.' The words belied the weakness of her conviction. Mabel stared at her untouched tea and then picked up the cup.

'Fresh pot!'

The waitress appeared suddenly and plopped down two cups of steaming brew. 'You don't want to be drinking that dishwater.' She took the cup out of Mabel's hand, picked up Evangeline's and left.

'Thanks,' Mabel called after her.

Evangeline stared after the waitress, looked back at Mabel and sighed.

'The father has no idea what's happened to his daughter?'

'No, he doesn't,' she said. 'And I suppose that's a blessing of sorts for him. Roxanne's mother has arrived from America.'

'I'm very sorry for them all,' Evangeline said still frowning, 'but I hope you're staying well away from them. I realise you have your Private Investigations division of Useful Women, but isn't this sort of thing getting a bit too dangerous even for that? I mean, with the *murder*' – she whispered the word – 'and all.'

It wasn't the first murder she'd been involved in, but Mabel hadn't told Evangeline about the other cases. 'I need to do what I can,' she said.

Evangeline tapped her spoon on her saucer. 'Why has the mother come from America?'

'I'm not sure she was too keen on Roxanne visiting her father. She'd told her daughter a few things that weren't exactly true, and I suppose she was afraid Roxanne would find out.'

'You don't think she's involved in all this business?' Evangeline said. 'Just to make her former husband look bad? Did they part on friendly terms or was there acrimony?'

'What?' Mabel asked, too surprised for a moment to go any further. 'No, she's only just arrived.'

'Is that her story or have you verified it?'

'Are you saying that MaryLou Arkwright should be a suspect?' Mabel asked, half laughing. 'Whyever would she kill Oswald Deuchar?'

'To make it look as if the father can't even keep his daughter safe? Think of all the years she's had to fume about what he'd done to her. And all those months to make this plan.'

Mabel didn't speak. This was preposterous. Wasn't it?

The morning before, Arkwright had been in his office at the house. Adelaide had gone off to a meeting, Cook had been in the kitchen, Dorcas held vigil at the bedside of her dying grandmother and Trigg... Trigg had been sent to the cobblers by MaryLou.

'What about Roxanne?' Mabel asked herself, but aloud. 'Where is she?'

'Hmmm,' Evangeline said. 'You've got me there. Perhaps they cooked something up together – mother and daughter?'

That brought Mabel up short. 'No, Roxanne would never stand for it.'

Evangeline laughed. 'It is a bit daft, isn't it? I suppose I've been reading too many of those detective novels.'

Mabel laughed along with Evangeline, but then remembered that Oswald read detective stories, too. It sobered her up. It may be a ridiculous notion, but it gave her something different to think about. She could at least find out why MaryLou had sent Trigg out to the cobblers. She finished her tea and offered the last slice of bread to Evangeline, who took it gratefully.

They each rummaged in their purses to pay the eight-pence bill.

'I've a sixpence,' Mabel said.

'I have only a threepenny piece.' Evangeline held it up.

'That's all right. We could leave the extra penny, don't you think?'

'Well' – Evangeline threw a begrudging look up to the counter – 'I suppose.'

They parted on the pavement outside the café. Mabel's original intention, to ask Evangeline if she'd be interested in a Useful Women job at the Arkwrights' for tea-making and what-not didn't seem such a good idea now. What if she accused MaryLou of murder?

'See you Monday morning?' Evangeline asked. 'I think you're right about being in Miss Kerr's line of vision when it comes to assignments. Out of sight, out of mind.'

'Yes, see you Monday.' Mabel said the words as rote, but she had no idea how she could ever get to Monday from that moment.

Evangeline walked back towards Mrs Oates' as Mabel asked herself, *Where to next?* She knew that when she stopped moving and planning and asking questions, the despair that dogged her steps would overcome her. She couldn't think of going home and the idea of bed made her feel ill. How could she pass another night not knowing where Roxanne was?

She would pay a hospital visit to Rupert Arkwright. He wasn't too far from Mayfair – only at King Edward VII's in Belgravia. Still, that seemed far from where she stood in Fulham. Already the streetlamps were blazing. If it had been daylight, she might have walked down the King's Road looking in at all the shops and if she arrived before closing time, she would've stopped to say hello to Cora at Milady's. Instead, Mabel hailed a taxi.

The hospital – red brick with white-trimmed bay windows that ran up to the roof – faced Grosvenor Gardens. When Mabel walked into the foyer, she understood this would not be the sort of place with cavernous wards and lines of beds that seemed to go on forever. A porter at the desk greeted her and when she asked for Rupert Arkwright's room, she received directions up to the second floor. Walking to the staircase, she passed a high-ceilinged room with bookshelves and a blazing fire. Several men in dressing gowns sat in upholstered chairs reading newspapers.

On the second floor, Mabel found a sister at a central station and said, 'Good afternoon.'

The sister turned. She looked a few years older than Mabel. She wore starched white from the cap that covered her hair to the white bodice of her apron pinned to her white dress and down to just above her black-stockinged ankles and black shoes. Mabel admired the woman's ability to appear so neat and tidy. She had nursed during the war and remembered her hair continually lacking enough pins and her apron a sorry sight of stains from spilled tea and... she pushed that memory aside.

'Can you tell me which is Mr Arkwright's room?' she asked the sister. The woman raised her eyebrows at the question, which caused her white starched cap to lift slightly. 'It's the room just behind you,' she replied. 'I'll bring in an extra chair.'

Mabel tapped lightly on the door and entered. Arkwright lay in a raised bed looking peaceful. A lamp burned at his bedside and another between the two armchairs occupied by Adelaide and MaryLou Arkwright. Next to Adelaide sat Miss Kerr.

There's a roomful for you, Mabel thought. She should've been surprised to see her employer, but instead, Miss Kerr's presence reminded Mabel that it was Friday and she had completely forgotten to collect her pay packet.

'Hello, Mabel,' Adelaide said. She smiled, but that only accentuated the lines of strain round her eyes and mouth. 'It's good of you to stop in.'

Mabel heard a supercilious sniff and knew it hadn't come from Miss Kerr.

'I hope I'm not intruding,' she said as the sister came in behind her with a ladderback chair and placed it next to Miss Kerr. 'I'm sorry I have no news.'

'It's all right,' Adelaide said. 'We've spoken with Inspector Tollerton. He assured us Scotland Yard is doing all they can.'

Mabel longed to know exactly what Tolly had said, but it didn't seem appropriate to ask.

'Sit down, please,' Adelaide continued. 'We've been telling stories about Roxanne. We thought it might be better to do that than talk about...' Her voice faltered.

'You see, it may be that Rupert can hear us even though he isn't awake yet,' Miss Kerr said in a detached yet caring tone. 'Some people believe that's true, and so until he does wake, we will entertain him.'

If he wakes. If Roxanne is found.

'Miss Kerr, did you know Roxanne before she left for America?' Mabel asked.

'Oh yes,' Miss Kerr said with a smile. 'Do you remember,

MaryLou, that you would bring her into the office on Friday mornings – the nanny's day off? We would keep her while you did your shopping and she'd crawl around on the rug and hide under her father's desk. Once when we weren't looking, she pulled a pot of ink off and it spilled all over her dress.'

'Irish lace,' MaryLou said. 'Ruined.'

'Roxanne told me she plays softball,' Mabel said, and MaryLou grunted.

Dear God, has it been this way all afternoon?

'Inspector Tollerton asked about you, Mabel,' Adelaide said. 'And Mr Winstone rang after that, hoping you were here.'

'Did he?' Had he found Ned Kettle and throttled the truth out of him? 'I'll telephone him before I leave,' Mabel said.

In the next moment of silence, there was a long intake of breath and a quick exhale. It came from Rupert Arkwright.

They all sprang out of their chairs and gathered round the bed.

'Is he waking?' Mabel asked.

MaryLou lay her hands flat on the bedcovers beside Rupert and in the bright light from the lamp, Mabel could clearly see a band of pale skin on her ring finger.

'I think he blinked!' MaryLou said.

'I'll get the sister,' Mabel said.

A quick word brought both the sister and a doctor who had been doing his rounds. A tall, thin, bald man, he had a harried look and spectacles perched on the tip of his nose.

'Stand aside,' he said, and the visitors stepped back and out of the way. The doctor leaned over the patient. 'Mr Arkwright, can you hear me?'

Rupert answered with a few unintelligible words, but then he spoke again in a clear, but sleepy voice.

'Where is my wife?' he asked. 'Adelaide, where are you?'

The doctor blocked Mabel's view of the patient, but she saw a hand reach out and Adelaide was there to take it.

'What's happened?' Rupert asked as the doctor went about checking his breathing, his eyes and his pulse.

'You're in hospital,' Adelaide said with a quaver of emotion. 'You were injured at home. Do you remember anything about that?'

Mabel crept a bit closer to the bed.

'I remember... I remember talking about coal,' Rupert said. 'I must've been asking Trigg for a fire. Is Roxanne here, too?'

'Don't tax yourself, Mr Arkwright,' the doctor said. 'Why don't you have a rest now?'

'That's a fine idea,' Rupert said, but held tight to his wife's hand. 'You won't go anywhere, will you, Adelaide?'

'No,' Adelaide said, 'I'll be right here. You sleep.'

'Good to have you back with us, sir,' the doctor said. 'Mrs Arkwright, I'll be back round to give him a closer look, all right?'

Without waiting for an answer, the doctor left with the sister following. Mabel moved Adelaide's chair up closer to the bed.

'Well,' she whispered, 'this is very good news, isn't it?'

Adelaide smiled, both relief and continued fear showing in the lines round her mouth. Now that Rupert was merely sleeping and not unconscious, she would have to prepare herself to explain about Roxanne.

'I'll be off now,' Mabel said.

'I'll leave with you,' Miss Kerr said and turned to MaryLou. 'Why don't we walk out together?'

MaryLou chewed on her bottom lip and seemed ready to plant herself on the spot in a defiant fashion.

'It'll be good for you to be at the house,' Adelaide said. 'You'll receive first word about Roxanne.'

That pushed her into action. 'Yes, I need to be there for my baby,' MaryLou said. 'I'm sorry to leave you here, Adelaide. I hope you don't mind.'

'Not at all.'

They all three went down to the ground floor where Mabel paused and asked the porter, 'Is there a telephone I can use?' When he gestured to a doorway off to his right, she turned to Miss Kerr. 'I need to ring home,' she explained.

Miss Kerr nodded. 'Come along, MaryLou. You and I will share a taxi.'

MaryLou offered a thin, stingy smile and followed.

'Hello, Mr Chigley, it's Mabel.'

'Miss Canning!' he exclaimed and called out, 'Mr Winstone, it's all right, she's on the telephone.' Mabel heard Park's voice from a distance – perhaps he was standing on the first-floor landing. 'Are you all right?' the porter asked her.

'Yes, I'm fine,' Mabel replied.

'Where are you?'

This was Park.

'I'm at the hospital. Good news – Rupert Arkwright is awake. Well, he's asleep now, but he's only asleep and when he was awake, he spoke quite coherently, although I'm not certain he remembers what happened.'

He sighed. 'That is good news. I've been looking for you.'

'Yes, sorry. I've been here and there and learned next to nothing. What about you?'

'I haven't found Ned. He's been gone all day from the Cornerstone. Mr Timpkins said Ned had found day work, but he didn't know where or what. I've put the word out again, and Mr Chigley knows I may get a message.'

'From Bootsie?'

'Yes, Bootsie. We'll talk when you get home.'

'Good. But first, I'm going to the Palais. I forgot to show the drawing of Fred Fredericks around. I just have a feeling... there's something up with him.'

'You don't think he was one of the kitchen workers, do you?' Winstone asked.

'Surely the chef has better judgement than that,' Mabel said. 'Still, it gives me something to do. I have to keep going until we find Roxanne, don't I?' Her voice rose and wobbled at the end.

'Come home first, Mabel. You need to rest, too. We will find Roxanne. We will.'

EIGHTEEN

'I'm still going to the Palais,' Mabel said to Park as soon as she arrived back at New River House and knocked on his door.

He drew her inside. Gladys, busy at her supper dish, didn't look up. Mabel took two steps in and stopped.

'I'm going,' she repeated. 'Don't try to talk me out of it. I can rest later.'

'I wouldn't think of trying. But listen – the laundry!' Winstone said. 'You were right to pursue that and Tolly thanks us for the tip. He sent a couple of constables to Bradford's. The last collection from the Palais had not been washed because one of their giant boiling machines had broken down earlier in the week.'

Mabel waited.

'They turned out each basket they'd taken and in one of them, they found a jacket, apron and hat rolled up into a ball. All splattered not with sauce but with blood.'

Mabel grabbed Park by the wrist. 'So we were right, the murderer worked in the kitchen! Did Tolly get anything else out of the chef?'

'He didn't say.'

'Well then,' Mabel said. 'Let's go and find out.'

'Let's have a meal first,' he said. 'The Palais doors won't open until eight – we might as well wait for them all to assemble.'

Mabel gave a brief thought to Mrs Norrell's Parisian gown, but this would not be an evening of dinner and dancing. They left Gladys with Mr Chigley and had a meal at the café the other side of Angel station. Mabel ate because she had to in order to keep going, but afterward couldn't have said if she'd eaten a chop or chicken. Winstone paid while Mabel went out to find a taxi and they were off. As they trundled through traffic, her meal sat like lead in her tummy.

At the Palais, they paid their five shillings each entrance fee so as not to call attention to themselves, and then went straight down the corridor behind the bar that led to the kitchen. Early in the evening the chaos seemed at a minimum – still, the chef didn't look best pleased to see them. He marched over to the doorway and started talking.

'Now what?' he asked. 'Police have already been here. I hire kitchen staff, not murderers. I took in four people that night – haven't I already told you this? Two men, two women. I don't take names, so I can't tell you any more than that. They'd scarpered by the time police arrived, but who wouldn't?'

'This man,' Mabel said, showing him the drawing of Fred Fredericks. 'Was he here that night?'

The chef drew back. 'Not in my kitchen, he wasn't. Is he the murderer?'

'That remains to be seen,' Winstone said.

They showed the drawing around, but no one at the Palais thought Fred Fredericks looked even remotely familiar. A few people recoiled when they saw the drawing. Mr Bryars winced.

'He's a one, isn't he?' he said. 'Never seen him before and hope I never do.'

Mabel examined the drawing again before she put it away in her satchel. Flea had captured the sly leer of Fred Fredericks, the man's unshaven face. You could almost smell him.

They walked out for a taxi and as they waited, Mabel looked up at the sky where she knew there were stars but couldn't see them for the clouds. This was the second night Roxanne had been missing. The thought hit her hard and she trembled. Park put an arm round her shoulder and kissed her hair.

'It's something,' he said.

'But what good has it done Roxanne?' she asked.

On the taxi ride to Islington, Mabel kept her fear at bay by going over the case and their suspects, then added, 'This is going to sound strange, but Evangeline brought it up and now I can't get the idea out of my head.'

'Miss Gregory from Useful Women?'

'Yes, I went by her boarding house earlier because...' Because she had needed cheering up and because she'd had the idea to ask Evangeline about working at the Arkwrights – neither of which had happened. 'Never mind. While we chatted, she asked, what about MaryLou?'

'She wasn't in the country when Deuchar died.'

'Or was she, but pretended she wasn't?' Mabel offered. 'Or does she have an accomplice?'

'What's her motive?'

'Deuchar found out about her son, and she was afraid he would tell Rupert?'

Winstone lifted his eyebrows.

'Not a strong enough motive?' Mabel asked.

'Oh no, people are killed for the pettiest of reasons,' he said.

'At the hospital,' Mabel said, 'I noticed that MaryLou wasn't wearing a wedding ring.'

'Well, she wouldn't, would she?'

'But she has worn one until quite recently,' Mabel said as she held up her left hand and pointed to her third finger. 'Because I saw where it had been.'

'A swindle? She's remarried and the two of them are trying to extort money from Arkwright?'

'*More* money,' Mabel said. 'Adelaide said Rupert left her quite well off when they divorced. Maybe her new husband is the accomplice.'

'Who is he?' Winstone said.

'Yes, who. And how do we get that information out of Mary-Lou?' Mabel asked, and noticed an odd, tinny sound to her own voice. 'Perhaps she has hidden Roxanne away, afraid that her daughter would tell me the rest of the story.'

There was silence in the taxi. Mabel had been looking out the window at nothing, but now she turned to Park. His face was grave, and his spectacles could not disguise the concern in his eyes.

'Mabel—'

She shuddered – from head to foot, the nerves in her entire body convulsed so that even her teeth chattered. She covered her face with her hands and sobbed. 'Oh my God, what am I doing?'

Park put his arms round her in a tight embrace and still she shook. 'It's all right. It's what we do – we look for any possibility, we try to make sense of senseless acts.'

'It makes no sense,' Mabel sputtered, 'I know it doesn't, but I want it to be silly, innocuous MaryLou that has cooked up some ridiculous plan, because that would mean that Roxanne is all right, really. But it isn't MaryLou and so—'

'And so we will keep looking until we find Roxanne and who has taken her,' Park said.

Mabel nodded – more of a spasm – but could not speak. She took long slow breaths and by the time the taxi pulled up in front of New River House her hysteria had subsided, and she could at least stand on her own two feet. While Park paid the cabbie, she found her handkerchief and dried her tears. She pulled her picture hat down a bit so that her face was in shadow when they walked in.

'Mr Chigley, I don't suppose there were any telephone calls?'

Mabel asked the question in as bright a voice as she could muster. She knew she shouldn't ask, because if someone had rung with news of Roxanne, the porter would've told her before he'd ever got to 'Good evening.' Still, she couldn't help herself.

'No, no,' he said. 'No.'

What did three 'nos' add up to? She glanced at Park. 'No?' she asked.

'No,' Mr Chigley said, 'it's been that quiet. Only time the telephone rang, it was one of those last-call calls.'

'What's that?' Mabel asked. Gladys trotted out from Mr Chigley's private quarters and under the counter to greet them. Mabel gave her a scratch.

'They come in every once in a great while, just after last call at the pubs. Some fellow's had a few too many, gives the exchange the wrong number and then sets the earpiece down and forgets about it.'

'And no one spoke?' Mabel said.

The porter cocked his head as if trying to listen again. 'No, that's the way they go. I could hear someone talking, but low against the pub noise in the background. Then there was a loud cheer and the call ended.'

For a moment, the three of them stood without speaking. Mabel tried to fashion Mr Chigley's account into a vital clue or some tiny piece of good news but couldn't see how. When Gladys trotted over to the door and *woofed*, the spell broke.

'Right, girl,' Park said to the dog, 'to the green.'

'Thanks, Mr Chigley,' Mabel said.

'Night, all,' the porter called.

Not long after, Winstone and Gladys came to Mabel's door.

'I only wanted to say good night.'

'Come in,' she said.

She had two glasses of blackberry wine waiting for them. Gladys stretched out in front of the cold gas heater and so Winstone fed it a few pennies then they sat on the sofa.

'I'm all right now,' Mabel assured him. 'I'm ready to carry on.'

'Good,' Park said, but looked closely at her.

'Tomorrow morning, I'll stop by the Arkwright house,' Mabel said. 'Trigg will have heard the good news about Rupert, I'm sure. Then, I'll... I'll decide what to do after that.'

They finished their wine in silence, Park set his glass on the table and stood.

'It's been a long day,' he said.

Mabel shot off the sofa. He was going without a by-your-leave? Without a suggestion that the evening might end another way? Well, fine, then let him.

'Yes, it has,' she said stiffly.

Park hesitated, but Mabel marched to the door and opened it.

He looked over at Gladys, who didn't move other than to open her eyes and look back at him.

'Well, then,' he said, as if at a loss for his next move, 'Gladys can keep you company.'

'Yes,' Mabel said. 'Thanks. Gladys will be lovely company.' Her face warmed at her silly words.

Park frowned and didn't move, but Mabel wouldn't look at him so he gave her a brief kiss and left.

She closed the door and stood staring at it. 'He could've said something.'

A throaty response came from Gladys, and Mabel looked over. The dog snorted.

Mabel gave a short, sharp laugh. 'Oh Gladys, are you saying I'm an independent modern woman and why couldn't I be the one to say something?'

Gladys yawned.

They went to bed, she and the dog, with Gladys on top of the counterpane and Mabel underneath, staring out the window at the glowing streetlamp.

The next morning, Mabel woke to a *woof*. Gladys stood with her paws on the low sill, looking out the window. Mabel rose and looked too and saw Winstone adjust his homburg and turn up his collar as he went off.

'I must have a plan today,' Mabel told Gladys. 'A plan of action that will make a difference for Roxanne's sake. Where do I begin?'

Gladys returned a look that Mabel interpreted to mean that they should begin with a quick visit to the green, and so she dressed and went out to the front room where she saw a flat brown envelope had been pushed under the door with a note on the outside that read: *One can never have too many details! Cora and I are out today but will be round later. Ring if you need us.*

Skeff's hand – her words strode across the page in a bold manner, reminding Mabel of the March of the Toreadors.

Mabel dropped the envelope on the table by the sofa and she and Gladys hurried downstairs.

On their way back, Mabel paused at the porter's counter.

'Mr Chigley, that telephone call – one of those last-call calls, you said.'

The porter looked up from sorting the morning post. 'Yes?'

'But it wasn't last call when it came in,' she said. 'It was too early.'

'You're right there,' he replied in a careful way. 'And that's been bothering me.'

'You heard a man's voice against the noise in the pub?'

'Eh, well now, I couldn't be certain, because it was so quiet. I couldn't make out any words.'

'You can't be certain it was a man. So, you mean, it could've been a woman?'

Mr Chigley held up a finger. 'Or a boy.'

'Can you ask the exchange where the call came from?'

'I'll get right on it,' the porter said.

Mabel set the kettle on the gas ring and put her last slice of bread under the grill to toast. She gave Gladys a Spratt's dog cake and said to her, 'I have something to do today after all. I will find out who rang Mr Chigley, mumbled something and then rang off. If it has nothing to do with the enquiry then at least we'll know. Then I will visit the Arkwrights and ask after Mr Arkwright and after that I will... I will stay busy.'

The dog cake had vanished in an instant. Gladys stretched out in front of the gas heater and looked at Mabel, who dutifully located a few pennies and fed it. She noticed Skeff's envelope on the table by the sofa and took it over to the kitchen table, then saved her toast before it turned to charcoal. She sat down and ate it with a scraping of butter and the last of last year's strawberry jam and finished with sticky fingers, which she washed before looking to see what Skeff had left her.

Two items, both from the *Intelligencer*. One article carried a date of 10 February 1909 and was no more than a few paragraphs about the men who had died in the rail yard.

The other article caught her eye first, because it included a photo of Rupert Arkwright at his desk. It had appeared a year later and offered details about his acquisition of the rail yard at Victoria Docks and his belief that Britain's rail system would be a shining example of... Well, so, he bought a rail yard. She went back to the first article.

It was as had been first reported, that the two men had climbed into an empty coal car with a bottle of whisky and had fallen asleep only to be killed when a load of coal had been dumped in. The coalman had not been to blame – who expected to find anyone sleeping off a night of drink at the bottom of a coal car? The tragic incident had occurred at Victoria Docks and one of the dead men was John George Gregory.

Mabel stared at the name, then looked round her flat as if she could find an explanation in the cushions or on the mantel. Could this be John George Gregory, Evangeline Gregory's father? Mabel recalled the small item Evangeline carried round with her – a brief report of the event. Her father's death, she'd said.

So, Miss Gregory's father had died at a rail yard that Rupert Arkwright bought a year later. The two events could have nothing to do with each other. And yet, such a coincidence.

Mabel would ask Evangeline about it. Most likely, she had no knowledge of this – she had been ten or eleven years old at the time of her father's death. What does a child know about her father's work? Mabel thought of the mother and daughter left alone. The mother falling ill and the daughter nursing her for years. How had they lived? Mabel pulled on her coat and buttoned it while the questions rose and flapped about inside her head like a clattering of jackdaws, so that when she reached for a hat, her hand went immediately to one of Cora's latest—a bicorn with a ribbon tied at one side that looked like a bird taking flight.

'Ah, Miss Canning,' Mr Chigley said and waved a small piece of paper when she and Gladys came down to the foyer. 'I have it for you. The telephone call was from the Fulham exchange and here's the number.'

'Fulham? Look, Mr Chigley, why don't I'll ring that number now for you?' she asked as if it had been the porter who wanted to track down the elusive caller.

Mabel stepped over to the telephone, took up the earpiece and depressed the hook, and when the exchange came on the line, she asked for the Fulham number. It rang and rang and someone answered on the other end at the same moment the door to the street opened and into the foyer of New River House tumbled an entire rugby team covered in mud and laughing and shouting.

'Sorry,' Mabel said into the mouthpiece, 'I didn't hear that. Who is it that I've reached?'

'I don't know who you were trying for,' a man's voice said, 'but you've rung the Elm Tree.'

NINETEEN

'Oh, yes, of course. Thank you.' Mabel replaced the earpiece and stared at the wall for a moment, then looked down at Gladys and said, 'Well, girl, I'd best be away. Fancy a visit with Mr Chigley?'

Mabel thought Mr Chigley's name and the word 'sausage' must be linked in the dog's mind, because Gladys wove her way through the forest of legs and under the counter into the porter's office.

Mr Chigley looked up at Mabel and nodded as he parcelled out the post to the rugby team. 'Learn anything?' he called out.

Mabel waved and called out, 'You're right – a pub!' and left before he could ask more.

Mabel couldn't sit still in the back of the taxi. Saturday morning and crowds of people were making their way to work or to shop – and every one of them in her way. Each time the taxi slowed for people crossing the road or when a bus pulled out in front of them, her anxiety level rose. At last, she tapped on the window and called out to the cabbie, 'I'm in a bit of a hurry.' He nodded, put the engine in gear and turned sharply to go round a horse cart carrying sacks of coal.

An urgency surged through Mabel as she approached the house. She must verify or discount suspicions that she couldn't quite put into words. Then, she would know how to proceed.

Instead of ringing the bell and alerting everyone, Mabel went round to the back of the house and knocked on the scullery door. She waited and knocked again before Trigg answered.

'Miss Canning!'

She glanced round behind him and asked in a low voice, 'Are Adelaide and MaryLou in? I'd rather no one knows I've stopped by.'

Trigg's eyebrows twitched. 'They are, indeed,' he replied, matching her volume. 'Come in.'

He closed the door and cocked his head out to the entrance hall for a moment. 'It's all right,' he said. 'Mrs Arkwright is in the morning room and Mrs Arkwright, of course, has remained in her room. Both Cook and Dorcas are in the kitchen.'

'Thank you, Trigg. What about Mr Arkwright?'

'I'm pleased to report that he should be home by this afternoon.'

'That's good, isn't it?' Mabel asked. 'But does he know about Roxanne?'

'He has not been told,' Trigg said. 'Mrs Arkwright is considering how best to do this.'

'I know this looks a bit irregular, Trigg,' Mabel began, hoping her request would sound reasonable – or at least, not mad – 'but I would rather not see anyone at the moment. I don't even want them to know I am here. I've stopped only because I need to check on something. I don't want to raise anyone's hopes.'

Too late – the butler's eyes lit up. 'Is it about Miss Roxanne?'

'It could be,' Mabel said, 'but it may come to nothing. Still, if you'll allow me to go up to Roxanne's room and then help me to slip out without being seen, I'd be grateful.'

Trigg held up a finger, walked out to the entrance hall and then came halfway back. He gestured for Mabel. 'The coast is clear – off you go.'

Mabel entered Roxanne's room, closed the door behind her and switched the light on. She didn't move as she took in the scene. The bed had been unmade on Thursday morning when Roxanne had disappeared, but now the counterpane had been smoothed and the pillows plumped.

There was the chair near the dressing table where Roxanne had been sitting the first time Mabel had met her. Mabel had been curious and then annoyed at Roxanne's obstreperousness until she realised the young woman's behaviour stemmed from being unsure of herself and her new surroundings. She had thought her father a tyrant and when one expects to be treated badly and has built strong defences against this, it isn't always possible to turn on a sixpence and tear those defences down.

Only a few days ago they had sat by the fire with Hildy. Roxanne had shown them photographs of her softball team and pointed out Flea's drawings, which she'd pinned up on the wall around her dressing table.

The drawings were the reason Mabel was here.

But now they were gone, and she remembered that they hadn't been there on Thursday morning when she'd come up looking for Roxanne. Nothing else in the room had been disturbed. Had Dorcas taken them down when she was tidying? Or had Roxanne hidden them away when her mother arrived?

Mabel moved to the dressing table and looked closely at the wall. She could see the pin holes and remembered there had been quite an array. Flea had proven himself a quick but expressive sketch artist, dashing off likeness after likeness at Roxanne's request.

The drawing of Roxanne was the one Mabel wanted. Mabel had returned the issue of *Tatler* to Cora that contained Roxanne's photograph and it wouldn't be wise to institute a search of the Arkwright house now for a photograph of her – it could give Adelaide and the staff false hope. But Flea's drawing of Roxanne would be as good as a photo – better, as he could always capture the sense of a person, not just what they looked like.

Mabel would show the drawing at the Elm Tree. It couldn't have been a coincidence that one of Mr Chigley's 'last-call' telephone calls came from a pub Mabel had only recently taken note of, because Evangeline Gregory could see it out the window of her boarding house room.

Where were the drawings now? If she had been talked out of the house and spirited away, held against her will, she wouldn't have had time to pack a bag. Mabel walked round the bedroom until she came to the wardrobe.

An image popped into her head of Roxanne holding a flat square box she'd retrieved from one of the wardrobe drawers. It had been the sort of box that would hold a necklace, but instead, it was where she'd hidden photographs she'd brought from Chicago.

Mabel opened the same drawer and there it was, the box. She took it out, released the clasp and the box popped open from the pressure of holding too much. Inside were the photos as well as the drawings.

It was a step, just one step and could come to nothing in the end, but Mabel wanted to shout for joy. Here they were. The drawing of Roxanne captured the ragged edges of her short bob, but in a kind way, and even showed the collar of her plaid coat, although not the emerald-green colour.

Here was Gladys looking noble, Skeff and Cora, heads

together laughing. A young woman wearing a beret and with a pouty smile. Was this Juliet?

Roxanne had persuaded Flea to draw a self-portrait, floppy newsboy hat and all, but who was this other boy with an unruly lock of hair that stuck straight out of the crown of his head? Was it Tommy?

He'd drawn Mabel, too, but how did he make her curls look so soft? And here was another woman, this one an amazing likeness of...

Evangeline Gregory.

Flea had captured the way the freckles that were scattered across Evangeline's nose seemed to dance when she laughed. He must've taken it from Roxanne's description, because under the drawing was written 'the funny one'.

Up Mudford and the funny one – Mabel remembered it had been Roxanne's way of differentiating the two women she'd chatted with in the powder room at the Palais. When, at Tollerton's request, Mabel and Roxanne had gone out to the big room to identify the beetle-browed man in the crowd, Roxanne had nodded at a woman sitting at a table. *Up Mudford,* she had said to Mabel, *not the funny one.* The funny one, it seemed, had already gone.

Evangeline Gregory had been at the Palais the evening Oswald Deuchar was murdered. She had talked with Roxanne and had never said a word to Mabel about it.

Mabel thought about the disjointed clues she'd gathered. Twelve years ago, Evangeline's father, having taken drink, died in a rail yard accident when a load of coal was dumped on him. A year later, Rupert Arkwright bought said rail yard.

Mabel had seen Evangeline's double photo frame with an image of her mother on one side and a copy of her death notice on the other. Behind the death notice, yellowed with age, was the brief item about her father's death – but it had been devoid of date. Had Evangeline's mother – or the girl Evangeline herself – been so deep in grief that they connected her husband and father's death with the unrelated rail yard's acquisition and blamed Arkwright? Or was the misconstruction entirely of Evangeline's making? She had been ten years old at the time and if no one had told her what had happened to her father, perhaps she created her own story. A person can believe something is true for so long that it no longer matters if it's true or not.

Could twelve years of built-up resentment suddenly burst forth into a murder, an attempted murder and an abduction?

Mabel jumped when a light tap came at the door, but it was only Trigg.

The butler took a step in, looked behind him to the corridor then closed the door.

'I thought you would like to know that Mrs Arkwright has left for the hospital and Mrs Arkwright remains in her room.'

'Thank you,' Mabel said. 'I'm ready to leave now.'

'May I get a taxi for you?'

'Yes, please.'

'Shall I ask him to wait two doors away?'

'Good thinking, Trigg. You have a bit of the detective about you.'

Trigg acknowledged the statement with a nod. 'A butler is an amalgam of many jobs, Miss Canning. Do you need me to telephone anyone?'

Mabel thought on this. 'No, thank you. I want to confirm an idea, and then I will ring Detective Inspector Tollerton and turn it all over to him. For now, there's no need to send him on a wild goose chase.'

'Wait here,' Trigg said.

While she waited, Mabel returned the photographs and drawings to the box except for the drawing of Roxanne and the one of Miss Gregory. She sat near the cold fire, looking only far enough in the future to know her next move.

Trigg returned.

'I've heard a stirring in Mrs Arkwright's room, so we'd best take care going down.' They went out and at the landing, he whispered, 'Follow me and avoid the right side of the third step down.'

A good servant knows which steps creak and which don't, Mabel thought as she carefully placed her feet where Trigg had trod. They made not a sound as they descended. Once through the entrance hall and out the door, Mabel gave the butler a wave and set off.

Grey clouds had muscled their way across the sky by the time the taxi pulled up to the Elm Tree in Fulham. Mabel paid the cabbie and then walked past empty casks at the kerb and through the open door of the pub, as the last ray of pale winter sun shot through the sparkling window glass and spilled onto the dark wood floor. Then it, too, vanished.

Not yet opening time, the air in the pub smelled of tobacco, beer and Brasso. At the end of the bar, a gangly boy several inches taller than Mabel slopped a wet mop back and forth in a wide arc on the floor.

'Where is the telephone?' Mabel demanded.

He looked up, startled, and he held the mop straight out in front of him as if it were a lance.

'We aren't open yet, ma'am,' he said, and his voice broke. 'And no one's allowed near the telephone even if we were. There's a post office down the road' – with the mop, he pointed out the door and to the right – 'and they have a telephone.'

'Thank you, but I don't want to ring anyone,' Mabel said. She took an easier tone of voice, the sort that calmed her Sunday school class. 'I'm sorry to startle you. My name is Miss Canning.' She held out her hand.

He rubbed the palm of his hand on his apron and shook. 'Pleased to meet you. I'm Donald.'

'Donald,' Mabel said, 'did you work last evening?'

'No, ma'am,' the boy said. 'My ma won't let me work evenings, because that's when she goes out to work and so I stay home with my baby brother.' He noticed the mop in his hand and rested it against the bar.

'Is there someone here now who was working last evening?'

'Well, Mr Hordern, ma'am, of course he was working last evening.'

'Good, thank you. Where is Mr Hordern? I'm looking for a young woman who came into the pub and used the telephone.'

'Mr Hordern doesn't allow that, ma'am,' Donald said. 'Not ladies nor the telephone. Also, it was the darts last evening.'

'Darts?' Mabel asked. Mr Chigley had said he'd heard a cheer go up in the background.

Donald nodded over to the dartboard on the wall. 'Heaving in here, it was.'

'How would you know if you aren't allowed to work in the evenings?' Mabel asked.

Donald's face darkened to the colour of beetroot. 'Don't tell my ma, will you?'

'Not a word,' Mabel said. 'Did you notice this young woman come in?' She took out the drawing of Roxanne and held it up for Donald to see.

He blinked, but didn't answer, because a roar came from other parts of the pub and a large man – in both height and girth – barrelled down the corridor towards them.

'We're not open and we don't allow women in the bar,' he said in a voice that could carry across the road and back again.

'You don't *allow* women in the bar?' Mabel asked.

'Ah now,' the man said, instantly dropping his belligerence for an injured tone. 'You've got the lounge. Can't you be satisfied?'

That was a battle for another day.

'You are Mr Hordern? My name is Mabel Canning and I want to know if you saw this woman in the pub last evening. She may have been using your telephone.'

'I told her, Mr Hordern,' Donald said, 'you don't allow anyone near the telephone.'

'Quite right, Donald, good lad.' Mr Hordern put his round face a bit nearer to the drawing and then backed off. He shrugged and stretched his neck as if his collar was too tight. 'Oh, that one. I don't think she was, you know, quite the full shilling, if you take my meaning.'

Mabel's pulse raced and she had to put a hand on the nearest table to steady herself.

'She was here?'

'It was the darts,' Mr Hordern said, 'or I would've noticed her earlier down there at the telephone.' He gestured towards the corridor. Mabel peered down the dimness and could just make out the telephone on the wall. 'Could hardly stand up and said something about fleas. That's an outright lie, that is. I don't have fleas here! I was going to tell her to go, but her friend came up and said something funny to me about "once bitten, twice shy" then gathered her up and out they went.'

Mabel held out another drawing. 'Was this her friend?'

Mr Hordern's brows lifted. 'Oh yeah, that's the one.'

Evangeline Gregory.

TWENTY

Mabel slammed the knocker hard against the doorplate of Mrs Oates' boarding house, then took it in her hand again. *Rap-rap-rap-rap-rap.*

She continued until the door flew open and Mrs Oates, with her arm raised as if about to strike, shouted, 'Stop that racket this minute!'

For one moment, they stood staring at each other. Mabel panted. Not from exertion, but with the fear and thrill of imminent victory. She had found her – she had found Roxanne. Upstairs. Captive. She was sure of it.

'I want to see Miss Gregory,' she said.

'Not in,' Mrs Oates replied, but her voice quaked as she dropped her hand. She glanced behind her.

'I don't believe you,' Mabel said and pushed past her. She put a hand on the newel and looked up the stairs. 'Which is her room?'

'I won't abide being told what to do in my own house!'

'You'll tell me, or you'll tell Scotland Yard,' Mabel shouted at her and took off. 'Third floor, I know that much. And I know she can see the Elm Tree out of her window.'

'I had nothing to do with this!' Mrs Oates called, hot on Mabel's heels. 'Let her say what she wants about where I get my gin. I'll not be a party to this sort of thing. I run a respectable establishment.'

Mabel whirled round and nearly lost her footing. 'Respectable? And how do you reckon that, what with one of your tenants keeping a young woman against her will?'

A few doors opened on the first floor and heads appeared. Mabel took the next set of stairs, but heard Mrs Oates behind her whisper hoarsely, 'Keep your voice down.'

'I will not keep my voice down,' Mabel said, but she did regardless, because she had run out of breath by the time she'd reached the third floor and was gasping. She'd lost her sense of direction and squinted down to one end of the dark corridor and then the other. Doors lined both sides. 'Which room?'

'I don't know what you mean "against her will". She said she had a sick friend and she needed to nurse her back to health,' Mrs Oates said, but fear had replaced outrage in her voice. 'She said not to tell anyone, that it needed to stay on the q.t., because of the girl needing protection from her beau. She gave me five pounds.'

'Which room?' Mabel shouted in the woman's face.

Halfway down the corridor, a woman stepped out wearing a dressing gown and carrying her towel and soap. She stopped and stared at them.

'Keep quiet, can't you?' Mrs Oates said. 'Third one on your right. The one there next to the bathroom.'

The woman who had come out of the bathroom scurried off as Mabel ran to the door of Evangeline's room and knocked.

'Miss Gregory? Roxanne? Roxanne?'

No answer came, and so Mabel turned the knob and went in. There was no one there.

The room contained a bed and bedside table, a small wardrobe, a chair and a dressing table – it could hold no more.

Mabel opened one door of the wardrobe and saw it held two dresses and a pair of shoes and she could tell at a glance they didn't belong to Roxanne. It came to her that it had been two days since Roxanne had been taken – or left voluntarily, it seemed – with nothing except the clothes she wore.

'Where is she?' Mabel asked Mrs Oates. 'Where is the young woman Miss Gregory brought up here?'

'How am I to know that? The girl wasn't too steady on her feet when I saw her. It isn't as if she could've run off.'

Had Roxanne been injured? Mr Hordern and now Mrs Oates thought something had been wrong with her. Where had Evangeline taken her now?

'When did you last see her?' Mabel asked Mrs Oates. 'Did you see her leave yesterday evening?'

'On her own? I doubt she could do that. Couldn't even put a proper sentence together.'

Mabel looked under the bed and opened the drawer of the dressing table, which rattled when she did so. Inside, she found a small dark blue bottle. She held it up to the light and saw it was empty but for a bit of liquid at the bottom. Mabel popped the cork off and smelled. It smelled of alcohol. It smelled acrid and at the same time sweet and herbal.

'Laudanum, is it?' Mrs Oates asked. 'Her mother, Winnie, nearly lived on it when she got sick that last year.'

Drugged? Mabel put a hand to her forehead and thought hard. If she could get a better picture of Evangeline in her head, perhaps she would know where the woman had taken Roxanne. She was alive, at least at last report, and that was the best news, but who knew what Evangeline might do next?

'Did you know Miss Gregory before she moved in here?' Mabel asked Mrs Oates.

'She came from only one street over. Right terror she was growing up, and always making up stories about how someone killed her father. What was she talking about? No one killed her father but himself. It was the sort of child she was – she made up stories and I suppose it was easier for Winnie to let her think it was someone else's fault.'

'Evangeline told me her mother had been sick for years, dying slowly because her husband's death had such a great effect on her.'

'Rubbish,' Mrs Oates said. 'Winnie Gregory didn't mind one whit that her drunkard of a husband caused his own demise.'

'But she couldn't work. How did they live?'

'They did all right. Limped along awhile on the bit of money Winnie got as the widow, but then a year later some rich fellow buys the rail yard and talked of a "clean slate". Instead of continuing to pay the few pennies a week she'd been getting, he starts paying her the same as her husband's wages would've been – and kept it up, too, until she died. Who does that?'

Rupert Arkwright, that's who.

'But why would Evangeline hold that against him?'

'Pish,' Mrs Oates said. 'She never would tell the girl about it. "She's only a girl," Winnie would say. "What does she care who pays for her milk?"'

Mrs Oates warmed to her memories of Evangeline. 'That girl always thought what she liked and did what she liked, but she took care of her mother to the end, at least you can say that about her. After that, she did turn a bit funny. Said now she had the proof how someone killed her father.'

'Where is she?' Mabel asked herself aloud, looking round at the nearly empty room. 'There must be something left behind to tell me where they've gone.'

She'd left the door of the wardrobe ajar and went to close it when the other door swung open. On it, inside, was a small mirror, barely big enough to show one's face, but not even Mabel's face would show in it for the newspaper cutting that had been stuck under the bracket that held the mirror.

Mabel had seen the cutting before, because Skeff had borrowed it from the *Intelligencer*'s morgue. It told of Rupert's acquisition of the rail yard. But this cutting, worn and creased as if it had been carried round for years, had been trimmed so closely that the date was missing.

With an explosion of energy, Mabel burst out of the room. By the time Mrs Oates reached the ground floor Mabel had looked around the dining room with its one long table already set for the evening meal. Then she headed for the kitchen.

'Here now,' the landlady said, and Mabel spun round.

'You knew what she was doing yet you said nothing?'

'She threatened me, she did,' Mrs Oates said.

Mabel waited for more.

Mrs Oates jutted out her chin as if refusing to speak, but Mabel narrowed her eyes and at last the landlady relented. 'You're a hard one,' she muttered. 'It's only that Miss Gregory threatened to tell the tax man I was getting the odd bottle of gin minus the excise duty. Who can afford to pay twelve shillings?'

That she allowed Roxanne, clearly in trouble, to be held captive for a cheap bottle of gin rendered Mabel speechless.

'Where is your maid?' Mabel demanded. 'She may know what Evangeline has done with Roxanne.'

Without waiting for an answer, Mabel turned and pushed the swing door to the kitchen open and found Sibylla cowering in the corner.

'Bring those bedclothes in before it starts raining,' Mrs Oates said to the maid, who skittered to the door.

'Wait, Sibylla,' Mabel said. The girl stopped. 'I don't mean to frighten you, it's only that I'm looking for my friend. Did you see the sick woman Miss Gregory was taking care of in her room?'

Sibylla looked with wide, fearful eyes at Mabel. 'I didn't ever see anyone.' She went out the door to the yard.

A sense of failure crept over Mabel, but she stopped it in its tracks. 'Roxanne is alive,' she said to herself. 'At least, she was last night. And I've found her. But now I've lost her again.'

'Well, Miss Canning,' Mrs Oates said as she opened her arms and shepherded Mabel out of the kitchen, 'As you can see, I've had no part in anything. I've not seen Angel today, and I won't mind if she doesn't come back at all.'

'Angel?' Mabel said.

'That's what her mother called her. Now, good luck to you and good day.'

Mrs Oates had managed to get Mabel all the way out and closed the door firmly behind her. Mabel plunged her hands in her coat pockets and started walking, not knowing where to go.

She'd just got to the corner of the house when she heard 'Miss Canning' whispered and turned to see Sibylla plastered up against the brick wall as if avoiding prying eyes.

Mabel approached and in a low voice Sibylla said, 'I did see her, ma'am. Your friend.'

Mabel took the drawing of Roxanne out of her satchel and held it out to Sibylla.

'Yes, that's the one,' the girl said. 'Only I can't let Mrs Oates know or I'd lose my position in a snap. I don't think your friend was sick. At least not in the proper way. It was a bit like she'd had too much drink, but Mrs Oates doesn't allow drink.'

Except for herself. 'When did you see her?' Mabel asked.

'I was told not to go into Miss Gregory's room to clean, which I would usually do on a Friday, you see. No one told me why, though, did they? That's a bit odd, I thought. So, last evening, Miss Gregory had gone out and I thought I'd just give her room a swipe with my cloth. That's my job, isn't it?'

'And that's when you saw her?'

'Yes, ma'am. I thought the room empty and so I nearly squealed when I saw her, your friend. She was sitting up in bed wearing a lovely green plaid coat but no hat. Her eyes were big, and she was sort of mumbling. I leaned in to listen and I heard her say, "telephone". I said the nearest telephone was at the Elm Tree and she sort of waked up then and got out of the bed and said, "Where?" and so I pointed out the window and she took my arm, and I led her downstairs really quiet like. Mrs Oates is in her own sitting room that time of the evening having a glass of gin, so we got to the door and she said... "Mabel".'

Mabel gasped.

'Is that your Christian name?' Sibylla asked.

'Yes.'

'Well then, she said your name and after that, I watched her walk to the corner and into the pub. I thought maybe she'd be back and so I started scrubbing the kitchen floor as I do every night and kept an eye out for her. A few minutes later, Miss Gregory came in and went up then came hurrying down the stairs and looking in all the rooms – even in the kitchen – and off she went again.' Sibylla's face wrinkled with worry. 'Will I be in trouble?'

Mabel squeezed her arm. 'No, you will not be. And I won't say a word. Well done.'

Sibylla nodded and dashed off to the back of the house.

If it hadn't been for Sibylla letting Roxanne free to telephone New River House from the Elm Tree, then Mabel wouldn't have got this far. Still, what did she have? Angel must've caught up with Roxanne at the pub and taken her... where?

Angel – Mabel had heard of someone called that recently. At the Mayfair house, they had been looking for staff, and Cook had referred to one of the maids Dorcas brought in as an angel, because she could do anything.

Who else had been in need of an angel? Freddy. She had yet to settle to her recent great fortune and seemed uncomfortably poised between being a servant and lady of the manor. She had difficulty carrying out even the most mundane tasks such as ordering coal, but hadn't her new under housekeeper done that for her? And the coal was to be delivered to Hanover Terrace that very morning at eleven o'clock.

In her mind's eye, a terrible scene emerged. Mabel saw men lifting the iron cover on the coal hole in the pavement outside Oswald Deuchar's house. She saw the men lifting sack after sack of coal and emptying them down the coal hole and the coal, like rocks, would fall into the cellar below, where Roxanne lay, trapped, drugged and unaware of her doom.

Mabel looked at her wristwatch – nearly ten thirty.

TWENTY-ONE

Mabel rushed back to the Elm Tree. Still not quite opening time, but regardless, a fellow stood at the end of the bar with a pint. When Mabel marched in, he jumped and put his bowler on top of the glass, but when he saw it was a woman and not a police constable, he resumed drinking.

The landlord, bent over behind the bar, straightened and caught sight of Mabel. He pointed a finger at her and his mouth opened, but before he could complain, she said, 'Mr Hordern, I need to ring Detective Inspector Tollerton at Scotland Yard. I will use your telephone to do so.'

She didn't wait for a reply but spun round and went down the corridor. She asked the exchange for Scotland Yard and called out, 'Donald!'

The boy appeared from the kitchen and said, 'Oh, ma'am, you shouldn't be—'

'Find a taxi for me, Donald, and don't worry, Mr Hordern knows I've commandeered his telephone.'

Off the boy went. Someone at Scotland Yard answered, but Mabel could barely hear his voice over her pounding heart and practically shouted into the phone.

Tollerton proved elusive. He'd been there only a moment ago but had gone out. She asked for Sergeant Lett. Seconds ticked away as the constable tried to find him. Mabel looked at the time – quarter to eleven. The constable came back on the line to report that Sergeant Lett had gone, too. She asked for WPC Wardle and the constable commented about wasting Metropolitan Police time to arrange a tea party. Mabel said that this was a matter of life or death and asked for the constable's collar number. Although that made him hop to it, it didn't do any good.

'Stepped out to assist a family,' the constable said when he came back on the line. Now rather more eager to help, he added, 'Is there someone else?'

'No, but I would like this same message left for each of them. Listen carefully.'

Mabel tried to be as succinct as possible, but she seemed to muddle things by trying to be clear. At the end, she repeated her name, Roxanne's name and Hanover Terrace. Time pressed in on her and every second was precious.

But before she could go, she rang New River House and learned from Mr Chigley that Park had not returned and Cora and Skeff had come and gone again. 'Miss Skeffington said there was something she needed to look into. Any messages?'

'Yes, please tell Mr Winstone "Hanover Terrace".' Mabel rang off and when she stepped out onto the pavement, there was Donald shivering coatless as he stood next to a waiting taxi. Mabel took long enough to pull a sixpence out of her purse and give it to the boy.

'For you,' she said and then handed him a threepenny piece. 'For Mr Hordern for use of the telephone.' She told the driver her destination, said it was an emergency and leapt into the back of the taxi.

In the moment before they sped off, Mabel looked across the road to the café where she and Evangeline had had tea only yesterday. There was the same waitress peering out the window. She must've seen Mabel and remembered her, because the woman gave her a big smile and waved.

'I'll get there, I'll get there.' Mabel repeated the words over and over to calm her nerves. The cabbie veered in and out of traffic and Mabel had to brace herself or slide back and forth on the seat. It couldn't've been a long journey but seemed to take forever.

When the taxi pulled up in front of number nine Hanover Terrace, Mabel tumbled out, paid and looked round. The road lay quiet, separated from the busy Inner Circle road that ran along Regent's Park on the other side of that strip of nearly leafless trees and shrubs. There was no sign of the coal lorry.

Freddy answered neither the bell nor the knocker.

'I'll go round the back,' Mabel said aloud, hoping she wouldn't have to scale a wall to get in.

Down to the corner around and then around again. She approached the back of the house and found the gate to the garden was closed but not locked. That meant that anyone – Fred Fredericks or Evangeline Gregory, for example – could come and go at will. Had Angel persuaded Fred to assist her in her plan, promising him a few bob for the pub? Quite likely.

Mabel looked round at the other back gardens but saw no one about. A fine icy mist had started to swirl and gain strength and now beaded up on the sleeves of Mabel's coat.

The gate creaked when she pushed it open. Mabel paused but saw no movement within. She slipped through and stopped behind a thorny tangle of roses. The land fell slightly from front to back and she spotted the daylight door she'd seen in the room where Fred Fredericks had set up his camp bed. She made for the door and found it, too, unlocked. Once in, Mabel held still and listened. All was quiet.

'Roxanne!' she called but no reply came. Had Evangeline assured Roxanne's silence with an extra dose of laudanum? Had Mabel arrived in time to save her life?

Mabel took two steps in and towards the coal cellar when a blow fell across her back. The force was so great it knocked her forward, and she put her hands out a second before she hit the floor, face first. She cried out as her hat went sailing through the air to a far corner and her satchel fell with a thud. As she pushed herself onto her knees, her arms were caught and forced to her side.

'Now Mabel,' Evangeline said in a cheerful voice as she pushed a knee into Mabel's back, dragged her up and manoeuvred her over to the chair. 'No need for all that. Calm down so we can enjoy the show to come.'

She fought to get free, but Evangeline only laughed as she kicked Mabel's feet out from under her, so that she couldn't stand or break free. Out of a coat pocket, Evangeline produced a thin rope. 'Thought I might need to use this for the little princess, but she's as docile as a cow.'

Evangeline threw the rope over Mabel several times and tied her to the chair then did the same for her feet. Mabel got in a kick or two, but they were only glancing blows.

'It won't work, Mabel, try as you might,' Evangeline said as she went about her work. 'I know how to shift a body that can't move itself. Dead weight, that is, and difficult. My mother could barely move for the last few months and so I was the one that got her out of bed and into a chair and to the lav and back again. She liked to sit in her chair and look out the window, but wasn't able to keep herself upright, so I would strap her in. Amazing the skills you learn that you can apply elsewhere, isn't it? Roxanne was as easy as my mummy. This tying you down – well, it's rather refreshing that you try to fight back.' She cinched the rope so that it cut into Mabel's arms.

Mabel stopped struggling and said, 'Evangeline, you must let Roxanne out of the coal cellar.'

'No, I mustn't,' Evangeline said. 'Her father murdered my father and here's how he will pay – by knowing his daughter died the same way.'

'He didn't murder your father. Your father and his friend had too much to drink, and they fell asleep in the empty coal car. It was an accident.'

Evangeline went on as if Mabel hadn't spoken, pacing back and forth in the short space. 'Mother never told me what happened – she wouldn't say a word about my father. But I knew – kids in my street knew. When she died, I found that newspaper clipping I showed you and it all became clear. I'm not stupid, you know, I looked into it and I saw the money in her post office account and found out where it was coming from. Mr Rupert Arkwright, owner of the rail yard where my father died.'

'He didn't own the rail yard when your father died there,' Mabel said. 'I saw the newspaper clipping in your room – the date had been cut off. I've seen the real newspaper article and Rupert Arkwright didn't buy the rail yard until after your father died.'

Evangeline leaned close. 'You can't cover for him, Mabel – it's no use.'

Mabel saw a vagueness in the woman's dark eyes and realised Evangeline was beyond reason.

Mabel tried again regardless. 'Your father died because of a foolish mistake. It wasn't Mr Arkwright's fault. Why are you punishing Roxanne?'

'I'm not punishing Roxanne,' Evangeline said in an oddly light-hearted manner as if Mabel were a bit slow understanding. 'I appreciate the part she's playing, though. It was when I saw her photo in *Tatler*, I knew what I had to do. I had to make Rupert Arkwright suffer as my mother had suffered. I've made a good start of it, but it's time I finished it.'

'Roxanne had nothing to do with it and neither did her father. Let her out and we'll say nothing.'

'You're a poor liar, Mabel,' Evangeline said and clicked her tongue. 'You'll need to—'

'Please, Evangeline,' Mabel said, squirming, 'please let her out. This is a mistake. Rupert Arkwright paid your mother out of kindness.'

'Blood money!' Evangeline shouted in Mabel's face. 'I'll have nothing to do with it!'

'Freddy is here,' Mabel said. 'She'll come downstairs any second now.'

'Freddy is not here,' Evangeline said, 'and you know it. I saw you ring the bell. I've been across the road waiting for the coalmen to arrive. I couldn't resist. I want to watch it all unfold and then telephone Scotland Yard to give them a tip. Imagine the scene, Mabel. Police cars come to a screeching halt in front of the house, followed by the family. Think of the grief on Rupert Arkwright's face. It could kill him, that grief – but not immediately, I hope. I want it to be a long, slow death.'

Mabel thought she saw movement out the window and her heart fluttered, but it was only the shifting of bare branches in a breeze.

'Rupert Arkwright is in hospital,' she said. 'Did you hit him with a glass paperweight – the other one you took?'

Evangeline grinned as she stuck her hand in her coat pocket, pulled out a paperweight, tossed it up in the air and caught it. 'Holyroodhouse,' she said. '"Why not take two" I asked myself.'

'You were the figure Ned Kettle saw wearing the apron at the Palais.'

'I don't know Ned Kettle from Adam,' Evangeline said.

'You took two glass paperweights from Mr Bryars' office.'

'The man should really lock his door.'

'Why did you murder Oswald Deuchar?'

'Such a busybody,' Evangeline said. 'Much like you, Mabel. I didn't even know who he was, but he'd seen me outside the Arkwright house. "Lurking," he said. I was only offering my services as I got the measure of Dorcas. Oswald actually handed me his calling card and said he would be "notifying Mr Arkwright of my interest in his family". Said he was there to protect little Miss Roxanne and I was to stay away. I had hopes of taking her that evening at the dance hall – right under your nose – but he got in my way. He annoyed me, the little midge, and that gave me every reason to knock him on the head.'

Knock him on the head many times over, Mabel remembered. A vicious attack.

'And you planted the paperweight in Rupert Arkwright's coat pocket when you were one of many working in the house that day.'

'Casting shadows,' Evangeline said. 'Worked, didn't it? Got the Yard all stirred up and the household – well they broke into little bits. And poor Dorcas and her dying granny. She needed both an extra pair of hands and, what do they call it? – "moral support".'

Mabel listened to the silence in the house. 'How did you get Freddy to give you a job?'

'I rang up,' Evangeline said and laughed. 'Remember little Ozzie handed me his calling card? Silly boy.'

'Freddy will be back soon. She's probably only gone to the shops. Let Roxanne go and I'll take her away and no one will hear of this.'

'Don't be tiresome, Mabel,' Evangeline said, peering out the back window. 'No one will hear about it, because there will be no one left to tell.' She studied Mabel for a moment as she took the glass paperweight out and tossed it in the air once, caught it and dropped it back in her pocket. 'But we'll get to that later.'

'Does Freddy know what you've done? That you murdered Oswald?'

'Good heavens, no,' Evangeline said. 'No one knows what's happened, Mabel. Except for you, of course.'

'They know who you are,' Mabel said.

'Who?' was Evangeline's sharp reply.

'Everyone. The police. We have a drawing of you – it's in my satchel there, go ahead and look.'

Evangeline opened Mabel's satchel, turned it out onto the floor and spotted the drawing.

'Who did this?' she said. 'It's quite good.'

'You see, they'll find you. It'll be so much better if you let Roxanne go and—'

A sound stopped her. The sound of something heavy being scraped across the pavement above. The sound of the iron cover to the coal cellar being removed. Then came a rushing noise, like rocks and grit tumbling down a dry hillside as the contents of the first sack of coal dropped. Mabel felt as if it were landing on her heart.

She screamed at the top of her lungs, wishing she could produce Roxanne's shrieking heights that would be heard across to Regent's Park.

'Shut it!' Evangeline slapped her.

'Here now,' said a complaining voice behind them. Evangeline whirled round, and in her haste she knocked into the chair, tipping it over and Mabel with it. Mabel fell hard on her right side and strained to turn her head far enough to see.

'Who are you?' Evangeline demanded.

Fred Fredericks stood in the doorway to the garden. 'I believe the true question here, young lady,' he said in his leisurely manner, 'is who are you, why are you in my living quarters and what are you doing to Miss Canning? That's three questions, isn't it?'

'Fred!' Mabel rocked but could not right herself. 'Open the coal cellar door – open it now. There's a woman trapped inside.'

Fred came closer, paying no attention to Evangeline. He leaned over Mabel and the smell of alcohol made her eyes water. She blinked and saw he had a black eye. With great effort, he righted her chair and shook his head. 'No, no,' he said, his usual leer turned down at the corners. 'It's too late now.'

'She will die if you don't let her out.' Mabel forced the words past the sob in her throat. 'You will be guilty of murder if you don't open that door this minute.'

She heard more coal falling onto the floor in a rocky *flump*.

'Pay her no mind,' Evangeline said in a cajoling tone. 'Fred, is it? Oh yes, I've heard of you. Do you know what you need to do, Fred?'

Another sack of coal dropped. Another and another.

Fred put his open hand on his chest. 'A lady can always rely on Fred Fredericks in a time of need.'

'She's only eighteen, Fred,' Mabel said, pleading. 'A girl.'

'Is she?' he asked in mock wonder. 'Awfully strong for one so young, though.'

More noise, but this came from other quarters – a cacophony of heavy thuds, shouts and a crash from above.

Mabel screamed and screamed and there was the thunder of footfalls on the stairs and a host of police officers burst into the cellar with Tollerton in the vanguard. Evangeline bolted out the door to the garden.

'She's the one!' Mabel shouted. 'She took Roxanne.'

Evangeline got no further than the tangled rose stems before two constables tackled her.

'Keep her out of the way,' Tollerton called out to them.

PC Drake took a penknife and cut Mabel free, and

Tollerton helped her stand. All the while, she heard more bags of coal being emptied and all the while she tried to make it clear it should stop.

'Roxanne is in the cellar! Stop them dropping the coal!' She pulled the cut pieces of rope off her, ran to the door of the coal cellar and took hold of the iron rod, struggling to push it aside with shaking hands. 'Tell them to stop!'

Tollerton shouted the order and a constable shot off up the stairs.

'Here, Mabel, let me,' Tollerton said. 'Stand back,' he added. 'In case.'

Mabel shut her mind to the possibilities and as the door creaked open and a cloud of coal dust billowed out, she shouted, 'Roxanne? Roxanne?'

There was no answer, and as the coal cloud settled, it became obvious why. In the middle of the cellar, and directly underneath the hole in the pavement into which the sacks had been emptied, stood a mound of coal at least four feet high and spilling down in all directions nearly to the walls. In the second of stunned silence, a single lump of coal at the tiptop loosened and tumbled to the floor.

'Roxanne!' Mabel screamed and dived into the cellar, pushing into the mound, throwing pieces right and left as she dug.

'Mabel.'

Park was behind her. He put his hands on her shoulders and said, 'Mabel, come away. They'll be quicker.'

She stumbled backward and he held on to steady her as the cellar flooded with police. Her right shoulder ached from the fall, but she welcomed the pain.

One of the constables picked up a coal shovel from the corner, but Tollerton shouted, 'Hands only!' He joined them grabbing the lumps and throwing them to the walls as quickly as they could.

Mabel felt a pressure on her legs and looked down to see Gladys looking up at her, brown eyes offering succour. Mabel sobbed. She thought of Roxanne's broken body beneath the coal and hoped that Evangeline had given her enough laudanum that she had not awakened to her fate.

The men worked as fast as they could without disturbing what might lay beneath. It felt incredibly slow to Mabel. But at last she could see the mound shrinking lower and lower until at the bottom, she spotted the edge of an emerald-green plaid coat.

TWENTY-TWO

Mabel cried out and tried to break away, but Park held her. 'Wait now.'

The men worked carefully to remove the last pieces of coal until all that was left was a thin layer of slack and dust and under that, Roxanne's coat.

But no Roxanne.

Mabel gasped and choked on coal dust. 'She isn't there,' she cried. 'She isn't there! She's alive!'

From outside came an anguished cry and Mabel looked to see Evangeline struggling to break free from the constables' hold and screaming in fury, 'No! No, it isn't true. That can't be. No!'

She caused such an uproar that Gladys ran out barking and growling and nipping at Evangeline's feet until the woman screamed, 'Get her off me!'

One of the constables responded, 'She hasn't touched you.'

'Gladys,' Winstone called. He gave Mabel a questioning look.

'I'm all right,' Mabel said. And she was – she felt light as a feather. 'You go on.'

Winstone went out and gave the dog a scratch, and Gladys leapt and wriggled and snorted.

'Good girl, Gladys,' Mabel called out the door.

Tollerton brushed his hands off. 'Mabel, who is that woman we're holding?'

'Evangeline Gregory,' Mabel said. 'She was in Miss Kerr's Useful Women ledger, but it was all a ruse.'

'Right, let's see if she'll tell us where she took Miss Arkwright.'

'No,' Mabel said, 'she hasn't taken her anywhere. Look at her – her plan is in ruins.' She looked out at Evangeline. 'Ruins!'

'Take her in,' Tollerton said to the PCs. 'So, if this Evangeline Gregory abducted Miss Arkwright and put her in the coal cellar, how did she get out and where has she gone?'

An unctuous voice came from the dark corner. 'Excuse me, Detective Inspector, sir, I might be able to help.'

Fred Fredericks stepped out of the dark, brushing off his coat and smoothing back his hair.

'Who are you?' Tollerton asked.

'No need to go into such detail,' Fred replied.

'Fredericks!' Sergeant Lett exclaimed as he came down the corridor from the stairs.

'Oh, Constable Lett, what a surprise.'

'It's detective sergeant now,' Lett said, pulling out his notebook. 'What do you have to do with this?'

'Nothing, nothing in the least.'

'Do you know how Roxanne got out of the coal cellar? Where is she?' Mabel demanded.

Winstone and Gladys returned, and the dog decided Fred Fredericks was the source of some interesting smells. She started sniffing round his boots and the hem of his trousers. Then, she sat down at his feet and offered him a paw.

Fred looked down at her. 'My, my, aren't you the polite girl,' he said and shook the paw. 'I say, Miss Canning, the thing is, perhaps you and I could talk just the two of us.'

'Not likely, Fred,' Mabel said. 'What do you know about Roxanne?'

'I don't know who this Roxanne is, but I am delighted to cooperate with Scotland Yard in any way I can' – his eyes darted to nearby police officers – 'so I will tell you my story and with your good graces, I will be on my way.'

Tollerton, Lett and Winstone all drew out pocket notebooks and pencils.

'Last evening, I returned here to my monastic cell, as it were.'

'What time?' Tollerton asked.

'It was just after closing time or possibly a bit later. I made my ablutions and retired to my bed, but I heard some stirring from the coal cellar. A fox, I thought, but I didn't fancy looking at that moment and thought I'd set the fellow free in the morning. But he kept up quite a racket and began beating on the door, which seemed a bit odd for a fox. Then, when he let out a shriek, I threw open the door and out tumbled a young woman in a terrible state. I tried to calm her, but that didn't go too well' – he pointed to his black eye – 'and so I backed off and she stumbled out the door, not terribly steady on her feet. I wasn't in too good a condition myself, and so, after I'd set the captive free, I shut the door to the coal cellar and went back to bed.'

'Laudanum,' Mabel said after imagining Roxanne, unsteady on her feet, wandering off into the night. 'She was drugged.'

Fred began to edge his way to the door. 'Mercy. Well, that's my part spoken, and so now I'd best be off. Good day to you all.'

Gladys followed him to the door and Tollerton frowned as Fred slunk off, deftly avoiding two PCs coming through the back garden by diving into the hedge.

The sound of a high garbled voice came rushing down the stairs just ahead of Freddy, who appeared with WPC Wardle right behind. Freddy held up at the sight of the crowd in the cellar.

'Inspector,' she began. 'Miss Canning, what is all this? Why have I just seen my new under housekeeper being taken away by police?' Then her head spun round, and she peered out the door. 'Fred Fredericks, what have you done now?' she shouted.

As Fred fought his way out of the hedge, Mabel said, 'He may very well have saved a young woman's life, Freddy.'

Fred came back to the door brushing dead leaves off his jacket. 'You see, my dear, I do you a favour by staying out of your way and I do Scotland Yard a favour by getting in theirs. I don't suppose my reward could be a spot of lunch, could it?'

Freddy drew herself up and looked down her nose at him. 'I demand an explanation.'

'Wardle,' Tollerton said, 'could you take the two of them upstairs and Mrs Fredericks could sort out a round of tea for us.'

Mabel frowned at this. 'Inspector—'

But Wardle shook her head. 'It's all right. Now, Mr and Mrs Fredericks, come along.'

As the three of them took the stairs, Tollerton turned to his sergeant. 'Do you think he knows any more?'

Lett shook his head. 'This sort of thing isn't in Fred's league.'

'Was she working alone?' Tollerton asked. 'It's quite a job for one woman.'

Mabel nearly pointed out that Useful Women could accomplish a great deal, but decided this wasn't a terribly good example.

'Ned Kettle's in the clear, so she wasn't working with him. Or at least, he didn't do her dirty work at the Palais,' Winstone said. 'When pressed, the doorman admitted to knowing him and said he would warn Ned when Bryars went on his rounds. He saw Ned out a good twenty minutes before Deuchar stumbled into Roxanne. The medical examiner said Deuchar would-n't've lasted twenty minutes.'

'Have you been talking to my medical examiner?' Tolly asked.

Winstone pointed a finger at him. 'You don't own Scotland Yard.'

That got a grin out of the inspector.

'I'm glad Ned is off the hook,' Mabel said. 'I liked him, although I liked Evangeline, too, so what does that say about my skills as a detective.'

'You think you're the only one who's had the wool pulled over their eyes?' Winstone said. 'Tolly and I could tell you a few tales.'

'We could that,' Tollerton said.

'I don't believe Evangeline had any help – this is all her doing,' Mabel said. 'And to think I was trying to get her more work with Useful Women. Now' – Mabel brushed her hands off although the coal dust remained embedded – 'we've got to find Roxanne. She must be in a terrible state.'

'Depending on the dose of laudanum, she couldn't've got far,' Winstone said.

'Evangeline gave it to her mother for pain during the last year of her life,' Mabel said, her emotions wheeling from high to low so quickly, it made her dizzy, 'and it sounded as if she became quite expert at dosage. Roxanne is still in grave danger. She's out there drugged and alone in London.'

'Right,' Tollerton said. 'We'll probably find Miss Arkwright in Regent's Park. I'll send the men out now and there won't be a leaf unturned. Also, we'll bring out the watermen to search the canal. Why don't you go home, Miss Canning, and we'll let you know.'

So, back to Miss Canning again, was it? He acted as if Mabel would faint at the idea that Roxanne might be floating in Regent's Canal. But Roxanne hadn't been under a mountain of coal, and that had buoyed Mabel's spirits. Roxanne had come to her senses long enough to get out of the cellar. She'd fought with Fred. Yes, she might've spent all her energy on that, but perhaps not. Could she find her way home to Mayfair? Or would she go somewhere else?

'I'll find her,' Mabel said. 'You look for her here, and I'll look elsewhere.'

'You can't mount your own search,' Tollerton said. 'Tell me, and after we're finished here, I'll send the men over.'

'No,' Winstone said firmly. 'I'll go with Mabel.'

She smiled and felt the tightness of dried tears on her cheeks. She wiped them and the back of her hand came away streaked with grit.

'Where will you go?' Tollerton asked.

'There's Mayfair,' Mabel said, 'but perhaps not first. I don't want to tell them she'd been found and lost again. It would be too upsetting for the family – it certainly was for me. But New River House – she knows where I live. Or perhaps she's gone back to the Elm Tree.'

'The Elm Tree?' Tollerton asked.

'It's the pub on the King's Road in Fulham near Evangeline's boarding house.'

'And how is Miss Arkwright to have gone off to any of those places – hailed a taxi in the middle of the night?'

'I don't know,' Mabel said, at once cross. 'Yet.'

To avoid further questions, Mabel made a show of searching for her hat, which she had espied under Fred's camp bed in the dark corner. She retrieved it, beat it once against her thigh and put it back on. The stiff ribbon tied at one side to look like a bird taking flight had lost a bit of its shape, but no matter. She stooped to collect what Evangeline had turned out of her satchel, including the drawings and her Bacon's walking map, which she unfolded and studied.

'I'll get Drake to drive you,' Tollerton said.

'No, WPC Wardle can drive us to Islington,' Mabel said as she folded the map up. 'We'll talk with Cora and Skeff, because they've met Roxanne and can help us with our search.'

Tollerton looked at Mabel as if he didn't believe it was going to be that easy to get shot of her.

'Tolly?' Park asked

'Yes, all right,' he said. 'You're to ring here to let me know what you've found. I've got someone upstairs at the telephone.'

Wardle flashed a brief smile when Mabel told her the plan, but then turned serious as she handed over tea-making to one of the men and left the Fredericks bickering about how much sugar Fred liked in his tea.

Mabel, Park and Hildy went upstairs and climbed into the police car with Gladys. Wardle took the driver's seat. They pulled away, and Mabel turned to Park.

'Hildy and I will leave you at New River House, because even if Roxanne isn't there, she may arrive.'

'Ah,' Winstone said. 'I thought you had something else up your sleeve. And where will you go?'

'The Waterman pub down at St Katharine Docks.'

Winstone lifted his brows. They'd both been at St Katharine Docks in the autumn where Mabel had made a gruesome discovery, but she would not let that overshadow her purpose.

'Roxanne knows Flea and Flea reminds her of her brother, Tommy.' Mabel said. 'She even mentioned Flea when she went to the Elm Tree—at least, the landlord said she mentioned "fleas".'

'Does the boy live at the pub?'

'I'm not sure, but they know him there. Look, it is broad daylight' she glanced out the window at the gloomy grey skies – 'and I'll have WPC Wardle with me.'

'And Gladys,' Winstone said.

'And Gladys.' Mabel took the dog's face in her hands and looked deep into her eyes. 'We're going to find Roxanne.' Gladys' back end wriggled.

'All right. I'll go to Islington,' Winstone said and knocked on the window.

Wardle pulled over at Marylebone Road and they explained the plan.

'I'll get a taxi from here,' Park said, 'but if I find nothing, I'm following you to the river.'

'Yes, good.' Mabel's eyes shone as she squeezed his hand.

He got out and when Mabel put down the window, he asked, 'How would Roxanne know where St Katharine Docks is – or the Tower of London, for that matter?'

'Because,' Mabel said, and gave him a quick kiss, 'she has a map.'

Mabel dropped that brave front as soon as they'd pulled away. A voice in her head told her how far-fetched it would be that Roxanne would look for help in a place she'd never been instead of going to her father's house or to Mabel's flat. But then, far-fetched suited Roxanne to a T.

But the argumentative voice in Mabel's head asked, what did it matter if Roxanne had located Tower Bridge and St Katharine Docks on her Bacon's walking map? How would she have got there from Hanover Terrace in the dead of night? Mabel, who had grown quite fond of London in the few months since she'd moved up from the country, knew there were many dangers in the city and that in certain neighbourhoods, those dangers multiplied after dark.

Roxanne's journey would've been nearly twelve hours ago, perhaps less, depending on when Fred Fredericks had returned to his camp bed. Now it was midday, and no one had rung Scotland Yard to say they'd found a young American woman wandering in the back garden and could a constable please come and collect her. Perhaps Tolly could send PCs door to door all the way from Hanover Square down to the Tower and the docks.

Hildy stopped along the road leading down to the river where Mabel could see Tower Bridge up ahead to the right, and the docks to the left with its warren of lanes leading down to wooden walkways and stretches of quays with ships alongside. The pub lay at the end of a path up ahead. Hildy got out and climbed into the back of the police car next to Mabel and said, 'Now what?'

'We need to find Flea, and I thought the pub the best place to ask. Park and Skeff will probably be on their way here soon enough, and she knows a bit more about the area, but we'll make a start of it.'

Mabel secured Gladys' lead and off they went, the dog zigzagging in front of them.

Midday on Saturday and the Waterman, which carried the usual pub smells of beer and tobacco with the addition of a brackish river odour, had a bar with no stools and a couple of tables with only benches along the wall for seating. A few men standing with their pints of beer or glasses of whisky looked as if they might be on their way to or from a job on the docks. The few others looked as if they might be part of the woodwork. Every one of them turned his head when Mabel, Hildy and Gladys walked in.

The women stopped in front of the bar, and Gladys sat at Mabel's feet.

'Hello, good afternoon,' Mabel said to the barman who stood with his beefy arms outstretched and his hands resting on the edge of the counter. He wore no collar, his sleeves were rolled up and his apron had long ago given up looking white.

'My name is Mabel Canning, and this is WPC Wardle. I'm a friend of Skeff's. Do you know Skeff?'

'You're a what?' the barman said to Wardle.

'Woman Police Constable,' Hildy said, standing tall and putting her hands behind her back. 'I'm with the Metropolitan Police.'

'What do you want with Skeff?' the barman asked.

'Skeff is a friend of mine,' Mabel repeated. 'Of ours. She lives quite near me in Islington.'

'What does that have to do with the price of tea in China?' a fellow propping up the end of the bar said. 'She isn't here. Have you tried Islington?'

'I'm not looking for Skeff,' Mabel said. 'I'm looking for a mutual friend named Flea.'

Conversation had fallen when Mabel and Hildy had walked in, but now it disappeared altogether. Mabel pushed on.

'I'm hoping Flea can help us find a... another mutual friend.'

'Just how many people are you looking for?' the barman asked.

'She's an American and she may have become lost,' Hildy said. 'It would do no one any good to keep information to himself if it might help us locate her whereabouts. She is a friend of Flea's and he'll be concerned when he hears. We believe he could help us find her.'

The silence in the pub, disturbed only by a hissing of the half-spent fire as the coal embers settled, went on for so long, Mabel nearly gave up hope. At last, the man at the end of the bar said, 'Is that a police dog?'

'This is Gladys,' Mabel said. 'Gladys, go say hello to the gentleman.'

Gladys stepped over and offered a paw, which was received with delight. 'Pleased to meet you,' the man said.

The barman leaned over to get a better look at Gladys and said, 'Used to have a ratter lived with me here. She was a lovely dog.' His comments were followed by several other of the men mentioning dogs of their past.

Then the barman said, 'Flea was up at the market first thing this morning and back and now he's gone out again, but he's due back here to peel potatoes.'

'The market?' Mabel asked.

'Smithfield?' Hildy suggested.

'A few scraps of beef,' the barman said defensively, 'a sausage or two. The boy isn't a thief – he pays. We aren't the Savoy, but I can fry up a bit of meat and a few spuds.'

That was the other smell Mabel had detected – well-used hot oil. No wonder Gladys' nose danced about on her face.

'When did this American person come down to the docks?' one of the men asked.

'You mean *why* did this American person come down to the docks?' another man said, and they all laughed.

'She could've been looking for Flea,' Mabel said. 'But she's not well and may be a bit disorientated. If she came down to the docks during the night, who would she meet?'

The men didn't look at Mabel or Hildy, but they glanced at each other and one or two bent down to pet Gladys.

'Any women round the quay that time of night?' Hildy asked.

'Ah now, leave 'em be,' the barman said. 'They don't do any harm.'

'I'll leave them be after I've had a word with them,' Hildy said.

'It's midday,' one of the men said, 'you won't find anyone.'

'No, Bessie'll still be out,' another said. 'You won't miss her red hair.'

Mabel and Gladys followed WPC Wardle out of the Waterman and headed towards the quay.

'Hildy, were you asking about women who... you know, work the quay?'

'Yes,' Hildy said. 'I asked to do a couple of night shifts when I first started. I was advised not to go. "It's not the sort of life you want to see, Wardle," I was told, but I pushed for it. It wasn't as if I was looking for training.'

Mabel laughed. 'Tollerton didn't say that, did he?'

'No, he's a good guv'nor.' She looked down at Gladys. 'Scotland Yard should assign dogs to constables doing rounds – people warm up to dogs easier than they do to humans.'

The ships creaked and squeaked as they rubbed up against the quay. Mabel and Hildy walked past men loading or unloading and up to a low building on the shore with a few doorways, one leading to a shop that sold the basics a man going to sea might need – sturdy trousers, braces and boots plus pomade and tooth powder. In one of the doorways, they found Bessie.

Even in the shadows, her red hair stood out, piled up on her head in an old-fashioned way. They paused and she shrank back, but Hildy said, 'Are you Bessie? We only want to ask you a question.'

Bessie stepped out into the grey light of day, and Mabel's first impression was that the woman didn't look young, but perhaps this was because of a difficult life. She wore heavy face powder and a dress with a neckline too low for evening, let alone midday.

'I'm on my way home,' Bessie said. 'There's nothing wrong with that.'

'No, nothing wrong,' Wardle said gently.

'What are you?' Bessie asked, looking Wardle up and down.

'Woman Police Constable.'

Bessie read off the badge on Hildy's shoulder. 'WPC. Who would've thought.' She looked down at Gladys and said, 'Well, I know what you are, so' – her gaze went up to Mabel – 'that leaves only you.'

'I'm Mabel Canning, and we're looking for a young American woman who might've been through here sometime during the night.'

Bessie squinted at Mabel. 'Is she working?'

'No,' Mabel said quickly. 'Not working. She's only visiting her father and ran into a bit of trouble.'

'And you thought she might've come down here?' Bessie asked. 'I hope you're wrong. I haven't seen her, but I've only been here since this morning. The girls from last night are asleep now and you'll have to wait until later to see them.'

'Do you know Flea?' Mabel asked.

'What's that boy up and done?'

'Not a thing untoward,' Hildy replied. 'At least, that we are aware of. It's only that he knows the American and so if we can find him, we might be able to find her.'

'Well, he just scampered through here not a minute ago,' Bessie said. 'I'm surprised you didn't see him or he didn't see you the way you came. Or it could be that he's gone off down the dock to see what might've floated in on the tide.'

'Thank you,' Mabel said, and they turned back down the path they'd come up. 'We could split up,' she suggested, but half-heartedly, because a cold mist had risen off the water and already crept on shore. Mabel shuddered. She'd seen a face under water in just such conditions.

'No, we'll look in the pub first,' Wardle said, 'and then we'll—'

From nowhere, Flea appeared in front of them on the path. Gladys *woofed* and leapt and wriggled, but the boy's face was etched with concern as his eyes went from Hildy to Mabel, his brows shooting up.

'It's Roxanne,' Mabel said. 'Have you seen her? That is, Skeff told you Roxanne is missing, didn't she? And in the pub they told you we were looking for you?'

A nod, but also questioning look.

'We'll tell you the entire story later,' Mabel said, 'but here's this much. She was being held captive and got loose sometime during the night, but she's been drugged and is in a bad way. Police are looking for her, and Mr Winstone has gone to Islington to ask Skeff and Cora if they've seen her. I thought she might try and find you. You haven't seen her?'

Mabel knew the answer even before Flea shook his head. He turned away from them and scanned the footways, the buildings down at the docks, as if he could see through solid brick and wood.

'You told her about the docks, didn't you?' Mabel asked. 'Any particular place?'

Flea spread his hands and threw his arms out. All of it.

'Where should we begin?'

Flea spun round at the sound of voices up on the road. Gladys barked and ran off, bringing back Winstone, Skeff and Cora when she returned.

'We've heard nothing from her, and we've left Mr Chigley to watch out,' Skeff said. 'Flea?'

Flea shook his head.

'They haven't seen her in the pub,' Mabel said.

'Right,' Winstone said, 'let's spread out. You know the place, Flea. You're in charge.'

The boy stood tall as he made assignments by snapping his fingers, pointing, and gesturing to indicate who should go this way or that. Wardle went back to Bessie's quay and would walk the length. Skeff and Cora made for the docks office to ask there. Winstone went down to the river's edge, but not before sending Mabel a questioning look.

'You go on,' she said. 'I'll go with Flea back towards the pub.'

'All right,' he said. When they moved off separate ways, Gladys looked first at one and then the other. 'Go with Mabel,' Winstone said.

The dog followed at her heels, and she followed at Flea's.

They crept along down the path with Flea stopping often or veering off to look under an upturned rowboat or behind a stack of rope coils. Meanwhile, Gladys inspected any tuft of grass along the shore no matter how dried and brown it might be. The fog had thickened, deadening sounds and giving Mabel the feeling that they were in a world of their own. When a strange man walked by, she started.

They worked their way towards the pub in a circular fashion, closing in on it as if it were a rabbit that might bolt. Taking their time, they spread out as they examined the accumulated detritus of the shoreline, picking up any bit of paper or piece of glass or broken smoking pipe. Mabel came across a crate missing its bottom with a stamp on the side that read East India Company in fading letters.

More crates were vaguely organised into stacks and then she saw a cask and a wall and realised she'd worked her way into the yard at the Waterman. She stood and surveyed her surroundings. Broken crockery, a blackened pan, a fire pit for burning rubbish and the compost heap covered in jute sacking. Just the bits and bobs that had been tossed out the back door of the pub when no longer useful.

Gladys trotted in behind her, stopped and sniffed the air.

'Yes, pungent, isn't it?' Mabel asked.

Gladys *woofed* followed by a growl followed by a bark as she raced across the yard to the compost heap, dancing around as if the jute sacking was playing a game with her.

Mabel's heart throbbed in her ears as she stumbled over and pulled the sacking away.

TWENTY-THREE

Roxanne lay nestled in the warmth of rotting potato peelings, trimmings from sprouts and the tops of beetroots, along with chicken bones and other less identifiable remains. Her skin was nearly translucent, dark circles showed under her eyes and she had bruises on her arms and a cut on her forehead. She wore a stained rose-coloured day dress blackened with coal dust and, of course, no coat, but she clasped her small leather envelope purse to her chest.

Gladys barked, Mabel cried out with a sob and Roxanne opened one bleary eye and then the other.

'Oh Mabel,' she said in a hoarse voice, 'there you are.'

'Flea!' Mabel shouted. 'Flea – she's here!'

Flea came running but stopped short when he saw Roxanne, who blinked at him.

'Tommy?' She shook her head. 'No, it's Flea!' Her voice was weak but triumphant. 'That's right, I came looking for you. It was too dark to see the name of the pub and I was so very tired.'

The boy grinned and pulled at his newsboy cap in greeting, then took what looked to be a police whistle from his pocket and blew three long blasts.

Gladys licked Roxanne's face and then ran off, barking.

Roxanne clambered up from the pile of rubbish holding Mabel's hands to steady herself.

'There, that's better,' Roxanne said, shaking a potato peel off her arm. The next moment, she swooned, and Mabel scooped her up before she fell to the ground. Roxanne opened her eyes again. 'I'm sorry, Mabel, it's just that I feel a bit odd.'

'Can you walk a few steps?' Mabel asked, keeping an arm around Roxanne's waist. 'We'll sit inside the pub by the fire, and you can warm up. How long has it been since you've eaten anything? Have you been out here all night?'

'Have I?' Roxanne said. 'I remember it was dark when I left there and dark when I arrived here.'

Flea blew the signal again, but there had been no need, because here came the others at a run, arriving from all directions. Gladys led the way with Hildy next, then Park followed by Skeff who waited for Cora to catch up.

When they saw Roxanne – on her feet, awake, alive – they all spoke at once, laughed and spoke again.

Bewildered, Roxanne looked from face to face. 'Are you all here for me?'

'You've been missing since Thursday,' Mabel said and saw Roxanne's eyes darken. 'Look, let's get you inside. You need to sit.' Mabel needed to sit, too – her legs felt like rubber with the relief.

'I'll tell Quaterman,' Skeff said and went off with Cora into the pub.

Flea approached Roxanne with care and the two of them had an exchange that might've included something about cricket. Or softball.

Winstone said, 'I'll go to the docks office and ring Tolly and tell him to bring an ambulance.' But he paused first and rested his hand on Mabel's arm. 'Well done.'

Mabel didn't answer – she didn't quite trust herself to speak – but covered his hand with hers.

Roxanne called after Park as he left, 'Thank you, Mr Winstone.' She turned to Mabel. 'An ambulance? Is someone hurt?'

'It's for you,' Hildy said.

'Oh, I don't need a doctor,' Roxanne said, 'but I will talk with Inspector Tollerton – is he "Tolly"? A cup of coffee would be nice. And maybe a sandwich.'

'I'll follow Skeff and Cora,' Hildy said, 'and see what we can find.'

When Hildy had gone and it was only Mabel and Gladys left, Roxanne wrinkled her nose. 'Ew, Mabel. What's that smell?'

'I'm afraid it's you, Roxanne,' Mabel replied and gave her shoulders a squeeze. 'And at this minute, it's better than perfume from Paris.' As they slowly walked round to the front of the pub, she added, 'You'll want to go to hospital and let the doctors take a look at you.'

'No,' Roxanne said, 'I can't go like this, I need a bath first.' She shook her arms and a woodlouse fell out of her sleeve. 'And Mabel, I'm sorry to say, but you could do with a wash yourself.'

The pub's landlord, Quaterman of the beefy arms, chased out the last customer, threw more coal on the fire and gave them the run of the place, which made no difference to him because it was after afternoon closing and before evening opening. He found three chairs in varying conditions and one short stool to add to the bench seats. He served Roxanne bread and cheese and a cup of black coffee that smelled as if it had been boiling on the back of the stove for a good long while. She took a sip and shuddered. 'At last,' she whispered, holding the cup to her chest. She heaved a great sigh as a tear ran down her cheek.

'There's more where that come from, luv,' Quaterman said.

She set to eating and Mabel gazed at her in amazement – that she was alive and relatively well and could tuck into food with such relish.

When Quaterman came out from the back again, he said, 'All right then, what'll the rest of you have?' It was beer all round, and he set to pouring pints. Winstone was ferrying glasses over to the table when Tollerton walked in with two police constables behind him.

'Serving after hours?' the inspector asked, and the landlord froze. Tollerton nodded to the full glass of beer in Quaterman's hand. 'I'll have the same.'

Mabel had expected Flea to disappear when the police arrived – she'd seen it before – but he stayed next to Roxanne, his eyes occasionally darting to Tollerton and away.

'Well, Miss Arkwright,' Tollerton said, taking the stool at the end of the table. 'We're all quite relieved to see you, as I'm sure your family will be.'

'Oh,' Roxanne said. 'Do they know?'

'I rang the house,' Winstone said, 'and spoke with the butler. Your mother and stepmother had gone to hospital to escort your father home. He will give them the good news when they return.'

'Hospital? Was Father ill?'

'He's fine now,' Tollerton said, 'and we'll get to that.'

'I can hear Mama now,' Roxanne said, '"Roxanne Louise, what have I told you before – you shouldn't take off on your own like that."'

'Your mother will be far too overcome with happiness that you're safe to say such a thing,' Mabel said and added to herself that if MaryLou tried to scold her daughter, she would have Mabel to deal with.

'But I didn't go off on my own,' Roxanne said. 'I went with your friend, Mabel. At least, she said she was your friend.'

'She lied, Roxanne,' Mabel said. 'She lied to you, and she lied to me.'

'Miss Arkwright, if you feel up to it, could you tell us what happened to you, starting with Thursday morning.'

Roxanne had made short work of her repast, but the hollow look had not left her face. Mabel took her hand. 'Or you could talk with the inspector later.'

'No,' Roxanne said, 'I'm all right. I'll tell you everything I can remember, but there are big, foggy parts.'

'Just do the best you can,' Tollerton said. He got out his pocket notebook and a pencil, as did Winstone. When Skeff did the same, Tollerton gave her a look, which she returned in kind. Mabel left her notebook in her satchel – she had no doubt she would remember everything and could write it up later. Roxanne took a deep breath and began.

'That morning, Thursday – wait, did you say it's Saturday now?' When assured that it was, she shook her head and continued. 'I ate breakfast by myself. Mother Adelaide had gone off to a meeting, Father was at the house but Trigg said he was in his office. Mama... well, Mama hadn't come downstairs yet. Then Trigg went off on some errand. I finished and was going upstairs when someone knocked on the door. I waited and no one came – where Dorcas had got to I have no idea – so I answered it. There was this woman on the doorstep, and she said "What luck" or something like that. I didn't recognise her at first, because she was wearing this very odd hat with a wide brim and what looked like a tiny birdcage attached, but when she took it off, I saw it was the woman I'd talked with in the powder room at the Palais.' Roxanne turned to Mabel. 'The funny one, not Up Mudford.'

'You had Flea draw a picture of her,' Mabel said. She took it out of her satchel.

'I did,' Roxanne said with delight. 'I was thinking of all the

people I'd met since I arrived. You're a true artist, Flea,' she said
to the boy. Flea attempted to shrink back into the shadows.

'Don't worry, son,' Tollerton said, 'you're a hero today. Go
on, Miss Arkwright.'

'Well, Angel – she told me that was her name – said she was
a friend of yours, Mabel, from Useful Women and she'd come to
collect me, and we were going to meet you at the Corner House.
Remember, Mabel, I asked if we could go there?'

'I remember,' Mabel said. 'Her real name is Evangeline
Gregory.'

'There's a mouthful,' Roxanne said. 'Well so, I knew it was
all right. I said come in while I get my coat and she said no, she
would wait on the doorstep. I went in and there was Dorcas and
I told her I was going out with a friend.'

'And you left with her immediately?' Tollerton asked.

'Yes, we just – no wait,' Roxanne said. 'She said, anyone at
home? And I said only my father back in his office and Mama,
but she was still in bed. So Angel... whatever her name is... said
was that Dorcas in the entrance hall and I said yes it was, and
Angel said she knew Dorcas and would just go in and say hello.'
Roxanne clicked her tongue. 'So I waited on the doorstep and in
a few minutes, Angel came back out and we left.'

'Did you go to the Corner House?' Tollerton asked.

'If that was the Corner House,' Roxanne said, 'then it's a
great disappointment. We took a bus and Angel chatted away –
she was just as funny as I remembered from the dance hall –
and then we got off and went to a small café to wait for you,
Mabel. Angel went to the counter and brought us back cups of
tea. I've gotta say, I'm getting pretty tired of drinking tea.' She
raised her cup and Quaterman was there in a second with his
coffee pot. 'That stuff at the café tasted awful.'

'She put laudanum in it,' Mabel said. 'I found a bottle in her
room at Mrs Oates' boarding house just off the King's Road in

Fulham. The café is quite near there. She must've kept you in a stupor the entire two days.'

'Wait now,' Tollerton said, jabbing his notebook with the tip of his pencil. 'A waitress from a café on the Fulham end of the King's Road rang Scotland Yard yesterday saying she'd seen a customer drug her companion the day before – that would've been Thursday – and said she'd seen the woman try it again yesterday with someone else. The waitress stopped her.'

Fresh pot! 'Yesterday – that must've been me,' Mabel said.

'The waitress had the good sense to keep the cup as it was,' Tollerton said. 'I only got wind of it this morning, but now I see how the pieces fit.'

'Quite convenient for Evangeline,' Mabel said. 'I'd gone to the boarding house, and she came out and led me to the café. She went up to the counter herself to get the cups of tea – the same as she did with you, Roxanne, and so she must've added the laudanum then. But just as I was about to drink it, along came the waitress. She took the cups away and replaced them.'

'I'm glad you didn't drink it, Mabel,' Roxanne said. 'Or you might not have been able to save me. Awful stuff – it's after that, my memory gets fuzzy. I remember she helped me up and we walked somewhere and climbed stairs. A woman said something in a sharp voice, but I don't remember what. Angel said I wasn't well and needed to lie down – I do remember that much. And then for a long time, it's all dim. Angel was around and then gone and then back. She gave me more to drink – sweet and bitter and...' Roxanne shuddered. 'I could only drink a bit at a time. I don't know how long she'd been gone when I thought I should leave and so I put my coat on, but then I had to rest. A girl came in and I told her I needed a telephone, and she helped me downstairs. But I can't remember if I made a call.'

'You did,' Mabel said. 'You walked to the Elm Tree on the corner and rang New River House. Mr Chigley answered, but he didn't know it was you and couldn't understand what you said.'

Roxanne looked at Mabel and frowned. 'Then Angel found me and she took me someplace else. I must've fallen asleep, because when I woke up I was in an empty coal cellar. It felt quite warm in there. I yelled, someone let me out and then I woke up here.'

'You don't remember anything from the coal cellar to here?' Winstone asked.

'You don't remember hitting the man who opened to door for you?' Mabel asked, thinking of Fred Fredericks' black eye.

'I did that?' Roxanne asked. 'I'm very sorry – I should apologise.'

'You came here looking for Flea,' Cora reminded her.

'Yes!' Roxanne's face lit up. 'I came here.'

'You could've gone to Islington,' Mabel said.

'You're right, I could've. Why didn't I?' Roxanne frowned. 'I was thinking of Tommy, I remember. Or maybe I was thinking of you, Flea.'

Flea looked both embarrassed and pleased.

'Had you been here before?' Tollerton asked.

Roxanne shook her head. 'No, but Flea had told me about it, hadn't you?' Flea gave a nod. 'And I found it on here.' She opened her small envelope purse and out popped an overly folded Bacon's walking map of London.

'Miss Arkwright,' Tollerton said, sounding if not vexed, then at least perplexed, 'you were trapped in the coal cellar at a house on Hanover Terrace and that is nowhere near here. Do you mean to say you found your way by looking at that?'

'She's very good with maps,' Mabel said.

'I am good with maps,' Roxanne said, 'but it's also true I didn't know where I was.' She squinted into the middle distance as if looking for the answer. 'I remember standing underneath a streetlamp looking at my map and a constable came up. He showed me where we were. I was cold.' She looked down at her dress. 'What did I do with my coat?'

'You left it behind in the coal cellar,' Mabel said. *And nearly frightened me to death.*

'What will Mama say? Oh well. And then... a taxi. I took a taxi.'

'And the taxi brought you to the Waterman?'

Roxanne fell silent, again staring off into space. Then, Mabel saw her eyes clear and her cheeks redden.

'I might've asked him to take me to the hotel near the Tower of London – I thought there must be a hotel near the Tower, because it's so famous. Once he dropped me at the hotel, I—'

'You looked at your map,' Tollerton said.

Roxanne nodded. 'But the fog had returned. It was in my mind, and all round me. I asked a woman for the way and knocked on a door, but there was no answer. Then I thought I'd rest. The next thing I knew, there was Mabel.'

There remained a myriad of questions to be answered, but at that moment, Tollerton had to be satisfied with the account Roxanne had given of her charmed journey. The inspector muttered something about finding the constable who had been on patrol near Regent's Park and the cabbie who picked up a fare, and that was that.

When Drake pulled up to the kerb in front of the Arkwright house in Mayfair there was still light in the sky – not even four o'clock. What a day. Mabel got out and walked Roxanne to the door.

'Come in, please, won't you?' Roxanne asked. She looked past Mabel to Park and Gladys in the taxi. 'All of you.'

'No, I only want to see you safely in the door,' Mabel said, thinking that the family should have some privacy. 'We'll come round tomorrow.'

The front door of the house opened wide before Mabel could pull the bell and a beaming Trigg stood aside. In the entrance hall next to the table with the pots of narcissus, Rupert sat in a side chair as if it were a throne and the bandage wrapped round his head a crown. He wore a dressing gown and an enormous smile.

'Roxy!' he said.

'Oh, Father!' Roxanne flew to him and sank to her knees at his side so that they could embrace. Adelaide came out from the drawing room and stood behind his chair and Roxanne rose to embrace her, too.

'Miss Canning?' the butler asked, with the door still open.

'Thank you, Trigg, but I won't come in,' she said. She waved at Adelaide, who lifted her chin in acknowledgement. Rupert pulled out a handkerchief and mopped the tears off his face. MaryLou was nowhere in sight.

Mabel turned away and as the door began to close, she heard Roxanne exclaim.

'Tommy!'

TWENTY-FOUR

Mabel spent Saturday late afternoon in the bath, soaking and scrubbing alternately, unsure if she would ever be rid of the coal dust or the lingering scent of rotting potato peel. She smiled as she imagined Roxanne doing the same. Mabel had great affection for the girl and a sense of accomplishment at helping to save her, but somehow those emotions were still entwined with useless remnants of fear at the image of Roxanne's coat at the bottom of the coal pile at Hanover Terrace.

She drained the water and filled the tub over again and put all other thoughts aside, sinking back into the hot water. She remembered when she had been quite young, before Papa had put a proper bathroom in their cottage, having her baths in a washtub set in front of the range in the kitchen. She must ring home.

Not long after Mabel had finished her bath, dried and dressed, Adelaide rang with an invitation to Sunday lunch for Mabel and Park, Skeff and Cora, WPC Wardle and Tollerton.

'It will be a bit of a crowd,' Adelaide said, 'but that's the celebration both Roxanne and Rupert want. We'd very much like it if you and Mr Winstone would arrive a bit early.'

Mabel heard a shout from Roxanne in the background. 'And Gladys!'

'Yes,' Adelaide said, 'and Gladys.'

In the evening, Mabel, Cora, Skeff and Park – the London Ladies' Murder Club plus their honorary gentleman – went off to dine at Vittorio's, a small and constantly busy Italian café nearby. On their way out, they stopped to leave Gladys with Mr Chigley. Park handed the porter a packet of sausages 'for the both of you' and a bottle of fine whisky 'yours alone, no matter how much she begs.'

'It's little recompense for your support, Mr Chigley,' Mabel said. 'And not just for filtering the news you give Papa, but for truly being a good friend.'

Mr Chigley blustered as his face glowed pink. 'Ah, now,' he said. He cleared his throat and patted the top of the whisky bottle gently. 'I'll save this for special occasions.'

'Roxanne is safe and sound,' Skeff said. 'I'd say that's special occasion enough.'

At Vittorio's, they ate and drank and laughed, crowded at a table too small for four people and just right for friends. They tucked their napkins into their collars and ate plates of macaroni and spaghetti, dressed with different sauces and redolent of faraway places by way of Clerkenwell.

'It certainly puts tins of spaghetti to shame,' Cora said as she dabbed a bit of tomato off her chin.

Skeff told them her uncle Pitt at the *Intelligencer* would give her a full page for coverage of the Arkwright story, but she wouldn't write it unless Rupert himself agreed to talk.

Park said he'd asked Ned about Harry Kettle. The boxer turned out to be an uncle who had been disowned by the family for his violent ways. 'Ned told me,' Winstone said, 'that in his darkest days, he had feared he would become like his uncle. But

Ned's been through the bad times and come out on the other side. He'll do fine.'

'You've found work for him, haven't you?' Mabel asked, and Park smiled. 'Boxing,' she muttered to herself. 'I never told Tolly about Mr Arkwright's past – the boxer who died after a fight.'

'Turns out he knew already,' Park said.

Cora informed Mabel that Mrs Norrell had decided not to enter holy orders after all, but that she had already begun to shop for new clothes and would sell the old frocks. 'They won't be a guinea a gown, I'm afraid,' Cora said. 'It's because she gives the money to the order for their good works.'

Mabel's heart sank. So much for keeping any of Mrs Norrell's lovely frocks – even a guinea was beyond her clothing budget. Ah well. 'Just which holy orders are these?' she asked.

'It's the Sisters of Saint Alkelda,' Cora said.

'Who?'

'Not actually within the church's jurisdiction,' Skeff said.

'They run their order the way they see fit,' Cora said. 'Still, they do good work for young women turned out by their families.'

Well then, Mabel would be churlish to complain about the cost. She set aside all thoughts of Mrs Norrell and her frocks.

In the foyer back at New River House, Mr Chigley came out with his cup of Bovril to say good night, Skeff and Cora continued up to their flat and Winstone took Gladys out and across the road for a last run on the green. Mabel stood at the bottom of the stairs watching them leave and before the door closed, Park looked back at her.

It was a quick run on the green, but not so quick that Mabel hadn't already undressed and thrown on her dressing gown. She stood with the door of her flat open, listening, and when she heard them return, she went out to the stairs and looked down at the first-floor landing.

'I've put pennies in the heater for Gladys,' Mabel said.

Gladys trotted on up the stairs without further ado, and Winstone waited, taking in the sight of Mabel, her bare feet and her dressing gown untied, but held closed with her arms crossed in front of her.

'Will you come up?' she asked.

'I will.'

Gladys stretched out in front of the heater. Park hung his coat on a peg and followed Mabel into the bedroom and closed the door. She stood close to him, so close he had trouble taking off his jacket, but he did and then dropped it as if he didn't care where it fell.

'My hands are cold,' he said a second before he slid them inside her dressing gown and onto her bare skin.

She gasped and then laughed. 'Yes, they are.' As she unbuttoned his shirt, she said, 'Well, I'll take care of that.'

'Mabel, there you are!'

Sunday midday, and they had just arrived at the house in Mayfair. Roxanne leaned over the banister from the gallery. She wore a lovely day dress in a dark raspberry that suited her hair colour. Apart from a plaster on her forehead, she looked none the worse for her travails. *Ah, the resilience of youth*, Mabel thought.

'We're not too early?'

'Oh no,' Roxanne said. 'We're a bit late. Hello, Mr Winstone. Hello, Gladys.'

'Miss Arkwright,' Park said, taking off his hat.

'Mabel!' Roxanne exclaimed. 'Aren't you the cat's pyjamas today.'

'Thank you – I think.'

Mabel put a hand to the copper-coloured velvet collar of her coat-frock – a soft wool gabardine dress in a delicious shade of mulberry with steel buttons to accent. She would be sorry to return it. It might be her favourite of all Mrs Norrell's, although she had said that about the Parisian number and the wool suit, making her sound much like Mr Bryars, who seemed to consider every one of his glass paperweights his favourite. Poor Mr Bryars, off the hook for murder, but without the Royal Pavilion at Brighton and Holyroodhouse until after the court case finished.

Roxanne looked behind her and in loud whisper said, 'No, you are not ready. Go comb your hair or Mama will have a fit.' She turned back to Park and Mabel and said, 'You go in the drawing room, and we'll be down soon. I have a surprise for you.'

Trigg took their hats and coats and gloves and went off to the boot room.

The two of them alone, Park stepped close to Mabel, drawing so near that she could feel his warm breath on her cheek.

'Mr Winstone, you're being rather forward,' Mabel said, moving not an inch, apart from lifting her lips to his. They kissed, and the entrance hall of the Mayfair house fell away to memories of the previous night and to waking up that morning with Park next to her in bed.

She had studied his face – so rarely seen without his glasses – and noticed the curl of his lashes. He'd opened his eyes and fixed them on her, smiling.

'Good morning,' he'd said.

'Yes, it is.'

That was all they'd had of their first morning in bed together – Gladys needed a walk, Mabel rang Peasmarsh and Skeff brought up the Sunday newspapers. No one had noticed the glow of intimacy that lingered around Mabel and Park, except perhaps Mrs Chandekar who, even over the telephone line, had heard a change in Mabel's voice and said to her, 'I'm happy for you.' The woman ought to be a detective.

Now, standing in the entrance hall at the house in Mayfair, Mabel and Park could do no more than gaze into each other's eyes until a *woof* alert from Gladys brought them back to the moment.

Trigg returned and said, 'Mr Winstone, you've been asked to join the gentlemen in Mr Arkwright's office. If you'll wait a moment to allow me to announce Miss Canning. Gladys, I believe you are expected in the kitchen.' He nodded toward the back of the house.

The butler left Gladys to trot back to the kitchen on her own, announced Mabel and closed the drawing room door on his way out. Adelaide and MaryLou were sitting on opposite sides of the fire and on the sofa between them sat Lillian Kerr.

'Miss Kerr!' Mabel exclaimed. 'I'm glad you're here. So you've heard what's happened? Not that I won't write up my usual report, of course.'

'I have heard, but I'm not one for tales of adventure, and so I was glad to know the ending first – that made the story tolerable.'

Adelaide rose and took Mabel's hands in hers. 'You're very welcome.'

'Thank you for asking us,' Mabel said and turned to Mary-Lou. 'You must be relieved that Roxanne is safe, Mrs...' She faltered as the fire flared, and Mabel caught a glint off Mary-Lou's left hand where she now wore a gold band.

'And here is our news,' Adelaide said. 'As it happens, I am the only Mrs Arkwright in the house. This is Mrs Jacob Burnett.'

MaryLou sat upright with her nose in the air. 'It was never my intention to keep my marriage to Jacob a secret,' she said, 'it was only that when I arrived, things rather got away from me and once unsaid, I... I had trouble saying it. Not that I have anything to hide.' *You mean, not any longer*, Mabel thought, and then MaryLou added, 'I look forward to introducing you to my husband, Miss Canning.'

But before the husband, came the son. Roxanne and Tommy burst into the room – followed by Gladys. Roxanne kissed Mabel on the cheek and then introduced her brother.

Tommy was a slight boy of about fourteen with a pale complexion and red-nearly-pink hair. A lock of it stuck straight up off the crown of his head. He inserted a finger between his collar and his neck and said, 'Hello, Miss Canning. I'm very pleased to meet you.'

'And I'm pleased to meet you, Tommy,' Mabel said. 'You look just as Roxanne described and just as Flea drew you.'

'I've shown him Flea's drawing,' Roxanne said, 'and now he's got it pinned up over his bed.'

'I do not,' Tommy said and punched his sister in the arm.

'Thomas Wayne, don't hit your sister,' MaryLou said.

'Yes, ma'am,' Tommy muttered.

When her mother wasn't looking, Roxanne punched him back. 'And Tommy, this is Gladys. She belongs to Mr Winstone.'

Gladys sat in front of Tommy and offered a paw.

'That's swell,' Tommy said as he shook. 'Digger can shake, too.'

'Tommy, you and your father must've been on a sailing behind your mother if you've just arrived,' Mabel said.

'Oh no, Miss Canning, we were on the same ship, but Pa and I have been in Scotland fishing, because Mama said we shouldn't intrude. We were a day late hearing about Roxy and came down to London after you rescued her.'

There was a burst of men's laughter from the entrance hall and in walked Park, Rupert Arkwright and Jacob Burnett all in high spirits and with glasses of whisky in their hands. Rupert still wore a bandage on his head, but a smaller one than Mabel had seen the previous evening.

Jacob Burnett was a short, rather roundish man with thinning pale red-nearly-pink hair that, although there wasn't a great deal of it, determined to make its presence known with a lock that stuck straight up from the crown of his head just as Tommy's did. He had a smile that went, as they say, from ear to ear and he held a fat cigar in his free hand.

'Jacob,' MaryLou said, 'you shouldn't be smoking in the presence of ladies.'

'Unlit, MaryLou my love. Now, could this be the Miss Canning I've heard so much about?'

'Hello, Mr Burnett,' Mabel said, shaking hands with him.

'Now, now, let's just leave it at Jacob.'

The bell sounded announcing the arrival of Skeff, Cora and Hildy followed soon by Tollerton. He had relinquished his coat to the butler and looked ill at ease. Trigg brought in a tray of sherry and more whisky as further introductions were made after which the group broke up into several conversations.

Park went over to keep Tolly company. Cora unwrapped a paper parcel to show Miss Kerr, Adelaide and MaryLou a hat with a turned-up brim in the front. She'd taken the beads from the cloche and sewn them on in a pattern of bold geometric shapes and offered it to Adelaide to try on. Skeff, Hildy and Jacob broke into loud laughter about something. All the while, Rupert stood with an elbow on the mantel and a smile on his face. Mabel watched as he caught his wife's eye and winked at her.

Trigg appeared and had a word with Roxanne, who nodded to her brother. The siblings slipped out of the room.

Conversations broke apart and reconfigured and Mabel found herself talking with Jacob.

'The thing is, Mabel,' he said to her, gesturing with his cigar-holding hand across the room where his wife, wide-eyed, stood talking with Skeff, 'MaryLou can twist me around her little finger, and that's the truth. The woman is the light of my life.'

The phrase *It takes all kinds* drifted into Mabel's head. 'How did you meet?' she asked.

'On the sailing to New York all those years ago when MaryLou and little Roxy were moving to Chicago. We married soon after. I thought MaryLou should tell Rupert immediately, but... well, the thing most people don't realise is that MaryLou worries, and she gets anxious so easily. She imagined he'd try to take Roxy away from her. That's hogwash, I told her, but neither was it my business in truth. I said all right, as long as Roxy knew about her father – I put my foot down there.'

'Had you met Mr Arkwright?'

'No, only read about him.'

'You seem to get along well,' Mabel said.

'Like a house afire,' Jacob said and laughed. 'In fact, Rupert and I might just be going into business together. I've had it with the stockyards. No, ma'am, it's aeroplanes for us.'

Roxanne and Tommy came back into the drawing room and the boy marched over to MaryLou.

'Mama, I'm going to eat in the kitchen,' he said.

'You'll do no such thing,' his mother replied with indignation. 'You'll sit at the table with us like a proper gentleman.'

'But Flea is here and he's going to eat in the kitchen. I can't leave him to have his meal alone, because that wouldn't be good manners and haven't you always said "manners make the man"? I'm only doing what you taught me.'

'Roxanne Louise,' MaryLou said, 'you are leading your brother astray.'

'Oh, Mama, you don't begrudge Tommy a friend, do you?'

'Who is this Flea?' MaryLou asked.

Trigg opened the door. 'Lunch is served.'

'Good thing, too, Trigg my man – I'm starving,' Jacob said. 'Come along, MaryLou, get a wiggle on.'

'Jacob!'

Cook had done herself proud. Having less than a day to prepare a meal for fourteen including the boys in the kitchen, she produced roast chickens, boiled ham, peas, three kinds of potatoes, cress salad with tinned oranges, a clear soup to start and apple Charlotte to end. A homely, delicious meal that didn't go on with too many courses and allowed conversation to flow.

'She never took your purse?' Hildy asked Roxanne.

'I don't recall she ever even looked for it,' Roxanne said, 'although I don't remember everything.'

'She wasn't interested in your money,' Mabel said. 'When her mother died and she saw that tiny undated clipping about you, Mr Arkwright, buying the rail yard, she added that to what little she knew about her father dying and came up with the wrong answer. She probably thought her mother blamed you, and so she did, too. In her grief, her mind became... unbalanced.'

Mabel had thought this through and with Roxanne safe, she found she could be charitable towards Evangeline. To a point.

'You were quite affected by those men dying at the rail yard,' Miss Kerr said to Rupert. 'Knowing one of them had a young child at home and thinking of your daughter.'

'It wasn't until a year later when I bought the yard,' Rupert said, 'that it occurred to me I should help. And I believe it was you, Lillian, who suggested it.'

Adelaide smiled, but MaryLou attended to her meal, chasing a pea round her plate.

'Now, Inspector,' Rupert said. 'Can you give us the details on Miss Gregory?'

Tollerton, who was seated between Cora and Roxanne, had toiled at polite conversation, but now that the subject turned to the enquiry, he was on firm ground. Trigg circled the table refilling wine glasses, and Tolly nodded to his own glass.

'Thanks to the lead from Miss Canning and Mr Winstone,' Tollerton said, 'we confirmed Miss Gregory worked in the kitchen at the Palais the Friday evening Mr Deuchar was killed.'

Mabel frowned. 'I mentioned we were going to the Palais in the office that morning and Evangeline was nearby collecting her pay packet.'

'If not then, she would've found another way to get at Roxanne,' Park said. 'It wasn't your fault.'

'Dorcas says she had been coming to the back asking for work,' Adelaide said. 'She may have heard Rupert and me talking about Useful Women.'

'It must've started when she saw Roxanne's picture in *Tatler*,' Miss Kerr said. 'She tried to get on here and then came to me.'

'Her mother dying, finding the newspaper clippings with no dates, seeing Miss Arkwright's photograph,' Tollerton said.

'It set her down the wrong path,' Skeff said.

'Now that we've her fingerprints,' Tolly said, 'we can match them to those found on the glass paperweights – both the Royal Pavilion at Brighton and Holyroodhouse, which she had in her coat pocket.'

'I can still feel that thing coming down on my head,' Rupert said, a look of anger scudding across his face.

'I shouldn't've let her back in the house on Thursday morning,' Roxanne said, regretfully.

'She was good at talking her way into almost any situation,' Miss Kerr said.

Rupert nodded. 'I opened my office door and there she was. She didn't seem unbalanced, but enthusiastic. She said that Lillian had sent her. "Miss Kerr wanted me to have a word with you about Miss Canning," she told me.'

'The nerve,' Mabel said.

'I led her into my office and well, that was that.'

No one spoke for a moment, then Roxanne said, 'But you found me, Mabel, so it's all turned out well. Miss Kerr, you must be quite proud of Mabel and her private investigations for Useful Women.'

Miss Kerr beamed. 'I am that.'

Other questions popped up from time to time, but over apple Charlotte, the conversation turned to lighter matters.

'Does your brother play baseball?' Park asked.

'Tommy plays,' Roxanne said, 'but he hasn't settled on anything in particular he likes best. He may become an explorer. He likes adventures. When he was nine, he ran away to join the circus.'

MaryLou shuddered.

'How far did he get?' Mabel asked.

'Indiana,' Jacob said with pride in his voice.

'Tommy is musical, too,' Roxanne said. 'Mabel, perhaps he could join in when you and Mr Winstone are on the piano. Tommy plays the tuba.'

'He was meant to learn the violin,' MaryLou said in an injured tone and with a look thrown at her husband.

'Mama enrolled him in a local music school,' Roxanne said, 'but he got Jacob to write a note saying he was to change to the tuba. It's because you can't play the violin in a marching band and that's what he wants to do.'

'He's always marching around the house with the thing,' Jacob said with a laugh. 'The boy's got high spirits.'

As everyone rose from the table and returned to the drawing room, Mabel and Park held back.

'High spirits, my eye,' she said quietly. 'I know the type. At eight he was a scamp, but now that he's fourteen, he's a terror.'

They settled in the drawing room and coffee was served MaryLou took a sip of hers and said, 'We'll be leaving on Tuesday, and you can be sure I won't let Roxanne or Tommy out of my sight.'

Roxanne set her coffee down and stood.

'Mama, I'm staying here.'

If MaryLou hadn't already been sitting, she might've hit the floor. As it was, she threw herself back against the sofa and, with a gasp, clutched her chest.

'I've only just arrived,' Roxanne went on, 'and I want to stay with Father and Mother Adelaide and see more of London. I'm old enough to make my own decisions and that's that.'

'Jacob?' MaryLou asked, pleading.

'Oh, give the girl a chance, MaryLou,' was his response.

'Roxanne Louise, your brother has been bereft without you,' MaryLou said. 'How could you do that to him?'

'Well, Mama, you see—' Roxanne started, but then a crash came from the entrance hall.

Tommy opened the door a crack and slipped into the drawing room. 'Sorry,' he said and glanced round, taking note of his sister standing in front of their mother.

'Did you tell her?' he asked.

Adelaide and Miss Kerr exchanged glances, but MaryLou's sharp gaze darted from Tommy to Roxanne. 'Tell me what?' she demanded. No one answered. 'Jacob?'

Burnett was examining the end of his unlit cigar. 'Got a match for this, Rupert?' he asked, and with that, all the men exited the room post-haste as if they sensed a storm brewing.

Roxanne wasted no time either. 'Later,' she said to her brother. 'C'mon, get Flea and his cricket bat. We'll go across to the park and I'll pitch. Put your coat on!'

'Roxanne Louise, I've told you before—'

'Yes, I know, Mama, I'm a tomboy,' she said, already out the door and turning to look back in. 'You'll just have to learn to live with it. Mabel?' Roxanne gave a quick nod towards the entrance hall and left.

Mabel followed. She saw the backs of Flea and Tommy as they dashed outdoors. Trigg crossed the entrance hall towards the boot room and Dorcas bent over the table, sweeping up one of the pots of narcissus that had inexplicably landed on the floor and broken. Roxanne drew Mabel to the side.

'It's only for a few weeks, Mama won't mind once she gets used to the idea,' Roxanne said. 'It's all legit, Mabel – it's a real Useful Women job.'

'I'm delighted to continue as your companion a while longer,' Mabel said, squeezing Roxanne's arm.

'Oh, not just me,' Roxanne said, her face aglow and her eyes sparkling, 'Tommy's staying too – you'll have both of us to look after.'

Mabel's face went numb.

Roxanne's high spirits dropped a notch. 'Miss Kerr did say it was up to you whether you took the job or not.' A pause. 'Tommy's a good kid, really, and I'll be there to keep him in line.' She looked at her toes. 'Jacob and Father are paying the bill, and I did happen to hear Miss Kerr say it would be double the usual fee, because of circumstances.' She looked back at Mabel and waited.

But Mabel, busy with an internal argument, didn't answer.

Roxanne forged ahead. 'We could do educational stuff, because Tommy will be missing school. Don't you have a Natural History Museum in London? Tommy would love that.'

Another moment of silence went by and she added, with knitted brows, 'What do you say, Mabel?'

The first answer that had wanted to burst out of Mabel's mouth – No! – had hesitated long enough to be reined in by the thought of the fat pay packet she'd receive for... what? Danger pay? In her mind's eye, a vision arose. She saw the dress she now wore – mulberry-coloured wool gabardine with a copper velvet collar hanging in her own wardrobe on a permanent basis alongside the Parisian gown with the crocheted bertha.

And how many others? All of Mrs Norrell's dresses were for sale with all monies going to the good works of the Sisters of Saint Alkelda.

An independent woman must always consider her budget and Mabel had already come to the disappointing conclusion she could not afford Mrs Norrell's prices. Until this moment. How difficult could it be watching Roxanne and Tommy – surely not as difficult as solving a murder?

'Although,' Roxanne continued thoughtfully, 'we'll need to keep him away from any dinosaur skeletons – you have no idea how rickety those things really are.'

Mabel put a hand to Roxanne's lips. 'Stop, please,' she said. 'I'll do it.'

A LETTER FROM MARTY

Dear reader,

I want to say a huge thank you for choosing to read *A Body at the Dance Hall*, book three in my London Ladies' Murder Club series. If you did enjoy it, and want to keep up to date with all my latest releases, just sign up at the following link. Your email address will never be shared, and you can unsubscribe at any time.

www.bookouture.com/marty-wingate

In book three, it's January 1922 and Mabel Canning has been one of Miss Kerr's Useful Women since September – and is proud to be in charge of the Private Investigations division. Still, it isn't always easy to be a modern, independent woman and Mabel has her hands full when she's assigned to be the companion to a young American woman who insists on going dancing. Dance halls were all the rage in the 1920s – all those young people letting off steam after the end of the First World War. Both fashions and attitudes were changing.

I hope you loved *A Body at the Dance Hall* and if you did, I would be very grateful if you could write a review. I'd love to hear what you think, and it makes such a difference helping new readers to discover one of my books for the first time.

I love hearing from my readers – you can get in touch through social media or my website.

Thanks,

Marty Wingate

www.martywingate.com

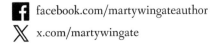 facebook.com/martywingateauthor
𝕏 x.com/martywingate

ACKNOWLEDGEMENTS

Here is the roll call of the many people who have helped make *A Body at the Dance Hall*, book three in the London Ladies' Murder Club, happen. My heartfelt thanks to each of you!

My agent Christina Hogrebe of the Jane Rotrosen Agency.

My editor Rhianna Louise, editor Eve Hall, associate publisher Jess Whitlum-Cooper, publishing executive Imogen Allport and the many others at Bookouture who have created a clear and easy-to-navigate publishing process.

My weekly writing group – Kara Pomeroy, Louise Creighton, Sarah Niebuhr Rubin and Meghana Padakandla.

My husband, Leighton Wingate ('No Oxford comma – are you sure?')

Continued thanks to these family members, fellow authors and dear friends who never mind listening to the latest results of my research, even if it is about the first commercial dog food in Britain: Carolyn Lockhart, Ed Polk, Katherine Manning Wingate, Susy Wingate, Lilly Wingate, Alice K. Boatwright, Hannah Dennison, Dana Spencer, Jane Tobin, Mary Helbach, Mary Kate Parker and Victoria Summerley. Cheers!

PUBLISHING TEAM

Turning a manuscript into a book requires the efforts of many people. The publishing team at Bookouture would like to acknowledge everyone who contributed to this publication.

Audio
Alba Proko
Sinead O'Connor
Melissa Tran

Commercial
Lauren Morrissette
Jil Thielen
Imogen Allport

Cover design
Emily Courdelle

Data and analysis
Mark Alder
Mohamed Bussuri

Editorial
Rhianna Louise
Nadia Michael

Milton Keynes UK
Ingram Content Group UK Ltd.
UKHW010858010424
440421UK00004B/373